RETHINKING DVOŘÁK

RETHINKING DVOŘÁK

VIEWS FROM FIVE COUNTRIES

EDITED BY

DAVID R. BEVERIDGE

CLARENDON PRESS · OXFORD
1996

Oxford University Press, Walton Street, Oxford OX2 6DP
Oxford New York
Athens Auckland Bangkok Bombay
Calcutta Cape Town Dar es Salaam Delhi
Florence Hong Kong Istanbul Karachi
Kuala Lumpur Madras Madrid Melbourne
Mexico City Nairobi Paris Singapore
Taipei Tokyo Toronto
and associated companies in
Berlin Ibadan

Oxford is a trade mark of Oxford University Press

Published in the United States
by Oxford University Press Inc., New York

British Library Cataloguing in Publication Data
Data available

Library of Congress Cataloging in Publication Data
Rethinking Dvořák: views from five countries /
edited by David R. Beveridge.
p.   cm.
The majority of the essays in this vol. were engendered by the
Dvořák Sesquicentennial Conference and Festival in America.
Includes bibliographical references and index.
1. Dvořák, Antonín, 1841–1904—Congresses. I. Beveridge, David R.
II. Dvořák Sesquicentennial Conference and Festival in America (1991:
University of New Orleans)
ML410.D99R48   1996   780'.92—dc20   95–2440
ISBN 0–19–816411–4

1 3 5 7 9 10 8 6 4 2

Typeset by Hope Services (Abingdon) Ltd.
Printed in Great Britain
on acid-free paper by
Biddles Ltd.,
Guildford & King's Lynn

DEDICATION

THE year 1991 marked not only the sesquicentenary of the birth of Antonín Dvořák, but also the seventieth anniversary of the birth of one of the most brilliant and dedicated of Dvořák scholars, Jarmil Burghauser. This volume, focusing on the life and work of the former, is dedicated to the achievements—past, present, and future—of the latter.

Demonstrating characteristic self-effacement and magnanimity towards others, Jarmil Burghauser scarcely mentions in his essay for this book, 'Metamorphoses of Dvořák's Image in the Course of Time', the role that he himself has played in effecting the more recent changes of view and reappraisals about which he writes. No one has done more than Jarmil Burghauser during the past half-century to enrich our understanding of Antonín Dvořák, his music, and the times in which he lived. And no one has done more to encourage scholars, performers, and even lay listeners to look at Dvořák's art and the Czech culture that spawned and nurtured it with an eye at once loving and critical.

In helping to prepare the revised editions of Otakar Šourek's four-volume biography of Dvořák during the 1950s, Dr Burghauser was able to enlarge upon the knowledge and appreciation of Dvořák's music he had gained as a young professional performer and composer by utilizing the training he had received at Charles University in musicology and psychology. His subsequent contributions to Dvořák research include innumerable critical editions of music and librettos; articles, programme and record-sleeve notes; a short biography published in five languages; the definitive thematic catalogue (now prepared for publication in a second edition); and a detailed study in progress that sheds new light on Dvořák's activities during his youth. These all reflect the workings of a brilliant mind attuned to the sensibilities of creative genius, enriched by an all-encompassing knowledge of social, cultural, and political historiography, governed by humanistic values, and directed by a sophisticated but unfailingly charming wit.

While maintaining an active life as a composer, pianist, choral conductor, and teacher, Dr Burghauser has managed to conduct musicological research not only on Dvořák but on Alexander Borodin, Bedřich Smetana, Zdeněk Fibich, Leoš Janáček, and others besides. In addition, he has published pedagogical materials and discourses on aesthetic and theoretical matters. The present collection of essays, prepared as a tribute to him, seeks to emulate his own high standards of critical enquiry, his depth of knowledge, and his breadth of perspective; its contributors can be justly proud if it succeeds to some small degree in this endeavour.

ACKNOWLEDGEMENTS

It is in the nature of a book like this that the names of the persons and institutions who furthered its genesis in one way or another are legion. A list of acknowledgements will inevitably omit, owing to space limitation or simple inadvertence, some who helped directly or indirectly to make the book possible. While begging the forgiveness of those who may be overlooked, I shall here venture to mention those whose contribution seems most conspicuous.

At the start I must thank all who helped me to bring about The Dvořák Sesquicentennial Conference and Festival in America (New Orleans, 1991), for which I served as Director and which was the original source for most of the essays in this book. I acknowledge with special gratitude the collaboration of Alan Houtchens of Texas A&M University, who served as Conference Coordinator, copiously and ably assisted by his wife Lucinda. I am immensely indebted also to the devoted work of my own Executive Assistant for the event, Emily De Moor Corbello. For general administrative support, thanks go to the University of New Orleans as host institution; among the countless personnel at UNO who assisted in one way or another, I should like to single out Anne Jakob, Coordinator of Conference Services, Metropolitan College; Robert Dupont, Dean of the Metropolitan College; Mary Louise ('Mike') Trammel, Office of Research; and Jeff Cox, Chair of the Music Department. Significant administrative support also came from Texas A&M University as co-sponsor, among whose employees I wish to thank especially, besides Alan Houtchens, the Head of the Music Program Werner Rose.

The conference was financed by generous gifts from, among others:

The National Endowment for the Humanities, an independent federal agency
The International Research and Exchanges Board (IREX), through the John
D. and Catherine T. MacArthur Foundation
The University of New Orleans Metropolitan College
The Czech Music Fund in Prague
The Czechoslovak Academy of Sciences in Prague (now Czech Academy of
Sciences)
The Ministry of Culture of the Czech and Slovak Federal Republic
The David M. Metzner, M.D. Foundation for the Arts in New Orleans
The University of New Orleans Student Government Association

And special thanks go of course to the more than fifty scholars and performers who contributed their insights in papers or panel discussions at the conference. Less than half of them are represented directly in this book, but all of them helped to create that 'melting pot' of ideas that the book hopes to capture (partially) in print.

With regard to preparation of the book itself, I again thank the International Research and Exchanges Board for major financial support. Among IREX personnel, Vivian Abbott and Beate Dafeldecker deserve special thanks for general encouragement. I also acknowledge supporting gifts from The Dvořák Society for Czech and Slovak Music (Great Britain) and the Czechoslovak Music Society (St. Louis).

The editors at Oxford University Press have been a pleasure to work with; I should like to single out Music Editor Bruce Phillips, along with Helen Foster, Elizabeth M. Stratford, and especially our meticulous and always courteous copy editor, Fiona Little.

For valuable advice of various kinds along the way I thank Michael Beckerman, John Tyrrell, Hugh MacDonald, and especially Jarmil Burghauser.

Permission for reproduction of illustrations was granted by The National Gallery in Prague, The Prague Conservatory of Music, and the Antonín Dvořák Museum in Prague; for help in obtaining the material for reproduction and the permissions I thank Jaroslava Dobrinčić and Markéta Hallová. I also thank the National Theatre Archive in Prague and Czech Radio in Prague for furnishing the contributors with unpublished musical manuscripts from which some of the music examples are drawn.

No small role was played by my research and clerical assistants during the long process of assembling and editing the book, communicating with the contributors, and making preparations for publication. Here I should like to acknowledge with thanks the work of Christine West, Mark Brill, Mark Nubio, and Nikolaj Kašpar.

D.R.B.

CONTENTS

LIST OF PLATES

(between pages 212 and 213)

PLATE 1. V. E. Nádherný *Dvořák Conducts the Orchestra at the World's Fair in Chicago*, 1893. Drawing. 38 X 23 cm. Courtesy the Antonín Dvořák Museum, Prague.

PLATE 2. Ludwig Michalek, portrait of Dvořák, 1891. Pastel, 72.5 X 52 cm. Courtesy the Prague Conservatory of Music, No. 261/1.

PLATE 3. Max Švabinský, *Antonín Dvořák*, 1898. Pen drawing, 33.3 X 26.5 cm. Courtesy the National Gallery, Prague, No. K-29.284.

PLATE 4. Max Švabinský, *Antonín Dvořák*, 1901. Lithograph, 60 X 48 cm. Courtesy the Antonín Dvořák Museum, Prague.

PLATE 5. Max Švabinský, Dvořák, standing figure. Pen drawing, 74.5 X 43 cm. Courtesy the National Gallery, Prague, No. K-6605.

PLATE 6. Max Švabinský, sketch for *Czech Spring* (writers), 1910. Oil on canvas, 105 X 100 cm. Municipal Museum, Prague, No. M-538. Reproduction courtesy the National Gallery, Prague, negative 75231.

PLATE 7. Max Švabinský, sketch for *Czech Spring* (artists and composers), 1910. Charcoal drawing, 105 X 97 cm. Municipal Museum, Prague, No. M-539. Reproduction courtesy the National Gallery, Prague, negative 75232.

Introduction

DAVID R. BEVERIDGE

THE 150th anniversary of the birth of Antonín Dvořák, celebrated on 8 September 1991, was no arbitrary milestone. Rather, it came at a time when a reconsideration of this composer was invited, even demanded, by world events. What bearing the politics of 1991 may have had on a musician of the nineteenth century may not be obvious. But Dvořák's image, rightly or wrongly, has always been conditioned by his status as a 'Czech nationalist'. And in 1991, thanks to the 'Velvet Revolution' in Czechoslovakia, the demise of the Soviet Union, and the rise of newly independent nations throughout the former 'Eastern Bloc', the world could better understand—better, perhaps, than at any time during or since Dvořák's life—the true significance of the Czech nation and its relation to European culture as a whole.

The political situation in 1991 presented a striking contrast with that during Dvořák's centenary year in 1941, when the Czech lands lay occupied by Nazi Germany. But that dark hour of history was only one link in a centuries-long pattern whereby Czech culture was stifled and distorted, both by armies and by ideas. From 1526 until 1918, the Czechs were ruled by the Habsburgs of Austria—an association that was voluntary and seemingly benign at first, but that led to a systematic suppression of Czech language and customs in favour of foreign models beginning with the Thirty Years' War. The influence of the Habsburgs lingers even today in the German names they used for Czech geographical features: the river Moldau, famous to us from Smetana's tone-poem, should by rights have the Czech name Vltava.

Following World War I and the demise of the Habsburg Empire, Czechoslovakia was established as an independent political entity, combining the Czechs of Bohemia, Moravia, and southern Silesia with their Slovak cousins to the east. Hopes of a national resurgence were aroused, but these hopes were snuffed out by Hitler in 1938, and the Nazis were only replaced by the next oppressor, Soviet Russia.

It is easy to forget, if indeed we ever knew, that things were not always so

for the Czechs. In the Middle Ages, Bohemia occupied an important place in
the arena of European civilization, and in its 'Golden Age' during the fourteenth century Prague was the seat of the Holy Roman Empire. The great
French poet and composer Guillaume de Machaut worked for a time in
Bohemia, and Emperor Charles IV established in Prague the first university
east of Paris and north of Italy.

With the 'Velvet Revolution' of 1989, the Czechs can rejoice in a truly
epoch-making achievement that inspires visions of recapturing their glorious
past. The Soviet empire is almost surely gone for good, and the threat of
Germanic hegemony seems more remote than in the early years of our century. Furthermore with the establishment of the Czech Republic in 1993, separated from Slovakia, the Czechs have for the first time since medieval days
an independent political state corresponding exactly with their national identity. It would appear, at long last, that the future of the Czechs lies in their
own hands.

Within this propitious environment, a series of conferences has been held
throughout Europe, Canada, and the United States over the past few years,
devoted to the study of one of the greatest figures in Czech cultural history—
Antonín Dvořák. The largest of these gatherings took place in New Orleans
in February 1991 in conjunction with the sesquicentenary celebrations, supported by major grants from the National Endowment for the Humanities and
the International Research and Exchanges Board. It attracted more than fifty
scholars as active participants, including almost every recognized authority on
Dvořák world-wide together with a strong representation of experts on the
music and culture of the nineteenth century generally and on Dvořák's special relation to the culture of America. A selection of twenty-one of the best
papers from the conference at New Orleans, revised in the light of ideas
exchanged there and afterwards, forms the core of this book. In combination
with three complementary essays from other sources (designated as such with
annotations on their opening pages), these studies form a symposium which
touches upon a wide array of issues concerning Dvořák's life and work, and
his place within a broad cultural context. It is a symposium unusual for the
diversity of background among its various contributors, offering a sample of
some approaches unfamiliar to the English-speaking audience: a good number of the contributions are by authors publishing here in the English language
for the first time.

That such a symposium should appear at this time is highly appropriate,
even without the change of political climate. For a scholarly reassessment of
Dvořák would be in order if only because of changes afoot in the reception
of his works among musical audiences. The two phenomena—political and
musical—are by no means unrelated; rather, the changed political climate

helps us to understand the patterns of past and present musical reception history. But before considering the relationship, let us examine some aspects of the purely musical situation.

In 1941, Gerald Abraham identified Dvořák as a great composer who, though popular with the public, was thoroughly misrepresented in the concert-halls:

[For most composers whom we know imperfectly,] what we see is generally characteristic enough, untrue only in the sense that a kindly caricature is untrue. A man has a heavy moustache and the caricaturist makes it a little heavier. . . . But the case of Dvořák is rather different. . . . Our conception of Dvořák's musical personality, if it is based mainly on, say, the *New World* and G major Symphonies, the F major ['American'] Quartet, the Slavonic Dances and the Carnival Overture, is nearly as false as a caricature that makes a man *all* moustache.[1]

Abraham knew that the works he mentioned were not necessarily Dvořák's best, nor even his most characteristic in style, and that their limitation to instrumental genres (mostly in the classical forms) gave a lop-sided picture of his compositional output. The fact is that, among composers of the Romantic era, few could match Dvořák's combination of overall fecundity and diversity of genre. A self-critical composer who destroyed many of his earlier efforts, Dvořák nevertheless bequeathed to us eleven operas, numerous choral pieces including several large works with orchestra, about a hundred songs, nine symphonies, four concertos,[2] five symphonic poems, several concert overtures, thirty-three chamber works of several movements each, and numerous short pieces for piano solo and piano duet.

Today, admittedly, the Dvořák favourites of the 1940s continue to occupy a disproportionate place in performances of his music. But a closer look reveals that, after all, a significant change is under way. Within the genres of absolute instrumental music, traditionally regarded as Dvořák's forte but only on the basis of a few pieces, there is much greater recognition of the lesser-known works. For example Paul Griffiths, in his book *The String Quartet*, now judges Dvořák's four quartets of the period 1876–81 (*not* including the 'American') to be the first completely successful string quartets after Beethoven. Even more significant is the degree of interest in genres that, according to conventional wisdom, were uncongenial to Dvořák. These include his programme music, songs, and choral works, all of which are much

---

[1] 'Dvořák's Musical Personality', in *Antonín Dvořák: His Achievement*, ed. Viktor Fischl (Westport, Conn., 1970), 192–3; 1st edn., London, 1943.

[2] Including an early Cello Concerto in A major, B. 10, left unorchestrated, but scored for orchestra recently by Jarmil Burghauser.

more commonly heard today than fifty years ago.[3] Most remarkable of all is the case of the operas, generally ignored in the past. Six of them have now been performed in America, with four having their premières just in the last fifteen years. And they have been advancing to ever more prestigious venues, most notably in the case of *Rusalka*, with its joint production by the Houston Grand Opera and Seattle Opera in 1990–1, followed by the Metropolitan Opera in 1993 (the first ever production of a Dvořák opera by a major company in New York).[4]

If musical audiences are indeed beginning to perceive Dvořák in a new light, placing value on previously neglected works and negating the composer's earlier image as a specialist in absolute instrumental music, this poses a challenge to scholars. Which image is proper—the earlier one or the new one? If the new image is proper, then why did it not surface until almost a century after the composer's death? In the recent conferences, scholars were able to address these questions, and to explore new avenues toward the understanding and appreciation of Dvořák's music, with the help of the new perspectives on Czech culture made possible by contemporary political events. Let us now explore some of these new perspectives.

The first lesson offered by recent events is one of simple geography. We have always tended to think of Bohemia as lying in Eastern Europe, and therefore outside the centre of European cultural development.[5] For Dvořák, this scenario has contributed to his portrayal in history and criticism as a composer on the 'periphery'. However, the image was determined largely by political conditions that have now evaporated. Bohemia is undeniably a Slavic land, and thus, for certain purposes, it is natural to think of it in connection with its

[3] One sign of this change can be seen in *Opus*, listing all compact disc recordings available in the USA through normal channels. The issue of spring 1992, e.g., showed that Dvořák's Piano Quintet in A major, B. 28, always overshadowed by his later quintet in the same key, B. 155, was available in four different recordings. The number of recordings of the long-neglected Piano Concerto was up to seven. The fourteen string quartets could be had in a complete recording by the Prague Quartet, with two more complete recordings listed as being in progress. Each of the symphonic poems was available on a number of discs. Among vocal works, the *Love Songs*, practically unheard-of until recently, were listed in three recordings, and there were five of the monumental Stabat Mater.

[4] The operas remain an important lacuna in recordings. *Opus* in spring 1992 listed only *Rusalka* in a complete rendition. However, nearly all the overtures to the operas were recently made available for the first time, and 1992 saw a landmark with the first ever commercial recording of *Dimitrij*. Regarding the recent live performances in America, see David Beveridge, 'The Reception of Dvořák's Operas in America: A Social, Political and Aesthetic Odyssey', in *Dvořák in America: 1892–1895*, ed. John C. Tibbetts (Portland, Oreg., 1993), 297–319. This study, however, is already significantly outdated by events of 1993, including the Metropolitan *Rusalka* as well as a *Jakobín*—in its second ever complete performance in America—at the University of Iowa. Outside America, 1991 was notable for the German première, with many successful repeats, of *Dimitrij* (concert performance at the Europäisches Musikfest, Stuttgart, 1991; staged production at the Bayerisches Staatsoper, Munich, 1992).

[5] e.g. this book was made possible in part by grants from the 'Eastern European Commission' of the International Research and Exchanges Board (IREX). However, this division of IREX was recently renamed, appropriately, 'Central and Eastern European'.

'sister' Slavic lands lying further to the east. But this linkage has been overemphasized, in the first place by ethnocentric attitudes on the part of Germans and their Austrian brethren—attitudes that tended to exaggerate the gulf between Teutonic peoples on the one hand and Slavic on the other. More recently, the Iron Curtain has played the determining role, placing Czechoslovakia on the eastern side of an artificial dividing line, lumped together with a myriad of Slavic and non-Slavic nationalities.

Now we can finally stand back and observe that Prague actually lies in the exact centre of Europe. To call it Eastern Europe is like calling Wichita in Kansas the Eastern United States. A true international crossroads, Prague may be found at the mid-point of straight lines connecting Stockholm and Rome, Moscow and Madrid, Bucharest and Newcastle. And the territory of Bohemia, in its more immediate environs, lies largely surrounded by German-speaking lands to the north, west, south, and even south-east. Prague is on the main railway link from Vienna on the south-east to Dresden and Berlin on the north-west.

In its cosmopolitan culture, Bohemia has reflected well its geographic centrality. During the 'Golden Age' of the fourteenth century, the Czechs chose as their rulers a dynasty from Luxemburg. In the seventeenth century, some of the most outstanding examples of baroque architecture were built in Prague by Italians. The Jewish influence in Czech culture has been notable as well, going back as far as the early medieval days when the Czechs themselves first came to the region.

In music historiography, a dichotomy between 'nationalist' composers of 'Eastern Europe' and the supposedly 'mainstream' composers of Germany, France, and Italy has been pervasive. But the error of this approach, especially when applied to Czech composers, is now increasingly evident (see Chapter 10). What, after all, is this 'mainstream'? If we are speaking of the 'Austro-Germanic' symphonic tradition of the Classical-Romantic era, we must remember that its first and last great exponents—Johann Stamitz (i.e. Jan Stamic) and Gustav Mahler—actually came from the Czech lands. And in the field of opera, again one of the seminal figures for the era, Christoph Willibald von Gluck, grew up in Bohemia. The concept of a 'mainstream', when used to separate Germanic from Slavic traditions, now appears to be more confusing than helpful, and has perhaps (*pace* Donald Tovey) outlived its usefulness.

Unlike Stamitz, Gluck, and Mahler, Dvořák retained Bohemia as his home base throughout his life. And, like practically all composers of the nineteenth century from all countries, he was indeed a nationalist in many respects. He was a patriotic Czech, and often expressed publicly and privately his views regarding Czech rights within the German-dominated Habsburg Empire. In some of his vocal and programmatic works he gave explicit expression to feelings of national pride. And of course, even in his 'absolute' instrumental works we may assume that he was influenced in some way by the environment in which he grew up, which was Czech.

Nevertheless, among great composers of the Romantic era, his cosmopolitan tendencies are conspicuous, probably equalled only by Liszt, Saint-Saëns, and Tchaikovsky. Indeed Dvořák's internationalism, though natural enough for a Bohemian, came in for criticism from some Czech patriots who were trying to establish a national identity in the face of Habsburg pressures toward amalgamation (see Chapter 11). Dvořák's works were published during his lifetime less in Bohemia than in foreign lands (including England, the United States, and especially Germany). His vocal works included settings of substantial texts in four different languages: Czech, German, English, and Latin. He travelled often to Germany and Austria, and near the end of his life became an honorary member of the House of Peers in the Austrian parliament in Vienna. He undertook concert tours once to Russia and eight times to England, where he received an honorary doctorate from Cambridge University. Most significant of all, he alone among major European composers of the nineteenth century took up residence for an extended period (three years) in America.

In Dvořák's compositions, certain features often viewed as signs of 'nationalism' can now be seen clearly as gestures of *inter*nationalism. The *dumka* is a case in point, often identified as a Czech genre but actually Ukrainian in origin (see Chapter 13). Commentators have sometimes spoken of Dvořák's Slavic operas *Vanda* and *Dimitrij* (set in Poland and Russia respectively) as reflecting a Slavic mentality, regionally limited in its appeal and incomprehensible to 'Westerners'. But Russia was actually rather exotic to Dvořák, and almost as far from his home as was, say, Egypt for Verdi. To group the Slavic nations together as some kind of monolith alien to 'Western' values is a mistake made plain in 1991 by the demise of the Soviet Union. With our new outlook, we need to reconsider even the significance of such a familiar item as the Slavonic Dances, drawn from the dance traditions of several countries but commonly viewed by non-Czechs as reflecting Dvořák's 'nationalism'. Dvořák's compatriots correctly perceived them as an international collection, and Smetana—a more thoroughly nationalistic composer than Dvořák—even reacted against them negatively for this reason, with his own specifically Czech Dances.[6]

Another aspect of Dvořák's traditional image, namely that he was 'naïve', is in part a corollary of his status as a Czech, as viewed from the perspective

---

[6] John Tyrrell, *Czech Opera* (Cambridge, 1988), 218, citing Mirko Očadlík. Additional problems in viewing the Slavonic Dances as expressions of Czech nationalism are that they were commissioned by Dvořák's German publisher Simrock, and explicitly modelled on the Hungarian Dances of Brahms.

of old Germanic attitudes toward the Slavic races. In part, too, this image arose quite independently of national prejudices, but nevertheless via a process that only now can be seen clearly thanks to a willingness to view Dvořák in the wider context of European music. This process involved the international dispute between advocates of absolute music (supposedly composed by intuition) and programme music or opera (involving conscious reflection). Amid the now laughable excesses of this dispute, every composer had to be pigeon-holed into one camp or the other. Dvořák in fact embraced both sides wholeheartedly, but was nevertheless deemed an 'absolutist'. This judgement tended to reinforce his image as a 'naïve' composer, and also contributed to the neglect of his vocal and programmatic works (see Chapter 18).

Despite the new perspectives of the 1990s, the recent achievements of Dvořák scholars (including those in this volume) are of course based on a foundation of previous research, whose progress had been accelerating already for some decades. Considerable feats had been accomplished by the Czechs themselves, and to them some of the 'new' vantage points represent merely a common-sense approach that they have practised all along. However, it must be cautioned that the reception history of Dvořák's music in his own country has been anything but simple, and distortions have existed there too (see, again, Chapter 11, as well as Chapter 1). Moreover, the limited resources of a small and struggling country have hampered the work of Czech scholars to some extent, while barriers in trade and in language have impeded the dissemination of that work in foreign countries.

The fundamental pillar of all Dvořák research is Otakar Šourek's admirable four-volume study, *Život a dílo Antonína Dvořáka* (The Life and Work of Antonín Dvořák), first published in 1916–33 and revised in the 1950s. Unfortunately the work in its entirety is still available only in Czech, and it has no counterpart remotely comparable in scope in any other language. A further indispensable tool is Jarmil Burghauser's thematic catalogue and bibliography, published in 1960 in Czech, German, and English.[7] Dr Burghauser, working with the late John Clapham, has now prepared for publication a greatly revised and expanded edition reflecting many important new discoveries and providing a new comprehensive bibliography as well as a new listing of all known performances of Dvořák's works through 1900.

The complete critical edition of Dvořák's works, begun in the 1950s in Prague, now covers all of the instrumental music and many of the vocal works, including numerous pieces not previously published in any form. Important gaps remain, however, chiefly in the operas. Indeed, three of Dvořák's operas—*Alfred*, *Vanda*, and the first setting of *Král a uhlíř* (The King

---

[7] *Antonín Dvořák: Thematický katalog—Bibliografie—Přehled života a díla* (Prague).

and the Charcoal Burner)—have still not been published in any edition, even in piano reduction, which makes an assessment of his stylistic development extremely difficult.

Much of Dvořák's correspondence, too, remains unpublished to date. A team of researchers under the leadership of Milan Kuna in Prague has nearly completed the preparation of a critical annotated edition of Dvořák's correspondence and of documents relating to his life. So far, the letters written by Dvořák through 1895 have been printed, in three volumes.[8] The fourth volume, covering Dvořák's final period, is expected in 1995. However, all of the letters Dvořák received from others, as well as the documents, lie still in typescript. For foreigners, a difficulty with this edition is that the majority of the letters are in Czech; German and English versions are provided only in the form of a brief summary. Persons not familiar with Czech must still rely largely on a highly selective collection edited by Šourek, published in English translation as *Antonín Dvořák: Letters and Reminiscences*.

An analytical study of great value is Antonín Sychra's *Estetika Dvořákovy symfonické tvorby* (The Aesthetic of Dvořák's Symphonic Creation), published in Prague in 1959 and later issued in a somewhat abbreviated German version. This substantial volume views Dvořák's music through the highly tinted glasses of Socialist Realism, but nevertheless sheds valuable light on his whole corpus of orchestral music, especially as regards its compositional genesis and its relation to folk-music.

If Dvořák historically has suffered an injustice resulting from Germano-centric attitudes, the Germans have in recent decades gone far to redress the damage, providing some of the most penetrating musical analyses as well as the most authoritative and objective studies of Dvořák's life and the reception of his works. Highlights in the former category are the study of Dvořák's chamber music (in reality only the middle and later chamber works, since the early works were unavailable for study) published by Ernst Kurth's pupil Hans Kull in 1948[9] and the excellent comprehensive study of Dvořák's fourteen string quartets by Hartmut Schick, published in 1990.[10]

Currently the most up-to-date overview of Dvořák's life and work in any language, and one that presents important new findings in the context of an overall authoritative narrative, is a German work published in the sesquicentenary year, *Dvořák: Leben, Werke, Dokumente* by Klaus Döge (Mainz, 1991; see also his essay on the song cycle *Cypřiše*, Chapter 4 below). However,

---

[8] *Antonín Dvořák: Korespondence a dokumenty—Kritické vydání* (Antonín Dvořák: Correspondence and Documents—Critical Edition), ed. Milan Kuna et al., i–iii (Prague, 1987–9).

[9] *Dvořáks Kammermusik* (Berne, 1948).

[10] *Studien zu Dvořáks Streichquartetten* (Neue Heidelberger Studien zur Musikwissenschaft, ed. Ludwig Finscher and Reinhold Hammerstein, xvii; Laaber, Germany, 1990).

intended as it is for a non-professional readership, Döge's book avoids technical analysis of the music, and omits from its bibliography those sources available only in Czech (though Döge presents some of the Czech scholars' recent findings in his narrative).

In the English language, the most accurate and comprehensive general coverage yet published lies in a pair of books from 1966 and 1979 by the late British scholar John Clapham, emphasizing respectively Dvořák's works and his life.[11] In the mean time, some lengthy specialized studies have begun to appear in the form of doctoral dissertations—by Jan Smaczny of Britain on the early operas, and by several Americans: M. Robert Aborn regarding Dvořák's influence on American musical culture, Alan Houtchens on the opera *Vanda*, and the present author on the sonata forms.[12]

Going back to 1942, we find already the idea of a book in English combining essays on Dvořák by a variety of different authors, namely the British compendium *Antonín Dvořák: His Achievement*.[13] In this tradition followed, remarkably, five further examples between the years 1989 and 1994, each offering at least some contributions in English. In 1989 appeared *Musical Dramatic Works by Antonín Dvořák: Papers from an International Musicological Conference Prague, 19–21 May 1983*, edited by Markéta Hallová and others, presenting papers mostly in German but with a few in English and one in Russian. From 1994 we have *Dvořák-Studien*, edited by Peter Jost and Klaus Döge, based mainly on papers from a colloquium at Saarbrücken in 1991, and *Antonín Dvořák 1841–1991: Report of the International Musicological Congress Dobříš 17th–20th September 1991*, edited by Milan Pospíšil and Marta Ottlová. The former has essays mostly in German but with several in English, while the latter includes German, English, and French. In the single year 1993 two collective volumes appeared in the United States, entirely in English. *Dvořák and his World*, edited by Michael Beckerman, combines specially written essays by five American and British scholars with an important selection of documents including many presented for the first time in English; among the essays, the opening one by Leon Botstein in itself constitutes a landmark in Dvořák-reception: 'Reversing the Critical Tradition: Innovation, Modernity, and Ideology in the Work and Career of Antonín Dvořák'. Meanwhile *Dvořák in America: 1892–1895*, edited by John Tibbetts, combines a large number of

---

[11] *Antonín Dvořák: Musician and Craftsman* (New York, 1966) and *Dvořák* (New York, 1979).

[12] Jan Smaczny, 'The First Six Operas of Antonín Dvořák', D.Phil. diss. (Univ. of Oxford, 1989); Merton Robert Aborn, 'The Influence on American Musical Culture of Dvořák's Sojourn in America', Ph.D. diss. (Indiana Univ., Bloomington, 1965); H. Alan Houtchens, 'A Critical Study of Antonín Dvořák's *Vanda*', Ph.D. diss. (Univ. of California at Santa Barbara, 1987); David R. Beveridge, 'Romantic Ideas in a Classical Frame: The Sonata Forms of Dvořák', Ph.D. diss. (Univ. of California at Berkeley, 1980). None of these has yet appeared in print.

[13] For which Gerald Abraham wrote the essay mentioned above (see n. 1).

essays by American authors with, again, reprints of some important documents, all pertaining to this particular phase of Dvořák's career.

From the *Musical Dramatic Works* and the *Dvořák-Studien*, the present volume differs in that it makes no claim to serve as a 'conference proceedings'; rather it is a selection of approximately half the papers from a very large conference, in some cases extensively revised, and with extensive complementary materials drawn from other sources. From the two American publications of 1993, it differs most conspicuously in its strong representation of foreign scholars, especially Czechs. Specifically, nine contributions come from the USA, eight from the Czech Republic, three from Germany, three from Great Britain, and one from Croatia. The foreign contributions are mostly by scholars who have made Dvořák their main field of research, while the American contributors have for the most part focused their primary energies not on Dvořák but in related fields; many of them have impressive qualifications to assess Dvořák's position in relation to nineteenth-century music as a whole, to Slavic music, to Czech music, to American music, and to the development of the African–American musical culture which so interested Dvořák. (See 'Contributors' Profiles', pp. 295–9.)

Though not a comprehensive survey of Dvořák's life or work, this book presents views on a panoply of topics that concern all phases of his career, his compositional process, his personality, the reception history of his music, and the musical content of his works in most major genres. Particular emphasis is given to Dvořák's overall image (Chapter 1), as well as to his often-neglected contributions in vocal music (Parts I and II). In accordance with our new understanding of Bohemia in the geography of Europe, and of Dvořák's position as not only a nationalist but an internationalist, the remainder of the book contemplates Dvořák in turn as a Czech composer (Part III), as a Slav (Part IV), as a European in the broadest sense (Part V), and in relation to the culture of America (Parts VI and VII). The Appendix, finally, fills in a long-standing gap in the publication of source materials by reprinting in English for the first time two important newspaper interviews given by Dvořák in London in the 1880s.

The reader is cordially invited to explore in these pages some new approaches to one of the nineteenth century's most prolific, most diverse, and most misunderstood composers, and to share in the process of rethinking Dvořák.

D.R.B.

Prague
1994

A Word about Opus Numbers

The opus numbers for Dvořák's works are notoriously misleading as a guide to chronology, and their use serves very little purpose. Vocal and programmatic works can almost always be unambiguously identified by their title, save for the two different settings of *The King and the Charcoal Burner*, where in any case opus numbers are no help because the first setting has none. Instrumental works in the standard genres can always be distinguished by mentioning the key, with only three exceptions: the two symphonies in D minor, the two string quartets in A minor, and the two piano quintets in A major. The symphonies can be identified simply enough as the Fourth and the Seventh. For the pairs of string quartets and piano quintets, as in any other case where a catalogue number needs to be assigned, this book uses the 'B' numbers referring to Jarmil Burghauser's thematic catalogue—a chronological listing that accomplishes for Dvořák what Köchel did for Mozart and Deutsch for Schubert. With few exceptions, the use of opus numbers is avoided.

1

Metamorphoses of Dvořák's Image in the Course of Time

JARMIL BURGHAUSER

WITH the passing in 1991 of the sesquicentenary of Antonín Dvořák's birth, it is well worth while to look back and reconsider the various and developing attitudes toward the man and the artist—attitudes of both the past and the present public, amateurs as well as professionals, music-lovers as well as musicologists. Not only books but also views have their fates.

The only opinions known to us about Dvořák from his early days in the Czech Provisional Theatre orchestra (1862–71) are of his person, not of his music, and are reported in later reminiscences rather than any articles published at the time. A very limited circle of musicians knew anything about a certain young man from the country, shy and reticent, but very intransigent and obstinate in the opinions he held. He had graduated from the Prague Organ School, but having been unable to find a post as an organist, had accepted a job as first viola player in the theatre and often helped out at orchestral concerts of various organizations around the city.

A still smaller circle of friends had any idea that he was composing. These included some of his fellow students at the Organ School, for example Václav Urban, who said:

We sat side by side and showed one another our works. Dvořák had—and still has— a testy temper. I do not make any bones about having rebuked him for mistakes in harmony here and there. Oh, immediately the fat was in the fire. He was 'himself'. . . . [On another occasion] Dvořák told me: 'Look here, I am composing a mass and have just finished the Kyrie.' At this, he drew my attention to the first bars, which I have retained in memory up to now. . . . When I took exception to a point . . . a dissonance, he retorted: 'You don't understand this!' And, hot under the collar, he left me and did not speak a word to me for the rest of the evening.[1]

---

[1] 'Sedávali jsme vedle sebe a druh druhu navzájem ukazoval své práce. Dvořák byl—je posud—prudké povahy. Netajím, že jsem mu někdy tu a tam vytkl nějakou chybu v harmonisování. Ó, to bylo hned zle! On byl "svůj". . . . Dvořák . . . pravil: "Podívej se, já komponuji mši. Už jsem dokončil 'Kyrie'." Při tom

Others of his inner circle were colleagues in the theatre orchestra, for instance Josef Jiránek, who recalled:

Already at the time some of the members of the orchestra were aware of Dvořák composing and studying scores, but nobody knew what he was actually writing. Dvořák never showed anything to anybody and therefore we never dreamed how great a creative talent was developing covertly. He won sympathy by his straightforward character, his sincerity and kindness. He knew how to tell the truth—even a disagreeable one—to his colleagues' faces, with the best of intentions, naturally, and was never blamed for it. They tolerated things from him that they never would have tolerated from anybody else. He never learned to pay lip-service to anyone.[2]

We find no published views about Dvořák as a composer before 1871, when several press reports in Prague mentioned that Dvořák, 'a member of the orchestra of the Czech Regional Royal Theatre', had finished a comic opera—*Král a uhlíř* (The King and the Charcoal Burner). This was the first of Dvořák's two settings of this libretto. The author of one of these reports was Dr Ludevít Procházka, a friend of Bedřich Smetana. Smetana was at that time musical director of the theatre. Procházka stated that having examined the score of the opera, he discovered that 'Mr Dvořák has adopted the most progressive position and displays, everywhere, the most genuine artistic effort, never falling back on banal resources.'[3]

Apart from the graduation concert given in 1859 upon Dvořák's completion of instruction at the Prague Organ School (when he played some of his academic-style preludes and fugues), the first known public performance of a work by Dvořák was of the song 'Vzpomínání' (Remembrance), from his five songs to words by Eliška Krásnohorská, B. 23, in December 1871. Next came

mne upozorňuje na první takty, které mám až posud v dobré paměti. . . . A když jsem se pozastavil nad tím místem . . . dissonance, odvětil, "Ty tomu nerozumíš." A rozlobený ode mne utekl a toho večera již se mnou nemluvil.' Quoted by Boleslav Kalenský in 'Antonín Dvořák: Jeho mládí, příhody a vývoj k usamostatnění' (Antonín Dvořák: His Youth, Experiences, and Development toward Independence), in *Antonín Dvořák: Sborník statí o jeho díle a životě* (Antonín Dvořák: A Collection of Essays about his Life and Work), ed. Boleslav Kalenský (Prague, 1912), 36–9.

[2] 'Již tehdy věděli někteří členové orkestru, že Dvořák také komponuje a partitury studuje, ale co píše, nikdo nevěděl. Dvořák nikomu nic neukazoval a proto jsme netušili, jak velký tvůrčí duch se tu skrytě rozvíjí. Sympatie získal si svým přímým charakterem, svojí upřímností a dobrotou. Dovedl říci svým druhům pravdu třeba nepříjemnou do očí, ovšem v nejlepším úmyslu a nebylo mu to vykládáno ve zlé. Od něho snesli, co by si od jiného líbit nedali. Pochlebovat někomu se do smrti nenaučil.' See *Smetanův žák vzpomíná: Vzpomínky a korespondence Josefa Jiránka* (Smetana's Student Remembers: Reminiscences and Correspondence of Josef Jiránek), ed. Blažena Pistoriusová and Luboš Pistorius (Prague, 1941), 105–6. 2nd, rev. edn.: *Josef Jiránek: Vzpomínky a korespondence s Bedřichem Smetanou* (Josef Jiránek: Reminiscences and Correspondence with Bedřich Smetana), ed. Blažena Pistoriusová (Prague, 1957), 57–62.

[3] 'Pan Dvořák stojí na stanovisku nejnovějších pokroků a jeví všude nejryzejší snahu uměleckou, neutíkaje se nikdy k prostředkům banálním.' 'Zprávy domácí', *Hudební listy*, 2 (June 1871), 150. The other reports were in the same vol. of *Hudební listy*, 134, and in *Světozor* (1871), 344. The *Světozor* art. mistakenly gives Dvořák's first name as 'Josef'.

another of the Krásnohorská songs, 'Proto' (The Reason), along with an individual song, 'Sirotek' (The Orphan), B. 24, in April 1872. In that same month Bedřich Smetana conducted the overture to the first version of *The King and the Charcoal Burner*, and later that year an Adagio from a lost piano trio (B. 25 or 26?) was performed along with the First Piano Quintet, B. 28. The general opinion in the reviews of these works was that Dvořák was an exceptionally talented young composer of the most progressive orientation. They unanimously praised Dvořák's rich creative fantasy and ingenuity, but found that he was sometimes too experimental, overflowing with beautiful ideas but as yet incapable of controlling the formal aspect of his works.[4]

When Dvořák's biographer Otakar Šourek later analysed one of his technical innovations from the early 1870s, namely the combination of Scherzo and Finale into one closing movement (as may be seen for example in the First Piano Quintet, B. 28),[5] he made the following observation: contemporary reviewers, who did not know Dvořák's compositional beginnings, seized on his works from this period as on the works of

an absolute beginner who in his very first œuvre experimented in a precarious and unnecessary way, owing to an exaggerated quest for novelty and to a lack of an unfailing knowledge of the established forms. . . . This basic error . . . is about the same as if somebody were to reprehend some of Dvořák's daring and provocative harmonic turns as an ignorance of basic rules of harmony.[6]

Certainly the reviewers would have formulated their reservations differently had they been aware of Dvořák's previous output. The works of the early 1870s, which were the first to receive public performance, were hardly his 'first fruits': in the 1860s he had composed, to name only works that survive today, four string quartets, a quintet, two symphonies, a cello concerto, a song cycle, and an opera. Moreover, he had already made a stylistic odyssey, taking late Mozart, early Beethoven, and Mendelssohn as his point of departure, but then—beginning with the last movement of the Second Symphony in 1865—almost losing himself in the Klingsorian world of Liszt and Wagner.

---

[4] The reviews were: 'Vzpomínání': *Hudební listy*, 2 (Dec. 1871), 356, 362; 'Proto' and 'Sirotek': *Hudební listy*, 3 (1872), 135; the overture: ibid. 143; the Adagio: ibid. 135, 235 as well as *Národní listy* (4 and 9 July 1872); the Quintet: *Hudební listy*, 3 (1872), 307, 363, 379, 395.

[5] Other examples are in the Third Symphony of 1872–3, the lost Violin Sonata, B. 33, of 1873, the Piano Quartet in D major of 1875, the Piano Concerto of 1876 (in a sense), and the Violin Concerto of 1879.

[6] 'jako naprostého začátečníka, jenž hned v prvních svých pracích z předpjatého novotářství a ne dost pevné znalosti ustálených forem povážlivě a zbytečně experimentuje. To však byl základní omyl, omyl právě asi takový, jako kdyby pro některé harmonické smělosti a přepjatosti byla se Dvořákovi vytkla naprostá neznalost základů nauky a harmonii.' Otakar Šourek, *Život a dílo Antonín Dvořáka* (The Life and Work of Antonín Dvořák), 3rd edn., i (Prague, 1954), 154.

A decisive success was the performance in March 1873 of the *Hymnus z Hálkovy básně 'Dědicové Bílé hory'* (Hymn from Hálek's Poem 'The Heirs of the White Mountain'), written in the spring of 1872. After an upswing of Czech political, social, and cultural activity at the beginning of the 1860s, connected with hopes for an equitable incorporation of the Kingdom of Bohemia into the Austrian Empire, the Czechs had again been denied their governmental rights toward the end of that decade and experienced a strong sense of disillusionment. This was the time of the Ausgleich, which created the dual monarchy of Austria-Hungary and neglected the other nationalities within the Empire. The patriotic verses of the *Hymnus*, by the much-praised poet Vítězslav Hálek, gave vent to these frustrations, and contributed greatly to Dvořák's victory. The composer was accepted as a fighter for the Czech cause and was immediately integrated into the progressive faction of the Czech cultural front. Of course, this point was not stressed very much in the reviews, for obvious reasons, but between the enthusiastic lines of praise for the music (the composition pushed all other items of the programme into the background) the political undertone was felt.

Dvořák's next orchestral composition, a nocturne entitled *Májová noc* (May Night—the second of the Three Nocturnes, B. 31), was performed at the end of the same month (March 1873) and praised in a similar way. One of the critics even wrote: 'We feel that our temples are touched by the breath of a genius!'[7]

Strengthened by these successes, Dvořák in 1873 completed his Third Symphony, which shares with the *Hymnus* an atmosphere of festive resolve, not to mention definite thematic relations. The year 1873, however, was a year not only of successes but also of a serious defeat: Smetana accepted his opera *The King and the Charcoal Burner* for production at the Provisional Theatre, but, after the failure of the operatic ensemble to do it justice because of its technical demands, Dvořák felt obliged to withdraw the work from rehearsals and resigned himself to the fact that it would not be performed.

Thus we have here the first comprehensive image of Dvořák the composer, which prevailed for several years: a young, very talented beginner, not well versed in theory and perhaps a little too sombre, a follower of the most progressive trends in music but also struggling for a distinctive Czech culture. This image was rather corroborated than weakened by the composer's sub-

---

[7] 'Cítíme, že ovívá spánky naše dech genia.' [František Michel], *Hudební listy*, 4 (1873), 111. Curiously enough, the work was lost before any further known performance. However, long after Dvořák's death the separate string parts were found. A recent reconstruction by the present author was made possible by the fact that Dvořák used exactly the same music for the first part of the original No. 7 of his piano *Silhouettes*, B. 32, later discarded. (He eventually inserted the theme—in a different rhythmic shape—into the fourth of his *Humoresques*.) The reconstructed *May Night* had its modern première during the Prague Spring Festival in May 1991.

sequent works, and only much later, in fact not before the analyses carried out by Otakar Šourek in the 1920s, did the public and reviewers realize the substantial, decisive turn in Dvořák's style that occurred in 1874. In that year Dvořák took the extraordinary step of composing an entirely new musical setting of the libretto for *The King and the Charcoal Burner*, employing a radically different style. This change was undoubtedly conditioned by the influence of Smetana, who now replaced Wagner as a model. For Dvořák's contemporaries it was enough that the new version of the opera (first performed on 24 November 1874) displayed 'a genuine Czech physiognomy' (according to V. J. Novotný).[8] Ludevít Procházka contented himself—after praising Dvořák as an 'excellent hand in dramatic composition' —with pointing out his surprising versatility even in 'depicting the more jolly aspects of human life', obviously a hint that his previous output was found too sombre.[9]

This turn from Wagner to Smetana was not so sudden in other compositions as it was with the two versions of the opera, but an analogous relation can be found by comparing the two string quartets written in this period—B. 40 in A minor from November–December 1873, and B. 45 in the same key from September 1874. This is especially true if we take into account the original version of B. 40. (B. 40 was subjected to an extensive revision, which, however, was never completed—B. 45 may have been intended as a replacement.[10])

The substance of the turn in Dvořák's development was grasped neither by the public nor by the reviewers, and the increasing simplification of the structure of his music was attributed to the technical maturation of a late beginner. They were not able (or enabled) to understand the extent to which Dvořák was engaged in a quest for a personal style, or that he had tried—and rejected—nearly everything possible offered by the evolution of European musical style up to that time. Only now do we comprehend that some weaknesses in his early works (most of them not yet performed at the time!) were due not to an ignorance of the academic rules and principles of composition, but to constant experimentation. Their success, to be sure, was often impaired by the fact that they were never put to the test of a live performance: in his works of the 1860s, Dvořák did not have the opportunity to engage with an interpreter or an audience.

Toward the end of the 1870s, Dvořák's image gradually began to change, as interest in him began to rise outside Bohemia. Through his applications for

---

[8] *Dalibor* (1874), 415.

[9] 'Literatura a umění: Zpěvohra', *Národní listy*, 26/324 (26 Nov. 1874).

[10] See Otakar Šourek, *Dvořákovy skladby komorní: Charakteristika a rozbory* (Prague, 1943), 89–99. Eng. version, trans. Roberta Finlayson Samsour: *The Chamber Music of Antonín Dvořák* (Prague, 1956). See also Hartmut Schick, *Studien zu Dvořáks Streichquartetten* (Neue Heidelberger Studien zur Musikwissenschaft, ed. Ludwig Finscher and Reinhold Hammerstein, xvii; Laaber, Germany, 1990), 137–65.

government stipends, which he obtained for five years in succession, Dvořák
came to the attention of influential musical personalities in Vienna, including
Johannes Brahms. Brahms recommended Dvořák to his own publisher, Fritz
Simrock, who soon published the existing Moravian Duets and commissioned
the first book of Slavonic Dances. After the resounding success of these works,
journalists too began to take an interest in Dvořák, not only as a composer but
as a person.

The first short biographies of Dvořák did not appear in his own country
but abroad. The earliest sketch was written by the well-known critic Eduard
Hanslick, a member of the jury for the government stipends, and appeared in
Vienna in the newspaper *Neue freie Presse* on 23 November 1879. Since the
article contains several minor and major errors, it seems that Hanslick combined some scant information supplied to him as a member of the jury with
some perfunctory verbal intimation by the composer himself.[11] Evaluating
Dvořák's music, he quotes the well-known article by Louis Ehlert from the
Berlin *Nationalzeitung* (15 November 1878), inspired by the two works mentioned above that Simrock had published. To Ehlert's characterization of
Dvořák's music as having a 'celestial naturalness', Hanslick added that it had a
'folk character, reminiscent of Schubert'.[12]

A more substantial and detailed biographical sketch by Hermann Krigar,
including an interesting list of works, was published in the Leipzig music journal *Musikalisches Wochenblatt* at the beginning of 1880. As the preserved documents show, the facts upon which this article was based were supplied in
written form by the composer himself and can therefore—*cum grano salis*—be
taken as authoritative. It is a serious fault of the literature of the twentieth century up to now that this article has never been taken into account. Its picture
of Dvořák's childhood and adolescence, particularly with regard to the
encouragement given him by his family to pursue a musical career, is truer
than that given in more recent studies, which emphasize his apprenticeship in
the butcher's trade—an apprenticeship that, we now know, never occurred![13]

Although knowing something of Dvořák's social origins, neither the public nor the reviewers around the year 1880 particularly stressed the rural or
folkloric quality of his music. His 'Slavonic colour', as it appeared in the most
serious application of supreme artistic technique, was mentioned from time to

---

[11] pp. 1–2, s.v. 'Concerte'. Section on Dvořák repr. with minor revs. as 'Anton Dvořák' in Hanslick,
Concerte, Componisten und Virtuosen der letzten fünfzehn Jahre. 1870–1885 (Berlin, 1886), 245–51.

[12] Ibid. 249.

[13] 'Anton Dvořák: Eine biographische Skizze', *Musikalisches Wochenblatt* (Leipzig), 11/1–8 (Dec.
1879–Feb. 1880), 3–4, 7, 15–16, 39–40, 67–8, 79, 91. Critical edn. by Jarmil Burghauser (Leiden, Holland:
Clipeus Press, 1992). Eng. trans. by Susan Gillespie in *Dvořák and his World*, ed. Michael Beckerman
(Princeton, NJ, 1993), 211–29.

time, but only in the case of Hanslick (typically for him, in fact) was it seen as an obstacle in the way 'to the heights of absolute universal art'.[14]

In England, the universality of Dvořák's art was understood from the beginning, thanks initially to his Stabat Mater, performed there in 1883 and many times afterwards.[15] (This work was not given in the German-speaking areas until February 1885, at Mannheim.)

The stress on the 'ruralness', 'folk character', and 'earthiness' of Dvořák's music, leading—with a substantial amount of misunderstanding—to characterizations like 'a peasant among composers', arose gradually during the 1880s. This 'angle' was undoubtedly promoted by the composer himself, who very keenly understood that it provided him with a very specific 'trademark', singling him out from his contemporaries who stressed their 'philosophical', literary, and/or esoteric positions within the general neo-romantic trends leading to the fashionable styles of the *fin de siècle*.

Dvořák had a very deep (and deeply hidden) sense of humour. (Surprisingly enough, Ehlert, in his famous article mentioned above, sensed it from the music alone!) He also displayed the natural absent-mindedness of a highly reflective intellect. Very often he uttered sentences sounding quaint to anyone who—deceived by his deliberate 'rural' behaviour—may have taken this for *naïveté*. Paradoxically, this misunderstanding arose first in persons who adored him as a god: his pupils, not experienced enough to see through his complicated double role.

After decades of good-willed acceptance of Dvořák's personal peculiarities, with no negative implications as to the superb music he was writing, it took a truly malicious mind to attempt a defamation of Dvořák's image before the public. This meant taking advantage of a situation where, among the whole musicological community, probably only Hanslick systematically commented on and analysed his works (Ehlert had died in 1884), and he found no reason to analyse the man.

The first instance of such a malicious attitude towards Dvořák was quite insignificant. A certain James Huneker, a minor piano teacher at the National Conservatory in New York during Dvořák's directorship there (only later becoming a known music reviewer thanks to his sharp, often poisonous pen), was offended by Dvořák's refusal to give him an interview, whereupon he made him a target for malevolent and fabricated defamations in his 'memoirs'.

---

[14] 'Wir wissen noch nicht, ob sein üppiges Talent . . . sich aus dem engeren nationalen Ideenkreise aufschwingen werde zur Höhe absoluter allgemeiner Kunst.' Hanslick, 'Concerte'.

[15] On 10 Mar. 1883 (London Musical Society, under Joseph Barnby), 20 Dec. 1883 at Newcastle upon Tyne (Amateur Vocal Society, under William Reed), 13 Mar. 1884 (Royal Albert Hall Society, conducted by the composer), and numerous other performances (according to information from John Clapham). The work was performed in the following five years at least nineteen times in England alone, as well as nine times in the USA.

This succeeded, however, only in misleading some later fiction writers unfamiliar with critical evaluation of sources, and it did not affect Dvořák's musical fame to any degree.[16]

The other instance was much more dangerous and, in fact, rather detrimental to the composer's reputation, at least in his own country. It began with Otakar Hostinský (1847–1910), head of the music department of the Charles University in Prague, who was a militant adherent to the aesthetics and philosophy of Richard Wagner. For him even Smetana (considered by the Czechs as being more Wagnerian than Dvořák) was not Wagnerian enough; his love was Fibich. Hostinský regarded Dvořák as a reactionary, conservative musician, even if he never dared to pronounce this publicly, considering the great popularity of Dvořák at home and abroad. The tension between the university and Dvořák certainly originated from the moment when the university awarded Dvořák an honorary doctorate in March 1891, only after his honorary doctorate from Cambridge had already been announced, and only through the delivery of a diploma without any ceremonial act—in comparison with the really splendid ceremony at Cambridge. This must have left a rather bitter after-taste in Dvořák's mouth.

Hostinský's attitude was only the preface to a much more intensive and protracted campaign against Dvořák waged by the musicologist Zdeněk Nejedlý (1878–1962), who was Hostinský's pupil. The reason why Nejedlý took such a consistently hostile attitude to Dvořák and his music has yet to be discovered.[17] His attacks, beginning in 1901 and continuing almost to his death, ranged from such apparently innocent articles as 'Z hovorů Ant. Dvořáka se Z. Fibichem' (From the Conversations of Antonín Dvořák with Z. Fibich),[18] only slightly though meaningfully distorting what Fibich's reminiscences of Dvořák may have in fact been, through his crushing review of the première of *Rusalka*,[19] and some very negative paragraphs in his short *Dějiny české hudby* (The History of Czech Music),[20] to finally his drumming-up of a group (mostly centred around the Department of Musicology at the Czech division of the Charles University in Prague) that systematically began to undermine Dvořák's standing as a composer. The members of this group included, especially, Josef Bartoš, Otakar Zich, and Vladimír Helfert. (The last-mentioned many years later, in a letter addressed to Otakar Šourek, expressed his regret at having shared Nejedlý's inimical views on Dvořák.)

---

[16] See Josef Škvorecký, *Scherzo Capriccioso* (Toronto, 1963; in Czech). Eng. trans. by Paul Wilson as *Dvořák in Love* (New York, 1986). See also Miroslav Ivanov, *Novosvětská* (The New World [Symphony]) (Prague, 1984).

[17] But see Ch. 11.   [18] *Smetana*, 2 (1911–12), 52–3.

[19] 'Dvořákova *Rusalka*', in a not-too-significant periodical, *Rozhledy*, 11 (1901), 205–9. It is doubtful whether Dvořák ever saw this review.

[20] (Prague, [1903]), 182–6, etc. This book had no great influence, and was soon forgotten.

The principal philosophy of this group was to depict Dvořák as a primitive, incapable of any artistic reflection, a conservative, even a reactionary in style, haphazardly mirroring the most diverse influences.

The storm burst in 1912, after a prolonged polemic between the periodicals *Smetana*, representing the views of the Nejedlý camp, and *Dalibor*, defending Dvořák. On 15 December of that year several leading Czech journals carried simultaneously a sharp protest against the defamation of Dvořák's work, signed by a large group of outstanding Czech musicians.[21] This act led to a long controversy, temporarily subdued a little by the outbreak of World War I, but then continuing all the way to 1951 when Nejedlý—in his position as Minister of Education and as the leading communist figure in the field of culture—prevented a Dvořák monument from being erected in Prague, despite all the necessary preparations having been made.

The anti-Dvořákians, a small party but a formally important one (since comprising graduate musicologists), did not hesitate to support their argument with far-fetched views, for example that of the composer Hugo Wolf, whose impartiality can certainly be doubted considering that he was rejected in one of his applications for the government stipend when Dvořák received it. Nejedlý's camp was served in print mostly by the periodicals *Smetana*, *Čas*, and *Česká kultura*; the most scandalous book, *Antonín Dvořák: Kritická studie* by Josef Bartoš,[22] was later withdrawn by the author himself and the remaining stock in print was destroyed at his expense.

Dvořák's case was defended by the vast majority of professional musicians, composers, and reviewers—many of them members of the important cultural organization Umělecká beseda (Arts Society). Among them were Leoš Janáček and, starting in 1915, Otakar Šourek.[23]

Šourek recognized at that time the justification of Professor Josef Zubatý's appeal of 1909 regarding the need to research and analyse Dvořák's life and work systematically.[24] Sharing only modestly in the polemic, he began his great *œuvre* of Dvořák research, its peak being the basic four-volume biography, *Život a dílo Antonína Dvořáka* (The Life and Work of Antonín Dvořák). The first edition of the first volume appeared in 1916, while the last edition of the fourth volume was published in 1957, a year after Šourek's death.

The principal merit of Šourek's work lies in the systematic assembling and

---

[21] Including such names as the members of the Bohemian Quartet (at that time Karel Hoffmann, Josef Suk, Jiří Herold, and Hanuš Wihan), along with Karel Hoffmeister, Jindřich Kaan, Rudolf Karel, Karel Kovařovic, Jaroslav Křička, Oskar Nedbal, Vítězslav Novák, Václav Juda Novotný, František Ondříček, Karel Stecker, Otakar Ševčík, Václav Talich, and Vilém Zemánek.

[22] (Kritické studie, iii; Prague, 1913), 448 pp.(!)

[23] Others were Ladislav Vycpálek, František V. Krejčí, R. Klíma, Miroslav Rutte, Antonín Šilhan, Antonín Srba, and Jan Löwenbach.

[24] 'Hlas volajícího na poušti?' (A Voice Crying in the Wilderness?), *Hudební revue*, 2 (1909), 161–6.

logical ordering of myriads of biographical details. This was accomplished
with the help of Boleslav Kalenský's clippings from periodicals as well as his
description of known autographs and, later, the assistance of other collaborators, for Dvořák's youth especially Jan Miroslav Květ. Šourek was the first to
establish the correct chronological order of Dvořák's works, to analyse them
systematically, and consequently to attempt a study of the composer's creative
process.

Aided by Otakar Nebuška, Šourek was the first to study Dvořák's sketches,
a field in which, later, the main role was played by John Clapham. Šourek and
Clapham, in succession, were able to show how deceptive was the apparent
straightforwardness of Dvořák's creative process, and how complicated it
actually was, from the first ideas jotted down, through the continuous sketch,
to the full score, where he still incessantly added and deleted.[25] It should be
mentioned that Clapham has contributed—besides the sketch studies—many
very substantial books and studies on Dvořák in general, including several
articles on the dissemination of Dvořák's music abroad.

The next and then the youngest generation of Dvořák researchers was left
to corroborate and complete (sometimes also to amend or to discuss) the general image built by Šourek and Clapham. There have been a number of larger
meritorious works which have added much to our knowledge about Dvořák's
life or understanding of his music, without however altering Dvořák's image
in any substantial way. In the mean time, numerous shorter studies on particular problems of Dvořák's life and work came into existence. Many papers
have been presented at various conferences, such as the Prague Spring
Conference of 1983 on *Musical Dramatic Works by Antonín Dvořák*, the papers
from which have recently been published by the Česká hudební společnost
(Czech Music Society) (Prague, 1989), or the six colloquia during the Dvořák
Five-Year Celebration (1987–91) in Prague and Slaný, systematically dedicated to various theoretical and historical spheres so as to cover practically
everything important in this field—Dvořák's structural procedures, his harmony, his melodic structures, his use of tone-colour, and his relations to
Vienna, Germany, England, and the USA. This series of conferences included
eighty-six papers by thirty-five Czech and twenty-three foreign scholars. And
then there are a number of recent doctoral dissertations; regarding these, and
other recent landmarks in Dvořák bibliography, see the Introduction.

Our knowledge of Dvořák's life has undergone meaningful expansions and
revisions (in some cases still not widely disseminated) even in the most recent
years, testifying to the continued state of imperfection in our understanding

---

[25] John Clapham's principal studies in this direction are on the 'New World' Symphony—*Musical
Quarterly*, 44 (1958), 167–83; on the F minor Piano Trio—*Musica*, 13 (1959), 629–34; on the Seventh
Symphony—*Music and Letters*, 42 (1961), 103–16; and on the Cello Concerto in B minor—*Music Review*,
40 (1979), 123–40.

of this artist. For example, Dvořák's receipt of government stipends in 1875–9, and his initial contact with Brahms via this avenue, have been the subject of considerable confusion and misinformation until recently. It has often been stated that he was rejected for the prize in one instance. However, in the first two biographical sketches of Dvořák, by Hanslick and Krigar, which as mentioned above have been generally neglected in the secondary literature, both authors rightly speak of five stipends in succession and no rejections. Another common error is to state that Johannes Brahms was a member of the jury that assigned the first stipend to Dvořák. In 1985 Milan Kuna discovered, in the archives of the Ministerium für Kultur und Unterricht in Vienna, the record of the jury's proceedings in 1874 (for Dvořák's first award in 1875). It shows clearly that the jury members were Johann von Herbeck, Felix Otto Dessoff, and Eduard Hanslick.[26] Brahms replaced Dessoff in the next year.[27]

Another instance is the case of Dvořák's supposed completion of an apprenticeship in the butcher's trade—a legend definitively laid to rest in my own study of this issue.[28] Attendant to this 'butcher legend' are several common errors regarding the dates of various events in Dvořák's childhood, and the general thrust of his early training in music. These too are touched upon in my study just mentioned, and elaborated still more in my paper delivered at the colloquium in Slaný of 1987.[29]

As to the later course of Dvořák's life, recent discoveries about the story of his courtship and wedding add an interesting aspect to our image of Dvořák the man. In 1865 the actress Josefina Čermáková held Dvořák spellbound, and was the inspiration at least for his song cycle *Cypřiše* (Cypresses), if not also for his first two symphonies, written in that same year. But Josefina never responded positively to Dvořák's feelings. On the other hand, her younger sister Anna and Dvořák took a mutual liking to each other and decided in 1873 to get married. The Čermák family, whose head was a well-to-do Prague goldsmith, strongly opposed this union. But the wedding eventually took place on 17 November 1873, after the couple resorted to a very old device used by lovers in such circumstances. (The first child, Otakar I, was

[26] See Milan Kuna, 'Umělecká stipendia Antonína Dvořáka' (Antonín Dvořák's Artistic Stipends), *Hudební věda* 29/3 (Dec. 1992), 295–300. The document is to be pub. in one of the last vols. of *Antonín Dvořák: Korespondence a dokumenty—Kritické vydání* (Antonín Dvořák: Correspondence and Documents—Critical Edition), ed. Milan Kuna et al. (Prague), probably in the late 1990s.

[27] See David Beveridge, 'Dvořák and Brahms: A Chronicle, an Interpretation', in *Dvořák and his World*, 59.

[28] Burghauser, 'Concerning One of the Myths'.

[29] 'Počátky hudebního vzdělání A. Dvořáka', paper read 17 June 1987. Publ. in Engl., ed. Graham Melville-Mason, 'The Beginnings of Dvořák's Musical Education', *Czech Music: The Journal of the Dvořák Society* 18/2 (winter 1994), 32–51.

born on 4 April 1874.) The frustrating courtship may have inspired Dvořák's composition just at this time of an orchestral overture (later destroyed) on the subject of Romeo and Juliet.[30]

One factor in Dvořák's artistic development which is just now coming to light, but which needs still to be more fully appreciated, is the influence of Leoš Janáček on his orientation toward the study of folklore from other Slavic nations. Janáček studied at the Prague Organ School from October 1874, and may have been present at the première of *The King and the Charcoal Burner* on 24 November that year, since Dvořák's name was becoming famous in Prague at the time; the personal contact, however, was more probably established because of Janáček's interest in the 'Caecilian reform' in church music, of which an important representative was Professor Josef Förster, *regenschori* of St Adalbert Church (the church of Svatý Vojtěch). Dvořák was then the organist at that church, and since he and Janáček lived around the corner from one another and had practically the same path to the church, they inevitably must have met then.[31]

There is no question but that, in the decades following the pioneering work of Šourek and Clapham, Dvořák's image has acquired still more new traits. New research will probably corroborate the refutation of the false ideas fostered by Nejedlý's camp, but also shared by several foreign, superficial reviewers, that Dvořák was a simpleton, a 'popular Brahms', incapable of deeper artistic reflection.

We have still to delve deeper into some aspects of Dvořák's personality in order to be able to appreciate fully the intrinsic value of his work. One field that needs more attention is the subject of Dvořák as a performing artist. A good study of Dvořák the conductor was published by Josef Bachtík;[32] Šourek's study on him as a viola player is also substantial;[33] Dvořák the pianist is the theme of a study by the Russian scholar Mstislav Smirnov,[34] which could be complemented by Josef Suk's large and detailed description of Dvořák's abilities in this field in an unpublished letter to Otakar Šourek of

[30] According to the report of *Dalibor* (1873), 206, 'obrav si za podnět basnický zejména scénu v hrobce' (the composer chose in particular the scene in the sepulchre for his poetic inspiration). He destroyed the work probably at about the time of his marriage to Anna, during his first self-critical survey of his works composed up to the time, undertaken—according to new discoveries and analyses—some time in Dec. 1873. The overture appears in the list of destroyed compositions he made *c.*1888.

[31] See Jarmil Burghauser, 'Dvořákova a Janáčkova dumka', *Hudební rozhledy*, 44/2 (1991), 86–9; based on 'Dvořák's and Janáček's *Dumka*', paper delivered at the Symposium of the International Musicological Society, Melbourne, Australia, Aug. 1988.

[32] *Antonín Dvořák dirigent* (Prague, 1940).

[33] 'Dvořák orchestrálním violistou' (Dvořák as an Orchestral Violist), *Hudební věstník*, 28 (1935), 7–9; repr. in *Z Dvořákovy cesty za slávou* (Dvořák's Path to Glory) (Prague, 1949).

[34] In *Antonín Dvořák . . . sborník statyey* (Antonín Dvořák . . . a Collection of Essays) (Moscow, 1967). Smirnov also pub. a book on Dvořák's compositions for piano, *Fortepiannoe tvorchestvo A. Dvoržáka* (Moscow, 1960).

June 1916. The least attention has been paid to Dvořák the organist, although his capacity here also must have been much above average. He held a regular organist's position only from 1874 to 1877, but he had graduated with distinction from the Prague Organ School in 1859. And as late as 1882 he was appointed as organist for the festive inauguration of the renewed independent Czech University in Prague.[35] A study of Dvořák the performer must take into account also his childhood beginnings as a violin player, when, for example, he played a violin solo in Antonín Liehmann's *offertorium* Ave Maria at the age of 13.

Other areas in need of research, of which I will suggest here only two, pertain to Dvořák the man. First, the spiritual background of his creation, which was based on his profound Christian faith, inherited in rudimentary form, and inspired later by his schooling in liturgical music and his short career as an organist, but then vitally rethought and refelt in the 1880s; secondly, Dvořák's very active involvement as a citizen. By this I do not refer to his patriotism, of which much has been said already, but to his willingness to join in public activities. I should like here to make only a few notes on the second of these themes—Dvořák's civic activities.

Already in 1872 Dvořák showed his sense of responsibility within the musical community by joining a group of Czech musicians who signed an open letter in support of Bedřich Smetana, when the latter was attacked by his adversaries. He later proved his loyalty to Smetana again by his joining the 'Association of Smetana's Followers' in 1882.[36]

In the course of his career Dvořák accepted innumerable appointments to committees and administrative posts having to do with musical matters. One of the first was during his work at St Adalbert's Church: in 1875 he was appointed to a committee to pass judgement on the competing bids for the reconstruction of the organ at the church and, following this, to the committee for overseeing the project.[37] In the same year, he was elected a member of the central committee of the Union of Czech Theatre Writers and

[35] The principal part of the service was the D major Mass by V. E. Horák.

[36] Dvořák's devotion to Smetana seems ironic in view of the later battle between supporters of the two. Further indication of his high regard for Smetana is given by his sending a funeral wreath with a moving inscription to Smetana upon the latter's death in 1884, and his attendance at a memorial service at Smetana's grave in 1887. The priest Adolf Pergl, present at the funeral service, described Dvořák as having crept into the back part of the church and wept bitterly—see 'Jak došlo k oslavě 60tých narozenin mistra hudby Dr. Antonína Dvořák' (How the Sixtieth Birthday Celebration of the Musical Master Dr Antonín Dvořák Came to Pass), in *Z pamětní knihy obce Nelahozeves o jejím slavném rodáku mistru hudby Dr. Ant. Dvořákovi na paměť 25. výročí jeho úmrtí* (From the Memorial Book of the Community of Nelahozeves Regarding its Celebrated Native Son, the Musical Master Dr Antonín Dvořák, in Memory of the Twenty-fifth Anniversary of his Death) (Prague, 1929), 3–4.

[37] His later donation of a new organ to the church at Třebsko, a hamlet near his beloved summer home Vysoká, must be taken more as a private matter, as a reminiscence of one of his former professions as well as of his Christian faith.

Composers. Still more interesting was his activity in the Umělecká beseda (Arts Society), of which he was elected a member of the executive board of the music division in 1878, and a year later its chairman. He worked on several juries of this board for music competitions, and on the editorial staff of its publishing house, Hudební matice.

In 1891 Dvořák was appointed to the committee that was to decide on the Czech music to be heard at the International Music and Theatre Exhibition in Vienna, and in 1894 he became a member of the artistic board of the Czech Philharmonic Orchestra, when this institution was being founded. In June 1897 he was appointed a member of the jury for government stipends to artists, as the successor to Brahms, who had died in April. (Did Dvořák ever dream of such a post when he, twenty-two years earlier, was awarded the stipend by the same board?) When, at the end of 1899, he was appointed a member of the board of directors of the fourth class of the Czech Academy of Sciences and Arts (of which he had been a member since 1890), it was surely owing to his previous activity and proven value in such posts, not only to his fame as a composer.

Even without formal appointments, he was often invited unofficially to give his opinion on musical matters, for example in 1880 regarding a Prague military band, before its departure to a competition in Brussels, or in 1885, to pass judgement on some arrangements as performed by the renowned brass band of the Twenty-Eighth Infantry Regiment, led by Rudolf Nováček (composer of one of the most popular pieces for this medium, the 'Castaldo March').

Interesting also are the activities in which he openly refused to share. An example is the competition for an Imperial March in 1898, for which the government officially invited him to submit an entry. This refusal, though, did not preclude his being appointed a member of the Ministerial Experts Collegium for Copyright in the field of music at the end of the same year, nor his being awarded the state decoration *Litteris et artibus* (after having already received the Order of the Iron Crown in 1889). Dvořák's appointment to the Austrian House of Peers (1901), however, was only an honour bestowed on an internationally renowned artist, meant by the Austrian Prime Minister Körber as a friendly (and noncommittal) gesture towards Czech political representation at that time; it could hardly be considered a genuine public activity in the sense we have been discussing.

The above remarks are not only formal additions to our image of Dvořák today; rather, they actually enlarge our grasp of the intellectual and moral background of Dvořák the composer. Apparently plain and uncomplicated, all his life he combined the utmost straightforwardness with a deliberate stress on one side of his profound and complex personality, namely the character of

a 'plain Czech musician'. But that designation was one that he alone was entitled to use, and which should not be improperly repeated as a fitting characteristic. It was, as a matter of fact, only a defence against the kind of
glorification which he detested as a true and humble Christian.

I

THE UNKNOWN DVOŘÁK:
A MINI-SYMPOSIUM ON THE
EARLY SONG CYCLE,
CYPRESSES

2

Cypresses: An Appreciation, and a Summary of Editorial Problems on the Eve of its First Publication

MIROSLAV NOVÝ

DVOŘÁK'S early song cycle *Cypřiše* (Cypresses) has received very little attention in the literature until recently. Besides Otakar Šourek's treatment of the work, contained in the first volume of his *Život a dílo Antonína Dvořáka* (The Life and Work of Antonín Dvořák),[1] and some smaller discussions in other of his books, Jaromír Borecký had been the only one to deal with this subject extensively, in his study on the composer's songs for the compendium *Antonín Dvořák: Sborník statí o jeho díle a životě* of 1912 (Prague).[2] But now this neglected musical work is suddenly arousing interest, as evidenced by Chapters 5 and 6.

To this day the work—except for some arrangements Dvořák made later of some of the songs—has remained unpublished. However, in the year 1991, marking the 150th anniversary of the composer's birth, the Committee for the Publication of Antonín Dvořák's Works made plans to publish this opus with Editio Supraphon in Prague, and it is hoped that the edition will appear soon. The editors are convinced that in spite of all its understandable signs of creative immaturity, Dvořák's original *Cypresses* is a work so spirited and worthy of publication that it will provoke a profound interest on the part of researchers, and attract performing artists as well. As one of the editors currently involved in the preparation of the edition (along with Jarmil Burghauser), I should like to review the known facts concerning the cycle, while also presenting my own findings on the work and the circumstances of its origin.

Cypresses was composed by Dvořák in the summer of 1865, between his First and Second Symphonies, when he was 24 years old. Set with piano

---

[1] 3rd edn. (Prague, 1954), 75–81.   [2] 'Antonín Dvořák v písni' (pp. 249–306).

accompaniment, the songs are based on lyrics from a collection of poems of the same title by Gustav Pfleger-Moravský (1833–75), a Czech poet, playwright, and author of novels. The *Cypresses* poems were published in 1862 by I. L. Kober's publishing house in Prague, and the appearance of the work was at that time clearly an important cultural event in the context of the rather undeveloped state of Czech poetry, in which every piece of new work was welcomed as a significant contribution and enrichment.

Dvořák set to music all eighteen poems from the part of the collection of poems called *Písně* (Songs). His full title for the song cycle, as given on the autograph manuscript, was *Písně vyňaté z 'Cypřiše' od Gustava Pflegera Moravského pro jeden hlas s průvodem piana* (Songs Taken from 'Cypresses' by Gustav Pfleger-Moravský for a Single Voice with Piano Accompaniment).

The *Cypress* poems fell into the hands of the young and, at this point, completely unknown composer Dvořák during the time of his intense romantic interest in the young Czech actress Josefa (Josefina) Čermáková (1849–95). Ms. Čermáková was an actress with the Provisional Theatre in Prague, in the orchestra of which Dvořák was playing the viola. She was the daughter of a Prague goldsmith, and became Dvořák's musical pupil. Dvořák's love for her appears to have been unrequited, but he later married her younger sister, Anna, and he maintained close contact with Josefina until her death in 1895. His summer house at Vysoká was on the estate of Josefina and her husband, Count Václav Kounic. In the B minor Cello Concerto of 1894–5 Dvořák paid tribute to Josefina by quoting a song of his that was one of her favourites (it is not one from *Cypresses*, however), and following her death he added the coda to the concerto as a memorial, quoting the same song again.[3] Dvořák's settings of the *Cypress* songs are dedicated not to Josefina but to his close musical friend Karel Bendl.[4] However, we may guess that only his shyness prevented him from dedicating the work to the one who actually inspired it.

The poems express, through bitter-sweet and sentimental verses, the passionate, tormenting, and resigned feelings of personal love which, after being disappointed, tries to find its fulfilment in love for the protagonist's homeland (Nos. 15 and 18). Dvořák apparently found in Pfleger's *Cypresses* an adequate expression of his own disillusioned love. Such a resonance gave birth to a spontaneous, deeply emotional, and extraordinarily intimate piece of music.

[3] Our knowledge of Dvořák's youthful feelings for Josefina comes from Šourek, *Život*, i; see also Jarmil Burghauser's notes to the critical edn. of the six songs rev. ?1881–2 (B. 123–4), based on six of the *Cypresses* songs (Prague, 1959), p. viii. Šourek wrote about Dvořák's relationship with Josefina as though it were publicly known. Unfortunately we don't know Šourek's sources of information; it appears that no letters by Dvořák have survived from the 1860s. Quite possibly the sources have been suppressed, considering the intimate nature of the relationship and Dvořák's known personal shyness. New research among the materials in the bequest of Dvořák's family may yet uncover primary sources concerning this episode.

[4] The autograph reads: 'svému dobrému příteli Karlu Bendlovi k milé upomínce věnuje . . . Chvála Bohu!' (to my good friend Karel Bendl in fond token I dedicate . . . Praise be to God!).

Cypresses is practically the first known vocal work of Dvořák, his first contact as a composer with the poetic word and at the same time his largest song cycle. By its origin it almost goes to the very beginning of his artistic creation. The work was written as if at one draft; within only eleven days in July of 1865 Dvořák composed fifteen songs, and after a short break he finished the last three in only two more days.[5] This testifies to the fervour with which he created this most personal statement.

The main, crucial inner meaning of the text, the spirit of each poem, is rendered in the songs in a remarkable way. Rather than an attempt at scrupulous attention to the verbal description, the main principle in forming the songs for Dvořák was the feeling for the overall mood, intensified by his own love, together with strong inspiration in a purely musical sense. Dvořák put the poems into music with a distinctive melodic line supported by vivid harmonies in the piano accompaniment. From the compelling sincerity of the song-settings follows a considerable amount of appealing 'coarseness' in their expression; however, the cycle as a whole already shows, in many details, a surprising indication of originality through which we may discern occasional flashes of a great talent.

Although this cycle is obviously the work of a remarkably talented composer, of course there can be found a number of imperfections, as in any other first fruit. The most evident one is an inaccurate or even faulty declamation of the sung word. This problem may be an unconscious reflection of the disputes current at that time between accentual and quantitative prosody in the Czech language (see Chapter 5). On the other hand it may result from the melodies having been conceived in a purely musical, instrumental way, and the words having then been placed beneath them without sufficient skill or experience in such matters. Another inadequacy can be found in a certain unevenness in both harmony and melodiousness, and, here and there, in a rather harsh stylization of the piano part, although we must admit that this roughness is often quite appealing.

Dvořák himself recognized imperfections in his work quite soon, mainly its declamatory faults, as can be seen in the comments he made on 21 September 1866, one year after he had finished the cycle. In an annotation to the autograph score, the composer acknowledged the validity of criticisms made by the dedicatee Karel Bendl, who had pointed out problems of declamation when Dvořák read through the songs for him at the piano: 'When I played these songs with Mr Bendl he told me that the declamation was wrong in many places; after a year, when by accident my prematurely born offspring

---

[5] Dvořák dated the completion of the songs on his autograph score as follows: 10 July 1865 (Song 1), 11 July (Songs 2–3), 12 July (Songs 4–5), 13–20 July (Songs 6–15), 26 July (Songs 16–17), 27 July (Song 18).

came back into my hands, I realized that his criticism was entirely justified.'[6] For this reason, undoubtedly, along with the extremely intimate character of the songs, Dvořák seems never to have made an attempt to have the songs performed or published in their original form.

But he kept returning to them in his later works, quite often with evident relish—apparently both for the memories of his love (conscious of what the songs meant for him) and for the sake of their musical qualities, of which he was well aware. In the beginning he made use merely of some of the melodies from the cycle when composing other works, as in the operas *The King and the Charcoal Burner* and *Vanda* and the piano cycle *Silhouettes* (a work of reminiscences which makes use also of others of Dvořák's earlier works—primarily his first two symphonies). But much later he worked with the whole texture of many of the songs. Twelve were revised with improvements in the declamation and piano accompaniment, while still preserving their original character, and were published as *Čtyři písně* (Four Songs), Op. 2, and *Písně milostné* (Love Songs).[7] Also, he chose twelve songs, including four that were never reused in any other way, and adapted them for a string quartet without voice. This collection he entitled *Ohlas písní* (Echo of Songs), referring to the origin of the pieces.[8] In this arrangement Dvořák preserved the form of the original work to the maximum degree; with no need to worry about declamation, he could simply transcribe the songs into the instrumental medium while keeping their original melodies, harmonies, and rhythms. The quartet version of the *Cypresses* has recently appeared quite often in chamber music concerts, with great success.[9]

As mentioned above, during his life Dvořák did not, to our knowledge, attempt to have the original *Cypresses* either performed or published. For a full eighty years after his death the work as a whole remained unperformed. Its first realization took place only on 1 May 1983, in the Dům umělců (House of Artists—previously and now again called the Rudolfinum) in Prague, when the Swedish singer Eva Serning sang all eighteen songs with piano accompaniment by Radoslav Kvapil, in English! (The translation was by Dr John Clapham.) This was the way in which the work, purged from Czech declam-

---

[6] 'Když jsem tyto písně s p. Bendlem hrál, pravil mně, že na mnoha místech je špatná deklamace; po roce, když jsem tento můj nedorozený výrobek náhodou do ruky dostal, nahlédl jsem k mému potěšení, že výrok p. Bendla úplně podstatný jest.'

[7] A preliminary compilation of *Six Songs* rev. ?1881–2 (B. 123), of which four were pub. as the *Four Songs*, Op. 2 (B. 124), and the remaining two included later in the *Love Songs*, was also dedicated to Karel Bendl, who had criticized the original declamation.

[8] Not pub. during Dvořák's lifetime. In the two posthumous edns., by Josef Suk (Prague, 1921) and by the editors of the complete critical edn. of Dvořák's works (Prague, 1957), the title is simply *Cypřiše* (Cypresses).

[9] For a complete tabulation of all Dvořák's uses of the various *Cypress* songs in later works throughout his career, see again Ch. 5.

atory imperfections by its translation into another language, was presented to the public for the first time. However, in 1991 a recording on compact disc was made with the British tenor Philip Langridge, again accompanied by Kvapil, singing the original Czech text.[10]

The autograph manuscript of the work, which is serving as the basis of our edition, was in the hands of Dvořák's family until it was acquired by the Muzeum české hudby (Museum of Czech Music) in Prague in 1980. For the time being, this autograph represents the only available source for the complete work. However, the illustrated journal *Zlatá Praha* (Golden Prague) published in 1905 a facsimile of fourteen bars from the cycle's first song, 'Vy vroucí písně' (You Ardent Songs), written in Dvořák's handwriting but differing in details from the known version of the song in the complete autograph. According to the anonymous accompanying article, 'Vzpomínka na Antonína Dvořáka' (Remembrance of Antonín Dvořák), this song was saved from destruction by Mořic Anger, because he refused to give it back to the composer despite his repeated requests.[11] (Anger lived together with the young Dvořák for some time; he later became a conductor at the National Theatre in Prague.) The autograph from which the facsimile was taken—which may be presumed to contain at least the one whole song—is missing today, and we know only those fourteen bars of it from *Zlatá Praha*. It seems to be an earlier, unfinished version of the work, but, of course, a question arises as to whether there might be still further autographs of the songs or even of the whole cycle.

It is necessary to point out that the surviving complete autograph contains an enormous number of mistakes and inaccuracies, which have to be identified and corrected. In some cases the string quartet score of *Cypresses* can be used as an auxiliary source which is, as mentioned above, closer to the original form of 1865 than are the later revisions of the songs. At some places in the autograph, locating the words beneath the notes is problematic as well, since Dvořák was a little careless in this matter.

Special care in preparation of the edition has been given to the words. *Cypresses* will, or course, be published with the original Pfleger poems upon which it was composed; but because its live performance in Czech would undoubtedly be undermined by the declamatory imperfections, it was necessary to provide new texts. Their author is Ivo Fischer, who died a short time ago. His poems are lively, of good literary quality, and suitable for declamation, but unfortunately their subjects are not the same as those of Pfleger's poems: the expression of spontaneous love is replaced by poetizing reminiscence. It might be appropriate to consider the possibility of a revision of

[10] Unicorn-Kanchana DKP (CD) 9115. [11] *Zlatá Praha*, 22 (1905), 57.

Pfleger's texts, even a radical revision, to preserve the inner relationship between words and music. The songs will also be published with German words by Dr Magdalena Havlová and with the above-mentioned English translation by Dr John Clapham.

3

Texts to Dvořák's *Cypresses*

GUSTAV PFLEGER-MORAVSKÝ

ENGLISH TRANSLATION BY
DAVID R. BEVERIDGE

THESE are the poems that Dvořák set in *Cypresses*, given here for the first time with a literal English translation. The translation adheres whenever possible to the original Czech word-order, even when it is not the most natural in English. It may be compared with the free translation for singing made by John Clapham, distributed by Unicorn-Kanchana with the recording by Philip Langridge (1991).[1] The source is the original edition of the poems, published in Prague in 1862. The volume is entitled *Cypřiše* (Cypresses); the poems Dvořák set form one section within it, called *Písně* (Songs).

I

Vy vroucí písně spějte
Tou nocí v mživou dál;
Všem pozdravení dejte,
Jež tíží tichý žal!

You ardent songs, go forth
through this night, drizzly, onward;
to everyone your greetings give,
whom burdens silent woe!

Tam spějte přes padoly,
Kde moje milka dlí,
A rcete, co mne bolí,
A proč letíte k ní!

Thither go, past the lowlands
where my beloved dwells,
and tell what me pains,
and why you fly to her!

A zapláče-li s vámi,
Povězte mi to zas:
Jinak ať dolinami
Zavane vítr vás!

And if she weeps with you,
bring tidings to me back:
else may through the marshes
the wind blow you about!

---

[1] DKP (CD) 9115. The version given with the disc reverses the order of Songs 9 and 10, as does Langridge in his performance, though preserving the original order in the trans. Also, the Czech text given with the disc differs in some points from the orig.

2

V té sladké moci očí Tvých
Jak rád bych zahynul,
Kdyby mně k životu jen smích
Rtů krásných nekynul.

Však tu smrť sladkou zvolím hned
S tou láskou ve hrudi:
Když mě jen ten Tvůj smavý ret
K životu probudí.

In that sweet power of your eyes
how gladly I would die,
if only to life the laughter
of lovely lips would not beckon.

But that death sweet I'll choose at once
with this love in my breast:
if me only those smiling lips of yours
to life will awaken.

3

V tak mnohém srdci mrtvo jest
Jak v temné pustině;
V něm na žalosť a na bolesť
Ba místa jedině,

Tu klam i lásky horoucí
V to srdce vstupuje,
A srdce žalem práhnoucí
To mní, že miluje.

A v tomto sladkém domnění
Se ještě jednou v ráj
To srdce mrtvé promění
A zpívá starou báj!

In so many a heart death dwells
as in a dark wasteland;
therein for grief and pain
is room, nothing else.

Here delusion and love's passion
into that heart enter,
and that heart in misery pining—
thinks that it loves.

And in this sweet presumption
itself once more to a paradise
this dead heart transforms
and sings the old tale!

4

Ó duše drahá jedinká,
Jež v srdci žiješ dosuď:
Má oblétá Tě vzpomínka,
Ač dělí nás zlý osud.

Ó kéž jsem zpěvnou labutí,
Já zaletěl bych k Tobě:
A v posledním bych vzdechnutí
Ti vypěl srdce v mdlobě.

Oh dear soul, the only one,
that in my heart has lived ever:
my memory hovers about you,
though parts us evil fate.

Oh, that I were a singing swan,
I would fly to you:
and in my last sighing I would
to you sing out my heart in swooning.

5

Ó byl to krásný, zlatý sen,
Jejž spolu jsme tam snili!
Ach škoda, že tak krátký jen
Byl sen ten přespanilý!

Tak sladká touha v bytosti
Se celé uhostila,
Až při loučení žalosti
Se slza dostavila.

A často chodím na horu
A za Tebou se dívám:
Však po dalekém obzoru
Jen žal svůj rozesívám.

Oh, was that a lovely, golden dream,
that together we there dreamed!
Oh a shame, that so short only
was that dream supremely gracious!

Such sweet longing in that being
whole resided
until upon parting's woe
a tear arrived.

And often I go to the mountain
and for you look:
but along the far horizon
only my woe do I see.

6

Já vím, že v sladké naději
Tě smím přec milovat:
A že chceš tím horoucněji
Mou lásku pěstovať.

A přec, když nazřím očí Tvých
V tu přerozkošnou noc;
A zvím, jak lásky nebe s nich
Svou na mne snáší moc:

Tu moje oko slzami
Se náhle obstírá,
Neb v štěstí naše za námi
Zlý osud pozírá! . . .

I know that in sweet hope
you I may indeed love:
and that you want thereby more ardently
my love to cultivate.

And still, when I look upon your eyes,
in that so-delightful night;
and learn how love's heaven from them
on me brings down its power:

here my eye with tears
suddenly overflows,
for in our happiness, behind us
evil fate stares! . . .

7

Ó zlatá růže, spanilá,
Jak jara zjevy ranní,
Ty's bol mi sladký vkouzlila
V mé celé žití, ždání.

Ta všecka Tvoje spanilosť
Se v hruď mi zakotvila,
Že jsem se dal Ti na milosť,
By's rány vyhojila.

Oh golden rose, fair,
like of spring visions in the morning,
you have sweet grief for me conjured
in my whole living, longing.

All your graciousness
is in my breast anchored,
that I have given myself to you in love,
you would soon cure.

A Ty v své lásce horoucí	And you in your ardent love
Mě jak sfinx objala jsi:	me like a sphinx have embraced:
A v moje srdce práhnoucí	and in my heart pining
Trn nový vrazila jsi.	a new thorn have you thrust.

8

Ó naší lásce nekvěte	Oh, to our love does not bloom
To vytoužené štěstí:	that longed-for happiness:
A kdyby květlo, na světě	and if it would bloom, in this world
Nebude dlouho květsi.	it will not for long bloom.

Proč by se slza v ohnivé	Why would a tear into fiery
Polibky vekrádala?	kisses steal?
Proč by's mě v plné lásce své	Why would you me in your full love
Ouzkostně objímala?	with anxiety embrace?

Ó trpké je to loučení,	Oh bitter is that parting,
Kde naděj nezakyne:	where hope doesn't beckon:
Tu srdce cítí ve chvění,	here the heart feels, trembling,
Že brzo bídně zhyne.	that soon in misery it will die.

9

Kol domu se teď potácím,	Around the house now I stagger,
Kde's bydlívala dříve,	where you used to live before,
A z lásky rány krvácím,	and from the wound of love I bleed,
Té lásky sladké, lživé!	of that love sweet, false!

A smutným okem nazírám,	And with a sad eye I watch
Zdaž ke mně vedeš kroku:	whether toward me you take a step:
A vstříc Ti náruč otvírám,	and toward you my embrace I open,
Však slzu cítím v oku!	but a tear I feel in my eye!

Ó kde jsi drahá, kde jsi dnes,	Oh where are you dear one,
	where are you today,
Což nepřijdeš mi vstříce?	why won't you come toward me?
Což nemám, v srdci slasť a ples,	Why don't I have in my heart the delight
	and joy
Tě uzřiť nikdy více?	you to behold ever again?

10

Mě často týrá pochyba,	Me often torments the doubt,
Zdaž láska Tvá je stálá:	whether your love is constant:
A zas mě naděj kolíbá,	and again me the hope caresses,
Že's věrně milovala.	that you have faithfully loved.

A znova doufám v lásku Tvou	And anew I hope in your love
A vroucněj tisknu Tebe,	and more warmly press against you,
Tvé vzdechy k sladké víře zvou	your sighs to sweet faith entice
A k blahu očí nebe.	and to bliss your eyes' heaven.

Tu hlavu skloním, srdce mé	Here my head I bend, my heart
Zní tajemnými hlasy:	resounds with mysterious voices:
My sotva šťastni budeme,	we scarcely happy will be,
A rozvedou nás časy!	and will separate us the times!

11

Mé srdce často v neštěstí[2]	My heart often in unhappiness
Se teskně zadumá:	itself gloomily loses in the thought:
'Ó že ta láska bolestí	'Oh, that this love [so many] pains
A tolik trnů má?	and so many thorns has?

Ta láska přijde jako sen,	This love comes like a dream,
Tak krásná, spanilá,	so beautiful, gracious,
A za kratinko upne jen	and after a moment will attach only
Se na ni mohyla!	on it the grave!

A na mohylu kámen dán,	And on the grave a stone placed,
Nad nímž tam lípa bdí;	above which there a linden watches;
A na kameni nápis psán:	and on the stone the inscription written:
'Zde srdce puklé spí! . . .'	'Here a heart broken sleeps! . . .'

12

Zde hledím na ten drahý list	Here I look upon this dear letter
Ve knížce uložený,	in a little book placed,
A Tvého srdce chci zas číst'	and from your heart I want again to read
Ty sladké pol-ozvěny,	those sweet half-echoes,

[2] Dvořák in his setting changed the word 'neštěstí' to 'bolesti', which means 'pain'.

Tu milým slovem povídáš,
Že věčně budeš mojí,
A až mě zase uhlídáš,
Že nic nás nerozdvojí!

Here with a dear word you say,
that always you'll be mine,
and until me once more you behold,
that nothing us will part!

A my se opět viděli,
Já poznal světa změny:
Mně nezbyl leč list zpuchřelý
Ve knížce uložený.

And we each other again saw,
I recognized the world's changes:
to me remained naught but the letter dusty
in a little book placed.

13

Na horách ticho a v údole ticho,

Příroda dřímá sladký sen;
A vzduchem táhne tajemné vání,

Ke kmenu v lese šepce kmen.

On the mountains silence and in the
    valleys silence,
nature dozes with a sweet dream;
and through the air draws a mysterious
    breeze,
to a tree-trunk in the forest whispers a tree-
    trunk.

A lesy šumí v modravou dáli,

Když dechne vání na lupen,
Šumí a šumí dále a dále,
S šuměním táhne tak mnohý sen!

And the forests murmur into the bluish
    distance,
when breathes a breeze upon the leaf,
murmur and murmur on and on,
with the murmuring comes along so many a
    dream!

14

Zde v lese u potoka
Já stojím sám a sám;
A ve potoka vlny
V myšlénkách pozírám.

Here in the forest by the brook
I stand alone, all alone;
and into the brook's waves
in thoughts I gaze.

Tu vidím starý kámen,
Nad nímž se vlny dmou;
Ten kámen vstoupá, padá
Bez klidu pod vlnou.

Here I see an old stone,
over which the waves rage;
that stone rises, falls
without rest under the wave.

A proud se oň opírá,
Až kámen zvrhne se:
Kdy vlna života mne
Se světa odnese?

And the current on it presses,
until the stone disintegrates:
when will the wave of life me
from the world carry away?

15

Mou celou duší zádumně
Bolestné dchnutí táhne,
A když i radosť v srdci vře:
Hned žalů mráz v ně sáhne.

Through my whole soul pensively
the aching sorrow draws,
and when even joy in the heart flares up:
at once woes' chill into it reaches.

A vše, co drahé, opadlo
Tož s mého srdce stromu,
Jen Ty's mi zůstal, národe,
A Tvoje strasti k tomu.

And everything that's dear has fallen
yea, from my heart's tree,
only you to me have remained, nation,
and your hardships as well.

Tvým celým dlouhým životem
Se táhne utrpení,
Ve věčném boji zoufalém
Tvé osudy se mění.

Through your whole long life
stretches suffering,
in eternal struggle wretched
your fates fluctuate.

Já k Tobě přilnul. Nad Tebe
Mi dražšího nic není:
Vždyť oba velkou žertvou jsme
Věčného utrpení! . . .

I have clung to you. Than you
to me dearer is nothing:
after all, we both a great sacrifice are
of eternal suffering! . . .

16

Tam stojí stará skála
U vchodu údolí,
Tak opuštěná, pustá,
Až srdce zabolí.

There stands an old rock
at the entrance to the valley,
so desolate, deserted,
that the heart aches.

K té staré skále často
Zabloudí noha má;
Já vzhůru k ní pozírám
Vlhkýma zrakoma.

To that old rock often
wanders my foot;
I upward toward it gaze
with misty vision.

A u té trvdé skály
Já dlouhé chvíle dlím,
A všechny své bolesti
Tu v srdci pouspím . . .

And by that hard rock
I long moments linger,
and all my pains
here in my heart I tranquillize . . .

Až umřu, v tuto skálu
Uložte srdce mé:
Tam na věčnosť se uspí
To všecko hoře mé! . . .

When I die, in this rock
lay my heart:
there forever will be soothed
all that sorrow of mine! . . .

17

Nad krajem vévodí lehký spánek,
Jasná se rozpjala májová noc;
Nesmělý krade se do lisří vánek,
S nebes se schýlila míru moc.

Zadřímlo kvítí, potokem šumá

Tišeji nápěvů tajemných sbor ...

Příroda v rozkoši blaženě dumá,
Neklidných živlů všad utichl vzpor.

Hvězdy se sešly co nadějí světla,

Země se mění na nebeský kruh:
Mým srdcem, v němžto kdys blaženosť
     květla,
Mým srdcem táhne jen bolestí ruch!

Over the countryside reigns a light sleep,
clear has stretched out the May night;
shy steals into the leaves a breeze,
from heaven has bent down peace's power.

Asleep the flowers, through the brook
     murmurs
more quietly of mysterious songs the
     chorus ...

Nature in delight blissfully meditates,
of restless elements everywhere has
     fallen silent the squabble.

The stars have come together like hopes'
     lights
earth is changing into a celestial sphere;
through my heart, in which once happiness
     bloomed,
through my heart draws only torments'
     bustle!

18

Ty se ptáš, proč moje zpěvy
Bouří zvukem zoufalým?
Proč tak teskně, proč tak divě,
Jako řeka ouskalím?

Neptej se mne, družko milá,
Upřímnou tou řečí svou,
Nesmím Ti to povědíti,
Jaké trýzně srdce rvou.

Ani lásky, ani slávy
Věnce dávno strhané,
Ani říší pranebeských
Krásy časem zmítané:

Ani štěstí uvadlého
Omešené skaliny,
Ani cizí vůkol zjevy,
A ty světa pustiny:

You ask, why my songs
rage with a sound despairing?
Why so darkly, why so madly,
like a river over rocks?

Don't ask me, companion dear;
with this sincere speech of mine
I may not you that tell,
what a heart they agonizingly tear.

Neither love's nor glory's
garlands long broken,
nor celestial empires'
beauties in time tossed about:

neither the fate of faded,
swept-away rocks,
nor strange apparitions,
and the world's wildernesses:

Ani vstek a rozruch vášní
V neukojném bouření
Nebudí těch mojich zpěvův
Divoteskné proudění.

Avšak jeden bol tak mocný,
Že duch můj jím zvrácen jest,
Užírá mi žití kořen,
Že nemůže bujně kvěst'!

A ten bol, jenž bez ustání
Vrývá v srdce velkou strast',
Jenž ty divé písně budí:
Ten bol mocný je má . . . vlast'.

neither the rage and fury of passions
in insatiable storming
does not awaken these my songs'
wild-gloomy torrent.

But one pain so powerful,
that my spirit by it is reversed,
consumes my life's root,
that it cannot freely flower!

And that pain, which without ceasing
embeds in my heart great distress,
which these mad songs arouses:
that pain powerful is my . . . country.

4

Dvořák's First Songs: Some Insights into *Cypresses*

KLAUS DÖGE

ANTONÍN DVOŘÁK's song cycle *Cypřiše* (Cypresses), composed in a short period during the summer of 1865, is among his earliest works, and represents essentially his first encounter with the problems of setting a poetic text. Here for the first time Dvořák had to dissect and analyse poetry with the intent of transforming its content, its form, and its poetic mood into music; he had, as Schumann once expressed it, 'to reweave the poem in its smallest details with finer material'.[1]

The words Dvořák underlaid to his songs are those of a set of eighteen coherent poems entitled *Písně* (Songs) within a collection named *Cypřiše*, published in 1862. Their author was Gustav Pfleger-Moravský, a Czech poet whom Dvořák possibly knew personally, because Pfleger-Moravský was a dramatic producer at the Provisional Theatre in Prague during the years 1862–3, when Dvořák was playing in the theatre orchestra.

Moravský's eighteen poems, very romantic in style, tell a sad story about an unhappy lover. The progress of the story is as follows:

Poems 1-2: E–G	The protagonist remembers his beloved and describes his present situation, which is full of longing and hope on his part.
Poem 3: F minor	In the moment of greatest pain, he realizes that, in his imagination, he can still recapture the lost past.
Poems 4-7: A flat–D flat–D flat–E	He dreams of the happy times with his beloved, but . . .
Poem 8: E flat	Suddenly he shifts his focus to the ill fate destined for their love.

---

[1] 'Das Gedicht mit seinen kleinsten Zügen im feineren Stoffe nachzuwirken.' See Karl H. Wörner, *Robert Schumann* (Mainz, 1987), 203.

Poems 9–11: E minor–G minor– E flat minor	He is overcome by dark thoughts. The dream has vanished; reality exists again.
Poems 12–14: A flat–B–E	He looks at an old letter from his beloved, the only thing of hers he now possesses. In the solitude of the countryside, he feels lonely and lost, and wants to forget. But in his attempt to find quietness and peace again, the pain cannot be banished.
Poems 15–17: F–E flat–A flat	He is led to think of his tortured nation and of an old lonely rock, where he wants to bury his unhappy heart, and even the peaceful natural beauty of a May night has not the power to alleviate his pain.
Poem 18: D minor	In his useless attempt to forget, suddenly he addresses his beloved again, for the first time since Poem 12. (In Poems 13–17 she is not even directly mentioned.) He explains to her the reasons for the sadness of his songs: pain has broken his heart, pain like that of his homeland.

In composing *Cypresses* Dvořák took into consideration the individual stages of the story and also the overall progress of its events. In other words: in his songs he respected the integrity of the complete cycle as well as the individuality of each poem, and thereby he created a song cycle in the manner of Schubert and Schumann.

To create a sense of unity embracing all eighteen poems, Dvořák used a variety of compositional devices. One of them is the key plan of the cycle, shown above. Whenever the story moves to a new stage, he chooses a key not closely related to that of the previous song.[2] Thus for example in Song 3 (transition from deep pain to dream), the key F minor follows the G major tonality of Song 2. In Song 9 (beginning of doubts after the happy dream), E minor follows E flat major. Furthermore in Song 15 (marking a return to pain), F major follows E major. And finally in Song 18 (sudden appearance of the beloved, and final resignation), D minor follows A flat major. This tritone relation between Songs 17 and 18 is quite startling, and may reflect the allusion to death contained in the sixth stanza of Song 18: 'jeden bol . . . užírá mi žití kořen, že nemůže bujně květ' (one pain . . . consumes my life's root, that it cannot freely flower)—an allusion that Dvořák acknowledges otherwise by drawing on elements of a funeral-march style.

For songs belonging to the same textual group, Dvořák uses keys that are

---

[2] In most cases the contrast in tonality is supported by a change of tempo.

more closely related. Often one finds here third-relations or enharmonic third-relations which, though perhaps not close in terms of the circle of fifths, were in the Romantic period quite normal. In this way Songs 1 and 2 are connected (description of the lover's situation, E major–G major) as well as Songs 4–8 (happy dream, all major keys A flat–D flat–D flat–E), Songs 9–11 (doubts—all minor keys E–G–E flat), Songs 12–14 (loneliness and abandonment in nature, A flat–B–E), and finally Songs 15–17 (pain, F–E flat–A flat). Song 8 constitutes a special case in this regard: while its key of E flat major represents a sharp break from that of the preceding song (E major), at the same time it relates closely to the A flat–D flat orbit which dominated the preceding *group*. This double meaning expresses well the function of this poem as a turning-point in the story.

Another procedure operating on a level above that of the individual song is the handling of phrase-structure. Dvořák usually set verses to music using phrases of two, four, or eight bars, and in his melodic invention squareness prevails. Thus it is significant that in three of the eighteen songs this principle is almost systematically abandoned, even though these songs show no difference from the others in the number of syllables per line. Those in question are Songs 9–11, which follow after the songs of the dream and which are based on the poems of doubt, despair and painful questions. For instance, the phrase-structure of Song 9 is as follows:

4 + 3	Kol domu se teď potácím,	Around the house now I stagger,
	Kde's bydlívala dříve,	where you used to live before,
4 + 3	A z lásky rány krvácím,	and from the wound of love I bleed,
	Té lásky sladké, lživé!	of that love sweet, false!
3 + 3	A smutným okem nazírám,	And with a sad eye I watch
	Zdaž ke mně vedeš kroku:	whether toward me you take a step:
3 + 3	A vstříc Ti náruč otvírám,	and toward you my embrace I open,
	Však slzu cítím v oku!	but a tear I feel in my eye!
2+1 +	Ó kde jsi drahá, kde jsi dnes,	Oh where are you dear one, where are you today,
2+1	Což nepřijdeš mi vstříce?	why won't you come toward me?
3 +	Což nemám, v srdci slasť a ples,	Why don't I have in my heart the delight and joy
3+3	Tě uzřiť nikdy více?	you to behold ever again?

The abandonment of square phraseology is anticipated in the middle section of Song 8, where painful questions similar to those in Song 9 make their initial appearance. Thus Dvořák clearly connects by musical means the hidden relations of content among the individual poems.

Further unifying devices are shown in some motivic and structural relationships. The first three songs all begin with a downward melodic triad (Ex.

Ex. 4.1 *Cypresses: a.* Song 1, opening; *b.* Song 2, opening; *c.* Song 2, near end; *d.* Song 3, opening

4.1*a, b, c, d*). The perception of this motivic connection is facilitated by the fact that each of these songs is in ABA form, so that the triad motif is present in both the opening and the closing sections. But Dvořák uses this motivic connection not only in the sense of a purely structural feature. He uses the relationship also as a dramatic device. Step by step he transforms the triad of the beginning of Song 1 (Ex. 4.1*a*) into the specific form of its appearance in Song 3 (*d*). At the opening of Song 2 (*b*) the triad is changed from major to minor (anticipating the minor-mode version in Song 3). Just before the end of Song 2 (*c*) we meet the motif again in the already known minor version, to be followed immediately by a varied repeat. This repeat, though returning to major, is motivically almost identical to the beginning of Song 3. By this method of motivic development Dvořák clearly reflects the continuity of text among the first three poems, which as mentioned above lead gradually to the first climax of the story.

Another motivic relationship is used in a similar manner. In the middle of Song 2 there appears a motif consisting first of three notes, then of four, which cannot be found in any other measure of this song (Ex. 4.2*a*). This motif then appears in the opening phrase of Song 3, after the descending triad (*b*). In both passages the text refers to death: Song 2 speaks of 'smrť' (death), and Song 3 has 'mrtvo jest' (it is dead). Dvořák may have remembered this motif and its semantic use in Songs 2 and 3 when he composed Song 11. There the text speaks about the lost love soon resting in a grave; on the grave is placed a tombstone ('A na mohylu kámen dán') with the inscription 'Here a broken heart sleeps'. The motif in the piano accompaniment here (Ex. 4.2*c*) could be understood as a reference to the descending step in dotted rhythm from Songs 2 and 3. The connection is strengthened by the appearance in the voice part

Ex. 4.2 *Cypresses*: *a.* Song 2; *b.* Song 3; *d.* Song 11

of the same fifth–octave structure that was used in the piano accompaniment of Song 3.

My last example of a musical connection between songs pertains to the junction between Songs 3 and 4 (Ex. 4.3). The piano begins Song 4 (Ex. 4.3*b*) with the third F–A♭, opening to a sixth as the note A♭ ascends to a C. Subsequently the tonic note A♭ follows in the bass. Thus the fourth song is the first one of the cycle to begin with a melodic ascent. And this is programmatic. The opening third emerges clearly from the F minor tonality of the previous song (Ex. 4.3*a*), and thus Song 4 appears at first as if it wants to continue in the same sorrowful vein as Song 3—but only for a brief moment.

Ex. 4.3 *Cypresses*: *a*. Song 3, piano postlude; *b*. Song 4, piano introduction

With the opening of the third to the interval of the sixth (the interval of musical beauty), and with the following bass note A♭, which makes it obvious that the song is *not* in F minor, the change in mood and content between the two poems is illustrated. The means are subtle but effective. This kind of compositional expression of textual relationships seems remarkable for a composer writing his first song cycle.

Sophisticated devices, similar to those discussed here in the context of the whole cycle, are met also in the handling of the individual poems. Just one example may suffice as illustration. In composing the *Cypresses* songs Dvořák usually respects the form of the poem with its structure of stanzas and verses, and he does not handle the poetic form in such a free, prose-like fashion as for example Hugo Wolf. However, Dvořák's understanding of the sense of the poem occasionally leads him to abandon this principle. So he did in Song 1. Lines 1–4 are handled in the usual manner: they are built as a single period and, corresponding to the stanza form of the text, they represent the first formal unit:

A	1	Vy vroucí písně spějte	You ardent songs, go forth
	2	Tou nocí v mživou dál;	through this night, drizzly, onward;
	3	Všem pozdravení dejte,	to all your greetings give,
	4	Jež tíží tichý žal!	whom burdens silent woe!

However, the second formal unit of the song consists surprisingly not, as one would expect, of the second stanza with lines 5–8, but rather lines 5–9.

B	5	Tam spějte přes padoly,	Thither go, past the lowlands
	6	Kde moje milka dlí,	where my beloved dwells,
	7	A rcete, co mne bolí,	and tell what me pains,
	8	A proč letíte k ní!	and why you fly to her!

	9	A zapláče-li s vámi,	And if she weeps with you,
A'	10	Povězte mi to zas:	bring me that back:
	11	Jinak ať dolinami	else may through the marshes
	12	Zavane vítr vás!	the wind blow you about!

Thus Dvořák does not adhere to the formal structure of the stanza. Rather, in his music he breaks the textual structure in order to give stronger emphasis to the words of line 9: 'A zapláče-li s vámi'. From the beginning of line 5 the music drives toward these words, which appear as the climax of a fourteen-bar passage (Ex. 4.4). More than the poem itself, Dvořák's music thus emphasizes the aspect of intensive hope, meaning that she simply *must* weep, that is, she must still have feelings for her former lover.

Ex. 4.4 *Cypresses*, Song 1

Ex. 4.4 *cont.*

In the Dvořák literature the *Cypresses* songs sometimes are treated in a rather negative sense. Certainly, the well-known faults of declamation and the sometimes rather reserved treatment of the piano accompaniment are not to be ignored. However, I hope I have been able to show that some positive elements of song composition may be found here as well.

5

Cypresses: A Song Cycle and its Metamorphoses

JAN SMACZNY

FOR a composer with such a reputation for compositional fertility, not to say facility, the fact that Dvořák could also be an almost compulsive reviser may come as something of a surprise. Three of his symphonies, two concertos, four of his eleven operas, and many other works were subjected to major revision or, in the case of the opera *Král a uhlíř* (The King and the Charcoal Burner), complete recomposition.[1] The sorts of processes involved are exemplified by the case of the Nocturne in B major for String Orchestra (B. 47), whose origins can be traced back from its performance and publication in 1883 through an earlier string orchestra version of 1875, then to a movement for solo strings that the composer rejected from the G major String Quintet of that same year, which in turn was a shortened version of a section from the much earlier String Quartet in E minor.[2]

Though the history of the Nocturne is complex, no work of Dvořák's had a more extensive history of revision than his first song cycle, *Cypřiše* (Cypresses). And no other work from his early years enjoyed such longevity, with the exception of a passage from the finale of the Second Symphony of 1865, which appears as the climactic musical statement of the opera *Rusalka* (1901).[3] The songs in the cycle were originally composed in 1865, and

This chapter is adapted from a paper of the same title first presented to the Royal Musical Association in Nov. 1990 and further elaborated for presentation at the Musicological Colloquium on Dvořák at Saarbrücken, Germany, as part of the Saarland Festival in June 1991, and subsequently pub. in *Music & Letters*, 72 (1991), 552–68, as well as in the conference proceedings from Saarbrücken (*Dvořák-Studien*, ed. Klaus Döge and Peter Jost, Mainz, 1994), 47–64.

[1] The works mentioned are the Second, Third, and Fifth Symphonies, the Violin Concerto, the B minor Cello Concerto, and the operas *The King and the Charcoal Burner*, *Vanda*, *Dimitrij*, and *Jakobín*.

[2] The date of the E minor Quartet is somewhat open to question. Burghauser's thematic catalogue gives 1869 or 1870; Hugh MacDonald, in 'Dvořák's Early Chamber Music (Dvořák's E minor Quartet)', in *Colloquium Dvořák, Janáček and their Time*, ed. Rudolf Pečman (Brno, 1985), 183–7, advanced the theory that this and the other quartets of the period—in B flat major and D major—were written rather earlier.

[3] Second Symphony: finale, first occurrence, mm. 133–40; *Rusalka*, Act III, mm. 1285–6 and, more fully, Act III, mm. 1345–8.

Dvořák's final reworking of their material came more than twenty-three years later, when he revised eight songs as the collection *Písně milostné* (Love Songs). At various times between 1865 and 1888, all but the fifteenth song of the original collection were treated to some sort of revision or arrangement, some more than once. The songs and their various incarnations are listed in Table 5.1.

Apart from one or possibly two Mass settings, now lost, *Cypresses* represents Dvořák's first attempt at word-setting. The cycle belongs to a year of great compositional fertility, probably the first in his career. The year—1865—saw the composition of the first two symphonies, the A major Cello Concerto, *Dvě písně* (Two Songs) for baritone (B. 13), and a clarinet quintet (B. 14) now lost. The importance of *Cypresses* is underlined by Dvořák's frequent return to the songs as a melodic fund. It is probable that they had a deep personal significance for him, based on his alleged feelings of unrequited love toward Josefa Čermáková at the time of their composition, which corresponds well with the subject-matter of the poems (see Chapter 2). The song cycle at this stage in Czech music was by no means a common means of expression, and it may have been special personal experiences that drew Dvořák to these poems.[4]

This extensive cycle from Dvořák's first year of confident creativity offers, both in its original form and in its later metamorphoses, a view of his style unparalleled in its breadth. The original cycle is a valuable indicator of the nature of Dvořák's early melodic and harmonic style. The fact that he was happy to return to the substance of this style in the 1870s and late 1880s indicates a confidence that it was still valid to represent him in the days of his most public maturity. On another level these songs indicate Dvořák's developing approach to the setting of his native language: as his first extant Czech settings they provide a bottom line for gauging his perception of a suitable treatment of Czech verse. His later revision of the declamation in the settings offers an insight into his changing view of accent and quantity. Turning to the final revision of *Cypresses*, in the eight *Love Songs*, it is possible to see the significance of these songs at a more metaphysical level with the composer indulging in self-quotation, an early sign of what was to become a favourite pastime in the 1890s.

As a benchmark of Dvořák's early style, *Cypresses* shows a considerable advance on the harmonic language of the first two symphonies and the A major Cello Concerto. Without doubt, the manuscript version of the songs

---

[4] Cycles and collections of solo songs to Czech words did not become common until the 1870s. *Večerní písně* (Evening Songs), Smetana's only cycle of Czech settings, to words by Vítězslav Hálek, dates from 1879. Dvořák did not compose solo songs with any regularity until the early 1870s. And while the young Fibich wrote over 100 songs before the end of 1871, they were all to German texts.

Table 5.1. Songs from *Cypresses* and their Reworkings

Cypresses 1865[a]	*Silhouettes*[b] ?1870	*King and Charcoal Burner*[c] 1871	*Vanda*[d] 1875	6/(4) Songs[e] 1881/82	*Cypresses* (String Quartet)[f] 1887	*Love Songs*[g] 1888
1. Vy vroucí písně spějte	—	—	—	1/(1)	3	—
2. V té sladké moci	—	—	—	—	2	7
3. V tak mnohém srdci mrtvo jest	—	—	—	—	9	2
4. Ó duše drahá jedinká	—	—	—	—	—	8
5. Ó byl to krásný, zlatý sen	—	—	—	2/(2)	1	—
6. Já vím, že v sladké naději	—	—	—	—	6	4
7. Ó zlatá růže, spanilá	—	—	—	—	4	—
8. Ó naší lásce nekvěte	—	Act II	—	4/(—)	7	1
9. Kol domu se teď potácím	—	—	—	3/(—)	—	3
10. Mě často týrá pochyba	—	—	Act I	—	—	—
11. Mé srdce často v bolesti	—	—	—	6/(3)	—	—
12. Zde hledím na ten drahý list	—	—	—	—	5	—
13. Na horách ticho a v údolí ticho	—	—	—	5/(4)	—	—
14. Zde v lese u potoka	1 & 5	—	—	—	8	6
15. Mou celou duší zádumně	—	—	—	—	—	—
16. Tam stojí stará skála	—	—	—	—	10	—
17. Nad krajem vévodí	—	—	—	—	11	—
18. Ty se ptáš, proč moje zpěvy	—	—	—	—	12	5

[a] B. 11. Cycle of eighteen songs composed 10–27 July 1865. Pages of the original MS have been pub. in facsimile, as follows: Otakar Šourek, *Život a dílo Antonína Dvořáka* (The Life and Work of Antonín Dvořák), i, 3rd edn. (Prague, 1954), between pp. 80 and 81: title-page and dedication to Karel Bendl; *Zlatá Praha* (Golden Prague), 21 (1904–5), 57: first page of Song 1; Otakar Šourek, *Antonín Dvořák*, 4th edn. (Prague, 1947): Song 4 complete; Václav Holzknecht, *Antonín Dvořák* (Prague, 1955): second page of Song 12; Antonín Hořejš, *Antonín Dvořák* (Prague, 1955): title-page and dedication, first page of Song 13.

[b] B. 98 (*Silhouettes*). A collection of twelve piano pieces pub. in 1880. A MS thematic sketch indicates that Dvořák may have conceived the cycle as early as 1870. The opening idea of Song 14 acts as a second theme in *Silhouettes* Nos. 1 and 5, to a first theme taken from the first movement of Symphony No. 1.

[c] B. 21. The first of Dvořák's two settings of this opera libretto (*Král a uhlíř*); still unpub. Song 10 is used as the melodic basis of a duet between the King and Liduška in Act II, Scene 2. Otakar Šourek's suggestion that Song 6 from *Cypresses* was also used in fragmentary form (*Život . . .*, i, 3rd edn., 134) is not borne out by scrutiny of the score.

[d] B. 55. Grand opera, still unpub. Song 10 is used as the basis for a short aria for Vanda in Act I, Scene 3.

[e] In each ref. here the first figure indicates the order in a selection of six songs from *Cypresses* rev. probably in 1881 (B. 123), not pub. in Dvořák's lifetime. Of these six, four were pub. in 1882, revised to some extent differently, as *Čtyři písně* (Four Songs), Op. 2 (B. 124); the second figure indicates the order in that set. Op. 2 and an appendix which gives the two remaining songs of the set of six were pub. in the Critical Edition, vi/2, in 1957.

[f] B. 152. Not pub. in Dvořák's lifetime, but now available in a critical edition. See Ch. 2.

[g] B. 160, pub. in 1889 as Op. 83, *Písně milostné*.

shows a sporadic crudeness, clearly visible in Ex. 5.1, which suggests that publication was not the first priority at the time of writing.[5] Dvořák's string quartet arrangement of the same passage from 1887 irons out some of these problems of texture (Ex. 5.2). Beyond this uncertainty of hand, some of these songs show an experimental, almost visionary, quality. For those familiar with Dvořák's later style, the fifth song, 'Ó byl to krásný, zlatý sen' (Oh, was that a lovely, golden dream) is extraordinary from a number of points of view. The melodic line looks forward some fifty years to the later work of Dvořák's younger contemporary Leoš Janáček. (Janáček is unlikely to have known the original version of this song, but he may have been familiar with the vocal line from Dvořák's arrangement of it in the published version of four of the songs of 1882.) Even apart from the free-wheeling vocal line, the harmony of the song suggests musical horizons which were a great deal broader than those observable in Prague in the 1860s. As may be seen in Ex. 5.3, the piano's canonic response to the voice comes to rest on an unresolved seventh above the tonic which later becomes the bass of a magical change of key to E major. The effect is unparalleled in the repertoire known to Dvořák and looks beyond his immediate surroundings to songs by Debussy dating from the late 1880s.

Ex. 5.1 *Cypresses*, Song 18

[5] All examples quoted in this chapter are taken from Otakar Šourek's copy of the composer's MS, which Jarmil Burghauser kindly lent to me.

Ex. 5.2 Selected songs from *Cypresses* arranged for string quartet, B. 152, No. 12

This song was a clear first step on a road that led through the acute harmonic, tonal, and formal experiment of the string quartets of the late 1860s to the first version of *The King and the Charcoal Burner*. The culmination of this first flowering of experimental writing was Dvořák's application to the charitable trust Svatobor on 14 May 1873 for funds to facilitate study with Liszt and to free him from having to give music lessons.[6] There is no record that he received funds from this source, and he certainly did not at any stage study with Liszt. In fact 1873 and 1874 marked the start of a move away from his early experimental style and an approach toward Viennese models, most notably Brahms, a process that went hand in hand with Dvořák's winning the Austrian state prize for poor composers between the years 1875 and 1879.

Some indication of the distance Dvořák had travelled by 1882 may be gauged from the revision of Song 5 in the *Four Songs*, B. 124 (Op. 2). The opening of the song in the version of 1882 (Ex. 5.4) reveals that the imitation has gone from the accompaniment and that the imagination that produced the exquisite unresolved seventh has been neutered.

6 See *Antonín Dvořák: Korespondence a dokumenty—Kritické vydání* (Antonín Dvořák: Correspondence and Documents—Critical Edition), ed. Milan Kuna et al., i (Prague, 1987), 119–21.

Ex. 5.3 *Cypresses*, Song 5, opening

Ex. 5.4 *Four Songs*, B. 124 (Op. 2), Song 2, opening

On the other hand, one palpable gain in these later revisions is the undoubtedly superior word-setting. Like all his Czech contemporaries, Dvořák cultivated a vocal style in *Cypresses* that was profoundly affected by German models. Thematic preconditions such as upbeat melodies and firm, final-syllable accents were brought to bear on a language that was in accentual terms fundamentally different from the German model that produced the anomalies. The resulting problems Dvořák frankly acknowledged in a note appended to the autograph regarding Karel Bendl's criticisms of the songs (see Chapter 2). Coming six years before the poetess Eliška Krásnohorská published a formative three-part article on Czech declamation in the magazine

Hudební listy,[7] which generated important debate on the question of word-setting in Czech opera and which had a perceptible effect on Dvořák himself,[8] Bendl's criticism was unusually perceptive for the mid-1860s in Prague.[9]

While Bendl's criticism of poor declamation suggests a complex fundamental fault, the immediate inadequacy of Dvořák's setting stemmed largely from misplaced accents. The principles of accentuation in Czech are extremely simple. For all practical purposes, and generally in speech, the accent falls on the first syllable of each word. Later syllables require lengthening where indicated by diacritical signs on appropriate vowels. An obvious and pertinent example is, of course, 'Dvořák', which despite its stressed first syllable, requires a lengthening of the second. In words of three syllables the first and third syllables can provide a neutral context for the second if a lengthening is indicated. Thus, a name like 'Janáček', in which the second syllable is lengthened, gives the impression of possessing a stronger accent there than on the syllable before and after it. The impression is almost that the 'Ja' portion acts effectively as an upbeat to the 'ná'. Nevertheless, the first-syllable accent is, and was in the nineteenth century, the characteristic stress in Czech, and accounts to a considerable extent for the particular sound of the language. In the 1860s this fact, obvious to a later age though not to a community in which German was often the first language, frequently eluded Czech composers. Eliška Krásnohoská neatly summarized the problem as it faced Dvořák in 1865, along with many of his contemporaries, in her *Hudební listy* article:

Let every Czech say: '*přílítlo jaro*', every musician will sing: '*přilítlo jaro*'. This is the consequence of foreign influence, foreign intonation, foreign rhythm and melody, to which we have become accustomed. So, above all, let the composer guard against declaiming the first syllable of a multi-syllable word weakly or as an upbeat: *there is not a single multi-syllable word in Czech that is weakly accented*, since each is pronounced with an accent on the first syllable; whether it is long or short, this strong syllable must be sounded on a strong beat.[10]

Otakar Hostinský, in an article on a similar subject written some thirteen years later, pursued a lengthier and deeper examination of musical declamation, but took fundamentally the same starting-point.[11] A much more recent study by František Daneš admits that there is a natural tendency toward reg-

---

[7] 'O české deklamaci hudební' (Concerning Czech Musical Declamation), *Hudební listy*, 2/1–3 (1, 8, 15 Mar. 1871).

[8] See Jan Smaczny, 'A Study of the First Six Operas of Antonín Dvořák', D.Phil. dissertation (Univ. of Oxford, 1989), 178–213.

[9] His ability to see the faults in Dvořák's setting of Pfleger-Moravský, however, did not prevent his making similar mistakes in his own setting of the first six poems in 1882!

[10] 'O české deklamaci'.

[11] 'O české deklamaci hudební', *Dalibor*, 9/1–8, 10–12, 18 (1 Jan., 10 Mar., 1, 10, 20 Apr., 20 June 1882); repr. under same title as *Rozpravy hudební*, ix, ed. Emil Chvála (Prague, 1886).

ularity in Czech, largely owing to the accentuation of first syllables.[12] His
work is supported by Josef Hrabák, whose study of the character of Czech
trochees and iambs, based on the huge corpus of verse by the nineteenth-century poet Jaroslav Vrchlický, suggests a link with simple syllabic verse.[13] The
main complicating factor for composers was that while many writers
attempted to incorporate standard metrical schemes into their poetry and
librettos, the complexity of these schemes militated against the natural accent
of Czech. Inevitably this had an effect on musical settings, since a composer
could easily create conflict with the metrical patterns even when he was faith-
fully following the correct accent of the spoken word.

Unlike Smetana, whose first language was German, Dvořák was primarily
a Czech-speaker. On many occasions, however, his setting of Czech in
Cypresses exhibits the faults outlined by Krásnohorská. There is a high proportion of second- and third-syllable accents in the cycle, as may be seen from
Ex. 5.5. Some melodic lines accommodate the accent correctly at the beginning of the poetic line, but by the end throw the accent onto the wrong syllable, as in Ex. 5.5*d*. Having accepted Bendl's criticism as valid in 1866,
Dvořák did not set Czech again until 1871, when he began working on the
libretto of the first version of *The King and the Charcoal Burner*. Krásnohorská's
article had now appeared, and the whole question of declamation must have
seemed a great deal clearer. Dvořák's revisions of a number of the songs in

Ex. 5.5 *Cypresses: a*. Song 1; *b*. Song 3; *c*. Song 9; *d*. Song 11

[12] *Intonace a věta ve spisovné češtině* (Intonation and the Sentence in Czech Literature) (Prague, 1957).
[13] *O charakter českého verše* (Concerning the Character of Czech Verse) (Prague, 1970).

1881–2 and 1888 usually correct the deficiencies in declamation of the originals, sometimes with only very small changes to the first version: for instance,
the simple shift of the word 'letíte' to the second half of the bar in Ex. 5.6

Ex. 5.6 *Four Songs*, B. 124 (Op. 2), Song 1

corrects the incorrect emphasis found in Ex. 5.5*a*, where the syllable 'le' acts
as an upbeat to the second half of the bar, thus placing undue emphasis on the
syllable 'tí'. In other cases Dvořák rationalized the vocal line so that a balanc-
ing phrase is replaced by one with different note-values; thus the heavy accent
placed on the last syllable 'ně' of 'pustině' in Ex. 5.5*b* is corrected in Ex. 5.7.

Ex. 5.7 *Love Songs*, B. 160 (Op. 83), Song 2

Elsewhere, more drastic alteration of the phrase or time-signature was
required. In the case of Ex. 5.5*c*, where the second syllables of 'domu',
'potácím' and 'krvácím' receive undue emphasis, Dvořák attempted in
1881–2 a version that kept the basic time-signature and character while altering the placing of the accents (Ex. 5.8). The first sounded syllable of

Ex. 5.8 *Six Songs*, B. 123, Song 3

'krvácím'—although there is no vowel in the syllable 'krv', it has full metrical value—is placed on a strong beat, and the last syllable 'cím' is given correct weighting in terms of length despite beginning on a strong beat. The
result is artificial, and Dvořák, possibly recognizing this, did not include the
song in the publication of 1882. The ultimate solution was to alter the time-
signature and the nature of the song to create an upbeat melodic figure with
greater character and more helpful pointing for the accentuation of the last

Ex. 5.9 *Love Songs*, B. 160 (Op. 83), Song 3

three-syllable words in the first and third lines of the verse (Ex. 5.9). The
resulting melody suits the accentuation of the words where originally the
melodic-rhythmic design had been fundamentally at odds with the verse.
Equally far-reaching are the alterations of Ex. 5.5*d* in time-signature, melodic
interval, and character made for the *Four Songs* of 1881–2, as a comparison
with Ex. 5.10 will show.

Ex. 5.10 *Four Songs*, B. 124 (Op. 2), Song 3

Even a cursory examination of the original *Cypresses* reveals that not all was
wrong with Dvořák's declamation, even in advance of Krásnohorská's article.
For Czechs whose first language was German, as was the case with most educated Bohemians, including Smetana, in the first half of the nineteenth century, there was little comfort to be derived from theorists. Josef Jungmann
(1772–1847), who did much to encourage the study and use of Czech, published a collection of poetry and prose translations—including some works in
the original tongue—with a lengthy glossary on accentuation.[14] More important, he added his thoughts on quantitative poetry in Czech, producing a system that rendered his translations completely unnatural when declaimed. Still
more ridiculous was Jan Kollár's epic poem *Slávy dcera* (Slava's Daughter),[15]
which took Russian models as the basis for quantitative metre. Not until Karel
Mácha published his epic *Máj* (May)[16] would Czech poetry return to a realistic system of accent rather than an imposed and complex quantitative metre
or equal metre. Erben's classic collection *Kytice z pověstí národních* (A Garland
of National Tales, 1853)[17] did much to aid the establishment of a simpler system of metre in which trochees dominate, rather than more complex
schemes. There is a predisposition to trochaic feet in Erben's folk-inspired
verse, owing to a large proportion of two-syllable words. But it is some indication of the confused state that faced composers by the late 1860s and early
1870s that Krásnohorská needed to state the obvious: 'Good declamation

[14] *Sebrané spisy veršem i prosou* (Collected Writings in Verse and Prose) (Prague, 1841).
[15] (Prague, 1824; 2nd edn. 1832).   [16] (Prague, 1836).   [17] (Prague, 1853).

requires also that every sentence attains its correct expression in song in accordance with its meaning and natural spoken delivery.'[18] The metrical aspects of verse were likely to be a vital factor in musical setting. Having stated quite reasonably that trochaic feet are the natural metre for Czech, with its strong first-syllable accent, Krásnohorská pointed out that iambic scansion does occur; despite its weak-beat characteristic it may start in a musical setting on a strong beat with some success:

Czech accent in origin is predisposed toward trochees, though it is possible to adapt it to iambics so that it can function as a possible metrical foot. However, the true substance of spoken rhythm is found in common speech: everywhere it is the case that our speaking proceeds from strong syllables to weak and never from weak to strong. An iambic upbeat will never be a characteristic sign of Czech music. However, it is possible for iambic verse to be set without an upbeat to good effect. Such is the case in Jeleň's song 'Kdes děvo má?' (see Ex. 5.11).[19]

Ex. 5.11 Alois Jeleň, 'Kdes děvo má

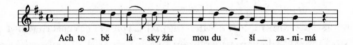

While Krásnohorská's example was doubtless useful, it was of course possible to set iambics satisfactorily with an upbeat if the metrical scheme continued with regular two- or four-syllable words. Some of the better word-setting in Dvořák's *Cypresses* illustrates this point (Ex. 5.12.)

Ex. 5.12 *Cypresses*, Song 1

There was an obvious need at this stage to provide a new kind of melodic writing that avoided the anacrusic pointing so common in German vocal setting, for since a definite article in Czech is never used before nouns there is a tendency for poetic lines not to start on a weakly accented single-syllable word. Equally pressing was the need to give final multi-syllable words in a line of verse an effective melodic and rhythmic treatment that avoided an

---

[18] 'O české deklamaci'.   [19] Ibid.

inappropriate accent on the final beat. Solutions were beginning to emerge. As early as the first version of *Cypresses* Dvořák was making use of appoggiaturas at the end of poetic lines as an effective way of setting potentially problematic final syllables (Ex. 5.13). These can be seen rubbing shoulders with misaccentuated words such as 'vstupuje', which is set as an anapaest. Right from the start of *The King and the Charcoal Burner*, probably begun in April 1871, only a few weeks after the appearance of Krásnokorská's article, there is a greater regard for accent and quantity than was apparent in *Cypresses*. But the early songs show Dvořák at the start of a journey toward an idiomatic style of setting Czech, presenting in many places an effective answer to problems felt by all his contemporaries, in many cases in advance of their own solutions.

Ex. 5.13 *Cypresses*, Song 3

A further aspect of the metamorphosis of this cycle opens up the question of its emotional significance for the composer, and provides an opportunity for speculation of a biographical nature. Josefina Čermáková probably never realized the full extent of Dvořák's feelings for her at the time of the composition of *Cypresses*. While his youthful ardour was later moderated by a number of factors, not the least of which was his marriage in 1873 to Josefina's younger sister Anna, Dvořák remained close to Josefina (see Chapter 2).

Any suggestion that Dvořák's final revision of *Cypresses* for the *Love Songs* in 1888 was prompted by some biographical circumstance involving Josefina cannot at present be substantiated. The nature of the revision of two of the songs, however, does prompt speculation that Dvořák was doing more than simply reworking earlier pieces prompted by a publisher voracious for small-scale compositions that would sell well.

The closing lines of Song 14 from *Cypresses* express a sort of death-wish that may be translated as follows: 'When will the flood of life bear me away from this world?' Dvořák's musical conclusion to the original song is given as Ex. 5.14*a*. In the revision for the *Love Songs* (*b*), he ornamented the cadence with a theme that prefigures rhythmically and intervallically the motif that dominates his setting of the Requiem Mass, B. 165 (*c*), begun within a year of the publication of the songs. Unfortunately, none of the sketches of the Requiem

Ex. 5.14 *a. Cypresses*, Song 14, conclusion; *b. Love Songs*, Song 6, conclusion; *c.* motif from Requiem

shows that the source for the theme was this song, but the sentiments expressed in the song suggest more than a passing link with the theme.

The next of the *Love Songs*, 'V té sladké moci očí tvých', provides a quotation that is conclusively retrospective and raises the question of a programmatic background to one of Dvořák's most familiar works, the Second Piano Quintet in A major, B. 155. Between the first two phrases of the song—'In the sweet power of your eyes' and 'I would gladly die'—Dvořák interpolated

Ex. 5.15 *a. Love Songs*, Song 7, opening; *b.* Piano Quintet, B. 155, second movement, opening

the main motif of the Andante con moto second movement of the quintet. The start of the song is given as Ex. 5.15*a* and the start of the slow movement of the quintet as *b*. There are three quotations of the theme in this form and two in a slightly curtailed version. The prominence of the quotation, as with that of the Requiem theme, inevitably prompts speculation that there may be a generalized emotional connection between the highly expressive motif from the quintet and the sentiments expressed in the song. Loosely paraphrased, the text tells of the lover who would gladly die for his beloved; having suffered the wounds of love, he chooses death in the knowledge that a smile from his beloved will restore him to life. The significance of the song to a young composer who in 1865 was in the throes of a frustrating, unreciprocated infatuation can easily be guessed. Quite why he chose to link these words with a thematic interpolation from the quintet some twenty-three years after the composition of the original song provokes speculation into an area of his life rarely examined.

As a key to Dvořák's early compositional horizons and an indicator of the experimental nature of his genius before the mid-1870s, the original *Cypresses* is as revealing as any of the compositions of this period. In its original form and later metamorphoses, *Cypresses* provides a crucial means of looking at many aspects of Dvořák's creativity, and anyone concerned with his music ignores it at their peril.

II

THE UNKNOWN DVOŘÁK: OPERAS

6

From the Vistula to the Danube by Way of the Vltava: Dvořák's *Vanda* in Vienna

ALAN HOUTCHENS

ANTONÍN DVOŘÁK maintained close relations throughout his life with many members of the Viennese artistic community, he travelled to Vienna fairly frequently, and he was especially keen on having his operas performed there. Yet the subject of his associations with people connected with the Court Opera in Vienna has been little more than a matter of passing interest to scholars. The first of Dvořák's operas to be considered for performance at the Court Opera was the five-act grand opera *Vanda*, and, although the performance did not materialize, fresh insight can be gained into Dvořák's burgeoning career by considering in detail the circumstances surrounding negotiations that took place in 1879 and 1880 for mounting this work in Vienna.

In a letter written on 23 November 1879 to his long-time friend Alois Göbl, Dvořák remarked that the director of the Court Opera, Franz Jauner, had become interested in *Vanda* partly because Johannes Brahms had spoken to him enthusiastically about his music.[1] The tone of this letter indicates that Dvořák was very excited about the prospect of having one of his operas performed in Vienna. Just a few weeks later he mentioned Jauner's interest in *Vanda* to the publisher Fritz Simrock, possibly hoping to get at least the new overture he recently had composed for it printed.[2]

An earlier version of this chapter was presented at a conference in Prague in 1983, and is pub. as 'The Proposed Performances of *Vanda* and *Rusalka* in Vienna' in *Musical Dramatic Works by Antonín Dvořák: Papers from an International Conference, Prague, 19–21 May 1983*, ed. Markéta Hallová, Zuzana Petrášková, and Jarmila Tauerová–Veverková (Prague, 1989), 173–81.

[1] *Antonín Dvořák: Korespondence a dokumenty—Kritické vydání* (Antonín Dvořák: Correspondence and Documents—Critical Edition), ed. Milan Kuna et al., i (Prague, 1987), 188. At this time Brahms and Jauner must have still been on good terms, for Brahms was asked to conduct the German Requiem at the Court Opera in the same month. Dvořák would have been able to discuss *Vanda* with Jauner during the several days he spent in Vienna before and after his Third Slavonic Rhapsody was performed by the Philharmonic under Hans Richter on 16 Nov.

[2] Letter of 2 Jan. 1880, ibid. 195. Upon the recommendation of Johannes Brahms, Simrock had earlier brought out some of Dvořák's works, thereby launching the Czech composer's international

Not wishing to let the opportunity of having the opera performed in Vienna slip away, Dvořák wrote to Jauner on 1 February 1880 for the purpose of inviting him to Prague to attend the first performance of the work in its newly revised, shortened version:

Most honoured Herr Director,
    During my last stay in Vienna you were so kind as to express to me the desire to come sometime to Prague to attend the performance of one of my operas.
    I am now in the fortunate position to inform you, highly esteemed Herr Director, that the performance of my opera *Wanda* is due to take place already on the 15th of February, and I herewith take the liberty of extending my most courteous invitation.
    Looking forward to your arrival with great anticipation
        Your very devoted

                              Anton Dvořák
Prague 18 1/2 80   Korngasse 10.[3]

In his reply dated 5 February 1880, Jauner accepted the invitation.[4] It is not certain, however, that he travelled to Prague for the performance, which in any case took place on Friday 13 February, not on the date Dvořák had indicated in his letter.[5]
    The performance probably was not as good as Dvořák would have wished. The facilities of the Provisional Theatre itself were not really adequate for the production of an opera like *Vanda*, which requires a large chorus, many super-numeraries, some reasonably sophisticated stage machinery, and elaborate

career. Dvořák eventually sold the pub. and partial performance rights for *Vanda* to August Cranz, who printed only the overture, first in a piano duet arrangement (1884), then in full score with parts (1900).

    [3] 'Sehr geehrter Herr Direktor! Bei meinem letzten Aufenthalte in Wien waren Sie so freundlich[,] mir gegenüber den Wunsch zu äußern, einmal zur Aufführung einer meiner Opern nach Prag zu kommen. Ich bin jetzt in der glücklichen Lage[,] Ihnen hochverehrtester Herr Dir[ektor] mitzuteilen, daß die Aufführung meiner Oper "Wanda" schon am 15. Februar stattfindet, und erlaube ich mir hiemit meine höflichste Einladung. Mit Sehnsucht erwartet Ihre Ankunft Ihr sehr ergebenster Anton Dvořák.' Here and in the following quotations from Dvořák's letters, I have transcribed the text unadulterated, directly from the original MS. My versions may be compared with those in the collected edn. of Dvořák's correspondence, where punctuation and spelling have been modified. See *Antonín Dvořák: Korespondence*, i, in this case p. 199.
    [4] Unpub. letter, Muzeum české hudby (Museum of Czech Music), inventory no. 749. Draft in the Haus-, Hof- und Staatsarchiv, Hofopernintendanz, Vienna, General-Intendanz Zeichen (Oper) 205/1880.
    [5] Such last-minute changes in schedule were common, and it appears that, in a two-week period, the performance of *Vanda* had been moved up, first to Saturday, 14 Feb., then to 13 Feb. This final date had been established without question by the 10th of the month, judging from an advance notice in the leading Czech daily newspaper: 'Literatura a umění: Benefice sl. Sittovy', *Národní listy*, 20/34 (10 Feb. 1880), [3].
    [6] Jan Bartoš, in his excellent study *Prozatímní divadlo a jeho činohra* (The Provisional Theatre and its Plays) (Prague, 1937), 75–8 and 82, has described very well the theatre's limitations of capacity, stage space, and accoutrements. The stage was small and the wings cramped. The auditorium also was small, but cosy, and was capable of seating a little less than 900 people under crowded circumstances. There were thirty-nine mezzanine boxes for no more than four persons each, while the main floor had 151 seats and perhaps 140 places for standing patrons. It was very dark and crowded in the parquet circle especially. Judging from

sets.[6] Aside from this, the month of February marks the height of the influenza season in Prague and a point in the opera schedule when the singers tend to flag terribly. The vocal soloists were grossly overworked during this particular season anyway. Antonín Vávra, for example, had been required to sing three major roles—in Smetana's *Prodaná nevěsta* (The Bartered Bride), Gounod's *Roméo et Juliette*, and Jan Josef Abert's *Astorga*—during the week before his performance as Slavoj in *Vanda*. The critics were quick to point out that he should not have pushed himself so much.[7] Not wishing to disappoint the distinguished soprano Marie Sittová, who sang the title role and for whose benefit the performance of *Vanda* was planned, Vávra agreed to attempt the part, but he soon became exhausted and could barely make it though the last act. After this performance, Vávra became gravely ill and had to curtail his appearances for almost a month, which led to the cancellation of several opera performances, including the next one of *Vanda*, scheduled for 16 February.

To make matters worse, the director of the theatre, J. A. Maýr, and the chief conductor, Adolf Čech, had difficulties throughout the season in finding enough capable personnel. A notice in *Dalibor* indicates that even after the season had begun in September 1879, they had not been able to secure a second bassoonist.[8] In addition, many of the better members of the opera chorus had resigned, and replacements could not be found. The adverse effects of such developments on the performances of *Vanda* were considerable, as the following excerpt from one of the reviews indicates:

In the first act, the ballet music was vigorous and pleasing, but perhaps more agreeable to listen to than suitable for dancing, at least so it seems in accordance with the unmistakable inconsistency of our ballet soloists, who are, nevertheless, always courageous. . . . The performance was not the best, although on the whole one must acknowledge the respectable effort on the part of all collaborators. In the first act the women's chorus was out of tune, which destroyed the impact of the ensemble. . . . As to the external trimmings it would not have been a bad idea if the princess Vanda had ordered neater and more tidy uniforms for her army. For the time being it would suffice to drive them off into the Vistula and wring them out a bit![9]

Bartoš's description and from illustrations showing the floor-plan and seating arrangements, it is difficult to imagine how *Vanda* could have been produced in this theatre with any success at all.

   [7] See esp. the reviews cited in nn. 9 and 10 below.
   [8] 'Z divadla: Zpěvohra' (Theatre News: Opera), *Dalibor*, 1/26 (10 Sept. 1879), 209.
   [9] 'V 1. jednání se zalíbením se poslouchala svěží baletní hudba, více milá k poslouchání nežli snad praktická k tančení, aspoň se tak zdá dle patrného kolísání našich vždy statečných baletních solistek. . . . Provedení nebylo z nejlepších, ač celkem uznati se musí dobrá snaha všech spoluúčinkujících; v prvním jednání dissonování ženského sboru zničilo účinnost ensemblu. . . . Co do zevní úpravy neškodilo by, kdyby kněžna "Vanda" své armádě předepsala nějakou novou úhlednější uniformu; prozatím snad by postačilo zahnat ji do Visly a trochu vyždímat!' From 'Zpěvohra' (Opera), *Pokrok* (17 Feb. 1880), [3].

V. V. Zelený, writing for *Divadelní listy*, and the critic for *Dalibor* likewise took exception to the poor set designs, which apparently were cheap and shoddy, and entirely unsuited to the grandiose, tragic nature of the opera.[10]

Thus far, only reviewers' negative comments have been mentioned in order to make a particular point: namely, that if Jauner was, in fact, present at the first performance of the new production, he would not have been overly impressed. Other aspects of the opera and its performance were highly praised. Sittová (as Vanda), Ema Maislerová (singing the part of Božena), Leopold Stropnický (Lumír), and Karel Čech (Velkokněz) sang exceptionally well; the costumes, designed by Göbl, were generally judged to be very effective; and Dvořák's music made a strong impression.[11]

Word quickly circulated around Vienna that Dvořák's *Vanda* was a significant new work. Toward the end of February, Dvořák received a letter of introduction from Ignaz Kugel (b. 26 December 1829; d. sometime before 1926), an impresario of sorts who ran a theatre and concert bureau in Vienna and was owner and chief editor of the weekly journal *Wiener Signale*. He wrote of having heard that the performance of *Vanda* in Prague was an 'outstanding success'.[12] This letter was the first in a series wherein Kugel tried to encourage Dvořák to let him serve as his agent, with the aim of getting Dvořák's operas performed throughout the Austro-Hungarian Empire, Germany, and Belgium. His next letter to Dvořák, dated 24 February 1880, just four days after the first, seems to indicate that Dvořák had responded favourably to his overtures.[13]

Already in the issue of *Wiener Signale* published on 28 February 1880—long before the Prague papers took up the story—Kugel announced that Dvořák would soon travel to Vienna for the purpose of finalizing arrangements with Jauner for a production of *Vanda*.[14] Kugel must have maintained close contact with Jauner, or at least with someone in the upper echelons of the theatre administration, because news about the most recent developments at the Court Theatre almost invariably appeared first in his journal.

---

[10] V. V. Zelený, 'Z divadel: Zpěvohra (Přehled za minulé čtvrtletí)' (Theatre News: Opera [Overview of the Last Three Months]), *Divadelní listy*, 1/1 (3 Apr. 1880), 13; 'Z divadla' (Theatre News) (unsigned), *Dalibor*, 2/15 (20 May 1880), 118.

[11] The identity of the costume designer, who was listed on the theatre posters and in various journals and newspapers only by the surname Göbl, is not known. It is certain, however, that he was not Dvořák's friend Alois Göbl.

[12] Unpub. letter, 20 Feb. 1880, Museum of Czech Music, inventory no. 801.

[13] Unpub., Museum of Czech Music, inventory no. 802. All of Kugel's letters to Dvořák that have survived may be found in the archives of the Museum of Czech Music. None have been published to date. I have not been able to locate any letters written by Dvořák to Kugel.

[14] 'Notizen', *Wiener Signale*, 3/9 (28 Feb. 1880), 70. The proposed Viennese production of *Vanda* was not mentioned in the Prague newspapers or journals until nearly three weeks later, when V. J. Novotný broke the news in *Národní listy*, 20/67 (18 Mar. 1880), [3]. Zelený subsequently made an announcement in *Divadelní listy*, 1/1 (3 Apr. 1880), 13. Nothing appeared in *Dalibor* until 1 June 1880, 127, under 'Drobné zprávy' (Brief Reports).

Negotiations between Dvořák and Jauner continued into April. Further performances of *Vanda* already planned for the Prague stage had to be postponed until Dvořák made some changes in the score and until Josef Srb-Debrnov's translation of the libretto into German could be underlaid in it.[15] This must have been accomplished by 20 April, judging from a letter Dvořák wrote to Jauner on that date:

Most honoured Herr Director!

I am taking the liberty of notifying you herewith that already I have taken care of the German translation of my opera *Wanda* and that the underlaying of the text is completed not only in the vocal score but also in the full score.

If it were your wish, I would be happy to undertake a trip to Vienna in order to discuss this matter in more detail.

I would bring the full score, vocal score and libretto along with me.

In the meantime, honoured Sir, your devoted servant signs himself

Anton Dvořák

Prague 18 20/4 80[16]

This letter is especially interesting because it reveals that a piano-vocal score had been prepared at least by 1880—and probably as early as 1876, for use in the rehearsals for the première.[17] Nothing from that time has survived. The only piano-vocal scores in existence today are the two located in the Music Archive of the National Theatre in Prague; one was prepared in 1925 by Josef Bartovský for the production of *Vanda* in Plzeň (and subsequently sold to the National Theatre, Prague, by the director of the Municipal Theatre in Plzeň, Bedřich Jeřábek), while the other is a copy of it.[18]

Dvořák apparently did not go to Vienna immediately. He probably wanted to wait for a reply from Jauner; or perhaps he hoped Kugel would be able to take care of matters for him. In any case, he was in Berlin from the end of March through the beginning of April.[19] Jauner's response did not come until

---

[15] See 'Literatura a umění' (Literature and Art), *Národní listy*, 20/105 (1 May 1880), 5; also V. V. Zelený, 'Z divadel' (n. 10).

[16] 'Sehr geehrter Herr Direktor! Ich erlaube mir Ihnen hiemit anzuzeigen, daß ich bereits die deutsche Übersetzung meiner Oper "Wanda" besorgt [habe] und daß die Unterlegung des Textes sowohl im Clavierauszuge also auch in der Partitur vollkommen fertig ist. Wenn es Ihr Wunsch wäre, würde ich sehr gerne eine Reise nach Wien unternehmen, um die Sache genauer zu besprechen. Partitur[,] Clavierauszug und Text würde ich mitnehmen. Inzwischen zeichnet sich Euer Wohlgeboren ergebenster Anton Dvořák.' Cf. the slightly adulterated version in *Antonín Dvořák: Korespondence*, i. 212.

[17] Dvořák composed *Vanda* between 9 Aug. and 22 Dec. 1875. The première took place on 17 Apr. 1876 in the Czech Provisional Theatre, Prague.

[18] The attribution to Bartovský is verified by Antonín Špelda in *Dr. Antonín Dvořák a Plzeň* (Plzeň, 1941), 157. The scores now in the Hudební archiv Národního divadla (Music Archive of the National Theatre) have the newly assigned inventory nos. 381–4 and 381–5, which replace 2D441 and 2D449 respectively.

[19] Concerning Dvořák's activities in Berlin, see his letter from Berlin to Alois Göbl, 1 Apr. 1880, in *Antonín Dvořák: Korespondence*, i. 204.

17 May.[20] While remaining relatively optimistic about the prospects of mounting *Vanda*, Jauner alluded to the fact that, contrary to the stipulations of his own contract, the Court Chamberlain, Constantin Prinz zu Hohenlohe-Schillingsfürst, had established once again the position of General-Intendant by appointing Leopold Friedrich Freiherr von Hofmann to that post. Jauner had enjoyed unprecedented freedom, independence, and power in the administration of the Court Opera, but with this appointment his position was weakened considerably. He resigned straightaway; in fact, he already had submitted his resignation by the time he wrote Dvořák in May, and he left the post in June 1880.[21]

Still, Dvořák had reason to believe that something would come of the proposed production of *Vanda*. In his letter of 17 May, Jauner indicated that as soon as Hans Richter, the Court Kapellmeister, returned from a visit to London (sometime in June, Jauner wrote), he (Richter) would go to Prague for the express purpose of discussing the details for bringing *Vanda* to Vienna.[22] Dvořák seems to have put a great deal of faith in this promise, for on 21 May he wrote to Göbl the news about Richter;[23] and then as late as 10 July, after having been to Vienna, he wrote his friend: 'Just now I am still waiting for Richter [to come] from Vienna. We need to go through *Vanda* together.'[24]

Dvořák must have felt that, should Richter ever have the opportunity to study the score and should he find the opera worth supporting, he could influence the next director of the Court Theatre. For a time, Richter himself was thought to be the logical choice as successor to Jauner, since he had had some experience as a theatre director at Budapest in 1874. But not wishing to become involved in administrative affairs, he wisely turned down any offers. The appointment eventually went to the German-speaking Moravian Wilhelm Jahn, but not until 1 January 1881. During the interim, Franz von Dingelstedt returned in the last half of 1880 to the position he had held between the years 1867 and 1870.

Concrete documentary evidence has not surfaced to explain why, in the end, *Vanda* was never performed in Vienna. Several factors can be isolated that may provide clues, however. In the first place, the turmoil within the administration of the Court Theatre would have made it difficult in the early part of 1880 to establish firmly the repertoire for the next couple of seasons. Nevertheless, Franz Jauner was still in a position to have some say in the mat-

---

[20] Unpub. letter, Museum of Czech Music, inventory no. 750.

[21] Jauner had begun to experience serious difficulties concerning his position as early as Mar. 1880, as noted in 'Notizen' in the *Wiener Signale*, 3/12 (20 Mar. 1880), 94. The announcement of his resignation appeared in 'Notizen' in this same journal on 8 May 1880 (3/19), 150. These arts. are unsigned.

[22] See n. 20.   [23] *Antonín Dvořák: Korespondence*, i. 218–19.

[24] 'Nyní ještě čekám Richtra z Vídně, musíme spolu prodělat "Vandu".' Ibid. 223. This last letter, especially, suggests that Otakar Šourek may have erred by maintaining in *Antonín Dvořák a Hans Richter. Obraz uměleckého přátelství* (Antonín Dvořák and Hans Richter: Portrait of an Artistic Friendship) (Prague, 1942), 22, that Richter became acquainted with *Vanda* when he visited Prague at the beginning of April.

ter. Since most likely he was the key person responsible for influencing the decision against *Vanda*, it is necessary to consider the basic tenor of his administration and to review his achievements as Director of the Court Opera.

As mentioned earlier, Jauner first conceived the idea of producing *Vanda* in November 1879. Up to that time he had devoted most of his energy as director to making a reconciliation on behalf of the theatre administration—indeed, on behalf of most of the Viennese public—with Richard Wagner. Jauner was a shrewd, adroit, brilliant theatrical manager. His first step as part of a personal ambition to provide exemplary, definitive productions of Wagner's operas in Vienna was to engage Richter as chief conductor. Then he managed to win Wagner's confidence by successfully negotiating, on terms favourable to the composer, matters concerning royalties and performance rights, with the result that *Die Meistersinger von Nürnberg*, *Lohengrin*, and the new Paris version of *Tannhäuser* were presented by the end of his first year as director. He even persuaded Wagner to supervise the production of the last two of these operas himself. As Viennese audiences and most of the critics clamoured for even more of Wagner's music, Jauner assuaged their thirst with the complete *Ring* cycle, a project that was completed by February 1879.

While the score of *Vanda* is not at all Wagnerian in style, it seems likely, in view of his particular artistic taste, that Jauner would have been attracted to such features of the opera as the broad, lyrical melodies; the occasional use of leitmotifs; the adventurous harmonic language; the formal structures made up of large-scale scene complexes in the grand-opera manner with impressive solo arias, intricate ensembles, and other set pieces joined together in such a way as to produce a continuous texture; the marvellous passages for chorus; and the colourful orchestration. Furthermore, it is clear that Jauner was eager not only to satisfy the prevailing taste among Viennese opera-goers but also to fashion that taste to some extent by presenting new compositions or those that might have an exotic appeal. He championed the music of Verdi (*Aïda*, *Ernani*, *Les Vêpres siciliennes*, *Rigoletto*, the Requiem), produced the first performance of *Carmen* outside France with great success, and, in 1880, initiated a cycle of operas by Mozart. He thus should have likewise been attracted to Dvořák's *Vanda*, for no opera by a contemporary Czech composer had yet been produced at the Court Opera, and the plot of *Vanda*—based as it is on a Polish legend—undoubtedly would have interested him very much.[25]

Certain reservations concerning the libretto may have been expressed, however, by the censor or by the Court Chamberlain, and Jauner may have been in agreement. After all, the main conflict in the drama centres around Polish resistance to domination by German-speaking peoples. In order to

---

[25] Another opera based on the Wanda legend, with a very different libretto by Theodor Bakody and music by Franz Doppler, was produced at the Court Theatre in 1862.

placate the gods and save her people, Vanda sacrifices her life by jumping into the sacred river Vistula. Still, if the court was willing to accept the works of Verdi, whose name had served as the battle-cry of the Risorgimento, there should not have been any objection to *Vanda*.

Indeed, the political climate in Vienna just at this time became somewhat more favourable for the Austro-Slavs, and especially the Czechs. The period immediately following the Ausgleich of 1867 had been a very difficult one for the Czechs, who embarked on a policy of passive resistance. Matters really became tense when Franz Joseph, buckling under pressure applied by the German-speaking and Hungarian nobility, reversed his Imperial Rescript by which he had recognized the Czech Crown. But in 1878, Czech deputies returned to the Bohemian Diet, and, after the fall of the German liberal ministry in 1879, the Czech nationalists took up their seats again in the Reichsrat and agreed to support the conservative coalition government of Count Eduard Taaffe. Although Austria entered into an alliance with Germany in 1879, the average Austrian citizen became increasingly wary of the great Prussian machine that once again was being fuelled by German ultra-nationalism. In short, even though a few anti-Slavic prejudices still held sway among German Austrians, the government was willing to grant certain political and cultural concessions to the Czechs.

If socio-political conditions in the Empire were changing ever so slightly to the benefit of the Czechs, the financial condition of the Court Opera was deteriorating. Jauner had been appointed director in the first place largely because he had proved to be a financial wizard while managing the Carltheater. When he came to the Court Opera, Vienna was still suffering from the after-effects of the financial crash of 1873, and all the wizardry in the world apparently could not have staved off an increasing deficit. By 1880 Jauner was receiving severe criticism from all sides, mainly for straining the budget with productions that were considered too lavish. He consequently would have found it difficult to justify a new production of an opera like *Vanda*, which requires an elaborate scenic apparatus, eleven principal singers, a considerable contingent of supernumeraries, and a large chorus.

Nevertheless, in his letter to Dvořák dated 17 May 1880, Jauner stated that he had recommended *Vanda* very strongly to the newly installed General-Intendant. Yet for any action to be taken, it was obligatory for the Director of the Court Opera to make such a recommendation in writing, and no evidence whatever can be found among the records kept by the offices of the General-Intendant or the Director of the Court Theatre to substantiate Jauner's claim. Apparently the idea of mounting *Vanda* on the stage of the Court Opera in Vienna died with Jauner's resignation, Richter's inaction, and Wilhelm Jahn's disinterest.

7

Vanda and *Armida*, A Grand-Operatic Sisterhood

JAN SMACZNY

DVOŘÁK'S last opera, *Armida*, must count as one of the composer's strangest works. This strangeness lies principally in its subject-matter: a fruitful concatenation of the story of Rinaldo and Armida with the tragic love of Tancredi and Clorinda taken from Torquato Tasso's epic poem, *Gerusalemme liberata*.[1] Dvořák was not alone in the community of Czech opera composers working at the turn of the nineteenth century in choosing a topic which bore no resemblance to *verismo*, a modish enthusiasm which had seized composers from the best-established (such as Richard Rozkošný and Karel Bendl) to the younger generation attempting to make their name (such as Josef Bohuslav Foerster and Leoš Janáček).[2] Dvořák's companion in this lack of conformity was his younger contemporary Zdeněk Fibich, who after rehabilitating himself with the critical community in Prague by his composition of the nationally based opera *Šárka*, considered a setting of Ibsen's play *The Woman from the Sea*, and serviced his liking for things Scandinavian in his last opera by composing *Pád Arkuna* (The Fall of Arkona), first performed in the National Theatre in Prague on 9 November 1900.

It is possible to pursue the parallels between *The Fall of Arkona* and *Armida* still further. Both tales involve the conflict between Christians and those of another persuasion. In *Pád Arkuna* the followers of Svantovit are involved[3] and in *Armida* the conflict that provides the context for the opera is the historical opposition of Christians and Muslims during the medieval Crusades. Beyond this resemblance further parallels emerge when the conclusions of the two operas are compared. In both cases the final catharsis is crowned by the singing of Christian songs. In *Armida* there is a chorus of pious Christians on

---

[1] The episodes are taken chiefly from cantos 4, 5, 7, 10, 12, 14, 16–18, and 20.

[2] See John Tyrrell, *Czech Opera* (Cambridge, 1988), and Jan Smaczny, 'Janáček and Czech Realism' in *Jenůfa, Káťa Kabanová*, ed. Nicholas John (London, 1985), 36–40.

[3] Arkona is a promontory in the north-east corner of the German island of Rügen in the Baltic Sea, and the site of the ruins of a temple to the Wendish deity, Svantovit.

their way to the holy sites of the promised land; in *Pád Arkuna* a triumphant
Te Deum is intoned by the chorus over the burning ruins of the pagan
temple.[4]

Dvořák may well have attended the première or subsequent performances
of *Pád Arkuna*, though spotting the composer at the opera at all, after his days
as violist in the Provisional Theatre orchestra (1862–71), is a thankless task.
We cannot be certain that he attended even important premières of Czech
operas, although it can be stated with some assurance that he went to the first
performance of Smetana's *Hubička* (The Kiss),[5] and on 8 September 1881 he
wrote to his friend Alois Göbl that he was looking forward to the première of
his old friend Bendl's opera *Černohorci*.[6] If Dvořák did not see *Pád Arkuna*, he
may have acquired the score, issued in 1901, from the publisher Urbánek.

A tempting interpretation would be to see *Pád Arkuna* as a significant part
of the background to *Armida*, especially since its publication came only a year
before Dvořák began work on his last opera. But beyond the structural resemblance of the finales the two works have little in common. In *Pád Arkuna*
Fibich made scant attempt to present closed melodic periods, and as a whole
the work is an advance on the through-composed texture of his mature
operas.[7] *Armida* is in many ways a backward-looking work after the more
obviously through-composed *Rusalka*. The libretto necessitates an
intensification of Dvořák's natural inclination toward number opera, held in
abeyance to some extent in *Rusalka*, and the adoption of the rigid structures
of grand opera.

If a model is to be found for *Armida* at this late stage in Dvořák's career, we
should look among his own earlier works and in particular at an opera that in
the dawn of the new century was very much on his mind. For Dvořák's 60th
birthday in 1901 the authorities of the National Theatre planned as complete
a cycle of his operas as possible.[8] Even the oratorio *Svatá Ludmila* (St Ludmila)
was drawn in, with Dvořák composing recitatives especially for a stage performance.[9] A handful of his early operas were left out, however,[10] to the
regret of one very influential commentator. In 1912 the musicologist and

---

[4] See vocal score (Prague, 1901), 168–9. This is in the second and major part of *Pád Arkuna*, called
'Dargun'. The prelude is known as 'Helga'.

[5] According to Eliška Krásnohorská, Dvořák had attended this première. See her letter to Smetana repr.
in *E. Krásnohorská – B. Smetana, vzájemná korespondence*, ed. Mirko Očadlík (Prague, 1940), 109–12.

[6] See *Antonín Dvořák: Korespondence a dokumenty—Kritické vydání* (Antonín Dvořák: Correspondence
and Documents—Critical Edition), ed. Milan Kuna et al., i (Prague, 1987), 260.

[7] See Tyrrell, *Czech Opera*, and Jan Smaczny, 'The Operas and Melodramas of Zdeněk Fibich',
Proceedings of the Royal Musical Association, 109 (1982–3), 119–33.

[8] Incl. the rev. version of Dvořák's second setting of *Král a uhlíř* (The King and the Charcoal Burner),
along with *Tvrdé palice* (The Stubborn Lovers), *Šelma sedlák* (The Cunning Peasant), *Dimitrij*, *Jakobín*, *Čert
a Káča* (The Devil and Kate), and *Rusalka*.

[9] Pub. as a supplement to the critical edn. of the vocal score, ed. Antonín Sychra (Prague, 1965).

[10] The as yet unknown *Alfred*, the first version of *The King and the Charcoal Burner*, and *Vanda*.

librettist Otakar Hostinský wrote the following in a long and important article on Dvořák's operas: '*Vanda* involves such interesting and impressive features, and is so important for understanding Dvořák's development in the field of drama, that it is deplorable that it was missing from the repertoire during the commemorative cycle of Dvořák's operas in 1901.'[11]

Although *Vanda* was missing from the cycle, there had been plans to include it. Indeed, the plans were fairly far advanced. The score, which had been sent to the publisher Cranz early in the 1880s (though the publication never materialized except for the overture), was returned for Dvořák's detailed perusal with a view to performance. Parts were copied, and Adolf Čech's memoirs tell us that there was even an orchestral rehearsal whose purpose was to 'try out the great triumphal march, which owing to the smallness of the [Provisional] Theatre [at the original première in 1876] had to be greatly reduced'.[12] But a lack of support among the theatre authorities frustrated the inclusion of the earlier operas in the cycle.

Much uninformed commentary on *Vanda* has fostered the impression of the work as an inadequate failure.[13] Čech's final comment on the work should be cited in defence of what has every right to be considered a neglected masterpiece. In the closing paragraph of his chapter on Dvořák, Čech stated that along with all the congratulations and good wishes the composer received on his 60th birthday, the one event that would have given him greatest satisfaction was that: 'he would have lived to see the glorious rehabilitation of his lovely opera *Vanda* perfectly realized on the stage of the National Theatre.'[14] Whatever the ins and outs attendant on the non-performance of *Vanda*, the opera was certainly very much in Dvořák's mind in 1900 and 1901, especially since the score and parts needed considerable attention. Within barely a year of these events, Dvořák was at work on the score of his last opera, *Armida*.

---

[11] 'Antonín Dvořák ve vývoji naší dramatické hudby' (Antonín Dvořák in the Development of our Dramatic Music), in *Antonín Dvořák: Sborník statí o jeho díle a životě* (Antonín Dvořák: A Collection of Essays about his Life and Work) [ed. Boleslav Kalenský] (Prague, 1912), 208–26.

[12] *Z mých divadelních pamětí* (From my Theatre Memories) (Prague, 1903), 93.

[13] Alec Robertson, in his *Dvořák* (London, 1945), 130: 'If the overture, the only part of the music published by Cranz, to whom Dvořák sold the score, is any criterion, *Wanda* deserved its fate. Dvořák never wrote anything else so utterly uninspired and conventional.' And Hans-Hubert Schönzeler, in *Dvořák* (London, 1984), 47–8: 'We now come to Dvořák's next—and perhaps most unfortunate—opera, *Vanda*, an effort in five acts (three would have been ample!) based on a Polish legend. Dvořák's choice of subject matter may have been caused by the pro-Polish feeling in Czechoslovakia at the time. However, when the first performance took place in April 1876, this general feeling had greatly abated because the Poles had aligned themselves with the Habsburgs against the Czechs. In *Vanda* Dvořák reverted to certain Wagnerian tendencies; not only is the opera unduly protracted, it is an affair of unmitigated gloom. The première was a fiasco of the first order, only three further performances were given, and the work is perhaps best ignored.'

[14] *Z mých divadelních pamětí*, 94.

The date of commencement for the full score of *Armida* is 11 March 1902.[15] Dvořák had begun the continuous sketch of the work precisely one month before, on 11 February.[16] Ten fragmentary sketches exist apart from the continuous sketch; none are dated, although three with separate inventory numbers are clearly from an advanced stage in the work on the full score, the third being a sketch for the prelude. The remaining seven contain ideas from all stages of the work, and may indeed predate the continuous sketch.[17]

The compositional process involved with *Armida* was, for Dvořák, unusually protracted. A quick comparison between the lengths of time spent on his last three operas offers a crude guide:

The Devil and Kate:	8 months
Rusalka:	7 months
Armida:	17 months

Even a cursory examination of the respective continuous sketches for each opera reveals that *Armida* gave Dvořák considerable problems. The sketches of *The Devil and Kate* and *Rusalka*[18] show every sign of fluency and a lack of hesitation. With *Armida*, on the other hand, there were two false starts to the first act on successive days. And while the rest of the first act proceeds relatively fluently in the continuous sketch, the end of the act presented clear difficulties, with no less than three different versions.

The versions of the opening do not show a clear evolution toward Dvořák's final solution in the full score. Some elements survived into the full score, others did not. The process involved does not suggest a natural growth toward a conclusion. In Exs. 7.1–7.8 selected passages from the sketch are shown beside the final version as it appears in the printed vocal score.[19]

The strong, declamatory unison opening of Act I in the continuous sketch of *Armida* (Ex. 7.1) has no counterpart in the final version (Ex. 7.2); indeed, the melody Dvořák uses is not to be found anywhere in the completed opera. The subsequent harmonized motif does, however, supply the basis for the opening of the final version of the opera, as may be seen from Ex. 7.2.

Ex. 7.3 shows the sketch of the first entry of the chorus with a curiously baroque-looking bass pattern in the latter portion—Dvořák's first inspirations could be expressed in an extraordinarily simplistic manner. At first glance Ex. 7.3 is quite different from the opening as it appears in the finished opera (Ex.

---

[15] See Jarmil Burghauser, *Antonín Dvořák: Thematický katalog—Bibliografie—Přehled života a díla* (Antonín Dvořák: Thematic Catalogue—Bibliography—Overview of Life and Work (Prague, 1960), 339–40 for details of the MS.

[16] The continuous sketch is held by the Muzeum české hudby (Museum of Czech Music) in Prague, for whose help I gladly acknowledge my heartfelt thanks.

[17] Also in the Museum of Czech Music.   [18] Also in the Museum of Czech Music.

[19] *Armida*, piano-vocal score by Karel Šolc, ed. Otakar Šourek (Prague, 1941).

Ex. 7.1 *Armida*, opening of Act I in continuous sketch

Ex. 7.2 *Armida*, opening of Act I in printed vocal score, p. 7

7.4). In fact, there is a passing similarity: if bars 9–11 of Ex. 7.3 are compared with bars 2–4 of Ex. 7.4, the similarity becomes clear. Interestingly, in the finished opera Dvořák made use of something rather similar to the beginning of Ex. 7.3 just a little later, when the men's chorus enters after the brief solo of the Muezin, as shown in Ex. 7.5. Here the semiquaver figure has been transferred to the orchestra; the time-signature is 3/4 rather than 2/4, and the choral line moves down rather than up. Nevertheless, the resemblance is quite clear.

The song of the Muezin himself in the continuous sketch (Ex. 7.6) is quite different from the final version (Ex. 7.7). The sketch shows a faint reminiscence to the opening of the prelude (the sketch version thereof—cf. Ex. 7.1),

Ex. 7.3 *Armida*, first choral entry in continuous sketch

Ex. 7.4 *Armida*, first choral entry in printed vocal score, p. 8

Ex. 7.5 *Armida*, choral entry after the first solo of the Muezin in printed vocal score, p. 10

but the rest goes its own way, remote from the prelude and from the final version. The only point of contact with the completed opera is in the setting of the concluding cry of 'Allah!'

Returning to the first choral entry in the finished opera (Ex. 7.4), we do eventually find a source for this passage in the continuous sketch. The second entry of the women's chorus in the continuous sketch (Ex. 7.8) gives the outline and some of the harmony of their first entry in the final version.[20]

This information is offered in part as an indication of Dvořák's working method in general, but by comparison with the continuous sketches of *The Devil and Kate* and *Rusalka*, it must also serve as evidence of an uncharacteristic hesitancy and uncertainty on the composer's part. As a whole the sketch and manuscript full score yield rich dividends for the student of Dvořák's compositional process. Two further examples must suffice here.

Perhaps unhappy about the wearisome process of using and writing all the flats in G flat major—the key of the final duet and chorus—Dvořák wrote the passage in G major and put at the beginning an arrow pointing down toward the indication *Ges*.

Ex. 7.6 *Armida*, first solo of the Muezin in continuous sketch

---

[20] By way of a general comment, the declamation is often different from the final version and occasionally rather poor, as in Ex. 7.8, where the last syllable of 'oasy' gets an uncharacteristic accentual thump.

Ex. 7.7 *Armida*, first solo of the Muezin in printed vocal score, p. 10

Ex. 7.8 *Armida*, second entry of women's chorus in continuous sketch

Another discovery in the sketch answers a question, or rather a perceptive complaint, made by John Clapham in his book *Antonín Dvořák: Musician and Craftsman*. In his discussion of *Armida*, Dr Clapham comments as follows: 'The motifs are usually used consistently, but we observe that the expected Cross theme is absent when Armida is baptized.'[21] In Ex. 7.9 I have reproduced the passage as it appears in the continuous sketch, revealing that the theme was present in Dvořák's original conception. The drum figure underpinning the passage in the printed score (Ex. 7.10) is a rhythmic survival of the presentation of the theme in sketch. Incidentally, it is worth noting that in the end of the sketch passage the descending vocal recitative is a D major arpeggio; in the finished version Dvořák resorts to baroque performance practice and turns the first D into an appoggiatura E.

Ex. 7.9 *Armida*, from final scene in continuous sketch

* Cross motif, crossed out!

Ex. 7.10 *Armida*, from final scene in printed vocal score, p. 375

These considerations are remote from the question of a model for the opera, but in one of these examples an incidental resemblance offers a way back into a consideration of *Vanda* in this connection. The fact that *Vanda*, the first of Dvořák's three grand operas, was on the composer's mind shortly

[21] p. 291.

before he began work on *Armida* has already been noted. A tempting point of speculation would be the passing resemblance between the opening of Act I in the continuous sketch of *Armida* and the corresponding passage in the completed score of *Vanda*—see Ex. 7.11.[22] Were this the only point of comparison, the justification for viewing *Vanda* as the model for *Armida* could not be sustained. There is however, much else.

Ex. 7.11 *a. Armida*, opening of Act I in continuous sketch; *b. Vanda*, opening of Act I in manuscript vocal score

The difficulty Dvořák experienced in coming to grips with the subject-matter of *Armida*, seen initially in the sketches, is echoed in the comments of the baritone Bohumil Benoni, who took the role of Ismen at the first performance. In his memoirs Benoni noted that:

Armida is Dvořák's tragedy. Dvořák was too naïve and literal a Christian, thus the magician Ismen is barely believable, and he [the composer] only responded to the political life of the crusader knights of Rome. . . . Eventually, Kovařovic, who had begun to set the opera in 1888, realized the false pathos and impotence of the libretto and stopped composing the opera he had begun. Dvořák was less critical; he was swayed by the name of the writer of his unfortunate libretto.[23]

Having been been bought back from Kovařovic by the author Vrchlický, the libretto of *Armida* was then considered by Bendl and Fibich, and eventually came to Dvořák via the director of the National Theatre, František Šubert. This was at a time when the composer was looking for a new role for Růžena Maturová, who had so successfully created the character of Rusalka.

---

[22] The excerpts from *Vanda* presented here and below are according to the MS vocal score in the Hudební archiv Národního divadla (Music Archive of the National Theatre, Prague, No. 381, made by Josef Bartovský).

[23] *Moje vzpomínky a dojmy* (My Memories and Impressions) (Prague, 1917), 308.

An additional problem for Dvořák may have been that he had not dealt with a central female role in a grand opera since *Vanda*. For all the importance of Marina, Xenie, and Marfa in *Dimitrij*, the central role belongs to the eponymous hero. There are other material resemblances between the outward structure of *Vanda* and *Armida*: both operas have a strong ceremonial element replete with fanfares and marches, and both conclude with the voluntary self-sacrifice of the heroine in scenes that are structured in remarkably similar ways.

Well before Dvořák's last creative period the contemplation of an earlier work or the work of another composer could stimulate him to a new, though related, endeavour. Dvořák spent much of 1887, in his own words, 'improving' old compositions with a view to sending them to Simrock.[24] Among them was his early Piano Quintet in A major, B. 28, composed in 1872. An attempt to 'improve' this particular piece led to the composition of the great Piano Quintet in the same key, B. 155.[25] In a reminiscence of Dvořák, Leoš Janáček noted that he frequently took the compositions of others as a starting-point, citing Škroup's 'Kde domov můj' ('Where is my Homeland'—the Czech national anthem), which Dvořák openly despised but which he eventually used in his overture (commonly known as 'My Home') and incidental music to Šamberk's play *Josef Kajetán Tyl*.[26] In the same connection Janáček mentioned that he had seen Dvořák looking at Berlioz's *Grand Messe des morts* and Liszt's *St Elizabeth* before composing respectively his own Requiem and *St Ludmila*. So perhaps it is no surprise to find Dvořák turning to *Vanda*, very much on his mind at the turn of the century, as something of a prop or inspiration in his difficulties with *Armida*.

Many aspects of the depiction of the heroine Vanda look forward to Dvořák's treatment of Armida. But to see this we must dispense with the notion that Dvořák failed to underline the dramatic points in *Vanda*.[27] There are numerous climaxes in the opera, all of which Dvořák negotiates with success. Dvořák's development of an effective way of dealing with climactic solo statements in fast arias in *Vanda* often anticipates his later operas. There is an interesting point of contact, for instance, between *Vanda* and *Rusalka*. Vanda's superb first-act aria 'Bohové velcí, bohové strašliví' (Great gods, fearsome gods) anticipates Rusalka's second-act outburst to the water goblin, 'Ó marno to je' (Oh, it is futile). The offbeat chords against the final statement and the

[24] See Dvořák's letter of 16 Aug. 1887 to Alois Göbl, in *Antonín Dvořák: Korespondence*, ii (Prague, 1988), 262.

[25] For part of which, as David Beveridge has shown, he turned to a model from another composer, namely the Piano Quintet by Schumann. See 'Dvořák's *Dumka* and the Concept of Nationalism in Music Historiography', *Journal of Musicological Research*, 12 (1993), 303–25.

[26] See *Antonín Dvořák: Letters*, 119.

[27] See the books by Robertson and Schönzeler cited in n. 13 above.

rising chromatic line leading to the final cadence look forward to the later
work. A similarly climactic moment in the fourth act of *Vanda* is also comparable to the end of 'Ó marno to je', but even more so to the brilliant conclusion of the aria 'Slyš, z hlubin bídy svojí' (Hear, from the depths of my misery)
in Act II, Scene 6 of *Armida*. This is where Armida herself calls for vengeance
on her supposed aggressors. In both the excerpt from *Vanda* (Ex. 7.12) and
that from *Armida* (Ex. 7.13), Dvořák makes telling use of the Neapolitan
chord.

Ex. 7.12 *Vanda*, from Act IV, Scene 2

The different demands of the various last-act finales in *Vanda*, *Dimitrij*, and
Armida—Dvořák's three works in the genre of grand opera—required appropriate and to some extent necessarily different treatment. It is not surprising
to find in the concerted first-act finales of *Vanda* and *Dimitrij*, where soloists
and chorus express strong positive sentiments, a strong family resemblance.
Where the requirements of the librettos are most evidently congruent it is
interesting to note Dvořák's response. In all three operas the conclusion is
brought about by the death of the heroine or (in the case of *Dimitrij*) the hero.
In each opera the demise of the main figure is followed by a chorus (joined in
Dimitrij by Basmanov and the Patriarch) with an orchestral postlude. While

Ex. 7.13 *Armida*, printed vocal score, p. 136

the presence of the chorus was dictated by the libretto, the quasi-liturgical atmosphere and the orchestral postludes reflect the composer's predilections. In *Dimitrij*, where the chorus actually sings 'Hospodin pomiluj!' (Lord, have mercy!), the decision to expand the single line of text probably came from Dvořák, in order to make an effective extended conclusion. In many ways, the conclusion of *Dimitrij* resembles and transcends that of *Vanda*. (Here it should be made clear that I am referring to Dvořák's revised ending of *Vanda*, made in 1880.)[28]

When, in *Armida*, Dvořák was presented with a conclusion that resembles more closely the end of *Vanda*, the ending emerges almost as a contrafactum of the earlier opera. In both cases the death of the heroine is followed by a choral verse and orchestral conclusion. Both begin *a cappella* and build through a crescendo to the orchestral conclusion—in the case of *Vanda* an apotheosis in the manner of Wagner's *Flying Dutchman*—which provides the peroration based on two of the major motifs of the opera (see Exs. 7.14 and 7.15).

Clearly, where Dvořák was presented with a situation and context that resembled those in the earlier opera where he had gained his experience, he

---

[28] The genesis, content, and revs. of *Vanda* are plotted in detail in Alan Houtchens's excellent study, 'A Critical Study of Dvořák's Vanda', Ph.D. diss. (Univ. of California, Santa Barbara, 1987). I am happy to acknowledge a debt to this in the preparation of this chapter.

Ex. 7.14 *Vanda*, final chorus and apotheosis

> Chorus: For her people, whom she loved, she gave her life; may her grave mound be light, and grant her everlasting glory. Let us bury her with love in her sacred, native earth—over her we shall raise a monument to her sacred and eternal memory.

reverted to the original solution. Apart from differences of material and a somewhat greater subtlety of treatment, Dvořák appears to be reaffirming the value of the experience he had gained in *Vanda*.

Many more examples may be adduced in pursuit of the debt owed to *Vanda* by *Armida*, the most convoluted of which is the strong similarity that exists between the major second-act duet of *Armida* and that to be found in the first act of *Vanda*—itself a transcription of the duet from the conclusion of Act I in Dvořák's first opera, *Alfred*. But more important than the debt owed by

Ex. 7.15 *Armida,* conclusion in printed vocal score, pp. 346–7

Chorus of crusaders: Again Christ's holy standard flies, further still!
Let us sacrifice all so that Christ's holy standard will fly further still!

Armida is the fact that Dvořák in his sixty-first year was prepared to turn to his earlier masterpiece for inspiration.

The message for all those who take the totality of Dvořák's *œuvre* seriously is that these early works do matter—they matter a great deal, and not just to a composer stuck with a libretto that exceeded the capacity of his original enthusiasm. What should be clear to us all regarding *Vanda,* not only from the trust that Dvořák, not to mention Hostinský, placed in this work, but supported also by the quality of the work itself, is that *Vanda* is an opera of extraordinary quality dogged from its première by ignorance and antagonism. Were it to receive the production it deserves and, to date, has never had, *Vanda* might prove to be a match for *Dimitrij* and, quite possibly, more than the equal of its successor, *Armida*.

Dvořák's *Dimitrij*—A Challenge to Editors

MILAN POSPÍŠIL

To most people, Dvořák is known as a composer who 'also wrote operas'. Already a renowned author of symphonies and chamber music, Dvořák, however, longed for international success as an opera composer. When late in 1880 he was offered the libretto for a grand opera, *Dimitrij samozvanec* (Dimitrij the Usurper) by Marie Červinková-Riegrová, he thought that by putting it to music he could finally achieve his aim of creating an opera that would earn him international acclaim.

The première of *Dimitrij* in Prague on 8 October 1882 was attended by prominent guests, including Dvořák's Berlin-based publisher Fritz Simrock and the Viennese critic Eduard Hanslick. Although the opera was well received, Dvořák failed in his efforts to have it produced elsewhere in Europe (Vienna, Munich, Hamburg, London, Budapest, St Petersburg, Moscow), and likewise failed to persuade Simrock to publish it. It was not until ten years after the première that the work was performed on a foreign stage—by the company of the National Theatre of Prague at an international exhibition in Vienna. In comparison with the response to Smetana's operas *Prodaná nevěsta* (The Bartered Bride) and *Dalibor* at this exhibition, *Dimitrij* failed, much to the disappointment of the composer.[1] This so shook his conviction about the values of the opera that in 1894, while in the United States, he decided to give it an overhaul so complete that his revision may be considered a new composition using the original musical material. In it he tried, in contradiction to the grand-opera character of the original, to satisfy the critics' demand for increased dramatic tension. The only form they recognized as suitable was the 'progressive' form of *Musikdrama*, which Dvořák more or less adopted in his revision.[2] Thus, the new *Dimitrij* is a different work altogether; Burghauser's

[1] See Walter Pass, 'Dvořáks Beitrag zur "Internationalen Theater- und Musikausstellung" Wien 1892', in *Musical Dramatic Works by Antonín Dvořák: Papers from an International Conference, Prague, 19–21 May 1983*, ed. Markéta Hallová, Zuzana Petrášková, and Jarmila Tauerová-Veverková (Prague, 1989), 167–72.

[2] On the origin and on the different versions of the opera, see Milan Kuna and Milan Pospíšil, 'Dvořák's *Dimitrij*: Its History, its Music', *Musical Times*, 120 (1979), 23–5, and three arts. by Milan Pospíšil: 'Dvořák:

thematic catalogue lists the first version under No. 127 and the second under No. 186.[3]

The fact that the two versions of *Dimitrij* are so different from one another that they cannot be published as one adds significance to the project of publishing it, in the context of the contemporary operatic world and musicological knowledge of Dvořák's complete operatic output. A critical edition should be a useful source for both study and production, and this is particularly important in the case of *Dimitrij*. Little known in the Czech Republic and hardly known at all in the world at large, *Dimitrij* is an opus whose full orchestral score has never been published in any form; even reliable rental material has been lacking.[4] This has affected the opera's performance history for over a century and contributed to the persistent belief that Dvořák's operas lack drama and are not particularly suitable for staging. Neither version has so far been issued in the complete edition of Dvořák's works by Editio Supraphon, which in fact includes only three of Dvořák's total of eleven operas (counting separately the two completely different settings of *The King and the Charcoal Burner*).[5]

In order to help make the opera known to a wider public, I have prepared and published, outside the complete works project, a critical edition based on the first version, which is generally considered the better one. Both musicologists (e.g. Dvořák's biographer Otakar Šourek) and practitioners (e.g. the conductor Karel Kovařovic) have preferred the first version to the second, but until now there has been no published version that adhered consistently to Dvořák's original.

To be sure, there are facts which might seem to counsel against favouring the first version. When offering the second version to the National Theatre, Dvořák prohibited productions of the first and did not even want its material to be lent out. Still, the restoration of the first version, performed fifty-one times in Prague before Dvořák withdrew it in 1894, cannot be considered harmful to Dvořák's reputation as an opera composer. Quite the contrary: publishing its critical edition is the only way to have the true worth of *Dimitrij*

Dimitrij (1882)', in *Pipers Enzyklopädie des Musiktheaters*, ii, ed. Carl Dahlhaus (Munich and Zürich, 1987), 94–8; 'Der Opernkomponist Antonín Dvořák', in *Europäisches Musikfest Stuttgart: Almanach* (Stuttgart, 1991), 196–210; and '*Dimitrij*, le grand opéra de Dvořák', in *Colloque Dvořák Macon, 24, 25, 26 novembre 1991* (Mouvement Janáček, xvi; Vanves, 1992), 11–14.

[3] *Antonín Dvořák: Thematický katalog—Bibliografie—Přehled života a díla* (Antonín Dvořák: Thematic Catalogue—Bibliography—Overview of Life and Work (Prague, 1960), 237–40, 316–17. The extraordinary divergence between the two versions of *Dimitrij* is exceeded only by the case of Dvořák's earlier opera, *Král a uhlíř* (The King and the Charcoal Burner), where the second version uses none of the original music and must be considered a completely separate opera.

[4] The available orchestral materials have been only Karel Kovařovic's arrangement of 1906 (from Dilia in Prague), described later in this chapter, and Honolka's Ger. version (from Alkor in Kassel).

[5] These are *Rusalka* (1960), *Jakobín* (The Jacobin) (1966), and *Čert a Káča* (The Devil and Kate) (1972).

recognized. If Dvořák preferred the second version to the first at a certain time, we need not necessarily identify with him, because the value and the life-span of works of art seldom depend on the judgement and the wish of their authors. Let us recall here the well-known case of Franz Kafka, who would be totally unknown to the world if Max Brod had complied with his will and destroyed the literary works the author left behind.

We therefore do not need evidence to prove what has become a traditional allegation in Dvořák literature, that toward the close of his life Dvořák regretted the reworking of *Dimitrij* and wanted to hear the first version of the opera. But for those who wish it, the evidence is available. When in 1904 a company in Plzeň became the first other than Prague's National Theatre to produce the work, Dvořák lent it an authorized copy of the score of the first version. The conductor, acting obviously on Dvořák's advice, interpolated certain passages from the second version: Shuiski's aria and the scene with Xenie in Act I (Scenes 3 and 4), Xenie's aria in Act IV (Scene 1), and the whole of Act III. The hire material for the Plzeň première has been preserved as testimony to the fact that Dvořák eventually placed both versions on a par and permitted their admixture.[6]

The director of the National Theatre opera company, Karel Kovařovic, pursued the same path in preparing a new production of *Dimitrij* in 1906, after the composer's death: he returned to the first version but combined it with certain parts of the second. His adaptation was in line with the demands of the time and was a success, but it gave rise to a false reception of the work, veiling its place in the historic genre of grand opera. Dvořák's own subtitle, *velká opera* (grand opera), was not mentioned.[7] In the Czech Republic Kovařovic's adaptations of other operas are still produced, and in the case of Janáček's *Její pastorkyňa* (*Jenůfa*), his version is considered the only form in which the work's full theatrical effect can be achieved. But world opinion is different, because *Jenůfa* is known elsewhere in Janáček's original as edited by Sir Charles Mackerras and John Tyrrell.[8]

It was the same John Tyrrell who initiated the British première of *Dimitrij* in Nottingham in 1979, restoring, with my assistance, most of the music that Kovařovic had left out. The success of the production was so convincing that attempts have since been made in Britain to restore Dvořák's original in full.

---

[6] See Milan Pospíšil, 'Dvořáks *Dimitrij* als Editionsproblem', in *Jahrbuch für Opernforschung 1986*, ed. M. Arndt and M. Walter (Frankfurt am Main, 1987), 87–108.

[7] The piano-vocal score of Kovařovic's adaptation was pub. in Prague by Hudební matice Umělecké besedy in 1912.

[8] With help from the Moravské muzeum (Moravian Museum) and John Tyrrell, Sir Charles Mackerras established the 'Brno' version of *Jenůfa*, which he performed in various preliminary versions leading to his recording of the work for Decca in 1982. A revised version by Tyrrell and Mackerras based on the original parts was first heard at Glyndebourne in 1990.

But the decision to favour the first version by no means solved all the problems in editing this work, for the first version is itself the result of a complex creative process. It is full of changes, of which I will mention only the most substantial. On the advice of Eduard Hanslick, who considered the murder of Xenie in Act IV to be insufficiently motivated and too ugly,[9] Dvořák asked the librettist Červinková to change the plot; he put the rewritten text to music in the summer of 1883. It was then that he also excised the fast part of the overture and adapted the slow part as an independent brief introduction. In 1885, he composed a new prelude for Act II, and wrote new music for Dimitrij's aria at the beginning of Act III, which had previously been omitted. It was with these and other changes, and with many cuts, that the piano reduction was published in 1886,[10] thus ending the period of creation of the 'first version'.

Though it was the only edition of *Dimitrij* in Dvořák's lifetime, the piano-vocal score cannot be considered the definitive form of the first version, and not simply because it is full of small mistakes—Dvořák seems not to have cared much about proof-reading—but, what is more important, because he did not notice more serious errors. Thus, after various cuts were made at the National Theatre, Dvořák changed the text of Marina's solo in Act III (Scene 4) to preserve her dramatic decision, 'Chci se Ruskou státi!' (I want to become a Russian!), though with different music. When, in the printed edition, Dvořák restored the passage originally cut, the new text was preserved so that the dramatic turn takes place twice![11]

In other places, the piano-vocal score preserves music that, in the mean time, the composer had changed in the score. This happened because at the time of the hectic preparations for the première, the piano reduction was first written by one person and later by three people who worked with the newly completed sheets of the score. The changes that Dvořák made in the score, even if he made them immediately after the piano reduction was finished, were for the most part not incorporated into it, resulting in numerous contradictions between the piano reduction and the orchestral score. Neither can the cuts be considered as definitive, as can be judged from Dvořák's later correspondence with Otilie Malybrok-Stieler, who translated the libretto into German.[12] In a letter to his publisher, Simrock, Dvořák described the piano-vocal score as only a provisional version necessary for negotiation with

[9] Hanslick's review repr. in his *Am Ende des Jahrhunderts: Musikalische Kritiken und Schilderungen* (Berlin, 1899), 140–8.

[10] (Prague, Em. Starý, 1886).   [11] Ibid. 244 and 247.

[12] See Dvořák's letter of 28 July 1887, in *Antonín Dvořák: Korespondence a dokumenty—Kritické vydání* (Antonín Dvořák: Correspondence and Documents—Critical Edition), ed. Milan Kuna et al., ii (Prague, 1988), 261.

foreign theatres.[13] The piano reduction is therefore not a convincing representation of Dvořák's definitive opinion about the first version.

Dvořák's continual reworking of *Dimitrij* should not necessarily be understood as a quest for an ideal form. We must realize that he had to conceive of an opera in part not as a finished work of art, but rather as a scenario for a single theatrical event adapted to the concrete conditions of the specific production. We are reminded of this traditional understanding of an opera by the circumstances in which Dvořák either reworked *Dimitrij* or contemplated doing so. He composed Act IV to a changed libretto having in mind a possible production of *Dimitrij* by the Court Opera in Vienna, and also a new production at the National Theatre, which had been rebuilt and reopened in 1883 after its destruction by fire. He wrote the new aria of Dimitrij in Act III inspired by the new casting of Antonín Vávra in the title role, and altered both this aria and the prelude to Act II in the hope that *Dimitrij* would be staged in Munich.[14] For the planned London production (which, like the Munich performance, never came to pass), he asked the librettist to consider introducing changes in Act IV.[15] Dvořák made smaller changes in the opera for each individual production and casting. I have already mentioned the last alteration of *Dimitrij* at the time of its Plzeň production, only five weeks before the composer's death. We can see from all the above that this opera was constantly evolving from the very beginning of its existence—a process which is normal for opera as a genre.

Because of the multitude of the changes and the fact that they were introduced in so many small increments—with the exception of the more sizeable revisions of 1883 and 1885—an exact dating of the individual phases of the first version's creation is not feasible. In my edition, the basis for restoration was the oldest finished form of the composition, that is the first version that Dvořák recognized as finished, and that he gave to the directorate of the National Theatre in Prague for its production in the summer of 1882. My intention was to publish this version in its entirety in the main text of the edition, and to give Dvořák's later changes and additions up to 1885 as variants juxtaposed to the respective passages. Thus the variants would be made equal in status to the original, because they were considered as such by the composer himself under certain conditions.

The basic principles observed in the edition were predetermined by its very subject, but they take into account also the approach adopted in modern

---

[13] See Dvořák's letter of 16 Mar. 1888, ibid. 317.

[14] See Julia Liebscher, 'Dvořák und München', *Musik in Bayern*, 39 (1989), 41–60.

[15] See Marie Červinková's note dated 15 Apr. 1884 (Archives of the Národní Muzeum (National Museum), Prague, Marie Červinková-Riegrová collection, box 11/9, p. 123). I thank Milan Kuna for this information.

editions of works with equally complex compositional histories (e.g. Verdi's *Don Carlos*).[16] The critical edition of the first version of *Dimitrij* thus brings together all the music that Dvořák wrote between 1882 and 1885 and that he considered suitable for production, making it accessible for interpretation. The edition enables the performance of the passages that were excised in Kovařovic's adaptation. Several substantial parts of the version from 1882 that Dvořák either recomposed or cut out are published here for the first time ever. The public is thus provided with an opportunity to become acquainted with and to hear, for the first time since 1882, some truly outstanding operatic music by Dvořák.

Even this very brief description of the complex development of *Dimitrij* hints at the difficulties that were encountered in restoring the first version and its various layers. Dvořák's autograph of the score was the chief source for the reconstruction, although it has not been preserved in full. Six sheets have been inadvertently lost, and other minor gaps were created by Dvořák himself when, in reworking the opera, he cut pages out of the bound score, pasted new pages on to old ones, and erased passages of the original version. Either these passages had to be fully reconstructed, or the individual versions had to be separated, with the help of the following secondary sources:

1. the copy of the score of Acts I and II (1882) from the archives of the opera company of the National Theatre in Prague;
2. the copy of the complete score made for Dvořák in 1884–5, preserved in the archives of the Plzeň opera; and
3. the manuscript piano-vocal score and orchestral parts made for the première in 1882.

The sources mentioned in group three were particularly valuable for the reconstruction of the original passage in Act IV dealing with Xenie's murder, which has not been preserved in the autograph. From these and other sources, the first version of the opera was thus restored quite reliably in all its different layers.[17]

The edition was to be published as rental material (orchestral parts, choral parts, and full score) and in the form of a piano reduction for sale. For provisional publication of the rental material (by the theatre agency Dilia in Prague), I have for practical reasons made the following arrangement (because the publisher insisted that the main text should be published without variants): in the main text the definitive introduction of 1883 follows the overture of 1882; I also have included the new prelude to Act II and the new aria for

---

[16] Piano-vocal score ed. Ursula Günther and Luciano Petazzoni (Milan, 1980).

[17] For more detailed discussion of the editorial issues see Pospíšil, 'Dvořáks *Dimitrij* als Editionsproblem'.

Dimitrij in Act III. The original versions of these parts, whose significance is more historical than anything else, are contained in a separate volume of addenda, along with the reworked version of Act IV (1883) and other revisions from 1882–5. Only minor instrumentation variants and negligible compositional changes have been omitted from the addenda.[18] It has already been the basis for new productions of the opera in 1989 and 1991, during which the conductors Gerd Albrecht[19] and Helmut Rilling[20] both decided in favour of the original Act IV but decided differently on the other variants.

I still hope that the edition will eventually be published properly, with the chief variants as part of the main text so that they can be employed conveniently at the interpreter's discretion. Until such time I can console myself with the thought that the unfinished character of the edition corresponds to the nature of the work itself.

[18] Using my critical edn., Dilia pub. the rental material (orchestral parts, choral parts, and full score) of four acts, not incl. the app. vol. The piano-vocal score was supposed to be pub. by Editio Supraphon, Prague. But both publishers ceased carrying the project. Dilia in Prague, together with Alkor in Kassel, is lending out the rental material based on my edn. illegally and without the consent of the editor. The complete critical edn., incl. critical commentary, exists so far only in an MS in the Ústav pro hudební vědu, Akademie věd České republiky (Institute of Musicology, Academy of Sciences of the Czech Republic) in Prague.

[19] For the concert performance in Prague, 9 Feb. 1989, and the first complete recording of *Dimitrij*, produced by Supraphon of Prague, No. 11 1259–2 633 (1992).

[20] For the concert performances at the Oregon Bach Festival in Eugene, 7 July 1991, and at the Europäisches Musikfest in Stuttgart, 8 Sept. 1991.

9

Rusalka and its Librettist, Jaroslav Kvapil: Some New Discoveries

MARKÉTA HALLOVÁ

ONE might think that more than enough has already been written about Dvořák's most-performed opera, *Rusalka*, and its libretto, and that there is no sense in adding more. However, my investigations have led me to conclude the very opposite.

In 1911 Jaroslav Kvapil, the author of the libretto for *Rusalka*, published the first serious recollections of how he wrote it: 'When in 1899 I wrote the libretto *Rusalka*, I did not anticipate that I was writing for Antonín Dvořák; I wrote it without knowing for whom.'[1] In the same article Kvapil went on to say that he gave the composer Oskar Nedbal the first act to read but the latter was too preoccupied with his opera *Pohádka o Honzovi* (Fairy-Tale about Johnny). Kvapil further stated:

I went on writing *Rusalka* for myself, and only when I had finished did I give it to several composer friends of mine, without making them an offer. Josef Bohuslav Foerster, Karel Kovařovic, and Josef Suk all read it. At the time all of them were engrossed in other work which I knew about, so I was not surprised that they showed only a friendly interest—and no more.

According to Kvapil's recollection, he did not 'dare' approach Dvořák, although he had known him for years. He says that it was only after he learned from the press that Dvořák, through the mediation of the National Theatre, was looking for a new libretto, that he turned to the theatre director František Adolf Šubert, saying he had a libretto that he could possibly offer Dvořák.

In an interview that Kvapil gave in 1936 he reiterated this information almost word for word,[2] as he did also in his book of memoirs published in 1946.[3] Naturally, Kvapil's account has been adopted in the secondary

---

[1] 'O vzniku *Rusalky*' (On the Origin of *Rusalka*), *Hudební revue*, 4 (1911), 428–30.

[2] 'O novou *Rusalku*' ([Efforts] Toward a New *Rusalka*), *Národní divadlo*, 13/15 (1936), 3–4.

[3] 'Skladatel *Rusalky*' (The Composer of *Rusalka*), in *O čem vím* (What I Know about), 3rd edn., i (Prague, 1946), 254–7.

literature. One comes across the same information in Šourek's four-volume monograph,[4] in Burghauser's lengthy introduction to the libretto dating from 1958,[5] in the critical edition of the score,[6] in the vocal score, and in later literature, most recently the article by Ivan Vojtěch in *Pipers Enzyklopädie des Musiktheaters*.[7]

It occurred to me to take another look at these facts (including the libretto itself) when I found a letter to Kvapil from František Šubert, dated 8 March 1897. This letter, written almost three years before the libretto for *Rusalka* came into being, states:

> Composer Dr Dvořák would very much like a libretto for an opera with a Czech fairy-tale plot. You would be the most likely and best person to write it. Wouldn't you care to do Dvořák a favour and go have a chat with him? Dr Rieger has taken this matter very much to heart and has talked it over with me twice already.[8]

(The reference is to the politician František Ladislav Rieger, who at that time was aiding Dvořák in matters of text as the composer revised his earlier opera, *Jakobín* [The Jacobin]; Dr Rieger was the father of *Jakobín*'s librettist Marie Červinková-Riegrová, who had died.)

This letter confirms that Dvořák was at that time already contemplating a new opera based on a fairy-tale and that Kvapil had received a direct offer to work on the libretto. Kvapil had at the time finished his fairy-tale play in verse, *Princezna Pampeliška* (Princess Dandelion), and offered it to the National Theatre. (Its first performance took place in the autumn of that year, with incidental music by Josef Bohuslav Foerster.) Šubert, as the theatre's director, interested in new repertoire, must have known the play as early as the spring of 1897. It is quite likely that he thought well of it and had possibly said so to Dvořák and Rieger. It seems clear, therefore, that Šubert contacted Kvapil in the matter of a libretto for Dvořák substantially earlier than has been thought.

Kvapil was not engaged in any other major work between writing *Princess Dandelion* (1896) and *Rusalka* (1899). Probably he actually forgot about the suggestion made by Šubert in 1897. While working on *Rusalka*, inspired by the landscape of the island of Bornholm where he was staying, Jaroslav Kvapil sent a letter to Foerster. I managed to gain access to this letter, hitherto

---

[4] Otakar Šourek, *Život a dílo Antonína Dvořáka* (The Life and Work of Antonín Dvořák), 2nd edn., iv (Prague, 1957), 124 ff.

[5] 'Vznik díla a hudební obsah opery' (Origin of the Work and Musical Content of the Opera), in *Antonín Dvořák: Rusalka* [libretto with commentary], ed. Jarmil Burghauser (Prague, 1956), 7–25.

[6] (Prague, 1960).

[7] 'Dvořák: Rusalka (1901)', *Pipers Enzyklopädie des Musiktheaters*, ii, ed. Carl Dahlhaus (Munich and Zürich, 1987), 101–6.

[8] Unpub. letter held by the Památník národního písemnictvi (Memorial of National Literature), Strahov, Prague (where part of Kvapil's bequest is preserved).

unknown, thanks to the kindness of a private owner. It was written on 30 September 1899 and contains some quite new facts:

Dear Friend. This time I am writing to make a little suggestion. Professor Jiránek from Kharkov approached me in the summer with a request for a libretto. He has just placed the opera *Dagmar* . . . and would like something new. Well, I was not particularly keen—but because an idea was buzzing in my mind, I got to work on it. Counter to all my expectations, the work began to go so well that I soon had regrets. Several friends whom I had let read the script are now persuading me not to give it to Jiránek. . . . Admittedly, he has again written from Russia and is pressing me, but I have not answered him, although I have finished it completely. I am too satisfied with the work to give it away to an uncertain address for a few gulden. And now I am telling you: I have a libretto that I think is valuable as a poetic piece and as a stage work. I am not offering it to you directly so that you will not be under the impression that I want to pin something on you that was originally meant for someone else. . . . It has three acts; it is an absolute fairy-tale, completely moonlit, but I think—if you'll forgive me—it has charm and is theatrically effective. There are elements (but only elements) drawing on Andersen's *Mermaid*, and on Fouqué's *Ondine* (however, it in no way overlaps with Lortzing's libretto).[9]

Foerster answered Kvapil's letter straight away, on 9 October:

Dear Jaroslav . . . I can only say now, that never before have I read such a libretto. You have written a rare work, and immediately the first scene captivated me. Such a lot of poetry, your verses sing in themselves, there is the sound of the sweetest melodies in them. Don't be offended that I am writing just these few words; a letter will follow. I'm incredibly busy here.[10]

We may assume from these words that there was a follow-up letter with a more thorough evaluation of the libretto. Perhaps it is this letter that is mentioned in a communication of 1943 from Otakar Šourek (Dvořák's biographer) to Kvapil:

Maestro Foerster has just written to say that when he received the libretto to *Rusalka* from you and read it, it occurred to him immediately that the only composer for it was Dvořák and with this in mind he also wrote to you. Please, do you happen to have this letter, and could you kindly lend it to me? Maestro Foerster is interested in it.[11]

Today it is impossible to ascertain whether the letter Foerster requested years later was actually returned. After 9 October, the next letter from

---

[9] Alois Jiránek was a Czech composer—now forgotten—who spent a long time in Kharkov, Russia. He died in 1950, the same year as Kvapil. He was the brother of the pianist Josef Jiránek. The Lortzing ref. is to the opera *Undine*, based on the composer's own libretto.

[10] Unpub. postcard, Memorial of National Literature, Strahov, Prague, in Kvapil's bequest.

[11] Unpub. postcard, 24 Sept. 1943, Memorial of National Literature, Strahov, Prague, in Kvapil's bequest.

Foerster to Kvapil to be found in any of the memorabilia of either Kvapil, Foerster, or Šourek is one dated 27 February 1900. This was two months before Dvořák started composing *Rusalka*. In it Foerster says, 'I think Dvořák could work real miracles with your libretto. A few days ago I heard his symphonic poem *Holoubek* [The Wild Dove], rich with rare poetry and tones that are akin to your poetry.'[12] Thus Foerster must be entered as another possible catalyst, along with Šubert and Rieger, for the Kvapil–Dvořák collaboration. There is still one more person who may have influenced the situation: the critic Emanuel Chvála. According to Kvapil himself, Chvála took a positive stance in evaluating the libretto to Dvořák when the two future collaborators met for the first time.[13] The meeting took place near the beginning of 1900, in the National Theatre.

From the present point of view it is on the whole irrelevant whether Foerster, Šubert, Rieger, or Chvála arranged the contact between Kvapil and Dvořák. What is truly important is that this was a happy encounter. Despite the great difference between the two artists in character and in age—Kvapil was born in 1868, twenty-seven years after Dvořák—their collaboration produced a harmonious work whose literary and musical aspects intermingle perfectly. It is a work whose beauty is outstanding—and not only in the context of Czech music.

Kvapil's instinct, which prompted him into thinking that his libretto would be wasted on a mediocre composer (though of course he did not state this blatantly), seems today to have been justified. The fact that the *Rusalka* libretto is decidedly superior to most Czech opera librettos produced in the nineteenth century goes without saying. However, Kvapil has been appreciated mainly as a theatre producer rather than a writer; he is considered to be the founder of Czech modern stagings.[14] Upon close study of his most important literary works, and in particular the stage works, the qualities of *Rusalka* become ever more apparent: in dramatic plan, language, and psychological essence it far surpasses his other dramatic works. It may be claimed without a doubt that *Rusalka* constituted a crystallization for Kvapil, and the height of his achievement as a writer. Soon after he completed *Rusalka* (in the same year, 1900) Kvapil turned his attention totally to theatrical production, so that *Rusalka* actually marked the end of his literary career.

It is questionable whether Kvapil really conceived *Rusalka* only as an opera libretto. He may have contemplated turning it into a straight play. He himself admits later in his memoirs that he would have written it as a play

---

[12] Unpub. letter from Hamburg, Kvapil's bequest, Memorial of National Literature, Strahov.

[13] *O čem vím*, i, 254–7.

[14] See Evžen Turnovský, 'J. Kvapil', in *Národní divadlo a jeho předchůdci* (The National Theatre and its Precursors), ed. Vladimír Procházka (Prague, 1988), 265–6; also Ivan Vojtěch, 'Dvořák: *Rusalka*'.

in its own right had it not been for the competition from Gerhard Hauptmann's *Die versunkene Glocke* (The Sunken Bell) (a play on a similar subject).[15] In any case, it is clear that Kvapil prized his *Rusalka* as a dramatic work: he included it in a collection of his stage works published in 1948.[16]

Some commentators have tried to interpret *Rusalka* in allegorical terms, as for instance M. Schlumpf in his essay for the programme book of the Darmstadt Opera (1984), saying that *Rusalka* represents an allegory of the disintegration of the Austro-Hungarian Empire and that with the kiss of death it heralds the decline of the House of Habsburg.[17] This view is difficult to reconcile with the words of Kvapil himself, who in his letter to Foerster of 1899 characterized *Rusalka* as 'an absolute fairy-tale, completely moonlit',[18] from which we may infer that the emphasis was on the actual plot.

The story of the water-nymph (Ondine-Rusalka) has been an attractive subject for folk-tales going back perhaps as far as Celtic days. The heathen visions of this story, evoked by the secretive nooks of nature, have long dwelt in people experiencing a certain psychic state, and are ever viable. The story probably entered literature for the first time in 1390.[19] In the many subsequent literary versions, each writer treated the basic theme according to his or her own imagination and creative potential, and according to the prevailing style of the period. It should be noted that the water-nymph theme is by no means exclusively linked to Western Europe. It is equally at home among the Slavs[20] and has a distinctive place in Czech myths and literature.[21]

The literature on Kvapil's libretto has concentrated almost exclusively on foreign influences, such as Friedrich de la Motte Fouqué, Andersen, Hauptmann, Grillparzer, and others. But it is not so important to determine the provenance of Kvapil's inspiration for his themes, or the models. The valuable contribution of *Rusalka* as such lies in the actual treatment. In keeping with the most modern artistic trends, the work makes an approach from the *fin-de-siècle* style toward impressionism. An immense dramatic conception is reflected in the structure of the work as a whole, and above all this conception has endowed the theme with the imprint of a profound

---

[15] *O čem vím*, i. 254.

[16] *Divadlo Jaroslava Kvapila* (The Theatre of Jaroslav Kvapil) (Prague). This is dedicated to Kvapil's first wife, Hana Kvapilová, a prominent actress in the Prague National Theatre company at the turn of the century, who usually played the leading roles in the plays written by her husband.

[17] 'Hütet euch vor Habsburg—oder Rusalka und die nationale Frage: Ein Märchen als politische Parabel', in *A. Dvořák: Rusalka—Libretto, Text, Bilder* (Staatstheater Darmstadt, 1984), 48–53. Adapted from a study by Ludwig Haesler pub. later as '*Rusalka*, aneb marnost pozemské lásky' (*Rusalka*, or the Futility of Earthly Love), *Hudební věda* 27/3 (1990), 237–43.

[18] See n. 9.   [19] Šourek, *Život*, iv. 119 n.

[20] See e.g. the poem about the water-nymph by Lesja Ukrajinka (1871–1913), written at about the same time as Kvapil's *Rusalka*.

[21] In fairy-tales by Božena Němcová, and also the stage fairy-tale *Česká Meluzina* by Václav Kliment Klicpera (Prague, 1848).

philosophical content. These features can be illuminated to some extent by a comparison of Kvapil's *Rusalka* with other works by the same author—a comparison that no one up till now has attempted.

The play *Princess Dandelion* (finished in 1896) apparently served Kvapil as preparation, as it were, for *Rusalka*. This is indicated by comparison of certain polarities shared by the two works: comic-melancholy and realism-dream. In *Princess Dandelion* these polarities are somewhat stilted and unclarified, but in *Rusalka* they are clearly marked. Moreover, whereas *Princess Dandelion* tends to move away from a realistic-romantic stance toward one that is more in step with the *fin-de-siècle* era, *Rusalka* reaches out even further in the direction of impressionism (which Dvořák fully understood as he projected his music toward this style). Hence it is impossible to agree with the opinion that the young composers to whom Kvapil had offered his libretto shied away from it because it was not sufficiently modern.[22]

Another parallel, hitherto unobserved, between *Rusalka* and *Princess Dandelion* is that both works focus on a conflict between two worlds. In *Princess Dandelion* the royal daughter, in spite of all her love for the stalwart country lad, is incapable of coming to terms with life in a country cottage and lapses into melancholic apathy until in the end she disappears, wafted away to eternity as it were by a frosty wind from the world of human beings. This same general theme, in fact, can be traced back to Kvapil's play from 1895, *Bludička* (Will-o'-the-Wisp); here too he was concerned with a woman hovering between two worlds—alienated from the one, and unable to accept the other.

And now at last let us take a look at the libretto of *Rusalka* from the standpoint of Dvořák. We should not forget that during his youth in the village of Nelahozeves, parties were often held at the nearby mansion park of the counts of Chotek in Veltrusy, where, as in *Rusalka*, guests were seen dressed as fairies and nymphs flitting among the trees. The local forester apparently used to go disguised as a water-goblin. However, popular lore of the region of Nelahozeves and Veltrusy has tended to exaggerate the importance of these youthful impressions for Dvořák's opera.

I therefore tried to investigate whether possibly Dvořák himself did not have some sway over Kvapil in choosing the theme. I was fascinated by this idea especially after finding Šubert's letter written in 1897. But it is clearly evident that Dvořák could not possibly have influenced Kvapil in his leanings toward this theme. Memories of his youth could have played a certain role in Dvořák's interest, but these should not be overestimated. The reason for

---

[22] Here I dispute the opinion expressed by Jan Smaczny in his art. 'Dvořák and *Rusalka*', in *Opera*, 34 (1983), 241–5.

Dvořák's interest in Kvapil's libretto must be sought in the very essence of the composer's colourful musical imagination, nurtured by his poetry-reading.

The extent to which various aspects of the story in *Rusalka* are accentuated mostly depends on the producer of the opera. It is well known, for instance, that the psychological level was underlined to the highest degree in David Pountney's production at the English National Opera. But, in any case, the reason for the success of the work up to the present day goes far beyond its simple narrative line: rather, the opera leads a sensitive and knowledgeable audience to far deeper contemplations. Armed with new information on the librettist's own regard for his work, and on Foerster's appreciation of its richness, together with the eminent suitability of Dvořák to provide the musical setting, we can more fully understand the deep dramatic and psychological impact of this landmark in Czech opera.

III

DVOŘÁK AS A CZECH COMPOSER

10

Dvořák and the Meaning of Nationalism in Music

LEON PLANTINGA

IN his article on 'Czechness' in music in *19th-Century Music*, my colleague and friend Michael Beckerman does me the honour of citing a passage in my book on the music of nineteenth-century Europe. What he says, among other things, is, 'The author's discussion of nationalism begins oddly with a discourse on the Viennese waltz.'[1] I might perhaps point out that I actually talk about the phenomenon 'nationalism' for a couple of pages before I get to the waltz, attempting, even, to provide a context of ideas and associations into which that dance might reasonably fit.[2] But let us focus here on the unanswered question: What is odd about discussing the Viennese waltz in the context of 'nationalism in music'? (And I do not for a moment deny that many might find it odd.) One might argue that the rage for the waltz in Vienna seems to fulfil some of the criteria that are often implicit in discussions of nineteenth-century cultural nationalism: the dance and its music were, or were perceived to be, products of an indigenous people, quite distinct from an international 'cultivated' tradition, and were celebrated as such by urban educated classes.

Now one reason why we don't usually think of the waltz as 'nationalist' music, perhaps, is that its swift rise to international popularity weakened its initial association with the Austrian countryside or the environs of Vienna. But there may well be a more basic reason. This is music from the centre of the Austrian Empire, which, despite some recent erosion of power and prestige—and there was soon to be more of this—occupied at the turn of the nineteenth century a position of political and cultural domination. And in our consideration of 'nationalism' as a force in the history of music and art we tend to limit our focus, by and large, to cultures of the powerless and the oppressed,

[1] 'In Search of Czechness in Music', *19th-Century Music*, 10/1 (Summer 1986), 61.

[2] Leon Plantinga, *Romantic Music: A History of Musical Style in Nineteenth-Century Europe* (New York, 1984), 341–2.

to those where there is a longing to throw off rule from elsewhere and establish indigenous nations. We applaud the Poles, their lands repeatedly redistributed among their more powerful neighbours, for stirrings of national pride and the celebration of their own language and literature; we view similarly the struggles of nineteenth-century Hungarians and Czechs to overcome that very cultural domination of Austria—to substitute, one might say, the csárdás and polka for the waltz. (In this regard Russia and its music seem to present a special case; though a great nineteenth-century political power, this country was regarded—even by Russians—as culturally and artistically peripheral.)[3] Among historians of European music, nationalism is almost always seen in this light; it is a benign thing, restricted mainly to those areas of the continent where it can be viewed as benign. It is more pleasing to observe the celebration of Czech cultural identity in the works of Smetana and Dvořák, surely, than to contemplate a similar impulse in the German Richard Wagner after the war of 1870.

Political and social historians of course tend to see this whole matter very differently. Among them 'nationalism' is frequently cited as the dominant organizing factor among most of the world's societies over the past two centuries—exceeding in force even, say, the competing systems of capitalism and communism. It is defined as a prevailing pattern of loyalties in which a person's first allegiance is owed not to a dynastic regime or a religious community—the old twin pillars of church and ruler—but to a 'people' or a 'nation'.

This last is not easy to define, and in their efforts to do so historians differ in their emphasis. Hans Kohn, in his good-sized volume *The Idea of Nationalism*, names a series of attributes that in varying combinations and strengths delimit 'nations': common descent, language, territory, customs and traditions, and religion.[4] Carlton J. H. Hayes singles out common language as the single dominant ingredient.[5] But there seems to be widespread agreement that the idea of nationality, upon which nationalism is founded, is first and foremost a state of mind, that, in Kohn's words, 'nationality is formed by the decision to form a nationality.'[6] (Another writer on the subject paints this picture in darker hues: 'a nation is a people united by a common dislike of its neighbors and by a common mistake about its origins.'[7]) Also generally agreed upon is this: that European nationalism was closely connected with the rise of the idea of popular sovereignty, and that its first great manifestation (though not its origin) is to be seen in the French Revolution. And Kohn expresses a

---

[3] On this subject I am indebted to a discussion with Malcolm H. Brown.

[4] *The Idea of Nationalism: A Study in its Origins and Background* (New York, 1944), 13–14.

[5] *Essays on Nationalism* (New York, 1926), 4–5.   [6] *The Idea of Nationalism*, 15.

[7] Quoted from an unnamed source by George Brock, 'An "Ism" that won't Go Away', *New York Times* (28 July 1990), 21.

common view when he writes, 'The modern period of history, starting with the French Revolution, is characterized by the fact that in this period, and in this period alone, the nation demands the supreme loyalty of man, that all, not only certain individuals or classes, are drawn into this common loyalty.'[8] Nationalism, thus, is seen as a pervasive set of assumptions that profoundly affected the course of European history, in the East and West, in countries large and small, weak and powerful.

One music historian who, as we might expect, has taken a broader view of the subject—more in accord with that of the political historians—is Carl Dahlhaus. In his essay 'Nationalismus und die Musik' he points to a 'bourgeois nationalism' as a pan-European phenomenon whose effects may be sought in German, French, and Italian music as well as in the so-called 'national schools' of central and eastern Europe. But throughout his article Dahlhaus seems to cling to another kind of restriction of the notion of nationalism. He consistently attaches a peculiarly German adaptation of this idea to the phenomenon as it appears in various contexts throughout Europe. This special adaptation is Herder's old notion of the *Volksgeist* (developed in the prefaces to *Stimmen der Völker in Liedern*, *Ideen zur Philosophie der Geschichte der Menschheit*, and elsewhere), that mysterious force that (in Dahlhaus's summary) formed the truly fundamental, creative, and stimulating element in art as in other human activities. According to this idea, for instance, it was the spirit of the people of Norway that demanded musical expression in and through Edvard Grieg.[9]

We ought to note here that the subject at hand is not, say, a mere interest in, or even a passion for, the cultural artifacts of one's own people. Rather it is this, that in the best traditions of idealist philosophy there is an unseen force underlying all manifestations of a nation's culture; that this force, the 'spirit of the people', plays a leading role in forming the character, thought, and artistic expression of all members of a nation. According to this theory it would presumably not have been necessary for Bartók and Kodály to undertake any sort of fieldwork in order to get at the nature of Hungarian folksong. As true Hungarians, they should have felt the genuine article welling up spontaneously within them.

Holding fast to this special variant as an essential factor in nationalism allows Dahlhaus to construct one of his beloved paradoxes: the composer who holds to such a tenet, who believes that *Volksgeist* is at the bottom of it all (whether this paradigm is accurate or not), will respond to such a belief in his music— belief in the theory is partly responsible for the phenomenon of which that

---

[8] *The Idea of Nationalism*, 12.

[9] Carl Dahlhaus, 'Nationalism in Music', in his *Between Romanticism and Modernism: Four Studies in the Music of the Later Nineteenth Century*, trans. Mary Whittall (Berkeley and Los Angeles, 1980), 81.

theory seeks to give an account.[10] But this mystical notion of the determinant force of the *Volksgeist* had currency mainly in Germany, and mainly from the time of Herder in the 1770s until the high tide of Hegelianism in the 1830s. Surely it will not do, without further evidence, to attribute such a belief to Grieg, whether he was in Bergen or Leipzig, to the leaders of the Risorgimento, or to Verdi as he promoted their cause, or to Smetana as he decided in 1862 to return to Prague.

Let us return for a moment to that other restriction of the idea of nationalism in music. Our habit of thinking about Norway or Hungary in this connection, and almost never about Austria and France, has a couple of unfortunate effects. The first of them (mentioned by Dahlhaus) is that it reinforces a distinction between 'central' and 'peripheral' nations and their music.[10] This is a distinction based upon a 'view from the centre', so to speak, and follows in traditions of ethnocentric musical historiography whose assumptions we may well wish to question. And it is a distinction whose obliteration was in some sense the programme of the composers of the 'nationalist' schools. The other effect of viewing nationalism as a force operative only in certain countries is that it easily lures one into the assumption that this is the central element in the music of these countries. Nationalism provides a convenient handle to grasp when one is looking for handy categories and unifying models of explanation. (And, to judge from the title of chapter 11 of my nineteenth-century book, 'Nationalist Music', one may easily conclude that I myself am not the least of offenders in this respect.)

Emphasis on national or regional elements in a musical style may arise from quite opposed sorts of presuppositions. It may reflect a belief in the intrinsic value of such elements as a 'voice of the people', and in their power to inform or enrich musical style with local colouring and associations. Or it may again reflect that 'view from the centre' with its assumption that 'regional' music is interesting only for its 'regional' traits, and hence is to be approached quite differently, and to be judged by criteria quite other than those invoked for the 'central' repertoire. Issues such as these have been addressed with a new care and sophistication in recent discussions of Russian music, discussions from which those of us in other areas may well profit.[11]

Dvořák participated energetically in various strains of musical practice to which he was exposed in that very active musical centre, Prague. His earlier compositions range all the way from a kind of Schubertian classicism to the

---

[10] Carl Dahlhaus, 'Nationalism in Music', in his *Between Romanticism and Modernism: Four Studies in the Music of the Later Nineteenth Century*, trans. Mary Whittall (Berkeley and Los Angeles, 1980), 81.

[11] See Richard Taruskin, 'How the Acorn Took Root—A Tale of Russia', *19th-Century Music*, 6/3 (spring 1983), 189–212; and also Taruskin, 'Some Thoughts on the History and Historiography of Russian Music', *Journal of Musicology*, 3/4 (autumn 1984), 321–9.

Wagnerian avant-garde and beyond. He made his first strong impression on an international public with pieces of a distinct regional cast with the publication of the Moravian Duets and the first set of Slavonic Dances, put out by Simrock of Berlin in 1878. Dvořák's subsequent fame in Europe and, particularly, in England and the United States, was surely coloured by perceptions of the composer as an 'exotic romantic', as representative of a valiant people and a picturesque homeland. But such perceptions, I suspect, do not begin to account for the great international acclaim he enjoyed by the 1880s and 1890s. Dvořák was seen, quite simply, as a great composer; people admired and were moved by his music in ways not very different, surely, from the way they responded to the works of, say, Mendelssohn or Brahms.

Eager pursuit of a Slavic or Bohemian component in Dvořák's music is unlikely, I think, to prove the most fruitful approach to a fuller understanding of this composer's works or their significance. Thoughts about Dvořák's 'Czechness' and the search for roots in folk and regional styles should not distract us from the straightforward analysis, appraisal, and criticism that this music deserves. None the less, recent discussion of nationalist elements in Dvořák and other composers have shown a welcome broadening of focus. Dahlhaus, in arguing for the legitimacy of audience perception and reception history as evidence for considering a music 'nationalist', writes, 'If a composer intended a piece of music to be national in character and the hearers believe it to be so, that is something which the historian must accept as an aesthetic fact, even if stylistic analysis—the attempt to 'verify' the aesthetic premise by reference to musical features—fails to produce any evidence.'[12]

And Beckerman's article, mentioned at the beginning of this chapter, appeals to many sorts of 'extramusical' associations—verbal, pictorial, historical, folkloric—to locate what he calls 'Czechness' in the work of Czech composers, while rejecting the notion that such a thing could be defined by the categories of musical style alone.[13]

Efforts to find convincing bases for the musical styles of the major 'nationalist' composers in specific and exclusive musical idioms of their own lands have proved mainly frustrating. I have been impressed with one or two of the identifications of folk sources such as those cited by Antonín Sychra in his

---

[12] Dahlhaus, *Between Romanticism*, 86–7. Note that Dahlhaus's formulation conforms to certain criteria for 'reference' proposed by modern philosophers of language (Kripke, Wettstein, and others). Suppose someone says to a companion, 'the man there at the bar drinking wine was recently released from prison.' If the speaker meant to refer to a particular man at the bar (intention), and his companion understood to whom he wished to refer (reception), then this example of 'reference' was successful even if the man at the bar happened to be drinking a diet cola from a wineglass.

[13] 'In Search of Czechness', 62–73. See also Beckerman's latest ideas on the subject, pertaining particularly to Dvořák, in his essay 'The Master's Little Joke: Antonín Dvořák and the Mask of Nation', in *Dvořák and his World*, 134–54.

book on Dvořák's symphonic music.[14] Clear and unambiguous relationships
to authentic indigenous music, however, remain hard to come by.

But 'authenticity' in this case may be a chimera not even very much worth
pursuing. An analogy with the invocation of exotic and folk styles in Western
art music at large may be helpful. At a performance of Mozart's *Die Entführung
aus dem Serail*, a knowledgeable eighteenth-century listener (even one who
has not bothered to glance at the title of the evening's offering) will know by
the ninth bar of the overture something of what the opera is about. The forte
entrance of piccolo, triangle, and bass drum unmistakably signals 'Turkish'.
And to ethnocentric Western European minds, this would bring on associations such as 'fierce', 'warlike', 'primitive', and, despite all this, 'a little comic'.
A good bit of communication has taken place here with a minimum of musical means. And for purposes of Mozart's audience, it really makes very little
difference whether that music resembles anything ever heard in Turkey or
not. (And *Die Entführung* might not play well in Istanbul for reasons more
basic than musical authenticity.) In Vienna this music performed the 'Turkish'
function expected of it simply because it was perceived to do so. And the
imagined properties of the Turks could even be transferred, on occasion, to
other nationalities simply on the strength of the associations such music carried with it. In Lesueur's Parisian opera *Ossian, ou les Bardes* (1804), the sav-
agery of the warlike Scandinavians is evoked with a generous dose of 'Turkish'
music.

A similar sort of communication took place in the evocation of folk idiom
in European art music. To cite another well-known example from Mozart,
the peasant scene from the first act of *Don Giovanni* (Scene 7) opens with a
round dance and chorus, 'Giovinette che fate all' amore', in which the music
is in the approved 'peasant' manner (though Mozart could not resist some
tongue-in-cheek tampering with its basic rhythm). This is of course the urban
sophisticate's notion of what peasant music is probably like. And for purposes
of Mozart's opera and its audience, whether that notion is right or wrong is
of little or no consequence.

Now I am aware that Mozart's adoption of a 'Turkish' or 'peasant' manner
is quite another matter from Dvořák's invocation of the native music of his
own homeland. The latter is an embrace of a very different sort. None the
less, a similar principle may be operating in the two cases. When Dvořák's
music was performed abroad, where audiences were innocent of any acquaintance with native Bohemian music, virtually any gesture that sounds folk-like
would probably be acceptable as a reference to the composer's origins. (Here
we might recall that Robert Schumann, when he first heard Mendelssohn's

---

[14] *Antonín Dvořák: Zur Ästhetik seines sinfonischen Schaffens*, trans. Gert Jäger and Jürgen Morgenstern
(Leipzig, 1973), 22–3.

'Scottish' Symphony, thought it was the 'Italian'. The drones reminded him not of bagpipes and heather, but only of a *Volkston*.[15] But this hardly allows us to conclude that he 'misunderstood' the symphony.) A mere lowered seventh scale-degree, when it sounds in the first theme of Dvořák's Cello Concerto, can easily be accepted as 'Bohemian'—even though it is the commonest cliché of modal colouring. What counts, again, is not the specificity or accuracy of a musical reference, but its perception. And I would expect that a situation not altogether dissimilar would prevail when Dvořák's music was played in Prague. Some in this urban and educated audience might recognize similarities to local idioms, and this might well prove an enriching experience. But such recognition would be in no way necessary for the basic communication of which we speak to take place. Elements of music that differ from an international cultivated style, and that are generally accepted as 'ethnic', can be perceived, also in Prague, I should think, as 'Czech'.

It mattered that Dvořák was Czech. And it is no denigration of his nationalist stance to say that the 'Czechness' in his works, like the very phenomenon of 'nationality' itself, was to a large degree a state of mind. For states of mind, the *Seelenzustände* of German theorists, have always been of crucial importance in the apprehension of music.

[15] *Gesammelten Schriften über Musik und Musiker*, ed. M. Kreisig, ii (Leipzig, 1914), 132.

11

The 'Dvořák Battles' in Bohemia: Czech Criticism of Antonín Dvořák, 1911–15

MARTA OTTLOVÁ

LET us begin with a testimony from the period:

God created in the desert an oasis and a crystal grotto;
and a Czech, with his typical uppishness, threw in a stone.[1]

With this metaphor, in his elegy to the death of Antonín Dvořák in 1904, the eminent Czech poet Jaroslav Vrchlický (1853–1912) expressed his feelings about the attitude adopted by university musicologists in Prague toward Dvořák's legacy. It was this attitude that later—exactly in the spirit of the metaphor—culminated in the 'Dvořák battles' of 1911–15. In this period of the battles for (or against) Dvořák (the preposition tells a lot about the position of those who waged them and the later interpreters) we can date the sad end of the idea of Czech national music, as formulated in the pro-Smetana camp amid the polemics of the 1870s. For the arguments and aesthetic judgements springing at that time from one of the period's major philosophical concepts of historical development appear later, in the Dvořákian disputes, in a perverted way, divorced from their historical context and their original content.

In view of the prestige and the unquestionable authority that Zdeněk Nejedlý (1878–1962), protagonist of the controversies, continues to enjoy among most Czech musicologists,[2] we should not be surprised that more

---

This chapter is an extended version of a text written originally together with Milan Pospíšil and read at an interdisciplinary symposium in 1990 in Plzeň. See 'Konce ideje české národní hudby' (The End of the Idea of Czech National Music), in *Čechy a Evropa v kultuře 19. století* (Bohemia and Europe in the Culture of the Nineteenth Century), ed. Petr Čornej and Roman Prahl (Prague, 1993), 81–6. In Ger. as 'Motiven der tschechischen Dvořák-Kritik am Anfang des 20. Jahrhunderts' in *Dvořák-Studien*, ed. Klaus Döge and Peter Jost (Mainz, 1994), 211–16.

[1] 'Bůh v poušti stvořil oasu a křišťálovou sluj | a Čech, má furiantství své, tam hodil kámen svůj.' J. Vrchlický, 'Za Antonínem Dvořákem' (Remembering Antonín Dvořák), *Zvon*, 4 (1904), 449.

[2] See e.g. Jaroslav Jiránek's ch. 'Zdeněk Nejedlý' in *Hudební věda: Historie a teorie oboru, jeho světový a český vývoj* (Musicology: History and Theory of the Discipline; Its Development Worldwide and in the Czech Lands), i, ed. V. Lébl and I. Poledňák (Prague, 1988), 172–82.

recent, post-war literature in Czechoslovakia[3] has approached the problem very cautiously and resorted to half-truths in explaining it.

It is generally admitted that Nejedlý's camp exhibited some degree of intolerance and a narrow aesthetic point of view.[4] The stark opposition to Dvořák at that time, however, continues to affect the historical treatment of the period in which modern Czech music was constituted, even if it is in the form of negation.

The controversies that raged in the period of the Dvořák polemics may seem impenetrable owing to their magnitude and the mode of argumentation,[5] all the more so because judgements based on music history and compositional technique were obviously used as a cover for cultural and political interests. Like the personality of Zdeněk Nejedlý, the 'Dvořák battles' cannot be fully explained from the point of view of one discipline. The musicological point of view can, however, help elucidate the nature and the motives of these controversies to some extent.

We have already referred to a connection between the Dvořákian disputes and the polemics concerning Smetana and Czech Wagnerism in the 1870s.[6] In many respects the combatants in the 'Dvořák battles' used the arguments formulated previously by the Czech aesthetician Otakar Hostinský (1847–1910), who had been the leader of the Smetana camp in the 1870s. Under the banner of Hostinský's idea of national music and progress, Nejedlý's camp (or Hostinský's 'school', as it called itself), grouped around the periodical *Smetana*, took a stand against Dvořák in the name of 'justice in the overall orientation of Czech music'—in the words of the musicologist Vladimír Helfert (1886–1945), as late as 1934,[7] when he had already begun to

[3] With the commendable exception of the new edns. of Otakar Šourek's *Život a dílo Antonína Dvořáka* (The Life and Work of Antonín Dvořák) (Prague, 1954–7). In the 1950s, Nejedlý was the Minister of Education and Culture and an influential communist ideologist. He formulated the main standpoint containing his attitude toward Dvořák, on the basis of which he posed later as an arbiter of Czech cultural and musical tasks, in 1901 with his *Zdenko Fibich: Zakladatel scénického melodramu* (Zdenko Fibich: Founder of Scenic Melodrama) (Prague, 1901) and in 1903 with *Dějiny české hudby* (The History of Czech Music) (Prague, [1903]), as well as in other works. In 1905, Nejedlý became the first *Privatdozent* (lecturer) specifically in musicology at Charles University.

[4] See Miroslav K. Černý, 'Antonín Dvořák ve světle české muzikologie' (Antonín Dvořák in the View of Czech Musicology), *Hudební věda*, 3/4 (1966), 396–414, esp. 401–5. Also Rudolf Pečman, *Útok na Antonína Dvořáka* (Attack on Antonín Dvořák) (Brno, 1992). The latter is more a continuation of the polemical arguments against Nejedlý than an analysis from the historical point of view.

[5] A list of polemical arts. and summaries of their contents may be found in M. Sobotka's 'Boj o Dvořáka' (The Fight over Dvořák), diploma thesis (Charles University, Prague, 1960). See also Ch. 1 above.

[6] For more information, see M. Ottlová and M. Pospíšil, 'K motivům českého wagnerismu a antiwagnerismu' (Regarding the Motives of Czech Wagnerism and Anti-Wagnerism), in *Povědomí tradice v novodobé české kultuře* (Consciousness of Tradition in Modern Czech Culture) (Prague, 1988), 137–54; in Ger.: 'Zu den Motiven des tschechischen Wagnerianismus und Antiwagnerianismus', in *Oper heute*, ed. H. Seeger (Almanach der Musikbühne, ix; Berlin, 1986), 165–82.

[7] 'Zde šlo o otázku spravedlnosti v celé orientaci české hudby.' 'B. Smetana a Ant. Dvořák', in Helfert,

revise his pre-war attitude toward Dvořák. The school shared with Hostinský the view that the alleged dispute concerning the main orientation of Czech music, differentiating between Smetana's progressive and Dvořák's conservative position, could and had to be resolved by scientific methods.

Hostinský's points of view, founded largely on the aesthetic categories of German music history and criticism with a neo-romantic orientation (the Neudeutsche Schule of Franz Brendel),[8] which, however, he continually corrected on the basis of his practical experience, were asserted in the arguments of Nejedlý's camp in a rigid and schematized form. According to Hostinský's idea of Czech national music, those creating its history had to pursue the only possible and unavoidable law of historical development, that is the progressive path, on which they must overcome lower stages of development. The most progressive contemporary stage of this path was determined by his concept of the 'progressive' genres, music-drama and symphonic poem. Hostinský himself, however, made this linear path relative by trying to incorporate into music history—often with great difficulty—all the variety and wealth of modern living music.[9] His understanding of history was reduced by Nejedlý's camp to an idea of linear progress as an uncompromising and universal gauge. In this conception, it was only progressive acts in the field of composition, according to the prescribed line of development, that justified a composer's inclusion in the history of national music. The musical work itself was reduced to a mere example for the future, and it was for the sake of the future that the dispute had to be resolved. The metaphor used in 1905 by the composer and writer Ludvík Lošťák (1862–1918), when he spoke about Hostinský's follower, the journalist and writer Václav Vladimír Zelený (1858–92), aptly describes the nature of our case: 'his brain was outlined with a ruler by the "progressive" master Otakar [Hostinský]'.[10]

Hostinský embraced a variety of coexisting tendencies, by considering works not only in terms of the single progressive line of development, but also as to their quality and the degree of empathy they aroused. This justified the existence within the framework of national music history of some so-called conservative works. On the other hand, Nejedlý and some of his followers, in

O Smetanovi: Soubor statí a článků (Regarding Smetana: A Collection of Essays and Articles) (Prague, 1950), 106–11 (quote from p. 107). First pub. in *Index*, 6 (1934), 49–51.

[8] See Carl Dahlhaus, *Die Musik des 19. Jahrhunderts* (*Neues Handbuch der Musikwissenschaft*, vi, Wiesbaden, 1980), 203–9.

[9] On this matter see his conclusion in his lecture 'Česká hudba 1864–1904' (Czech Music of 1864–1904) (pub. Prague, 1909), which can be regarded as the nucleus of Vladimír Helfert's later concept, formulated in *Česká moderní hudba* (Czech Modern Music) (Olomouc, 1936). There, Hostinský began to view Smetana and Dvořák as two complementary creative types participating in the shaping of Czech musical creativity as a whole.

[10] 'jeho mozek . . . byl kolem dokola ohraničen pravítkem "pokrokového" mistra Otakara.' 'V. V. Zelený' in *Chromatické hromobití* (Chromatic Thunderclaps), v (Prague, n.d. [after 1903]), 10.

an attempt to make Dvořák's work part of national music history, had to construct, in an unhistorical and totally speculative way, a line of development
whereby Dvořák, as a composer who typically wrote in what they called 'old'
or 'classical' forms, was presented as a composer belonging to the pre-Smetana
and even pre-Beethovenian period, and 'Dvořák [thus] supplied *ex post facto*
what had been lacking before Smetana'.[11]

In this variant of historical construction Dvořák was still lucky enough to
be included in Czech national music. But this view preceded the period when
the 'Dvořák battles' degenerated into newspaper polemics and the pronouncement of verdicts. 'I am not interested in Dvořák,' wrote Nejedlý in
1912:

For me, he represents a past and dead chapter in Czech music where there is nothing
much to research. . . . Dvořák means the same to me as Mendelssohn, on a reduced
Czech scale . . . and my knowledge of history tells me enough about the fate of the
Mendelssohnian type of personality. . . . He belongs to the past and we must wait
until time eats away what has to be eaten away.[12]

As in the rigid conception of musical progress mentioned above, here, too,
reference was made to the verdict and the irreversible course of history, which
were integrally linked to the idea of progress. The mention of Mendelssohn
points to another, closely related, topos of nineteenth-century criticism that
appeared in this context, namely novelty and originality. Arguments about
originality and eclecticism entered here into the dispute about the orientation
of Czech national music in the function of scientific evidence and, together
with other factors, determined a composer's ranking in national history.
Dvořák's value as a composer was assessed from this point of view by the aesthetician and composer Otakar Zich (1879–1934).[13] As in the case of
Mendelssohn and his placement in the history of German music according to
Wagner's judgement, 'evidence' of Dvořák's eclecticism (meaning that he
contributed nothing new) led to the conclusion that he meant nothing for the
development of Czech music, and to the following verdict by the critic and
aesthetician Josef Bartoš (1887–1952):

The analysis of all of Dvořák's work is also a reminder to us: the Czech music of
which we can boast to the world must not be superficial, it must not content itself

---

[11] 'Dvořák ex post facto dodává, co chybělo před Smetanou.' Nejedlý, *Zdenko Fibich*, 173.
[12] 'Mne Dvořák nezajímá. . . . Pro mne jest to odbytá mrtvá kapitola z české hudby, kde pro ducha
bádavého . . . není mnoho co dělati. Pro mne Dvořák jest arci co Mendelssohn, ovšem ve zmenšeném
českém vydání . . . a znalost historie mne dostatečně poučuje o osudu zjevů Mendelssohnovského typu.
. . . Patří minulosti, ale nutno sečkati, až doba na něm stráví, čeho jest třeba.' 'Boj proti Ant. Dvořákovi'
('The Fight against Antonín Dvořák'), *Česká kultura*, 1/6 (1912–13), 187–8. Repr. in *Smetana*, 3 (3 Jan.
1913), 106.
[13] 'Dvořákův význam umělecký' (Dvořák's Artistic Significance), *Hudební sborník* (Musical Symposium),
1/3 (1912–13), 145–80.

with external exoticism, even if that was the road leading to world success; the originality of our nation consists in something much more profound than that, and as the
price of this truth we must renounce in view of the future a musical personality as
remarkable as was Antonín Dvořák.[14]

Nejedlý's camp endeavoured to support its position with arguments based
on compositional and technical features of the music. In the eyes of its oppo-
nents, many of whom were musicians and composers, it was these arguments
that betrayed the camp most. Innovative form was considered the main criterion of progress, but for example its concrete analysis, based on a study of
Smetana's *Prodaná nevěsta* (The Bartered Bride) published in 1908 by
Nejedlý,[15] who limited himself to seeking and identifying melodic fragments
as leitmotifs, was quite justly subjected by the composer Ladislav Vycpálek
(1882–1969) to a crushing critique, including examples of Nejedlý's ignorance
of harmony.[16] This was at the time when the controversy about Dvořák was
just beginning, and from that time on Nejedlý never again illustrated a problem with concrete musical examples.

The evidence of Dvořák's eclecticism, cited by Zich as justification for
considering him insignificant in the history of Czech national music, consisted
in identifying reminiscences of individual elements, idiom, and stylization
from the work of other composers. Wherever Zich heard something Czech
in Dvořák, he always found a reminiscence of Smetana. He thus applied *ad
absurdum* the approach to a musical work taken by Czech critics in the 1860s,
when the opening of a permanent Czech theatre (the Provisional Theatre,
1862) stimulated activity in the field of Czech national opera. Amid the
national particularism of nineteenth-century Europe, even the musical world
was understood as a sort of competition among nations, and the idea was current that a nation could contribute to European art as a whole only that which
was nationally distinctive and felt to be original. Efforts were increased by
Czech critics in the 1860s to pass categorical judgements as to what was
dependent on 'alien' models, and to separate it from what seemed to them
purely Czech. On the basis of associations whose motivation often cannot be
fully reconstructed today, various compositions were atomized into the parts

---

[14] 'Jest nám tedy zároveň rozbor Dvořákovy životní práce i mementem; česká hudba, ona, kterou se
můžeme pochlubiti před cizinou, nesmí ulpívati na povrchu, nesmí se spokojiti vnějšnostním exotismem,
byť tato cesta byla cestou vedoucí k světovým úspěchům; náš národní svéráz jest něco mnohem hlubšího
a za cenu této pravdy musíme se před budoucností zříci i hudební osobnosti tak markantní jako byl
Antonín Dvořák.' *Antonín Dvořák: Kritická studie* (Kritické studie, iii; Prague, 1913), 427.

[15] 'O hudbě Prodané nevěsty' (Regarding the Music of *The Bartered Bride*), in K. Sabina, *Prodaná nevěsta*:
Text k zpěvohře Bedřicha Smetany (*The Bartered Bride*: Text to the Opera by Bedřich Smetana), ed. Z. Nejedlý
(Prague, 1908), 101–63.

[16] 'Prof. Zd. Nejedlý a Prodaná nevěsta' (Prof. Zdeněk Nejedlý and *The Bartered Bride*), *Hudební revue*,
4 (1911), 313–19.

considered original and the parts inspired by alien examples.[17] This model of
originality led Nejedlý's camp to view Dvořák's music as a heterogeneous
mixture of foreign influences, exposed by scientific methods. As Bartoš put it,
'The world did not check where Dvořák took his property from; they
thought everything was his own invention, and that is why they believed he
was so original.'[18]

If we examine the concept of originality applied by the pro-Dvořák camp,
characterized in the Czech musicological literature as 'publicists of a rather
eclectic mould' whose arguments were mostly emotional,[19] we shall see that
their understanding of originality was undoubtedly closer to the modern concept than was that of the university circles as far as Dvořák is concerned. The
music teacher and composer Antonín Srba (1881–1961) argued with Zich that
'the similarity of several elements weighs little; it is the structure of the composition as a whole that counts. . . . When one passage is found to resemble
another there can be no objections if it follows from the preceding content.'[20]

An attitude very close to this one was adopted by Nejedlý himself in his
study of Mahler, with the reservation that according to Nejedlý only a genius
could give positive value to the cultural wealth of the past—and Dvořák was
no genius in his eyes.[21] Nejedlý was prepared to find categorical arguments at
any time. His mode of argumentation is shown for example in his answer
(from the very beginning of the disputes) to the question of whether Dvořák
had become a progressive artist after he had turned toward the 'progressive'
genre of symphonic poem:

Following the decline in Hanslick's influence, and following Smetana's success . . .
Dvořák extricated himself from the influence of the conservative party and embarked
on the path of modernity. But he did not become a progressive artist himself, because
once an artist decides to adhere to modern currents only after a quarter of a century
of conservative artistic activity, and only after the progress achieved by truly progressive artists becomes common property, to which all contemporary composers of some
significance, with only a few exceptions, adhere, he cannot be regarded as a progressive artist but rather as one who has succumbed to the predominating, victorious
power of artistic progress.[22]

[17] See M. Ottlová and M. Pospíšil, 'K otázce českosti v hudbě 19. století', *Opus musicum*, 11 (1979),
101–3. In Ger.: 'Zur Frage des Tschechischen in der Musik des 19. Jahrhunderts', in *Music of the Slavonic
Nations and its Influence upon European Musical Culture*, ed. R. Pečman (Brno, 1981), 99–104.

[18] 'Svět nekontroloval, odkud Dvořák svůj majetek bral, on pokládal vše za jeho vlastní vynález a proto
mu přisuzoval takovou originalitu.' *Antonín Dvořák*, 17.

[19] Vladimír Lébl, 'Moderní hudba' (Modern Music), in *Hudba* (Music), ed. M. Očadlík, R. Smetana, et
al. (Prague, 1971), 243 (*Československá vlastivěda*) (Czechoslovakia's own Scholarship), IX/iii.

[20] 'podobnost několika prvků na váhu nepadá, protože záleží na stavbě celé kompozice. . . . Vyskytne-
li se místo jinému podobné, není proti němu námitek, jestliže bylo z dřívějšího obsahu vyvozeno.' *Boj proti
Dvořákovi* (The Fight against Dvořák) (Prague, 1914), 34.

[21] 'Gustav Mahler', in *Hudební sborník*, 1/1 (1912–13), 1–38; repr. (1958), 87.

[22] 'Úpadkem vlivu Hanslickova, úspěchem Smetanovým . . . Dvořák vymanil se z vlivu konservativní

The present chapter can only suggest that the arguments of Nejedlý's anti-Dvořák camp for a 'scientific decision' as to the proper future of Czech national music, arguments which had to be cited 'in the interest of justice', were based on stereotyped judgements rooted in writings about Czech music in the 1860s and 1870s, and in Otakar Hostinský's approach above all. The judgements became separated from their original contents and historical context, particularly from the context of Hostinský's idea of Czech national music. They became requisites and were introduced as decisive criteria for ranking composers within a single line of development of Czech national music—a line that had been preliminarily constructed using Smetana and his music to stand for a rather vague complex of ideas about what should be considered exemplary. This 'Smetanism' embodied Hostinský's gauge of progress.

The vehemence of the anti-Dvořák campaign was explained in the Nejedlý camp by the fear that Dvořák's international success could overshadow Smetana's legacy, and the reverence for Smetana has later often been used as a weighty argument without any further interpretation. Miloš Jůzl still writes, for example: 'It was . . . not Hostinský (and later Nejedlý, Helfert and others) who brought the case of Dvořák versus Smetana to a head, but rather the traditional anti-Smetana group, all of whom concentrated on the promotion and glorification of Dvořák.'[23] Nejedlý and his followers applied the contrast between a successful though conservative Dvořák and a suffering progressive genius, Smetana, back to the time when Hostinský formulated his idea of Czech national music in a different way: on Smetana's relationship to the so-called progressive, contemporary European tendencies, exemplified particularly by Wagner.[24] Nejedlý wrote as early as 1903:

With *Dimitrij*, Dvořák opposed manifestly and quite deliberately Smetana's endeavours. . . . Dvořák's reactionary stance was encouraged by his success in England. That non-musical country, where the tradition of Handel's oratorios had for centuries been as strong as had been the Mozartian tradition in this country, was so impressed by the Stabat Mater oratorio . . . that Dvořák was invited to conduct it himself. In March 1884, he triumphed. . . . Thus, Dvořák was acclaimed for his conservative works at the time when the most progressive of our masters was dying.[25]

strany a dal se cestou moderní. Sám tím pokrokářem se však nestal, neboť přilne-li umělec k moderním proudům teprve po čtvrtstoletí umělecké činnosti konservativní a to teprve tehdy, když pokrok docílený mistry pokrokovými, stal se všeobecným majetkem, k němuž se hlásí, až na malé výjimky všichni dnešní znamenitější skladatelé, nelze to nazvat pokrokářstvím, nýbrž podlehnutím vše si podmaňující vítězící síle uměleckého pokroku.' *Dějiny české hudby*, 236.

[23] 'Ne tedy Hostinský (a později Nejedlý, Helfert aj.) vyhrotili problém Dvořák kontra Smetana, ale tradiční protismetanovská skupina, která se celá soustředila k podpoře a oslavování Dvořáka.' *Otakar Hostinský* (Odkazy pokrokových osobností [Legacies of Progressive Personalities]), lvii; (Prague, 1980), 264–5.

[24] See n. 6.

[25] ' "Dimitrijem" postavil se Dvořák zjevně a sice vědomě proti snahám Smetanovým. . . . Na této

In 1934 Helfert paraphrased this statement to read, 'At a time when Smetana's tragedy culminated at the Jabkenice gamekeeper's lodge and when the unfortunate genius was waging his superhuman fight with fate, Dvořák's world fame grew into unexpected dimensions.'[26] As late as 1980 we can read in Miloš Jůzl's monograph on Hostinský: 'It was in the year when Smetana became deaf (1874) that the young Dvořák scored his first significant success as a composer. . . . In the year when Smetana died (1884), Dvořák triumphed in London; in 1892, when Smetana's music at last won international recognition, Dvořák, a famous composer by then, was about to leave for the United States.'[27]

These short examples show, in a telling way, the persistent wandering of stereotypes in Czech musicological literature. As mentioned in the opening of this essay, standpoints formulated in the anti-Dvořák camp still influence the historical analysis of the entire period of development of modern Czech music (coinciding with the period of the emancipation of the Czech nation in the nineteenth century) by predetermining to a large extent the stereotyped questions musicologists ask. Belief in the written word as mediator of music, which was yet another topos of the nineteenth century and which Nejedlý's camp shared with Hostinský, was applied in the fullest measure here.[28] Czech Dvořákian research can still be aptly described by the words of Antonín Srba, written at the time of the 'battles': 'the truth about Dvořák that we feel while listening to Dvořák's music will only be told . . . when a historian arrives who is unconfused by Hostinský's theories and Nejedlý's judgements.'[29] We can say with little exaggeration that only then shall we establish not only the true worth of Dvořák's music but also its meaning for those who defended him at

reakcionářské cestě utvrdil Dvořáka úspěch v Anglii. Tato země nehudební, kde tradice Händelových oratorií jest po celé století tak silna jako u nás někdy tradice Mozartova, oratoriem 'Stabat mater' . . . nadchla se tak, že Dvořák pozván k dirigování tohoto svého díla. V březnu r. 1884 slavil tu triumfy. . . . Tak slaven byl Dvořák za svá konzervativní díla v době, kdy nejpokrokovější náš mistr umíral.' *Dějiny české hudby*, 208.

[26] 'V době, kdy v jabkenické myslivně vrcholila tragedie Smetanova, naplněná nadlidským zápasem tohoto nešťastného genia s osudem, tehdy začala vyrůstat světová sláva Dvořákova do netušených rozměrů.' 'B. Smetana a Ant. Dvořák'. See n. 7 above.

[27] 'V roce Smetanova ohluchnutí (1874) začínají první větší skladatelské úspěchy mladého Dvořáka. . . . V roce Smetanova úmrtí (1884) dosáhl Dvořák velkých úspěchů v Londýně, v r. 1892, kdy konečně Smetanova hudba pronikla přesvědčivě a úspěšně za hranice, odjížděl slavný Dvořák do Spojených států.' *Otakar Hostinský*, 265.

[28] This means not only the conviction of historians and critics (the German Franz Brendel, or the Czechs Hostinský and Nejedlý, etc.) that progress in music would be influenced, in a large measure, by criticism and the theory and history of music, but also the remarkable development of musical journalism and its impact in the 19th cent. in general. In musicology, the influence was sometimes reflected quite paradoxically in the fact that contemporary judgement of music was not the subject of a historical analysis but rather the subject of polemics, and that these judgements of music sometimes replace the works themselves and knowledge of them.

[29] 'pak vysloveno bude o Dvořákovi, co cítíme při poslechu . . . až dostane se mu historika nezmateného theoriemi Hostinského a úsudky Nejedlého.' *Boj proti Dvořákovi*, 71.

the time of the 'battles'. We shall find out that the frequent picture of Dvořák as a naïve, joyful, and earthly artist was not so much tied to questions of composition or creative type, as musicology has been claiming and disclaiming since that time, but that rather he was seen as a man creating from the depth of European tradition a picture of the harmony and order of the world as an integrated whole, that he was understood as a positive contrast to the world of 'strength, reason, reflection, and creative sadness, an escape from the world of reality', as a figure contrasting to the 'weak and sick world',[30] and we shall understand what Vrchlický meant by the oasis in the desert and the crystal grotto created by God.

[30] Typical quotations and paraphrases from contemporary reviews and articles; see e.g. K. Hoffmeister, 'Antonín Dvořák ve skladbě symfonické' (Antonín Dvořák in Symphonic Composition), *Dalibor*, 23/33–7 (1901), 273–5.

12

Dvořák in the View of the Artist: Portraits by his Contemporaries, and his Portrayal in the Patriotic Mural *Czech Spring*

JAROSLAVA DOBRINČIĆ

ONCE a man emerges from anonymity owing to outstanding achievements in some field of human activity, society takes an interest not only in what he has done, but in what he looked like too. It is part of the mentality of the public to want to visualize the people it adores.

In the case of Antonín Dvořák this problem was solved by the development of photography, which ensured that the composer's physical image was preserved. Fortunately quite a number of his photographs, both studio and amateur ones, have survived. In Dvořák's time, the documentary function of painting, previously so important, was thus taken over by this totally new medium. (The invention and widespread dissemination of photography covers, in fact, exactly Dvořák's life-span.)[1]

Does this mean that portrait painting had lost its purpose? Once the acquisition of portraits ceased to be a matter of preserving a family tradition, many personages including Dvořák had to wait to become quite famous before being immortalized by a painter. For a long time there were no significant artistic likenesses of him other than various small sketches and caricatures recalling his musical performances. Examples are a sketch in the magazine *Humoristické listy* (Humorous Pages) of 1878[2] and one made in 1893 portraying Dvořák as conductor at the World's Fair in Chicago (Plate 1).

The first serious artistic portrayal was made on Dvořák's 50th birthday in the year 1891. It was a pastel portrait (Plate 2) by the Viennese painter Ludwig

---

[1] Leon Botstein recently noted this coincidence in his essay 'Reversing the Critical Tradition: Innovation, Modernity, and Ideology in the Work and Career of Antonín Dvořák', and drew an interesting analogy between the particular type of 'realism' embodied in Dvořák's musical expression, and the 'realism' of the new art of photography. See *Dvořák and his World*, ed. Michael Beckerman (Princeton, NJ, 1993), 45–8.

[2] With accompanying unsigned art., 'Antonín Dvořák', *Humoristické listy*, 20/7 (16 Feb. 1878), 1–2.

Michalek, now a little-known artist but well established in his time. Born in 1859 at Temesvar (now Timisoara, in western Romania), but living during Dvořák's lifetime in Vienna, Michalek was a portrait and landscape painter. According to an unsigned article in the *Hudební revue* (Musical Review) in 1908, Michalek visited Dvořák on a recommendation from Johannes Brahms with a plan to include Dvořák's portrait in his collection of heads of famous writers and musicians.[3] This fine pastel later found its way to the Prague Conservatoire and is presently held in its archives. Its existence is almost unknown; it is mentioned in literature seldom, and usually mistakenly as an oil-painting.[4]

Dvořák did not find a portrait artist who could make his image widespread and everlasting until almost the end of his life. This artist was Max Švabinský (1873–1962). Toward the end of the last century, Švabinský was a well-accepted member of the rising artistic generation in the Czech lands. He was an admirer of the most important personality in nineteenth-century Czech fine art, the painter Josef Mánes, and he was a follower of all artists belonging to the so-called 'Generation of the National Theatre'. The young painter was also an outstanding master of graphic art. From the very beginning of his career he devoted himself to portrait painting. His first subjects were in his own family, but he soon concentrated upon his famous contemporaries. He executed a number of psychologically oriented and very accurate portraits of contemporary personalities in literature (for example Jaroslav Vrchlický and Julius Zeyer), as well as in the arts, in science, and in politics, and specialized also in representations of great people belonging to the past (the writers Jan Neruda and Božena Němcová and the composer Bedřich Smetana, to name a few).

The National Gallery in Prague possesses Švabinský's pen-drawing of Dvořák from the year 1898, made on the basis of a photograph (Plate 3).[5] Three years later, however, Švabinský made a second drawing of Dvořák, this time from life, depicting the artist in dignified but slightly eccentric form. It was Dvořák's 60th birthday, and the likeness became practically his official portrait, primarily through two lithographs which Švabinský executed on the model of his original drawing, both in the same year, 1901.[6] The Antonín

---

[3] 'Neznámý obraz A. Dvořáka' (An Unknown Portrait of A. Dvořák), *Hudební revue*, 1 (1908), 288.

[4] Otakar Šourek, *Antonín Dvořák*, 2nd, rev. edn. (Prague, 1941), illus. 44. This portrait also appears, without attribution or description other than the date 1891, as the frontispiece to Šourek's *Život a dílo Antonína Dvořáka* (The Life and Work of Antonín Dvořák), iii, 2nd edn. (Prague, 1956). The reproductions in Šourek's books are quite poor.

[5] See Milan Kuna, 'Švabinský a Dvořák', *Hudební rozhledy*, 44/4 (1991), 179.

[6] Letter from Max Švabinský, 26 Oct. 1958, to the composer's son Otakar Dvořák. Copy in the archive of the Národní galerie (National Gallery), Prague.

Dvořák Museum in Prague holds in its collection a print from one of these lithographs (Plate 4).

Švabinský knew what Dvořák looked like both from direct contact and, undoubtedly, from having seen the famous composer and conductor in public. He used this precise knowledge several times. One of these instances was in the Obecní dům (Municipal Hall) in Prague, for a very realistic image of Dvořák in a large and important mural painting. Dvořák was not alive at the time of Švabinský's work on the mural, but the painter was able to picture the composer easily from memory.

The idea of the Municipal Hall, intended as a centre for Czech cultural and social life, originated in 1901. The building was designed by the architects Antonín Balšánek and Osvald Polívka, and constructed between 1905 and 1912. Its style is that of the late art nouveau, which ruled the whole lifestyle of the turn of the century.[7] It must have been very satisfying for Švabinský to have been commissioned for the decorations in one important social space of the house, the so-called 'Rieger Room'—named after the famous politician František Ladislav Rieger (1818–1903) whom Švabinský had also painted. Here our painter was to face the important task of depicting various representatives of cultural development from the time of the Czech national revival in the mid-nineteenth century up to his own time. These included writers, musicians, and artists. Ten of them had to be assembled in a large space of two oblong panels requiring almost life-size proportions.

The idea of depicting a series of historically important people dates back to antiquity and had a strong tradition in the Italian Renaissance. One thinks of the so-called *uomini famosi* found in studies and drawing-rooms in palaces in Ferrara (the d'Este family), in Mantua (the Gonzagas), and elsewhere. In the Municipal Hall this idea was applied once more as a reflection of neo-Renaissance thinking. But here, instead of great warriors, statesmen, and similar heroes, we find celebrities of the cultural world. It is not surprising that Antonín Dvořák found his place among them.

Under the symbolic title *Czech Spring*, meaning the time of the revival of Czech culture, leading figures in the various arts were brought together. On the one side are poets and writers: from left to right, Svatopluk Čech, Jaroslav Vrchlický, Jan Neruda, Božena Němcová, and Julius Zeyer. On the other side are composers and fine artists: the sculptor Josef Václav Myslbek, the painters Mikoláš Aleš and Josef Mánes, and the composers Smetana and Dvořák. The very first glance at this group, assembled in an awakening spring-like countryside, reveals that Švabinský depicted his heroes in a monumental but utterly realistic manner. In this respect, his work differed from other works in the

[7] See E. Poche and J. Janáček, *Prahou krok za krokem* (Through Prague Step by Step) (Prague, 1964), 129.

Municipal Hall. The other artists such as Jan Preisler and Jiří Mucha followed much more precisely the current trends of symbolism and art nouveau.

Švabinský worked on his commission in 1910 and 1911. He proceeded as was customary: from initial sketches, through quite a few full-figure studies of individual people, to the overall design. He made large composite studies which were the final preparatory step before his work on the walls of the building. The National Gallery and the Municipal Museum in Prague have preserved some of the original sketches, including a pen-drawing of the full figure of Dvořák (Plate 5), a study in oil for the group of writers (Plate 6), and a charcoal study of the full group of artists and composers (Plate 7).

Note that the sketch in Plate 5 is rather unflattering. In the composite drawing (Plate 7), however, there are slight changes in posture, and a clearer though more conventional definition of the face. (The large sketch bears also a typical though almost invisible network of lines serving as a support to the future execution of the design.)

Švabinský worked on the final murals in the Rieger Room between the beginning of 1910 and the spring of 1911, when the section with Dvořák was completed. In this essentially decorative painting, intended as a commemoration, he managed to reveal some of the most down-to-earth, realistic portraits of the given personalities.

How was Švabinský's achievement received by his contemporaries? In the first place, it must be realized that there were voices critical of the whole idea of the Municipal Hall from the ideological, financial, and artistic point of view. At the time of its completion the edifice was very modern and functionally efficient, yet from a stylistic point of view very conservative. Just imagine that only a few steps away stood a cubist building, erected at exactly the same time (Josef Gočár's 'House of the Black Madonna', 1912). Young artists (for example the painter Miloš Jiránek) were right to have criticized the art nouveau style of the building at a moment when the Czech avant-garde was keeping pace with that of the whole of Europe. On the other hand, in the context of the time, of the prevailing fashion and taste, it could be understood that such critical opinions could not shake the popularity of the building and its decorations.

In 1917 the magazine *Zlatá Praha* (Golden Prague) wrote about Švabinský's painting and published the first good reproduction of the *Czech Spring*. The critic Antonín Macek wrote approvingly of the successful decorative approach, mixed unconventionally with an understanding for character and the artist's deeply realistic viewpoint.[8]

---

[8] 'Max Švabinský', *Zlatá Praha*, 34/28 (4 Nov. 1917).

With the passing of time, criticisms of the decorations in the Municipal Hall mellowed considerably. From the 1960s on, the art nouveau style has been gradually rediscovered, and it is now highly valued. This admiration seems permanent. The Municipal Hall, constructed with unusual solidity and perfection from both a structural and an artistic point of view, has remained preserved in its entirety up to the present day. In particular the drawing-rooms, which were closed to visitors for long periods of time, have survived in very good condition, including the Rieger Room, where Švabinský's mural is placed. Since 1989 this space has been open to visitors. Unlike other portraits of Antonín Dvořák, which are held usually in deposit or storage rooms of museums and galleries, *Czech Spring* is thus available to the public.

IV

DVOŘÁK AS A SLAVIC COMPOSER

13

Dvořák's Slavic Spirit, and his Relation to Tchaikovsky and Russia

MILAN KUNA

THE several conferences on Dvořák held in Prague in 1987–91 dealt with the relations of the composer to various cultures outside his Czech homeland. However, the Slavic spirit of Dvořák has been omitted from the topics of discussion—and this aspect is one of the most characteristic facets of his work. Dvořák's Slavic spirit was not engendered by any extraordinary appreciation of his work in the various Slavic countries; in his lifetime there was apparently no deep interest in his music coming from those regions. Rather, the roots of Dvořák's Slavic spirit lay in the specific conditions of the Czech nation in the nineteenth century, which often focused on the so-called 'Pan-Slavic Movement', on the notions of mutual solidarity and mutual help among Slavic nations.

In the Pan-Slavic Movement the Czech nation saw a way out from its unfortunate vassal's position within the Austro-Hungarian Empire, under whose government it had been oppressed for several centuries. The Czechs were struggling for new legal rights of organization that would give them a dignified life, and one part of this struggle was the idea of Slavic ties. Several times during Dvořák's life Czech society experienced waves of sympathy for other Slavic nations that were either fighting for their liberation—Poles, Ukrainians, South Slavs (Yugoslavians), and the Slavic Balkan nations—or that, as in the case of large and powerful Russia, posed a constant threat to the chief foreign oppressor of Slavs—the Habsburg dynasty.

This was not, of course, a unified political movement; on the contrary, the forces of the two most influential Czech political parties—the Staročech (Old Czech) and the Mladočech (Young Czech) parties—were divided in their attitude toward pan-Slavism. It was the conservative Old Czechs who inclined more toward the idea of Slavic solidarity.

Such contradictory applications of pan-Slavism to life were reflected in the arts as well. Dvořák's association with the Slavic spirit gave rise to a myth

about a reactionary, conservative background to his work. Legends arose
about the composer's close relationship to the main representative of the Old
Czech concept of pan-Slavism, František Ladislav Rieger, and to his daughter,
Maria Červinková-Riegrová, who provided librettos for Dvořák's operas
Jakobín and *Dimitrij*. In the framework of such associations, Dvořák was placed
artificially in opposition to his older contemporary Bedřich Smetana, who had
never made any effort to express pan-Slavism in his music, and whose supporters were recruited above all from the ranks of the Young Czechs, thus
from the camp precisely opposite to that in which Dvořák was placed.[1]

This attitude toward Dvořák was false, sometimes even malicious, and
unfortunately it has survived in some respects even to the present day. It arose
because some were too quick to associate Dvořák's artistic orientation toward
sources of inspiration in the eastern Slavic lands on the one hand, and political viewpoints and the goal of Slavic solidarity on the other, in an over-
simplified way. This error caused great harm not only in the case of the
evaluation of Dvořák and his relation to Smetana, but also in the assessment
of his entire compositional school. From Dvořák's orientation toward Slavic
music came most of the arguments for his alleged conservatism and cos-
mopolitanism (i.e. lack of nationalism). Today, when ideas of Slavic solidarity
are gone, and have proved through the experience of history to be unreal, we
must re-evaluate the sense and the significance of the Slavic spirit in general,
and particularly as manifested in Dvořák.

Dvořák's entire work is—more or less—living up to now. Pan-Slavism, to
the extent that it is represented in his work, actually helped open for him the
gates to the world. The works of his that embody this spirit became attractive
to all continents of the world precisely because of this orientation. Therefore
it is necessary to speak of Dvořák's Slavic spirit not in a political sense but
rather in the sense of his musical discovery of the Slavic East. We should
understand this as meaning his discovery of a mysterious ancient mother
source of inspiration, with its own keys, modulations, melodic structures, and
dance rhythms or other musical elements, which Dvořák encountered for the
first time in Moravia (lying just to the east of Bohemia) and which he then
pursued further to the east, in Slovakia and then other Slavic nations. In this
way he pioneered a previously unknown path, not only for himself but for
other Czech composers like Vítězslav Novák, Josef Suk, Rudolf Karel, and
also Leoš Janáček, all of whom then carried this inspiration and experience

---

[1] The association of Smetana with the Young Czechs and Dvořák with the Old Czechs, as well as the
inclination of the Old Czechs toward pan-Slavism, is discussed briefly but cogently by John Tyrrell in
Czech Opera (Cambridge, 1988), 10–11, 48, 116–17, 124–5. Tyrrell asserts (p. 125) that 'Dvořák was the
most prominent Pan-Slav Czech composer', citing the Slavonic Dances, his many *dumka* movements
(Ukrainian), and his two operas with Polish and Russian subject-matter (*Vanda* and *Dimitrij*.)

further and made further spiritual expeditions to the sources of Slavic, particularly rural, folklore.[2] This discovery of Dvořák came at the eleventh hour. Several decades later the eastern village folklore was overwhelmed by the progress of civilization and, in its genuine purity, was almost destroyed.

An entire book could be written on Dvořák's Slavic spirit. It is a large topic that has not yet been fully explored. For Dvořák it was not just a matter of superficial enchantment with exotic-sounding folklore, but rather an inspiration with a deep social, sometimes even political, background.

We see the first expression of Dvořák's conscious Slavic spirit in the String Quartet in D major from the year 1869. This was the period when the Czech nation was outraged by the establishment of equal status within the empire for Austria and Hungary—an arrangement the Czechs viewed as an insult and an unjust disregard of their own rights. As a response to this great wave of Slavic sentiment Dvořák based the third movement of his quartet on the song 'Hej, Slované!' (Hey, Slavs!), which at that time was officially forbidden because Czech people sang it as their song of liberty. 'As long as the Slavic language lives, the Slavic nations will live for ever as well' was the motto of this song, originally Polish but commonly adopted in Bohemia. On Dvořák's part, it was a political gesture intended to support the Slavic spirit in Bohemia.

It has often been said in the literature on Dvořák that the composer's Slavic spirit is primarily linked to the spread of his musical curiosity to Slavic lands lying to the east, including Moravia and Slovakia, and to the use of the musical sources of the Slavic nations. But with Dvořák this process was much more profound than it would appear at first glance. The composer's method was not only borrowing folk elements such as tunes of songs or characteristic features of folk-dances, according to some naïve theories about Slavic music, as has been stated from time to time even in the Czech press. These 'songster' theories, to put it simply, were not viewed as important by Dvořák.[3] There was something else that was much more meaningful. Dvořák let himself be inspired by the whole atmosphere of Czech culture of the time, particularly by Czech literature, which tried for various reasons to compete with the culture of the Slavic nations.

---

[2] It is probable that Dvořák's and Janáček's interest in the music of the Slavic East went hand in hand. In 'Dvořákova a Janáčkova dumka', *Hudební rozhledy*, 44/2 (1991), 86–9, Jarmil Burghauser even hypothesizes that it may have been Janáček who suggested to Dvořák the idea of composing *dumky*. But this is only a hypothesis (see Ch. 1 above).

[3] For statements of the 'songster' theories in Dvořák's time, see Max Konopásek, 'Rozbor otázky slovanské hudby' (An Analysis of the Question of Slavic Music), *Hudební listy*, 5/33–44 (13 Aug.–29 Oct. 1874), 174; K. V. Zap, *Rozmluva o slovanské hudbě* (A Discussion of Slavic Music), iv (Vlastimil, 1840); Ludvík z Rittersbergu, *Pravlast slovanského zpěvu* (The Ancient Homeland of Slavic Song) (Prague, 1846), 34, and 'Myšlenky o slovanském zpěvu' (Thoughts on Slavic Song), *Dalibor*, 4/27–36 (1861); Ján Levoslav Bella, 'Slovanská hudba a zpěv slovenský' (Slavic Music and Slovakian Song), *Dalibor*, 8/8–9 (10, 20 Mar. 1869), 57–8, 65–6.

The most characteristic example of this complicated artistic transformation was the case of Dvořák's so-called *dumka* (plural *dumky*), through which the process can be best demonstrated. In connection with this musical form, slanderous criticisms were spread to the effect that Dvořák was composing something that he didn't know in its original folk form, and whose proper meaning eluded him.[4] This was obviously not true. The greatness of Dvořák's genius lay not only in the fact that in his *dumka* he created an original musical form unknown in classical music until that time. More than that, with this supreme artistic form he expressed the desire of Czech society to be more deeply connected culturally with the other Slavic nations, some of which (like the Czech nation) were fighting for recognition and their right to liberty.

In the middle of the nineteenth century, it was above all on the Ukraine that this Slavic interest of the Czechs concentrated most strongly, that is on the so-called 'Little Russians', who at that time escalated their desire for national identity and who gave the world proof of the beauty, specificity, and originality of their folk-art. Many editions of Ukrainian folksongs reached as far as Bohemia.[5] Knowledge of these had already been used in full measure since the middle of the century, primarily by Czech poets who wrote so-called *ohlasy* ('echoes') in their spirit (i.e. they combined their new poetry with themes taken from the distant Slavic culture). These works of the Czech poets often bore titles like *My Dumky, Cossack Dumky, Evening Dumky, Melancholic Dumky, Night Dumky*, and so on, which Dvořák apparently knew from Czech literary reviews.

The fact that Dvořák was influenced by these literary *ohlasy* is indicated in that he, like the poets, did not differentiate between the authentic Little Russian *dumka*, the finest flower of Ukrainian lyrics, and the so-called *duma*, the most brilliant expression of Ukrainian epic poetry. Dvořák's *dumky*, whether created as separate works for piano or included in his Slavonic Dances, Violin Concerto, E Flat major String Quartet, A major String Sextet, A major Piano Quintet (the later one, B. 155), or the six-movement Piano Trio entitled *Dumky*, represent an ingenious synthesis of these two folk forms. Dvořák takes from the *dumka* its softly elegiac, lyrical tone, and from the so-

[4] Dvořák's pupils spread this point of view as a joke. But it was accepted by Josef Bartoš in his book *Antonín Dvořák: Kritická studie* (Kritické studie, iii; Prague, 1913) with the serious intention of injuring Dvořák's reputation.

[5] As early as 1861 a detailed bibliographic listing was published of all eds. of Slavic folksongs, of which however most contained only text, not music: see [V. Dunder], 'Přehled sbírek národních písní slovanských', *Dalibor*, 4/29–30 (10, 20 Oct. 1861), 232–3, 238–99. Dvořák probably knew the coll. with music *Pisni, dumki i šumki ruskovo naroda na Podoli, Ukraini i Malorossii* (Songs, Dumky, and Šumky of the Russian Nation in Poland, Ukraine, and Little Russia), ed. Kocipiński, and also the excellent study by A. Rubec, 'Několik slov o maloruských národních písních' (A Few Words about Little Russian National Songs), *Hudební listy*, 2/25, 30 (16 Aug., 20 Sept. 1871), 203–5, 250–1.

called *duma*, epically verbose and narrative, he uses the variative and imitative method of theme-elaboration.

Dvořák is said to have taken also from Ukrainian folk-music the strong internal contrasts of tempo generally found in his *dumky*. Although this opinion is shared by almost all Dvořák researchers, it cannot be documented. If we study Ukrainian *dumky* and *dumy* in, for example, the collections of Kolberg, Kocipiński, Rubec, and Lysenko, as well as of the Czech folklorist Ludvík Kuba, we encounter this feature only exceptionally, as a slight acceleration or slowing in certain parts of the small song form. The strong contrast of tempo found in most of Dvořák's *dumky* is utterly his own invention, his own formulation of the *dumka* genre in art music.

It is also noteworthy that the typically Czech *furiant* dance (energetically defiant), or music in some similar style, is as a rule placed within Dvořák's *dumka* or as one of its structural components. Not without basis is the hypothesis that even this principle of the division into two emotional worlds was derived by the composer from the Czech *ohlasy*, in which *dumy* and *dumky*, in a Czech context, were often combined with heroic subjects, as for instance in the story of the Ukrainian Cossacks' fight for freedom (an allegory for Czech patriotism directed against the Austrians).

Unfortunately, we have no direct evidence that Dvořák engaged in direct study of Ukrainian music. He had at his disposal primarily the collection *Slavia*, edited by Ludevít Procházka, containing Slavic and even specifically Ukrainian songs,[6] but not until 1885 did he, little by little, acquire the collections of Slavic songs arranged for piano by the Czech folklorist Ludvík Kuba.[7] Yet we cannot say that Dvořák had no contact with this Slavic music before. The fact that in some *dumka* movements (for example in the second Slavonic Dance) he uses simple counterpoint in a continuous countermelody, or imitative technique, as a means of stylization (in the Ukraine it is called *podgolovski* technique) may indicate that Dvořák in fact had some practical experience with the music of the Slavic East.[8]

Remarkable is also a statement of Piotr Ilyich Tchaikovsky regarding Dvořák's opera *Dimitrij*, that in the parts where Dvořák musically represents the Russian setting, he works largely with the character not of Russian but rather of Ukrainian music.[9] It is a statement that has passed unnoticed by

---

[6] *Slavia: Sbírka národních písní slovanských* (Slavia: A Collection of Slavic National Songs) (Prague, n.d.).

[7] *Slovanstvo ve svých zpěvech* (Slavic Lands in their Songs) (Prague, 1885).

[8] I have written about this matter in greater detail in my study 'První dumky Antonína Dvořák' (The First *Dumky* of Antonín Dvořák), *Hudební rozhledy*, 9/8 (1956), 313–15. See also David Beveridge, 'Dvořák's *Dumka* and the Concept of Nationalism in Music Historiography', *Journal of Musicological Research*, 12 (1993), 303–25.

[9] See Marie Červinková-Riegrová, 'Zápisky' (Manuscript Notes), MS from 1888, Archives of the National Museum, Prague.

Dvořák researchers up to now. One illustration of Tchaikovsky's point is the entry march of the Russian people, assembling before the Kremlin.

There is no doubt that Dvořák's Slavic spirit, even if it can be traced to some degree in almost all his works, has its epicentre in his works of the late 1870s and early 1880s. Already significant in this regard is the opera *Vanda* of 1875, whose mythological subject comes from Polish history. With the opera *Dimitrij* of 1881–2, we find the pinnacle of his conscious Slavic spirit. Here Dvořák employs a whole variety of Slavic musical elements, especially for the differentiation between the Polish and Russian factions. He works with dance rhythms, such as that of the Polish mazurka, but also with the harmonic peculiarities of old Russian songs tied to the church modes. The important thing is that the composer—for the first time in his career—had in his hands an excellent dramatic text, which not only dealt with a glorious historic period of a great Slavic nation but was really on a 'world' theme. No less than the German dramatist Johann Christoph Friedrich Schiller also worked on a drama based on the Dimitrij theme.[10]

Dvořák's attempt to introduce the Slavic East into Czech music is here multiplied by his desire to give the world proof of the effort Czech music was making to keep in step with European culture, to gain recognition in a wider international context. That he had the requisite talent and artistic power for the task, and that this path was feasible and propitious for him, was indicated to him by the favourable foreign reception of the Moravian Duets, Slavonic Rhapsodies, Slavonic Dances, Violin Concerto, chamber works with *dumky*, and so on.

To put *Dimitrij* on the world stages was Dvořák's biggest lifelong desire.[11] Here he could not only show the depth, breadth, and genuine inspiration of his Slavic musical orientation, but also prove that this orientation of his work in connection with the world theme could succeed even in the context of the highest musical art in Europe and the world. However, the dream was not to be realized, and this was one of Dvořák's greatest disappointments. To be sure, the work was given an enthusiastic reception at its Prague première in 1882, and was reviewed very favourably by Eduard Hanslick in the *Neue freie Presse* in Vienna.[12] Nevertheless, despite the composer's efforts in various countries, it was never performed outside Bohemia during his lifetime, except by the Czech National Theatre company at an international exhibition in Vienna in 1892. Dvořák was especially persistent in attempts to have the work staged in

[10] See Jarmil Burghauser's commentary in his edn. of Červinková-Riegrová's libretto, *Antonín Dvořák: Dimitrij* (Prague, 1961).

[11] See my study 'Dvořák a Rusko' (Dvořák and Russia), *Hudební rozhledy*, 30/9 (1977), 386–97; also Ch. 8 above.

[12] 17 Oct. 1882.

St Petersburg and Moscow, assuming that companies there might be interested in the subject, but to no avail.[13]

Despite this failure to have *Dimitrij* performed on the world stages, Dvořák could claim the distinction of being the only Czech composer to have elevated the problem of Slavic music to a truly universal level—by his choice of the subject, as well as the depth and the manner of dramatization. And in this he realized the aspirations of many other artists at work in Czech culture of the time. To attain the level of world art with his music and with the Slavic opera theme was, at the turn of the 1870s and 1880s, an intention corresponding to that of the new generation of Czech writers—to the efforts of the Czech poets who, headed by Jaroslav Vrchlický and Julius Zeyer among others, tried to project European currents of thought and stylistic criteria on to Czech poetry and thus to find their place in the context of poetry world wide. From such a point of view Dvořák's Slavic spirit appears to us as one of the most progressive cultural developments of Czech music.

In 1888, six years after the première of *Dimitrij*, Dvořák established one of the most important of the personal relationships he had with great composers of his day when he met Piotr Ilyich Tchaikovsky. Despite the brevity of their direct contact, the relationship of the two men was deep, sincere on both their parts, and full of respect, and it is only to the detriment of the biographies of both renowned artists that their relationship has not been fully analysed and characterized.

Before Tchaikovsky's arrival in Prague that year, the artists did not know each other. To be sure, Dvořák knew such music of Tchaikovsky as was commonly performed in Prague, but that was not much. Nevertheless he took an interest in his art, as we know, for example, from his correspondence with Fritz Simrock (even if at the beginning his interest showed signs of negative criticism); he even played for himself at the piano Tchaikovsky's symphonies written up to that time—a decade before he met him personally.[14] This interest was understandable. Dvořák, who consciously composed Slavic music, had to devote his professional attention to the culture of other Slavic nations, above all to Russian music. When he was still a member of the Provisional Theatre orchestra, Dvořák gained an intimate familiarity with both of Glinka's operas, *A Life for the Tsar* and *Ruslan and Ludmila*, and also met Mily

---

[13] After the performance in Vienna, another century passed before *Dimitrij* was staged outside Bohemia. But the past decade has seen a remarkable awakening of interest in the work, with concert performances at Carnegie Hall, New York in 1984, then at Eugene, Oreg., and Stuttgart, Germany, in 1991, and a staged performance by the Bavarian State Opera in Munich, 1992.

[14] See Dvořák's letter to Simrock of 8 Apr. 1879 (*Antonín Dvořák: Korespondence a dokumenty—Kritické vydání* (Antonín Dvořák: Correspondence and Documents—Critical Edition), ed. Milan Kuna et al., i (Prague, 1987), 170–1. 'Diesen Brief schreibe ich nicht einmal zu Hause, soeben beim Klavierspiel, wo ich eine Symfonie [probably the Fourth in F minor], die fürchterlich ist, von Tschaikovsky spiele . . .'.

Alexeyevich Balakirev, leader of the 'Mighty Handful'. From a Prague performance he knew also Tchaikovsky's opera *The Maid of Orleans*, composed to Schiller's drama; from here it was a short step to the study of other works of Tchaikovsky, which were published by Jurgenson and appeared with increasing frequency on the shelves of Czech and German music shops.

Dvořák met Tchaikovsky on 12 February 1888, only one day after the latter's arrival in Prague. It was during the interval at a performance of Verdi's new opera *Otello* in the National Theatre that the two were introduced, by the Czech politician František Ladislav Rieger. Surrounded by the famous personalities, Tchaikovsky turned the conversation to Dvořák's *Dimitrij*, which interested him enormously. He wanted to know to what extent its authors, the librettist Marie Červinková-Riegrová and Dvořák, had worked from Schiller's drama *Demetrius* and Pushkin's *Boris Godunov*, and how the action of Dvořák's opera related to these models. During this evening further meetings between Tchaikovsky and Dvořák were agreed upon.

From this moment there was not a single day during Tchaikovsky's spring and autumn stays in Prague in 1888 when the Russian guest did not meet Dvořák on some public or private occasion. These daily meetings, of which we have detailed accounts from the notes kept by Marie Červinková-Riegrová (who likewise was in daily contact with Tchaikovsky), were something unprecedented and surprising for those who knew Dvořák.[15] Dvořák would visit Tchaikovsky at the Saxon Court Hotel, and Tchaikovsky came to Dvořák's home for a festive luncheon with his family (where he was enchanted by Dvořák's wife Anna and impressed with her excellent management of the household). The two masters would meet also in small circles of friends at private banquets *chez* Červinková-Riegrová; from the diaries of this unique woman we know that these gatherings were the occasion for lively debate on the character of Slavic music and the most suitable material for Slavic operas.

Important meetings between Dvořák and Tchaikovsky took place also at concerts of Tchaikovsky's music in Prague and at rehearsals for the autumn première of *Eugene Onegin*, all of which were attended by Dvořák. But neither did the Russian master miss any opportunity to hear some of Dvořák's work. He was enthusiastic, for example, about the Piano Quintet in A major, B. 155, in particular the *dumka* in the second movement;[16] Dvořák gave to Tchaikovsky the piano reduction of *Dimitrij*, which the latter was unable to

---

[15] See Červinková-Riegrová's handwritten 'Zápisky'. See also my book *Čajkovskij a Praha* (Prague, 1980).

[16] Kuna, *Čajkovskij a Praha*.

see staged in Prague owing to various intrigues, and also the printed score of his Seventh Symphony in D minor.[17]

Although at the time of Tchaikovsky's arrival in Prague Dvořák was still bewildered by the scores and piano arrangements of his works, little by little he developed a deep appreciation for his friend's music and came to be very fond of it. According to the testimony of Oskar Nedbal, Dvořák's pupil and a member of Czech Quartet, in the beginning Dvořák was startled by the unusual character and originality of tone-colour in Tchaikovsky's music, in particular the Fifth Symphony in E minor, but he soon understood its greatness and profundity.[18] Dvořák's letter to Tchaikovsky of 14 January 1889, in which he confesses his admiration for *Eugene Onegin*, is one of the most beautiful declarations that Dvořák—except for his letters to Johannes Brahms—had ever written to another composer.[19] And when Tchaikovsky died and Dvořák heard his 'Pathetique' Symphony, its effect on him was so strong that he was completely overwhelmed by the experience.[20]

Tchaikovsky was the only Russian composer who understood Dvořák's creative greatness and the significance of his art for European music. As a perfect professional, well informed about the artistic circumstances of Western European music, he knew the place that Dvořák occupied in that world, and he strove to enable the Czech master to visit Russia and, through several concerts of his music—under the auspices of the Royal Russian Music Society in Moscow and St Petersburg—to help break the conservatism of Russian musical life. When Dvořák showed reluctance to make the journey to Russia, and several people recommended to Tchaikovsky Czech musicians other than Dvořák, for example the composer Karel Bendl or the conductor Adolf Čech, Tchaikovsky would not listen—it would be either Dvořák or no one. In his letters Tchaikovsky urged Dvořák so strongly and convincingly that he finally agreed.[21]

But for Dvořák, his stay in Russia in 1890 (unfortunately during Tchaikovsky's absence) was a small tragedy that hurt him considerably. For he did not suspect there would be an abysmal gap between the sincerity of his friend Tchaikovsky and the attitudes in official Russian musical circles. Responses to Dvořák's concerts in Moscow and St Petersburg were a real

[17] This score with Dvořák's dedication is preserved in the Tchaikovsky Museum at Klin.

[18] Regarding Dvořák's initial puzzlement at the Fifth Symphony, see one of Oscar Nedbal's reminiscences of the meeting between the two maestri, MS in the bequest of O. Nedbal in the Theatre Department of the National Museum, Prague. See also Kuna, *Čajkovskij a Praha*.

[19] *Antonín Dvořák: Korespondence*, ii (Prague, 1988), 359–60.

[20] See Josef Bohuslav Foerster, *Poutník v cizině* (The Traveller Abroad) (Prague, 1942), 38 ff.

[21] The two composers' discussion of the trip is recorded in detail in Červinková-Riegrová's 'Zápisky'. Tchaikovsky's letters to Dvořák from 1889 will be pub. in *Antonín Dvořák: Korespondence*, vi. See also John Clapham, 'Dvořák's Visit to Russia', *Musical Quarterly*, 51 (1965), 493–506.

disappointment for everyone who wished to strengthen by means of these events a progressive orientation in Russian music, especially in its relation to the music of western Europe. Unfortunately the Tsar's critic found Dvořák's music imperfect, its inner life insufficient, its musical ideas failing to soar with fantasy. For the official Russian musical circles it was too contrived and showed no spontaneous inspiration. It was even said that Dvořák's compositions were lacking in greatness of spirit, originality, and invention, that his ideas were mundane, ordinary, grey. Even his instrumentation was viewed as heavy-handed, cold, and trivial.[22]

Almost the only exception in the dozens of critiques was the review by the so-called 'Russian Hanslick', G. A. Laroche. He alone, in the spirit of Tchaikovsky's intentions, recognized Dvořák's greatness, and from Dvořák's failure he drew conclusions in the form of a warning to the Russian musical public and the press. After finding out the position that Dvořák held in Western European musical culture—comparable to that of Brahms, Wagner, Liszt, Mendelssohn, Schumann—he appealed to the Russian musical circles to follow Dvořák as a Slavic composer who through all his work had achieved a high degree of recognition in the West.[23]

Dvořák was deeply disappointed by the response to his work in Russia, and complained more than once of this ironic lack of understanding of his work and artistic contribution: 'Oh, so-called Slavic ties, where are you?'[24] And he had a right to complain, for at that time, in 1890, he was already a world-famous master, and one of the first to recognize through his music the greatness and inspirational potential of Slavic folk culture for all European and world music.

Laroche, already impressed with the success Dvořák had achieved throughout Europe, could not know that shortly he would become a hero in America as well. As director of the National Conservatory of Music in New York, Dvořák was expected to provide guidance in the field of so-called 'American national music'—to indicate the points of departure and direction that the music of this continent should take into consideration. The gauntlet was thrown down, and Dvořák took it up without hesitation, fulfilling with the confidence of a genius and in the shortest possible time the secret hopes of the whole culture of America.

Dvořák could do this precisely because of his extraordinary ability to enrich his musical expression with the characteristic musical elements of distant

---

[22] See Kuna, 'Dvořák a Rusko', and Clapham, 'Dvořák's Visit to Russia', 501–4.

[23] See *Moskovskoje vědomosti*, 117 (30 Apr. 1890).

[24] 'Ó tak zvaná slovanská vzájemnosti, kde jseš?' In Dvořák's letter of 23 Mar. 1890 from St Petersburg to his friend Gustav Eim in Vienna: see *Antonín Dvořák: Korespondence*, iii (Prague, 1989), 32. For an Eng. trans. of the letter, see Clapham, 'Dvořák's Visit to Russia', 505–6.

nations and to enter into the spirit of their own musical poetics, as he after all had been doing for more than a decade in his Slavic music. Regarded analogically, we may speak of a transfer from the folk-music of the Slavic East to that of the original culture of the American nation. This is admittedly an observation that has not been fully expressed so far, but I consider it the most likely explanation of Dvořák's success in the field of American music.

Dvořák's orientation to the elements of American folk-music, whether of Native American or African-American origin, was similar to his orientation to the folk-music of the Slavic East. In both cases it meant the enrichment of Czech music with a new spiritual dimension; it was something that invited other composers to imitation in the wider musical context and that made Dvořák a supranational master, an artist of real world importance—the very dream of the poets of Dvořák's generation. Dvořák was probably the only living European composer at that time who could go to America with the above-mentioned mission and go down in American history in a way that exceeded all hopes and expectations. And it was, in large measure, because of his experience with Slavic music.

14

Dvořák's Eighth Symphony: A Response to Tchaikovsky?

HARTMUT SCHICK

DvoŘÁK's Eighth Symphony in G major ranks inarguably among the composer's most popular works. And yet no other work by Dvořák has received such a peculiarly divided reception as this symphony. Among the wide spectrum of concert-goers, the Eighth enjoys much greater esteem than, say, the Seventh; it also surpasses its predecessor in D minor by far in terms of the number of recordings. The judgement of the 'experts', on the other hand, is precisely the opposite. While Dvořák's Seventh is usually cited in the musicological literature as his greatest symphony, the Eighth is judged with conspicuous reserve, irritation, or open criticism.

In his *Führer durch den Konzertsaal*, Hermann Kretzschmar discusses Dvořák's Seventh and Ninth Symphonies each in ten pages, but devotes just one and a half pages to the Eighth, stating plainly that according to the prevailing views held by the European musical world since Haydn and Beethoven, Dvořák's Eighth can hardly be called a symphony: 'It is far too underdeveloped, and its fundamental conception is too strongly grounded in loose invention. It inclines toward the character of Smetana's tone-poems and of Dvořák's own Slavonic Rhapsodies.'[1]

Likewise Gerald Abraham: he completely denies any symphonic character in the first movement, and regards all the movements of the symphony except the third as musically weak, and, further, as failed experiments.[2] To be sure, Abraham overlooks a series of thematic relationships in this work, but within

---

A slightly different version of this chapter, in Czech trans. by Milan Pospíšil, appeared as 'Dvořák a Čajkovskij: Poznámky k Dvořákově Osmé symfonii' (Dvořák and Tchaikovsky: Remarks Concerning Dvořák's Eighth Symphony) in *Hudební věda*, 28/3 (1991), 244–56.

[1] '. . . dafür ist sie viel zu wenig durchgearbeitet und in der ganzen Anlage zu sehr auf lose Erfindung gegründet. Sie neigt zu dem Wesen der Smetanaschen Tondichtungen und dem von Dvořáks eigenen Slawischen Rhapsodien.' *Führer durch den Konzertsaal, 1. Abteilung: Sinfonie und Suite*, ii (Leipzig, 1921), 584.

[2] 'Dvořák's Musical Personality', in *Antonín Dvořák: His Achievement*, ed. Viktor Fischl (Westport, Conn., 1970), 235–7.

the criteria he applies (which are obviously Brahmsian), it is difficult to contradict his assessment. Even authors who judge the symphony positively diagnose a rhapsodic character and a rather loose succession of musical ideas throughout, and seem themselves unable to explain properly the impression of unity that the work nevertheless conveys.[3]

It has been established often enough that Dvořák pointedly distanced himself from Brahms in this work, without enquiry as to the reasons for this distancing. We should remember that immediately before the G major Symphony Dvořák composed a piano quartet (in E flat major) that in character and in construction still belongs thoroughly to his 'Brahmsian' works.[4] I believe that a better understanding of the symphony's peculiarity requires a more careful consideration of the circumstances related to its origin, and that a clue is offered by the name Tchaikovsky.

During his second visit to Prague in late 1888, Tchaikovsky invited Dvořák to Russia, and in the following summer he commissioned Vasilij Iljich Safonov to settle the details with Dvořák. On 24 August 1889 (several days after completion of his Piano Quartet in E flat major) Dvořák wrote a letter to Safonov regarding the programme for his concert in Moscow, scheduled for early 1890. In this letter Dvořák cites a number of his own works that he could bring with him to Moscow and conduct there himself. He suggests the *Husitská* Overture, the Symphonic Variations, the *Scherzo capriccioso*, and, as a fourth work, one of his symphonies. 'But which?' he asks; 'I have three symphonies: D major, D minor, and F major (all three published by Simrock in Berlin).' Safonov should make the choice or discuss the matter with Tchaikovsky.[5]

---

[3] This judgement coincides roughly with that of Brahms himself, who, according to his friend Richard Heuberger, commented on Dvořák's Eighth Symphony in 1891 as follows: 'Too much that's fragmentary, incidental, loiters about in the piece. Everything fine, musically captivating and beautiful—but no main points! Especially in the first movement, the result is not proper. But a charming musician! When one says of Dvořák that he fails to achieve anything great and comprehensive, having too many individual ideas, this is correct. Not so with Bruckner, all the same he offers so little!' ('Zu viel Fragmentarisches, Nebensächliches treibt sich darin herum. Alles fein, musikalisch fesselnd und schön—aber keine Hauptsachen! Besonders im ersten Satz wird nichts Rechtes draus. Aber ein reizender Musiker! Wenn man Dvořák nachsagt, er komme vor lauter einzelnen Einfällen nicht dazu, etwas Großes Zusammenfassendes zu leisten, so trifft dies zu. Bei Bruckner aber nicht, der bietet ja ohnedies so wenig!') See Richard Heuberger, *Erinnerungen an Johannes Brahms*, 2nd edn. (Tutzing, 1976), 47. Trans. of this passage according to David Beveridge in 'Dvořák and Brahms: A Chronicle, an Interpretation', in *Dvořák and his World*, ed. Michael Beckerman (Princeton, NJ, 1993), 82.

[4] Cf. Hartmut Schick, 'Konstruktion aus einem Intervall: Zur harmonischen und tonalen Struktur von Dvořáks Klavierquartett op. 87', in *Antonín Dvořák 1841–1991: Report of the International Musicological Congress Dobříš 17th–20th September 1991*, ed. Milan Pospíšil and Marta Ottlová (Prague, 1994), 91–102.

[5] 'Das wäre also: 1. eine Ouvertüre, "Husitská", 2. dann die "Sinfonischen Variationen", dann 3. ein "Scherzo capriccioso", und 4. eine von meinen Sinfonien (aber welche?). Ich habe 3 Sinfonien: D dur, D moll und F dur (alle bei Simrock in Berlin). Dann habe ich ein Violinkonzert und ein Klavierkonzert, welche Herr Hřímalý oder Herr Sapelnikov spielen könnte. Das sind nur so mein Vorschläge. Bitte also, wählen Sie selbst oder besprechen Sie sich mit Herrn Tschaikowsky!' *Antonín Dvořák: Korespondence a dokumenty—*

Just two days after this letter, on 26 August 1889, Dvořák began outlining a new symphony in G major, his Eighth, and it is easy to imagine that, while he was considering which of his symphonies might be suitable for Russia, he came to the idea that indeed an entirely new symphony should be written for this occasion.

This presumption is supported by two further letters from Dvořák to Safonov. On 2 October 1889, Dvořák gave Safonov a new programme recommendation, in which he indicated as a fifth item 'a symphony—either the D minor or F major, or I will bring a *new one*, which is still in manuscript form; I am however uncertain if I will be finished with the work.'[6] And on 8 January 1890—the Eighth Symphony meanwhile completed—Dvořák wrote to Safonov, 'Most honoured Herr Direktor! To your esteemed enquiry regarding the symphony, I beg to recommend the new Symphony in G major, still in manuscript form.'[7] Should Simrock be unable to provide the printed version in time, Dvořák would bring the manuscript score and parts with him to Russia. He wanted to have it performed not only in Moscow but in St Petersburg as well.

Nevertheless, Dvořák decided soon thereafter not to perform the new symphony in Russia, but rather to leave the first foreign première to the London Philharmonic, to which he owed a gesture of gratitude. The symphony was not only performed but also published in England (by Novello) and soon took the nickname 'The English'. However, we now see that it would be much more appropriate to call it 'The Russian', in view of its origin. This would also apply to some internal features.

To write a symphony for Russia meant, of course, to compete with the symphonies of Tchaikovsky. We know—from the testimony of Janáček, for example[8]—that Dvořák studied the newest compositions of his contemporaries very carefully, and that they often provided a stimulus for his own compositions. It would therefore have been nothing out of the ordinary for him to react in a similarly creative manner to Tchaikovsky. To my knowledge, however, no Tchaikovskian influence has been ever pointed out in Dvořák's music.

Kritické vydání (Antonín Dvořák: Correspondence and Documents—Critical Edition, ed. Milan Kuna et al., ii (Prague, 1988), 387. The correspondence between Dvořák and his Russian interlocutors may be found in Eng. trans. in John Clapham, 'Dvořák's Visit to Russia', *Musical Quarterly*, 51 (1965), 493–506.

[6] '*Eine Sinfonie.* Entweder die D moll oder F dur, oder bringe ich eine *neue*, die noch Manuskript ist, ich weiß aber nicht *bestimmt*, ob ich mit dem Werke fertig sein werde.' *Antonín Dvořák: Korespondence*, ii. 393. The first four items were now the First Slavonic Rhapsody, the Symphonic Variations, the Violin Concerto, and the *Scherzo capriccioso*.

[7] 'Sehr geehrter Herr Direktor! Auf Ihre werte Anfrage bezüglich der Sinfonie erlaube ich mir, Ihnen also die neue *Sinfonie in G dur*, welche noch Manuskript ist, vorzuschlagen.' *Antonín Dvořák: Korespondence*, iii (Prague, 1989), 15.

[8] See Leoš Janáček, *Musik des Lebens: Skizzen, Feuilletons, Studien*, ed. Theodora Straková (Leipzig, 1979), 45.

We know that Dvořák received his introduction to Tchaikovsky's Fifth Symphony on 30 November 1888, when Tchaikovsky himself conducted it in Prague just a few weeks after its world première. On this occasion Tchaikovsky also presented his new opera, *Eugene Onegin*, which made a deep impression on Dvořák, as he reported subsequently in a letter to Tchaikovsky.[9] In this letter Dvořák didn't mention the symphony; however, his pupil Oskar Nedbal later remembered that Dvořák was initially startled by the unusual character and originality of tone-colour in Tchaikovsky's music, in particular the Fifth Symphony, but soon understood its greatness and profundity.[10] And there is some evidence that he had studied this symphony very carefully when, a few months after Tchaikovsky's visit, he began writing his own Eighth Symphony.

When Dvořák deals with the work of another composer in his own music, he usually selects the same key or a very closely related one. (Cf. for example his String Quartet in C major, modelled in part on Schubert's C major String Quintet, or his Sixth Symphony in D major with its relation to the Second Symphony in the same key by Brahms.) And so he does here. After the gloomy D minor of Dvořák's Seventh Symphony, Tchaikovsky's key of E minor would hardly have been considered; instead Dvořák chose the most closely related major key, namely G. Writing his symphony in major, he nevertheless follows Tchaikovsky by beginning in the minor (G minor) and likewise with a self-contained, elegiac introductory theme preceding in both cases the main theme of the sonata form—a feature that is very unusual for Dvořák, who begins nearly all his larger works with either the main theme itself or a motivic prototype thereof.[11]

Except for the initial note-repetitions, the opening melody of the Eighth Symphony has admittedly nothing melodically in common with the 'Fate' theme at the beginning of Tchaikovsky's Fifth (see Ex. 14.1, Theme 1 in each symphony). But structural similarities are present throughout: the wide-reaching minor-mode melody in the tenor range with subdued dynamics, the clarinets carrying the melody low in their range (combined with, in Dvořák's case, the cello, bassoon, and French horn), and the accompaniment of striding crotchets separated by rests, which in Tchaikovsky's case vividly suggest a funeral march.

---

[9] See Dvořák's letter of 14 Jan. 1889, in *Antonín Dvořák: Korespondence*, ii. 359. This letter was written in Czech.

[10] This information I owe to Ch. 13.

[11] To be sure, Dvořák's introductory theme in the Eighth Symphony is not a slow introduction like Tchaikovsky's but a calm melody in the main tempo, felt to be not yet the main theme, but a bit more than an introduction, whereas the following main theme in turn seems perhaps too lightweight for this function, and is introduced more as an episodic figuration. Regarding this ambiguity and its formal implications, see Jaroslav Volek, 'Tektonické ambivalence v symfoniích Antonína Dvořáka', *Hudební věda* 21/1 (1984), 18 ff.

In the first movement of Dvořák's G major Symphony, the numerous themes and motifs, closely following one another without apparent logic, have always annoyed commentators—at least, the more critical of them. A comparison with the opening movement of Tchaikovsky's E minor Symphony shows, however, that for every one of Dvořák's themes (with one exception) there is a counterpart in Tchaikovsky.

The main themes of the respective opening movements (Ex. 14.1, Theme 2) have, again, nothing melodically in common. But both are introduced by solo wind instruments piano or pianissimo, and dotted rhythms play an important role in both cases (also in the ensuing elaborative passage). In both movements, the primary key-area of the exposition culminates in a fortissimo repetition of the main theme, and both composers proceed from this to the second group without any real transition.

Particularly striking are the parallels between the two works during the second group of the exposition, in which three distinct themes follow one another. The initial theme of the second group is in both cases transient and tonally unstable (Ex. 14.1, Theme 3, shown with the full texture in Ex. 14.2): it does not yet establish the true secondary key, but rather, at first, the dominant of the primary key—B minor in Tchaikovsky, D major in Dvořák—and in both cases these keys are not actually confirmed, but only implied by their dominants. The instrumentation is identical: rich four-part strings (violins, violas, and cellos), with conspicuous waves of crescendo and decrescendo. Furthermore, to the octave figure of the winds interspersed throughout Tchaikovsky's strings theme, Dvořák provides a perfect parallel: the octave decorations in the flute and clarinet.

In both movements there follows a strongly contrasting theme, static but very rhythmic, made up of repeated wide leaps (octaves or fifths) and a closing scalar passage (Ex. 14.1, Theme 4). Both composers assign this theme to the woodwinds (answered in Tchaikovsky's case by the strings), and in both cases it is immediately repeated without change. With the arrival of this theme Tchaikovsky has achieved his tonal aim—the secondary key, D major—but Dvořák not yet completely. Dvořák presents this theme in B minor, the minor variant of his secondary key, B major.

The third and final theme of the second group is in both movements a wide-ranging, highly melodic major-mode theme which starts at piano and soon begins to rise in dynamics (Ex. 14.1, Theme 5). Dvořák's theme begins like the Tchaikovsky theme with the third scale-degree, then ascends step by step in a similar manner, quite nearly paraphrasing the Tchaikovskian melody in another metre.

Finally, the closing section of the exposition in both movements begins with a fortissimo tutti in which the brass blares out a reduced version of the

Ex. 14.1

a. Tchaikovsky, Symphony No. 5, first movement

main theme (Ex. 14.1, Theme 6), namely its transformation into a pure trumpet signal. Once more the motivic shapes are very different, but basically the same thing occurs in both movements. And even at the end of the exposition, Dvořák's repeated descending fifths in the flute and oboe (mm. 121 ff.) seem to be hinting at Tchaikovsky and the close of his exposition.

The key-schemes of the two expositions may be compared thus:

	Intro.	First group	Second group
Tchaikovsky:	E minor	E minor	(B minor)–D major–D major
Dvořák:	G minor	G major	(D major)–B minor–B major

In these tonal designs, several common features become apparent. In addition to the opening in minor, mentioned previously, we have in both cases the ending in an abnormal key (neither dominant nor relative major) and a tonal cross-relation, B minor–D major (Tchaikovsky) and D major–B minor

Ex. 14.1

b. Dvořák, Symphony No. 8, first movement

(Dvořák), in the second group. Both second groups begin with tonally unstable material in the dominant and proceed to the respective relative major or minor of this dominant. Without question, Dvořák's key-structure has inherently greater tension owing to the major-minor contrast between the introduction and the first subject, and again between the second and third theme of the second group.

One theme of Dvořák's exposition has not yet been mentioned: the march-like theme from m. 39 (Table 14.1, Theme 2*a*), a supplementary theme without Tchaikovskian counterpart. Why does Dvořák introduce this additional theme? Its powerful motivic resemblance to the second half of the introductory theme (mm. 7–10) provides an obvious answer: it binds together the first main section and the introduction. A further motivic bond can be found in the fanfare version of the main theme in the closing section (Ex. 14.1, Theme 6), which, in its second half, falls back upon the same passage of the

Ex. 14.2 *a*. Initial theme of second group in Tchaikovsky, Symphony No. 5, first movement; *b*. The same in Dvořák, Symphony No. 8, first movement

introductory theme. Gerald Abraham's assertion that this introductory melody is 'unconnected with the rest of the thematic material' is an obvious mistake.[12]

While Tchaikovsky's introductory 'Fate' theme is heard only at the opening and then plays no further role in the movement, Dvořák's introductory theme is thus brought directly into the thematic process of the exposition. Moreover, Dvořák reintroduces the entire theme twice at the movement's formal seams—immediately after the exposition and, played by the trumpets in a triumphant tutti, between the development and the reprise.

Compared with the first movement of Tchaikovsky's symphony, whose numerous themes are neither interrelated nor developed from each other, but rather are decisively contrasted to each other, Dvořák's opening movement is thematically quite coherent. If Dvořák's movement, more than Tchaikovsky's, nevertheless gives the impression at first glance of being a rhapsodical succession of too many themes and motifs, this is a result of the different durations of the two movements: Tchaikovsky's requires sixteen minutes, while Dvořák's requires just ten. Tchaikovsky repeats each theme at least once, and then stretches it out widely before proceeding to the next idea. Dvořák, on the contrary, often forgoes immediate repetition and proceeds much more quickly from one theme to the next.

To be sure, some puzzling facts remain, for instance that—quite atypically for Dvořák—no consequences are drawn from the very first measures of the movement, the beginning of the introductory theme. And it cannot be altogether overlooked that the first movement of Dvořák's Eighth Symphony lacks the intensity of developing variation and thematic work to be found in his Seventh Symphony or F minor Trio. Of course, Brahmsian construction is not the only means by which a symphony can be written. However, the fact that Dvořák followed Tchaikovsky in so many respects, but not in what is perhaps the most important of his traits, namely the lyrical expansiveness so typical of his music, appears to me indeed as a problem with this symphony.

In the third movement, too, Dvořák follows Tchaikovsky's Fifth Symphony by writing an elegant waltz in the place of the usual scherzo—a waltz that, with its supple melody, reminds one of Parisian salons and Tchaikovskian ballets, far removed from the *furiant*-style scherzi of the Sixth and Seventh Symphonies. (Even in Tchaikovsky's ballets, however, there are not to be found many waltzes of such a filigreed, refined orchestration, and the other movements of Dvořák's symphony, too, show a skill at instrumentation rarely attained in Tchaikovsky's symphonies.)

As is well known, a crucial aspect of the whole conception of Tchaikovsky's

---

[12] 'Dvořák's Musical Personality', 235.

E minor Symphony is the cyclic connection of the four movements by means
of the 'Fate' theme. The introductory theme of the first movement returns
episodically in both middle movements and then, converted from minor to
major, becomes the introductory theme of the finale. Within the first movement, the 'Fate' theme remains strangely isolated, and its reappearance in the
middle movements is rather arbitrary and not internally motivated in purely
musical terms. Certainly, according to Schumannian or Lisztian aesthetics
these recurrences are poetic moments in their own right. However, within
Dvořák's more conservative aesthetic such citations always have to be prepared and 'legitimized' on the level of motivic-thematic work. This is, at least,
what Dvořák's early works show us quite clearly, and so do the later works,
in which such reappearances of themes play an increasing role again (cf. the
Ninth Symphony and the Cello Concerto).

In his own symphony, Dvořák completely relinquishes the repetition of the
introductory theme in the other movements. I believe, however, that the
afore-mentioned twofold repetition of the introductory theme at the seams of
the opening movement is itself a reflection of Tchaikovsky's symphony: a pro-
jection, as it were, of the symphony's cyclic form on to a single movement. It
seems to be no coincidence that Dvořák's introductory theme in its third and
final appearance—after the development—is orchestrated in a manner very
similar to that of the 'Fate' theme in its last appearance during the finale of
Tchaikovsky's symphony (Ex. 14.3). The originally sombre, elegiac character
of the theme is here converted to a triumphant climax, with trumpets playing
the theme as a fortissimo solo and the violins and violas accompanying in a
very similar manner with runs of notes in triple octave doubling.

But Dvořák does also tie together the four movements of his Eighth
Symphony in cyclic unity, though using means that are somewhat more subtle than those of Tchaikovsky. Thus the first two movements are clearly
related to one another by a pastoral element: the pentatonic main theme of
the first movement, played by the flute over a static background (Ex. 14.1,
Theme 2), is unmistakably a nature theme resembling a bird-call, as is also the
flute theme in the second movement (Ex. 14.4). The way in which the flute
theme in the slow movement is eventually reduced to merely its descending
fourths, repeated continuously with a 'natural stillness', gradually dissolving,
relates directly to the reprise of the first movement, where the octave-leap
theme (Ex. 14.1, Theme 4) is accompanied by a similar repeated bird-call
motif of descending fourths in the flute, gradually dissolving. And in the finale
one notices an echo of this pastoral sphere in the strikingly frequent use of the
solo flute.

Motivically, the finale's main theme (Ex. 14.5a), with its ascending triad,
refers quite clearly to the main theme of the first movement. Yet otherwise,

Ex. 14.3 *a*. Tchaikovsky, Symphony No. 5, finale, coda; *b*. Dvořák, Symphony No. 8, first movement

Ex. 14.4 Dvořák, Symphony No. 8, second movement

the themes and motifs of the various movements are not interrelated by the contours of their melodies (i.e. not by diastematic means), but rather by a certain resignation of melody, specifically the feature of pure note-repetition. Even the main theme of the Finale originally shows—as revealed by the sketches—no ascending triad at the beginning, but a simple note-repetition. (Compare its second sketch version, Ex. 14.5*b*.)[13] And then, when Dvořák decided upon the more melodic shape, he placed before the main theme a fanfare-type theme in the solo trumpets (Ex. 14.5*c*), composed essentially of note-repetitions.

Ex. 14.5 Dvořák, Symphony No. 8, finale: *a.* main theme, final version; *b.* main theme, second sketch version; *c.* opening fanfare added before main theme in final version

We have seen that in the first movement Dvořák takes from the introductory theme precisely the measures with note-repetitions as material for constructing themes later in the exposition (see Ex. 14.1, Themes 1, 2*a*, and 6). In this context the octave-leap theme (Theme 4) can also be understood as being constructed of note-repetitions, separated in this case into octaves. Compare, finally, the essential role of note-repetition in the second subject of the last movement (Ex. 14.6).

The foremost impression created by note-repetitions is that of rhythm. And in rhythm, the themes of the opening and closing movements are extraordi-

---

[13] Regarding the evolution of themes in the sketches, see John Clapham, *Antonín Dvořák: Musician and Craftsman* (New York, 1966), 32 f.

Ex. 14.6 Dvořák, Symphony No. 8, finale, second subject

narily homogenous. The majority of themes and motifs are based upon march rhythms such as those in Ex. 14.7. No two themes are exactly identical in terms of rhythm, nor do they altogether trace back to any one specific fundamental rhythm, but rather they function, in a quite abstract manner, as various realizations of the pure idea of the march—most concretely realized in Themes 2*a* and 6 from the opening movement (see Ex. 14.1), in the trumpet theme at the onset of the finale (Ex. 14.5*c*), and in the same movement's second subject (Ex. 14.6), which itself is a proper funeral march in C minor, the key of Beethoven's 'Eroica' march.[14]

Ex. 14.7 Dvořák, Symphony No. 8, typical march rhythms

The slow movement, too, despite its pastoral elements, has a march-like quality and even has been characterized by commentators as a funeral march, although the key of C major prevails. It is truly ingenious how Dvořák, here and in the entire movement, on the one hand plays the pastoral and march-like elements against one another, while on the other hand allowing them to pass into and interlock with one another until they are completely united at the end: the repeated descending fourth is at once both bird-call and trumpet signal. The supposed antitheses—military march and nature—penetrate one another as the 'naturalness' of the drum tattoo and trumpet signal becomes clearly obvious and the repetitive, non-developmental character of both corresponds with the bird-call. The inner relationship to the music of Gustav Mahler, whose First Symphony incidentally received its world première two weeks after the completion of Dvořák's Eighth, is not to be overlooked.

The comparison between the two symphonies of Dvořák and Tchaikovsky has shown that both works employ the march, and especially the funeral march, in order to create a cyclic unity among the four movements. But while

---

[14] Dvořák used C minor for a funeral march again later, in the symphonic poem *Holoubek* (The Wild Dove): Andante, marcia funebre. See Ch. 19.

Tchaikovsky attempts to achieve this unity with a single, solidly outlined theme, which does not always seem properly integrated within its context, Dvořák works in a much more abstract way with the basic idea of the march. In different ways, this march idea is present in most of the themes—especially in their rhythm, but also by means of instrumentation such as the soloistic use of trumpets and drums. Thematic work within the diastematic parameter—traditionally the most important field of play—moves to the background. More than any other factor, it is this, in my opinion, that engenders the difficulties one encounters when approaching this work with Brahmsian criteria. Like Schubert, Dvořák is essentially a rhythmist—a fact already demonstrated in his early D major String Quartet, where the rhythm, specifically that of the mazurka, likewise ties the four movements together in cyclic unity.[15]

My comparison with Tchaikovsky's Fifth Symphony has not, I hope, given rise to the impression that Dvořák simply entertained a foreign influence, thereby composing less originally in his Eighth Symphony. Precisely the opposite is the case. It is when critically dealing with Tchaikovsky's symphony that Dvořák shows his own originality most clearly, by the way he selects only certain aspects from Tchaikovsky and develops them into a unique conception quite typical of himself. His aim apparently is not imitation but rather 'to go one better than Tchaikovsky'. This of course does not mean that for us Dvořák's symphony is necessarily better than Tchaikovsky's, lacking as it does, for example, the overwhelming lyricism of the latter work. But in any case, the comparison may bring us a little closer to an understanding of Dvořák's musical thinking.

Finally, one could speculate whether it is only coincidence that Dvořák's next work in this genre, the 'New World' Symphony, is written in the same key as Tchaikovsky's Fifth, and begins with a true, and similarly sombre, slow introduction (though of the classical, theme-generating type). The reappearance of several themes in the last three movements, too, may be inspired by Tchaikovsky's Fifth Symphony, although here Dvořák probably rather had in mind Beethoven's Ninth, an idea confirmed by the similarities between the openings to his and Beethoven's scherzo movements. Dvořák's G major Symphony, at least, proves that his relation to his Russian colleague was more than merely a matter of personal acquaintance or friendship, and reveals a new facet of Dvořák's participation in the ongoing 'discussion in notes' which is perhaps the essence of music history, especially in the nineteenth century.

---

[15] See Hartmut Schick, *Studien zu Dvořáks Streichquartetten* (Neue Heidelberger Studien zur Musikwissenschaft, ed. Ludwig Finscher and Reinhold Hammerstein, xvii; Laaber, Germany, 1990), 68 ff.

V

DVOŘÁK AS A EUROPEAN COMPOSER

15

Dvořák's Contribution to Progressive Trends in the European Symphony, 1865–95

MIROSLAV K. ČERNÝ

IN view of the traditional belief that Dvořák was a conservative composer for his time, the title of this chapter may provoke some scepticism. But new approaches are needed. Today we can no longer say that Dvořák was conservative on the basis of his failure to follow the Wagnerian conception of *Musikdrama*, and this is not only because he did in fact use some elements of Wagner's conception and practice—for instance the 'leitmotifs' in *Dimitrij*, generally considered a 'conservative' opera in Meyerbeerian style. Similarly, the fact that Dvořák, contrary to the ideas of Berlioz and Liszt, composed many works in the old forms of sonata and symphony does not allow us to label him as conservative—and again, this is not only because in his last decade he abandoned these forms and composed nothing but operas and symphonic poems.

Our views have changed. We no longer think the symphony is dead, as Richard Wagner thought in his time. The evolution of European music from the end of the nineteenth century to the late twentieth century has brought a great number of important and aesthetically valuable symphonies, from Mahler to Shostakovich and Martinů, to name only a few. We must consider the long-term evolution of the symphony and its form, an evolution that began much earlier than the second half of the nineteenth century. We can by no means speak either of a decline of the symphony after Beethoven, or of an 'ideal *typus*' of the genre as usually described in textbooks.[1]

What was Dvořák's position in the development of the European symphony? What did he contribute to that development? Certainly he played a role in the 'second life' of the genre, to use Carl Dahlhaus's phrase, after the

---

[1] The existence and power of different types of symphonic 'dramaturgy' was convincingly shown as early as the 1940s by the Russian musicologist I. Sollertinsky. See 'Istoricheskije tipi simfonicheskoj dramaturgii' (Historical Types of Symphonic Drama) in his *Muzykalno-istoricheskij etjudy* (Studies in Music History) (Leningrad, 1956), 301–11.

gap following Schumann's Third Symphony.[2] But I would not emphasize this role, for the supposed 'gap' did not really exist. There were not only two great cyclic symphonies by Liszt, but also works of other composers, if not very outstanding ones. We might mention the symphonies by Felix Draeseke, Robert Volkmann, Joachim Raff, Niels Gade, Anton Rubinstein, Georges Bizet, Jan Bedřich Kittl, Václav Jindřich Veit, Leopold Eugen Měchura, and Bedřich Smetana.[3] It is true that these symphonies didn't substantially change the traditional form of the genre and didn't enrich its aesthetic value. But neither, at first sight, are the symphonies of Brahms, Bruckner, Dvořák, Tchaikovsky, or Franck revolutionary works destroying the old traditions. Each of these composers brought to the symphony many new features (even if only in details) which prolonged the vitality of the genre, giving it space for development and a broad appeal which has lasted until our time. We must consider the role of Dvořák in the light of this process, which is not always obvious at first sight. Let us examine some of these details.

Norbert Jers tried in 1979 to define Dvořák's progressive style by showing the 'developing variation' technique found in Dvořák's Ninth Symphony, 'From the New World'.[4] This technique was described by Arnold Schoenberg, in relation to the compositions of Johannes Brahms, as the procedure that had opened the way to progress toward his own methods and intentions.[5] David Beveridge found the same technique in Dvořák's very first opus, the String Quintet in A minor, and in his other early works.[6] In my own previous analyses I have come to similar results;[7] some further examples will be offered later in this chapter. Unquestionably, the tendency to condense and concentrate musical form on thematic material that is interrelated or derived from a single nucleus, excluding filler material and subthematic sections, is a

---

[2] *Nineteenth-Century Music*, trans. J. Bradford Robinson (Berkeley and Los Angeles, 1980), 78.

[3] See also the symphonies by Edvard Grieg and Vilém Blodek, discussed by Jarmila Gabrielová in Ch. 16.

[4] 'Dvořák der Progressive: Entwickelnde Variation in der 9. Symphonie', *Musica*, 33 (1979), 258–62.

[5] 'Brahms the Progressive', in *Style and Idea: Selected Writings of Arnold Schoenberg*, ed. Leonard Stein (New York, 1975). This essay contains a clear description of the phenomenon, though Schoenberg does not actually use the phrase 'developing variation' until a later essay, 'Symphonies from Folksongs'. There he refers to Beethoven's Fifth Symphony, which he views as being constructed on the interval G–F, but this derivation seems to me too strained, related rather to Schoenberg's twelve-tone methods, and not acceptable as a useful definition of developing variation.

[6] 'Romantic Ideas in a Classical Frame: The Sonata Forms of Dvořák', Ph.D. diss. (Univ. of California at Berkeley, 1980), 43 ff.

[7] See my essay 'Zum kompositorischen Typus Antonín Dvořák', in *Colloquium Dvořák, Janáček and their Time*, ed. Rudolf Pečman (Brno, 1985), 155–63, and my art. in *Opus musicum*, 22/3 (1990), vi–xi, based on a paper read in 1989 at a conference in Prague on Dvořák's harmony: 'Byl Dvořák Semantik? (K harmonické výstavbě a modulačním plánům v sonátových větách Dvořákových symfonií)' (Was Dvořák a Semanticist? Regarding the Harmonic Structure and Modulatory Plans of Sonata Form Movements in Dvořák's Symphonies). The problem will be explored further in my forthcoming study of Dvořák's musical language.

progressive trait, parallel, as Dahlhaus explains, to the sequential principle of Liszt and Wagner.[8]

But problems arise in trying to establish concretely these types of procedure, because variative techniques were used not only in the form of 'thema con variazioni' in middle movements, but also in thematic elaboration in the sonata forms, and in symphonies particularly, going back at least to the beginning of the nineteenth century; moreover, some of the 'classical' procedures of thematic development such as transposition, diminution, augmentation, and possibly also fragmentation can be considered kinds of variation in the broader sense of the word. In the Ninth Symphony of Dvořák, Jers evaluates not only the true variations (for instance of the introductory theme and 'first theme' of the first movement), but also relationships and similarities between motifs far removed from each other in the piece and in different parts (for instance motifs from the 'second themes' of the first and the third movements),[9] which brings his concept very near to that of Schoenberg.[10] Taking into consideration also rhythmic relations, he differs from the concept of Dahlhaus, as will be discussed below. The procedures he analyses reach far beyond the usual borderlines of variation. Beveridge emphasizes the heard logical continuity of change: 'Developing variation requires that each new unit of melodic or figural material be derived by some natural-sounding process of alteration from the foregoing material.'[11] Dahlhaus sees the substance of it, as practised by Brahms, in the diastematic (pitch-contour) identity or similarity of motifs.[12] If I understand this correctly, an example would be the formation of the second theme in the first movement of Brahms's Third Symphony (Ex. 15.1). This practice would be the opposite to that of Bruckner, in which relationships are based on the common rhythmic substance of themes.

Ex. 15.1 Brahms, Symphony No. 3, first movement

These differences in definition of the concept make it difficult to determine precisely the borderlines of this special type of developing variation in Dvořák's compositions. There are many forms of variation present. They play

---

[8] *Between Romanticism and Modernism: Four Studies in the Music of the Later Nineteenth Century*, trans. Mary Whittall (Berkeley and Los Angeles, 1980).

[9] 'Dvořák der Progressive', 260.

[10] Schoenberg, 'Symphonies', 228. Compare Schoenberg's derivation of the 'bridge' and 'second theme' in Beethoven's Fifth Symphony.

[11] 'Romantic Ideas', 43 ff.   [12] *Nineteenth-Century Music*, 255–7, 272.

an important role not only in the middle movements of the cycles (for instance in the second movement of the Fourth Symphony, and in certain places in the second movement of the Third), but also in the first movements and some finales of the symphonies (e.g. the Eighth). What is important is that in Dvořák's compositions, especially in the sonata forms, variative techniques are ubiquitious, ranging from the usual types to those close to the techniques of 'developing variation' as characterized by various authors. The intensity of Dvořák's use of these procedures warrants his classification as progressive, because they contribute to the trend of nineteenth-century music toward 'logical form'.

It is common for Dvořák to vary or develop his themes by different alterations just after their initial presentation. Such 'expositional developments' largely replace the subthematic material heard in many works of Haydn and Mozart, and fill large spaces of both the exposition and recapitulation sections. As a result, the differences between the main parts of the sonata form (exposition, development, and recapitulation) are greatly diminished. This is in accord with the general trend in the late nineteenth century, which continued through Mahler deep into our own century—maybe even to Shostakovich. Though Dvořák was not the first who participated in this trend, the frequency of these techniques in his works makes his contribution of great importance.

Most of these variative procedures fulfil the conditions mentioned above for 'developing variation', though not necessarily all at once. Continuity in the change of variants, which is of great importance (as Beveridge asserts), can be observed very often. Mostly we find small changes in the intervallic structure, expanding or contracting the pitch-range of the theme or only of its characteristic interval. Thus in the first movement of the Third Symphony (1872–3), the upward leap of a perfect fifth in the first theme (Ex. 15.2a) is expanded during the repetition to a sixth (b), and later contracted to a third (c). When this motif appears as counterpoint to the second theme, the interval appears in different parts as a unison, third, fourth, and sixth (d, e).

But not only this head-motif is varied and repeated. Dvořák also subjects the entire first theme to 'developing variation', by repeating it with small changes within the opening part of exposition in G flat major—the flat mediant, which is also the tonality of the second theme—then again in the tonic and once more starting in the flat mediant at the transition to the development section.

The expanding or contracting of the pitch-range of themes can be found in many other symphonies of Dvořák and, even more clearly, in some of his chamber works (for instance the String Quartet in D major from 1868, and the String Quartet in C major from 1881). An outstanding case of the 'stretch-

Ex. 15.2 Dvořák, Symphony No. 3, first movement

ing' of the pitch-range occurs in the Ninth Symphony, where the main theme of the first movement appears initially in the slow introduction with a total pitch-range of a diminished seventh (Ex. 15.3*a*), is expanded to a tenth to form the main theme (*b*), and is further changed at new appearances not only in the first movement but in others as well.

In the first movement of the Fourth Symphony (1874) similar changes are connected with the variation of the inner structure of a theme by translating the fanfare triad motif to the different degrees of the tonic chord (Ex. 15.4). (The term 'translation'—in Czech *translace*—was introduced by J. Hutter, Professor of Musicology at the Charles University in Prague during World War II. Translation is to transposition as tonal sequence is to real sequence.)

Ex. 15.3 Symphony No. 9, first movement

Ex. 15.4 Symphony No. 4, first movement

The method in question is applied also in the finale, where it is combined with the device of extending the motif from two to four measures. It appears in the first movement of the Fifth Symphony as well (Ex. 15.5).

Ex. 15.5 Symphony No. 5, first movement, opening

Returning to the first movement of the Fourth Symphony, we find that the process of variation leads to a new shape for the first theme, marked 'grandioso'. This new shape appears later—especially in the recapitulation—as a proper main theme. The idea of the grandioso, which constitutes a specific trait in most of Dvořák's symphonies, is a survival from the fortissimo repetitions of the theme just after its first presentation, as heard in Haydn and Mozart. But Dvořák ushers in his grandiosi only after a long variative development or elaboration of the first theme. In his First, Third, Sixth, Seventh, and Ninth Symphonies (probably also in the original, destroyed version of the Second, as shown by the remnants of the old pagination), he then returns at the grandioso section to the theme in its initial form. (In the First, Seventh, and Ninth, the grandioso is not actually marked as such, but a fortissimo dynamic indication creates the same effect; in the Third, 'grandioso' is marked some measures before the return of the theme.)

The principle of these variations is the preservation of the rhythmic basis while changing the diastematic one. The opposite, demonstrated in the Third Symphony of Brahms (Ex. 15.1 above), is very rare in Dvořák.

But there are still further procedures identifiable as developing variation, if only on the basis of the continuity of change. One might mention the construction of the theme from the opening bare interval of a fourth in the first movement of the Sixth Symphony, or the variation of the second half of the first theme of the Ninth Symphony, which evolves toward the shape of the second theme.

Among Dvořák's variation procedures there are two that occupy an extraordinary position. The first is a change of intervallic structure by altering the harmonic basis under the same position of melody, which I have described as 'modal variation' because the resulting variants resemble, in their structure, the medieval modes. This type occurs frequently in the First Symphony, as I showed in 1989 at the conference in Prague on Dvořák's harmony,[13] and can be considered Dvořák's specific method (Ex. 15.6).

Ex. 15.6 Symphony No. 1, first movement

The other special variation procedure is what I suggest calling the 'timbre-variation'. Though not invented by Dvořák—we can find many previous examples for instance in Schumann—because of its frequency and function in the elaboration of Dvořák's themes, it is a very specific trait and represents a personal contribution to the development of the European symphony. The Andante sostenuto of the Fourth Symphony consists of variations limited almost entirely to changes in instrumentation and sound-articulation (including changes of accompanimental figuration and countermelodies), without

[13] 'Byl Dvořák sémantik?'

any change in the melodic or harmonic substance of the theme. This is the only such movement in Dvořák's work. But the technique of purely orchestrational 'timbre-variation' appears in more limited passages in the initial elaborations of themes in many sonata-form movements, for instance at the beginning of the first movement of the Fifth Symphony. More often it occurs in combination with transposition or other small changes—a characteristic example is the beginning of the Seventh Symphony.

Besides these variative techniques, there are in Dvořák's symphonic sonata forms many other peculiarities. Very striking and important are his experiments with thematic contrast—including the *diminishment* of thematic contrast—which can be traced through his entire output. We find them in the Second as well as the Ninth Symphony.

Dvořák used various methods to diminish thematic contrasts, such as motivic affinities, incorporation of elements from the first theme into the second, the joining of the two by counterpoint (as in the Third Symphony), restriction of the frequency of one of them, and so on. The clearest case of this restricted contrast occurs in the finale of the Second Symphony in its original form from 1865. Here Dvořák replaced the proper second theme with two of the three elements from the first thematic group in reverse order, transposed to the dominant (in the recapitulation they appear in the tonic).[14]

The other way that Dvořák modifies thematic contrast in his sonata forms is by the choice of tonality for the second theme. In the Third to Eighth Symphonies, in all opening and some closing movements, the second theme is in neither the dominant nor (if the main key is minor) the relative major, but rather most often in an abnormal mediant or submediant key. (The same observation applies to most of Dvořák's chamber works.)[15] But I should like to emphasize that this practice has very few parallels among Dvořák's predecessors in the symphonic genre—except maybe early Schubert and Beethoven's Ninth Symphony—and so we can consider it an important contribution by Dvořák to the loosening of the stiff 'textbook' shape of the sonata form—to a trend that has been common since the second half of the nineteenth century. ('Irregular' choice of the second key is also common in Brahms, but Dvořák developed his practice quite independently, for he did not become well acquainted with Brahms's works until the 1880s.)

There are still more contributions to the evolution of the European symphony that should be mentioned, but let me recapitulate those described here, which in my opinion are the most important:

[14] See František Bartoš, 'Vydavatelské poznámky' (Editorial Annotations) in the critical edn. of Dvořák, *II. symfonie B dur, op. 4* (Prague, 1959), 39 ff. The fourth measure of the cut passage presents the theme from mm. 37 ff. in the first theme-group; the eleventh measure presents the main theme, from m. 11 (the identity of measure nos. is coincidental).
[15] 'Byl Dvořák semantik?'

1. Equalization of the main parts of the sonata-allegro by diminishing the difference in degree of thematic development.
2. Intensive variation of the themes by various means just after their exposition (leading to point 1).
3. Special forms of thematic variation—'modal variation' and 'timbre-variation'—with intensive application.
4. The restriction of thematic contrasts by, among other methods, introduction of 'irregular' tonalities in the exposition of the second and possibly third theme-groups, together with melodic affinities.

Dvořák thus had an important part to play in the overall evolution and enrichment of the European symphony and sonata form, and in the progressive trends in the evolution of music.

16

Dvořák's Early Symphonies in the Context of European Symphonic Writing of the Mid-Nineteenth Century

JARMILA GABRIELOVÁ

THE first period of Dvořák's creative activity (1861–74) constitutes an astonishingly productive starting-point for his career as a composer. His fecundity was manifested during this period in practically all the main genres of nineteenth-century music, both vocal and instrumental: symphony, solo concerto, chamber music, song, and opera. In these years, however, he seems to have concentrated mostly on the large cyclic forms of instrumental music. The symphony is especially well represented, with four works completed by 1874.

The historical explanation of this fact is ambiguous, and it is also difficult to evaluate. The 1850s and 1860s in European music generally were a period of programme music (tone-poems) and of music-drama; both of these genres were proclaimed as 'music of the future' by their adherents. And considered from the point of view of the domestic situation (in Prague), the 1860s were the period of national opera. The genre of symphony, in Prague as well as in the wider context, seems to have been almost 'out of fashion'—undeserving of any serious compositional and aesthetic attention. To write symphonies at that time meant not to believe very much in public performance and appreciation and not to seek them. However, there was a renaissance of the symphony in the late 1870s and 1880s,[1] and Dvořák's mature works became a distinguished part of that renaissance. The early symphonies of Dvořák may

This chapter is a small part of my more comprehensive study on the early instrumental works of Dvořák. I have already presented the results of my research to the annual Dvořák Seminars in Prague during 1987–9, and my book on the same subject, *Rané tvůrčí období Antonína Dvořáka* (The Early Creative Period of Dvořák), has recently been published by the Charles University Press (Karolinum: Prague, 1990). I am indebted to Dr Hartmut Schick for sending me the score of the Symphony in C minor by Grieg and Werner Korte's book *Bruckner und Brahms*, and especially to Dr David Beveridge for his critical re-examination of my paper and for his considerable help with the preparation of the printed version.

[1] See Carl Dahlhaus, *Nineteenth-Century Music*, trans. J. Bradford Robinson (Berkeley and Los Angeles, 1989), 265 ff.

be considered and evaluated as a forecast or foreshadowing of that development.

But let us discuss the situation of the 1860s and early 1870s in more detail. In spite of the leading role of programme music, there were still many symphonies composed during this time. However, if we consider the names of the composers, we find that they were either second-class, rather inferior and eclectic authors, or very young ones at the beginnings of their careers. Among the latter, there were some who later contributed considerably to the new rise or (as Carl Dahlhaus terms it) the 'second life' of the symphony in the 1870s and 1880s. But there were also some composers of that generation (born about 1840) who did not pursue the symphonic genre any further after their first efforts.

For the greater part of the nineteenth century, aesthetic, critical, and analytical approaches to the symphony (or individual symphonies), as well as value judgements of it, were profoundly influenced by the idea of symphony as a large-scale, monumental form. This idea originated from the music of Ludwig van Beethoven, especially his Third, Fifth, and Ninth Symphonies,[2] and has been associated with such phrases as 'teleological form' or 'goal-directed structure', 'symphony as drama' or, in Karl Heinrich Wörner's terminology, the German expression *Finalcharakter*.[3]

However, for actual composition in the years around 1860, we can say (with an inevitable simplification) that the most prevalent models were the symphonies of Felix Mendelssohn, above all his Third and Fourth Symphonies (the 'Scottish' and the 'Italian'). Mendelssohn's conception of the symphony represented, in fact (around 1830–40, when the works were composed, as well as around 1860), the only relevant alternative to the Beethovenian model. The dominating role of the works by Mendelssohn around 1860, especially for composers of Germany and the Austrian Empire,[4] can be demonstrated in two typical examples:

1. Edvard Grieg (1843–1907) composed his Symphony in C minor in 1863–4 at the age of 20. The Mendelssohnian links were mediated here by the composer's studies in Leipzig. The Symphony in C minor remained Grieg's only work in this genre and, moreover, was not published during his lifetime (except for the second and third movements, which were arranged for piano, four hands, and published as Op. 14 in 1864). As a whole, this symphony has attracted the interest of audiences only recently, in the 1980s, when it was

---

[2] See Carl Dahlhaus, *Nineteenth-Century Music*, trans. J. Bradford Robinson (Berkeley and Los Angeles, 1989), 152 ff. ('The Symphony after Beethoven').

[3] *Das Zeitalter der thematischen Prozesse in der Geschichte der Musik* (Regensburg, 1969), 1–63.

[4] i.e. for the composers who were born here or had been associated with this area through their professional training and activity. The Leipzig Conservatoire played a leading role in this development.

published and performed in its original form for the first time.[5] Ex. 16.1 presents the exposition of the main theme of the first movement, in reduction.[6]

2. The Czech composer Vilém Blodek (1834–74) composed his First Symphony in D minor in 1865 (the same year as Dvořák's first effort in this genre). On the whole, it is a well-made composition. Blodek, in fact, was a very gifted and promising composer of his generation. He was interested in helping to create a Czech national opera tradition (as most Czech composers of his time were), but being a flute virtuoso and professor of flute at the Prague Conservatoire, he was involved in the problems of instrumental music as well. Ex. 16.2 shows, like the Grieg excerpt, the exposition of the main theme in the first movement, in reduction.[7]

In both symphonies, the inspiration from the Mendelssohnian model follows its outward or surface features only. The modest dimensions of the individual movements and of the symphony as a whole are a common feature, along with the reduced orchestral scoring—two each of the woodwinds and trumpets, two horns (Grieg) or four horns (Blodek), one trombone (Blodek) or none (Grieg), two timpani, and the usual complement of strings. Also notable are the even rhythmic flow and texture, the regular metrical structure, and the non-contrasting thematic material. What is missing here (as compared with the works of Mendelssohn) is above all the fine contrapuntal elaboration of the texture or, more specifically, the combination of the song-like thematic material with counterpoint and motivic association.[8]

Other composers representing the most advanced state ('the last word', so to speak) in the development of the symphony at mid-century were Robert Schumann, whose Third Symphony was completed in 1850, and Franz Schubert, whose symphonic and chamber works began to achieve wide dissemination in the 1850s and 1860s. The impact of Schubert and Schumann, however, does not seem to have been as evident and unmistakable as that of Mendelssohn.

To the best of my knowledge, there were only two composers in central Europe who wrote symphonies after 1850–60 and, rather than adhering to the Mendelssohnian model, tried to follow their own paths from the very beginning of their careers: Anton Bruckner (1824–96) and Antonín Dvořák (1841–1904). Both of them re-established the monumental form of symphony, and both did so with a striking and surprising self-confidence even in

---

[5] *Sinfonie c-Moll*, Studienpartitur, ed. Finn Benestad and Gunnar Rugstad (Frankfurt, New York, and London, 1984). The first performance was at the Bergen Festival in Norway, in 1981.

[6] All music exs. in this chapter are given in piano reduction by David Beveridge.

[7] Based on an MS copy made by the conductor Karel Moor (1873–1945) in the 1920s or 1930s, now in the archives of Czech Radio, Prague. The autograph is missing, and the symphony remains unpub.

[8] See Dahlhaus, *Nineteenth-Century Music*, 157.

Ex. 16.1 Grieg, Symphony in C minor, first movement, opening of Allegro

Ex. 16.2 Vilém Blodek, Symphony in D minor, first movement, opening of Allegro

their first works. However, the compositional procedures used by them were 'non-Beethovenian' to a great extent and had almost nothing in common with the Beethovenian model discussed above.

Bruckner's approach had not yet fully crystallized in his earliest symphonic attempts, the Symphony in F minor from 1863 and the Symphony in D minor from 1863–4. However, it can be seen clearly already in his Symphony No. 1 in C minor, composed in 1865–6, especially in the exposition of the first movement, mm. 1–93. Ex. 16.3 shows the opening of the movement. The form appears here as a succession of blocks of music, that is of clearly demarcated and sharply contrasting sections of music, each averaging about forty to fifty measures (in this case, mm. 1–44, 45–66, and 67–93). The dominating and distinguishing feature of each block is a repeated rhythmic motif along with a prevailing orchestral colour and texture. Thematic material and thematic development in the classical sense (i.e. developing variation and thematic links based on pitch-contour) are less important here in relation to the integrity of the form).[9]

The traditional 'logic' of functional harmonic relations (harmonic cadence and rules of modulation) seems to be suspended here to some extent, in detail as well as on a large scale. In its place, we find here more often simply successions of remote chords or tonalities. The blocks of music are consequently interchangeable to some extent: they can be substituted for one another (or replaced by a section having the same or similar rhythmic and dynamic characteristics but different thematic content) without affecting the basic form, idea, or integrity of the whole symphonic movement. The form that originates from these procedures is, of course, not a 'teleological' form (see above), despite the numerous gradations and triumphal tuttis in the development and reprise sections. It is more apt to remind us of a circle or of a spiral[10]—a formal idea not often found in music until the latter part of our own century. It is not necessary to stress that the traditional categories of sonata form such as exposition, development, recapitulation, first and second subject, transition, and so on are not adequate any more. They are used here mostly because of the lack of better ones. But at the same time, they can convince us that in spite of the radical novelty of this symphonic idea there are still some important links to the previous tradition.

Let us turn our attention at last to the early symphonies by Dvořák. If we listen to them and investigate them in detail, we can find some surprising similarities and analogies to the above-mentioned procedures of Bruckner. We cannot, however, speak of any direct influence. Bruckner and Dvořák created

---

[9] See Dahlhaus, *Nineteenth-Century Music*, 272.
[10] Matthias Hansen, *Anton Bruckner* (Leipzig, 1987), 152.

Ex. 16.3 Bruckner, Symphony No. 1, first movement, opening

their works quite independently, in the 1860s as well as later. They did not meet each other until 1896—shortly before Bruckner's death.[11]

Most of the Brucknerian features can already be found, in my opinion, in Dvořák's Symphony No. 1 in C minor from 1865, especially in its first movement. Ex. 16.4 shows the opening of the exposition, from m. 9. As with

Ex. 16.4 Dvořák, Symphony No. 1, first movement, opening of Allegro

[11] See Otakar Šourek, *Život a dílo Antonína Dvořáka* (The Life and Work of Antonín Dvořák), iii , 2nd edn. (Prague, 1956), 276–8, and also Jiří Vysloužil, 'Proč Anton Bruckner a Antonín Dvořák?' (Why Anton Bruckner and Antonín Dvořák?), *Opus musicum*, 15/3 (1983), 82.

Ex. 16.4 *cont.*

Bruckner, the form consists here of a succession of large, extensive blocks of music each internally integrated (and differentiated at the same time from the others) by its own orchestral texture, rhythmic motif, and dynamic level. In Dvořák's works, too, these sections of form are to some extent 'arbitrary' or interchangeable in their placement.

Again, there are situations here where the harmonic procedures, in detail as well as on a large scale, are not regulated by the logic of harmonic (functional) cadence or by the tonal plan of the classical sonata form. It is normal in these early works of Dvořák that the exposition of a sonata form does not close in the dominant, but rather returns at the end to the tonic. The development does not modulate to remote tonalities, and the reprise need not re-establish the superiority of the tonal centre again.

The characteristics of the individual formal sections no longer correspond to their traditional names and functions. For example, the 'transition' section in the exposition of the first movement of the First Symphony (mm. 129–72), placed between the first and the second thematic groups, does not actually constitute any 'transit' or 'mediation' between the thematic and harmonic content of the two groups. On the contrary, it is a very self-contained section, more a dividing than a connecting one. Moreover, the 'development' here (mm. 289–498) hardly brings any possibilities for the developing or variation of thematic material that were not already present in the exposition. And the 'reprise' (mm. 499 ff.) is not a literal recapitulation of the beginning and by no means returns to the initial 'state of affairs'.

But there is something in the First Symphony that is rather different from Bruckner. What we can find here is a complex structure or network of thematic and motivic links extending through the whole symphonic movement and its individual sections. This structure involves the following features, among others:

1. The traditional succession of thematic or motivic variants within the main thematic groups as well as between them (from the first subject to the second one, etc.) and between the main sections of the form;
2. Variation procedures involving the rhythmic figure (ostinato) of the first bars of the Allegro (mm. 9 ff.); this figure not only permeates the first movement, but appears in all the remaining movements as well—either integrated into the texture and rhythmic flow or, by contrast, isolated and marked out as an extraneous quotation (for the latter possibility, see e.g. the second movement, mm. 193–4); and
3. The thematic meaning or function of a specific instrumental colour—here the colour of the brass section.

These detailed procedures can be described as 'redundant', because (as mentioned above) the idea or dramaturgy of the form does not directly depend on them. On the other hand, they make the form 'plastic', 'multi-dimensional', more elaborate, and more convincing.

In contrast to Bruckner's style, which did not change much during his career (his early works, including Symphonies Nos. 1 and 2, appear to a large extent as a direct foreshadowing of his mature style),[12] Dvořák's style and his

---

[12] See Werner F. Korte, *Bruckner und Brahms. Die spätromantische Lösung der autonomen Konzeption* (Tutzing, 1963), 21–2, etc.

approach to the problem of the symphony underwent profound and essential transformations. His creative development was much more complicated and not free of reversals or breaks.

In its compositional problems, Dvořák's Second Symphony in B flat major is very similar to his First Symphony. It seems, however, to be less elaborate and less sophisticated. What is not present here, in comparison with the First Symphony, is the 'plasticity' or 'multi-dimensionality' of the whole structure. More precisely: the procedures that could remind us of the First Symphony— such as the thematic function of instrumental colour or of rhythmic osti-nato—are present here only in fragments, without being developed consistently and projected to the level of the whole symphonic cycle.

The next symphony, the Third in E flat major of 1872–3, is very different from the previous ones.[13] With reference to the above-mentioned dichotomy between the Beethovenian and Mendelssohnian symphonic models, we can speak of an inclination toward the Mendelssohnian pole, or of Dvořák's very specific and very individual adaptation of the Mendelssohnian approach, espe-cially in the first movement.[14] The even rhythmic flow of figuration and the non-contrasting thematic and motivic material are typical here. At the same time, the traditional architectonic concept of form—including the more-or-less regular return and repetition of the individual thematic and motivic units as well as the large-scale tonal structure—is more important and more marked here than in the previous two symphonies.

As far as the extensive final movement is concerned, some of its distin-guishing features (the formal shape, the character of thematic and motivic material, etc.) are analogous, in my opinion, to corresponding symphonic movements of Schubert (the 'Great' C major Symphony) and Schumann (the First Symphony in B flat major).

The Symphony No. 4 in D minor (1873–4) stands at the end of the series of Dvořák's early symphonies. At the same time, it is among the first works by Dvořák in which the profound change of style characteristic of his approaching maturity begins to be manifested unmistakably.[15] Two features

[13] As far as we can judge from the preserved version, which is the result of later changes and rewritings. It is impossible to reconstruct the original version of this symphony from the surviving autograph score. The same is true of Symphony No. 2. See František Bartoš, 'Vydavatelská zpráva' and 'Vydavatelské poznámky' (Editorial Report and Editorial Annotations) in the critical edns. of Dvořák, *II. symfonie B dur, op. 4* (Prague, 1959) and *III. symfonie Es dur, op. 10* (Prague, 1963).

[14] The 'Wagnerian' traces some earlier scholars think they have found in the Third Symphony are, in my opinion, a product of vague and passing associations: rich and dense orchestral texture, brass instru-ments in solo roles, etc. For a more detailed discussion of this problem, see Gabrielová, *Rané tvůrčí období*, 14, 109, etc.

[15] Again, we can know it only in the revised version, coming from the late 1880s, and not from the original one, which can scarcely be reconstructed. See František Bartoš, 'Vydavatelská zpráva' and 'Vydavatelské poznámky' (Editorial report and Editorial Annotations) in the critical edn. of Dvořák, *IV. symfonie d moll, op. 13* (Prague, 1962).

foreshadowing Dvořák's later stance are striking here: the simplification of the whole of the structure, and the economy of thematic and motivic material. However, we can still recognize relations and references to the previous stage of Dvořák's symphonic writing, in the ambiguity of formal functions of the individual parts of the form (see, e.g., the first thematic group of the first movement, mm. 1–25 and 25–52) and in the orchestral texture of some sections (above all in the tutti fortissimo sections: see the first movement, mm. 26, 136, 218 ff., etc.).

The whole context of Dvořák's early works and of his creative development in the first ten to fifteen years of his career reveals that these works did not result simply from uncontrolled, spontaneous expression. They were not (as is often said of his music generally) products of a naïve, vernacular musicianship, but on the contrary the results of a high level of reflection and of a very arduous and very conscious endeavour. However, it is in the nature of Dvořák's music that all 'artificial' features and compositional calculations remain hidden until they are revealed by a thorough analysis.

Compared with the techniques of his more or less prominent contemporaries, Dvořák's response to the state of compositional thinking in the 1850s and 1860s reveals a varied yet highly individual adaptation of the most significant contemporary impulses. In mentioning composers—Beethoven, Schubert, Schumann, Mendelssohn, and others—as well as particular works that influenced Dvořák's youthful style, earlier Dvořák scholars have tended to portray that style as being derivative, in a pejorative sense. In my opinion, this idea seems to be rather simplistic and not to be justified by the facts.

Dvořák's turn toward an apparent 'simplification' of style, of which signs can be seen starting with the Fourth Symphony, was the result of a conscious decision on his part. His situation in these years can perhaps be compared to the situation of Franz Liszt at the end of the 1840s. These two composers perhaps represented different types of creative orientation; both of them, however, had to solve a dilemma between tendencies toward rhapsodic, loose musical thought and structural principles on the one hand, and on the other hand the need for formal order that would establish and confirm the validity and definite character of the musical work of art. Each composer reached a reconciliation between the two antagonistic tendencies which seems to be rather 'non-academic' and 'non-schematic'. And that means at the same time, as far as Dvořák was concerned, that many, and indeed most, of the achievements from his first period of creative development were taken over and became significant components of his mature style.

17

Schubertian Tonal Plans Reinterpreted: Dvořák's 'Shadow-Key' Sonata Forms

JOHN K. NOVAK

IN his dissertation 'Romantic Ideas in a Classical Frame: The Sonata Forms of Dvořák', David Beveridge comprehensively examines Dvořák's use of sonata form throughout the composer's life.[1] Beveridge begins with the young, progressive Dvořák, who leaned towards the grand and fantastic Liszt–Wagner school in both harmony and developmental procedures. Dvořák's persistence in writing in supposed sonata forms despite this inclination resulted in the composing of many movements with confusing tonal plans, whose fundamental designs were sometimes a far cry from the classical models of sonata form. As Dvořák's style evolved and matured, his sonata forms became increasingly tight, logical, and, in a word, classical. As Beveridge traces this development, he singles out works of one particular period that are further away from the classical model than the other pieces of that period as 'regressions'.[2] One such work is the first movement of the String Sextet in A major. However, a disadvantage of using the classical models of sonata form with their tonic–dominant polarity (as codified by Donald Francis Tovey, Charles Rosen, Edward Cone, James Webster, and others) as a yardstick for any piece in sonata form is that it can diminish one's ability to examine the individual logic of the work.

Notwithstanding the development of Dvořák's formal clarity through his career, some of Dvořák's most mature and revered works in sonata form continue to deviate from the standard models. Such is the case with the first movements of the C major String Quartet, the Piano Quintet in A major, B. 155, and the Ninth Symphony in E minor, 'From the New World'. All of these movements contain recapitulations in which the final theme-group closes outside the tonic key, and awaits harmonic resolution in the coda. Such a procedure opposes one of the fundamental traits of classical sonata form:

[1] Ph.D. diss. (Univ. of California at Berkeley, 1980).   [2] 'Romantic Ideas', 258.

Cone's 'sonata principle', which states that the most important ideas and the strongest cadential passages from the second group must reappear in the recapitulation transposed to the tonic.[3] It also is different from the procedure of Schubert's three-key sonata forms, whose third key, always the dominant, is transposed to the tonic at the end of the recapitulation.

Among the many Dvořák movements whose recapitulations close outside the tonic, none have such a unifying and at the same time dramatic purpose for this anomaly as do the first movements of the 'regressive' String Sextet in A major and a work that in many ways is its formal predecessor, the Piano Quartet in D major. In this study I should like to examine the formal logic of the key-structures of these movements, which gives rise to their unique modified sonata forms.

Dvořák composed his D major Piano Quartet (the first of two works he wrote in this genre) in 1875, the year of the String Serenade and the Fifth Symphony. The quartet is imbued with Dvořák's natural gift for writing chamber music: it contains a kaleidoscope of textures and timbres, and approaches an even distribution of writing among the instruments.

The opening melody outlines the tonic triad while emphasizing the third scale-degree, F# (Ex. 17.1). The inflection of the F sharp minor triad at the beginning of the second measure immediately propagates the Czech flavour of the piece. But more surprising is the sudden modulation to the major submediant, B major, in m. 9. Startling as this may seem, Dvořák has been single-minded about the preparation for the tonicization of B from the start. The F sharp minor harmony, which has been emphasized through the use of metric placement and accents, becomes F sharp major in m. 8, thereby preparing the key of B. In m. 10, the opening motif returns in this new key transformed: originally it began on the first scale-degree of D major, and leapt to the third scale-degree; but here it begins on the fifth scale-degree of B major, and leaps to the tonic. After a mutation to B minor (m. 17), the key of D major returns (m. 26). Thus the brief B major episode recedes, but it leaves the listener to expect some manner of consequence.

The opening key-area, D major, might be said to be related to its subordinate area of B major as an object to its shadow. The shadow, while generated by the object, remains subordinate to it. Its appearance is clearly differentiated from the actual object. Had the B major area been an actual minor-third transposition of the D major area, the result would have been a banal lowering of tension. Instead, the melody thrusts further upward from what was originally the third scale-degree, thereby propelling the piece forward. This situation is similar to that of the openings of two late piano sonatas of Schubert, the G

---

[3] Edward T. Cone, *Musical Form and Musical Performance* (New York, 1968).

Ex. 17.1 Piano Quartet in D major, first movement, opening

major (D. 894) and B flat major (D. 960). The first theme-groups of both of these works are organized in ABA form. In both cases, the B section contains a melody in an indirectly related key that is a subtle transformation of the opening theme.

In the Dvořák quartet, the return to D major in m. 26 is followed by what appears to be a transition, which at m. 45 prepares again the shadow key of B. Measure 54 reveals this to be only a ploy, for an unexpected German augmented sixth chord starts a transition back to the opening theme in D major, which in turn begins a dependent transition (i.e. a transition that begins with the first theme in the original key). The key of A is finally prepared, beginning in m. 85. In Mozartian fashion, Dvořák deceptively touches on A minor before presenting the second theme in A major. The theme is shown in Ex. 17.2. This is a transformation of a motif from the transition section. After a

Ex. 17.2 Piano Quartet in D major, first movement, second theme

thirty-six-measure stretch in the key of A major, the music takes repose on the local subdominant at m. 133 before a short chromatic transition takes place. Its tonal goal, F sharp major (m. 147), is first prepared traditionally through the dominant of the dominant (G♯, B♯, D♯, F♯—m. 142). A linear chromatic passage ensues beginning on the dominant note C♯, and cadences on an F sharp major chord via an Italian augmented sixth. The closing motif in m. 147 (Ex. 17.3) is a hybrid of two previous motifs: it begins like the motif that opened the first transition section (m. 26), and ends like the opening theme. The structural function of the short tonally stable section that follows (fifteen measures) is simply to close in F sharp major, the dominant of the B major shadow key.

In review, not only are the themes of the first group related to the themes of the second group, but the key-areas of the two groups are also related:

Ex. 17.3 Piano Quartet in D major, first movement, closing motif of exposition

the dominant key-areas of both the tonic D major and its shadow key B major are presented in the second group. Because no return to A major is made at the end of the exposition, the resulting form might be considered a three-key exposition with the key-scheme D major–A major–F sharp major, with the shadow key B major subsumed into the larger first key-area, D major. What distinguishes this three-key exposition from those of Schubert is that Schubert's third key (not his middle key) is the dominant. Schubert's outer keys therefore articulate the classical sonata-form model with its tonic–dominant polarity. Dvořák's form, on the other hand, hints more at a double polarity: the first polarity of the tonic D major to its dominant A major; the second of the shadow key B major to its dominant, F sharp major.

The development need not concern us, with the exception of one feature: it contains not one but two false recapitulations, the first in F sharp major (m. 201) and the second in the shadow key of B major (m. 227). A false recapitulation is not an uncommon occurrence, but the second preparation and presentation of the opening theme in the key of B major further correlates the tonic and shadow keys.

The true recapitulation restates the opening theme in the tonic key, followed again by the shadow passage in B major. The transition section begins as before in D major, but here Dvořák wisely eliminates the exposition's lengthy meanderings toward B minor and back to the first theme in D major. Instead, the transition is shortened and recomposed. The ascending chromatic scale that was formerly used to lead back to first theme in the tonic now leads to the second theme in the tonic. From this point until the coda all material is transposed up a fourth from the exposition. The shadow key assumes its position of greatest prominence as the sonata form proper ends in the key of B major. The coda sums up the movement: the tonic key returns, and in mm. 394 ff. the first and second themes are presented simultaneously. A little later, in mm. 418–19, the B minor triad is featured prominently, representing the shadow key's tonic.

From the traditional view of the sonata form, the form of the first movement of Dvořák's Piano Quartet in D major contradicts a fundamental precept of sonata form: Cone's 'sonata principle'. But from a dramatic standpoint that takes into consideration the guidelines that the work itself sets up, the result is fulfilling.

Yet the work is not without its problems of structural balance. First, the lengthy double transition in the exposition is difficult to follow, and the return half-way through of the first theme in the tonic key seems retrogressive. Second, the F sharp major area that closes the second theme-group is prepared so curiously and lasts for such a short while that its integration is dubious.

Lastly, after the extended quasi-developmental transition section, the long development section proper seems laboured.

Dvořák must have nevertheless been pleased with the innovative key-structure of the quartet, because three years later, in 1878, he composed another work whose first movement operates under virtually the same precepts: the String Sextet in A major. Ideas for the ebullient sextet may have occurred to Dvořák while composing his first set of Slavonic Dances, for he composed its first version as soon as he had finished the piano version of the latter.

The first page of the sextet (Ex. 17.4) is virtually identical in structure to the opening of the Quartet. The opening again emphasizes melodically the third scale-degree. A modulation is made in m. 12 to the major submediant, where a transformed version of the first theme begins on the first scale-degree of the new key.[4] The genesis of this key is in the chromatic neighbour-note of the third measure, A♯. The A♯ next becomes harmonic in the bass of m. 6; finally it becomes a diatonic degree of the shadow key in m. 12. (Note also that no chromatic inflection from F sharp major occurs in m. 14, the passage parallel to m. 3.) The developmental Allegro con brio explores other keys before

Ex. 17.4 String Sextet in A major, opening, outer parts only

----

[4] The critical edn. of the Sextet, ed. Otakar Šourek (Prague, 1957), counts the opening upbeat as a measure, so that the first full measure is m. 2. However, I am using the numbering found in most other editions, whereby the first full measure is m. 1.

returning to the first theme in the tonic key (Tempo I, m. 40). Here a cadence with the tonic triad in second inversion seamlessly joins the tonic return to the preceding developmental passage. This section becomes a dependent transition.

Besides the buffering second-inversion chord at the return to the key of A, there are two other elements that render this two-part transition fundamentally different from that of the quartet. In the quartet, the presentation of the shadow key is followed immediately by a return to tonic. After a transition passage that seems to prepare for a return of the shadow key, the tonic key returns yet again. In the sextet, the shadow key is not immediately followed by the major tonic, but by a fleeting tonic minor. The transition passage mutates only once to A major, at the return of the opening theme, before preparing for the second key-area. The resultant structure is more compact than that of the quartet.

In the measures that lead up to the second theme-group in the sextet, Dvořák prepares neither E major (the dominant of the tonic A), nor C sharp major (the dominant of the shadow key F sharp). Instead, he prepares the unlikely key of G sharp minor. However, by the third beat of the second theme (Ex. 17.5), G sharp minor is lost.

Ex. 17.5 String Sextet in A major, first movement, second theme

What results is a section whose tonal centre floats between E major, its submediant C sharp minor, and its mediant, G sharp minor. Beveridge's chief complaint against the sextet is that the internal tonal structure of this group 'makes a mockery of its clearly delineated tonal frame'.[5] But Dvořák achieves a self-contained drama here through the continual alternation of these three key-areas: a tonal circularity whose effect is fundamentally different from either a stable one-key theme-area or a forward-propelled transition section. Three diatonic third-related keys compete to be the tonal centre. Shortly after the section begins to repeat (m. 79), E major seems to get the upper hand, but in the ensuing 'fortissimo molto tranquillo' at m. 89 a broad theme derived from the opening melody appears in the key of C sharp major (the dominant

---

[5] 'Romantic Ideas', 261.

Ex. 17.6 String Sextet in A major, first movement, closing theme

of the shadow key). See Ex. 17.6. The relationship of this theme to the opening melody is highlighted by the echo of the latter in the lower strings. Like the closing section in the quartet, this passage is based largely on tonic and dominant harmonies, though it differs from the quartet in its cantabile character and extended length.

The development section, much shorter than that of the quartet, contains no false recapitulations. In the recapitulation, the second theme (transposed down a fifth from the exposition) begins in C sharp minor, but soon finds the tonic A major and its submediant F sharp minor contending for tonic status. This area becomes an actual secondary development section that explores many keys before settling in the shadow key F sharp major at the 'molto tranquillo'. After such rhythmic and tonal restlessness, this closing section seems all the more tranquil, and the shadow key all the more like home. The shadow key has indeed reached its apotheosis. As in the quartet, Dvořák brings back the original tonic in a formal coda. The tonal transition to the tonic, leading also to a return of the opening theme, is again made smooth by the tonic 6–4 pedal.

Charles Rosen, in the introduction to his book *Sonata Forms*, proposes that 'an investigation of the function of the elements will enable us to examine the work of all the composers of a period without regard to the deviations from a supposed norm'.[6] I propose that the function of the second theme-area of the sextet is to challenge playfully our notions of key-stability before surprising us with the dominant key-area of the shadow key. The result appears not at all like the product of a fatigued Dvořák, as Beveridge suggests, but like that of the gleeful Dvořák who, in his good nature, mocks only our expectations.

[6] Rev. edn. (New York, 1988), 7.

18

The 'Uncomfortable' Dvořák: Critical Reactions to the First Performances of his Symphonic Poems in German-Speaking Lands

KARIN STÖCKL-STEINEBRUNNER
TRANSLATED BY DAVID R. BEVERIDGE

MUSICAL criticisms are often influenced by local musical and cultural politics, by the predilections and creeds of the reviewers themselves, and even to some extent by world politics. Moreover the image constructed by the critics, of the composer and the work, necessarily reflects just these critical stances more than any impression arising from an unprejudiced hearing of the music itself. How much Dvořák's works, regardless of their actual traits, have been subjected to a pre-formed critical opinion is shown perhaps most clearly by the reviews of his symphonic poems.

In this chapter I have omitted the discussions of Dvořák's last symphonic poem, *Píseň bohatýrská* (A Hero's Song), because it is constructed on a different type of model from his other works in this genre, and also because this last symphonic poem was received in a quite special way owing to its close temporal proximity and similarity of title to Richard Strauss's *Ein Heldenleben*. This almost purely external similarity led naturally to a comparison of the two works—a comparison that was often problematic in terms of their content.

Included in the present study, on the other hand, are the four symphonic poems all based on ballads by Karel Jaromír Erben, namely *Vodník* (The Water-Goblin), *Polednice* (The Noon Witch), *Zlatý kolovrat* (The Golden Spinning-Wheel), and *Holoubek* (The Wild Dove). Dvořák wrote these works

This chapter originated in a presentation (in Ger.) at the Dvořák conference held during the Saarland Festival in Saarbrücken, June 1991, pub. as 'Der unbequeme Dvořák: Reaktionen der Musikkritik auf die ersten Aufführungen der Sinfonischen Dichtungen im deutschsprachigen Raum', *Dvořák-Studien*, ed. Klaus Döge and Peter Jost (Mainz, 1994), 190–6. It has also appeared in a slightly different version, in Czech trans. by Jitka Slavíková, as 'Nepohodlný Dvořák', *Hudební rozhledy*, 14/8 (1991), 369–72.

in rapid succession in the year 1896,[1] thus after his nine symphonies, in the time of his full recognition and maturity when the critics had become accustomed to viewing him in a particular light. This circumstance is especially important for the reception of the symphonic poems and needs to be kept in mind from the beginning.

The reviews discussed here relate to the first performances of these four works in German-speaking lands, occurring from late 1896 to early 1900 in Vienna, Frankfurt, and Berlin, and are found in *Musikalisches Wochenblatt: Organ für Musiker and Musikfreunde* of Leipzig, *Signale für die Musikalische Welt*, also of Leipzig, *Die Zeit* of Vienna, and *Die Gegenwart: Wochenschrift für Literatur, Kunst und öffentliches Leben* of Berlin. The reviews are unsigned; in cases where the city of publication is different from that of the performance, the reviewer presumably is a correspondent who resides permanently in the city of the performance. Table 18.1 gives, for each work, the place and date of performance; the reviewing journal; and volume and issue numbers, date, and page number(s) of the review.

Table 18.1. The first performances of four Dvořák symphonic poems in Germany and Austria

The Water-Goblin			
Vienna	22 Nov. 1896	*Signale*[a]	54/70 (22 Dec. 1896), 1107
		MW[b]	28/23 (3 June 1897), 316 f.
The Noon Witch			
Vienna	20 Dec. 1896	*Signale*	55/9 (29 Jan. 1897), 132
		MW	28/23 (3 June 1897), 316 f.
The Golden Spinning-Wheel			
Frankfurt	29 Dec. 1896	*Signale*	55/5 (15 Jan. 1897), 68 f.
Vienna	3 Nov. 1901	*Die Zeit*[c]	29–30/371 (9 Nov. 1901), 91
		Signale	59/64 (13 Nov. 1901), 1019
		MW	33/3 (9 Jan. 1902), 39 f.
The Wild Dove			
Vienna	3 Dec. 1899	*Die Zeit*	21–2/271 (9 Dec. 1899), 157
		Signale	58/7 (15 Jan. 1900), 105
		MW	31/8 (15 Feb. 1900), 99 f.
Berlin	2 Mar. 1900	*Signale*	58/23 (10 Mar. 1900), 359
		MW	31/36 (21 June 1900), 347 f.
		Gegenwart[d]	59/27 (7 July 1900), 14

[a] *Signale für die Musikalische Welt* (Leipzig).
[b] *Musikalisches Wochenblatt: Organ für Musiker und Musikfreunde* (Leipzig).
[c] *Die Zeit* (Vienna).
[d] *Die Gegenwart: Wochenschrift für Literatur, Kunst und öffentliches Leben* (Berlin).

[1] *The Water-Goblin*: 6 Jan.–11 Feb.; *The Noon Witch*: 11 Jan.–27 Feb.; *The Golden Spinning-Wheel*: 15 Jan.–25 Apr.; *The Wild Dove*: 22 Oct.–18 Nov.

In comparing all of these critiques, one finds that many reviewers had problems, some of a general nature and some more particular, with Dvořák's symphonic poems. Let us begin with the particular problems; essentially, there are two of these. The first could be called 'Vienna'. To put it succinctly, it consists in the fact that in Vienna some of the critics not only have their own reservations about the works, but they speak also of a reserved reaction on the part of the public. Moreover when the public seems to exhibit enthusiasm, that too apparently contributes to a sense of concern. Thus while the *Signale* attests to 'hearty applause' (*reichen Beifall*) at the Vienna performance of *The Wild Dove*, the *Musikalisches Wochenblatt* reporting on the same concert says the piece 'had to content itself with a *succès d'estime*, and even that not undisputed'.

What background such extraordinary contradictions may have had is betrayed by the very same reserved critique from the *Musikalisches Wochenblatt*, which says that the 'unadulterated Czech' sound of Dvořák's music could 'only arouse divided loyalties in a Vienna concert-hall, given the current political relations'. The resentments of the German-speaking population of Vienna against the national self-interests springing up in the non-German parts of the empire had been brought to a preliminary crisis by the Badeni Language Decree of 5 April 1897, intended as a friendly gesture toward the Czech segment of the population.

The second particular problem in the Vienna critiques could be called the 'Mahler problem'. Gustav Mahler, who had conducted the première of *The Wild Dove* just mentioned, was quite controversial in his position as director of the Vienna Philharmonic Concerts, and viewed by some as radical and unsound in his advocacy of modern music. When the conservative Josef Hellmesberger took over the directorship, just before the Vienna première of *The Golden Spinning-Wheel*, reviewers focused attention on the implications of this shift. Thus the review of this concert in the *Signale* is nothing more than an appreciation of the return to normality represented by Hellmesberger's leadership; musical discussions are totally absent here. And even the more progressive *Musikalisches Wochenblatt* devotes a large segment to this change of director, lamenting the conservative slant of the programming for the new season and calling the followers of Hellmesberger a puritanical community that had greeted gladly the total absence of a 'progressive' (*Fortschrittspartei*) composer like Liszt or Strauss. This certainly did not indicate an especially auspicious starting-point for a symphonic poem, which according to the *Musikalisches Wochenblatt* remained in the programme only to provide a cloak of liberalism with regard to the Viennese mix of nationalities. The *Musikalisches Wochenblatt* also lamented the loss of the 'almost demonically seductive mental power' (*suggerirenden Geisteskraft*) of a Mahler, which always

held out the prospect of relatively new, highly interesting experiences, even
if they occasionally provoked disputes—as was often the case with regard to
the modern 'touching up' (*Übermalung*, or *Übermahlerung* as the Viennese liked
to say) of classical originals, a practice much favoured by Mahler.

Mahler had to struggle during his whole period of office in Vienna with
attacks against his manner of programming as well as his performance of the
chosen pieces, so that the works and composers he had selected were always
burdened with the double-edged gift of divided critical opinions. Common
belief held that Mahler the composer could establish through music a wilful
(*willensmäßig*) impetus, which he tried to create also as a conductor and
believed to be present in the music that he chose to perform. Mahler's programming was inclined toward the (new) expressive music (*Ausdrucksmusik*),
and that meant for him, after the works of Beethoven, mainly the so-called
New Germans, the composers of programme music. On this level lay also
Mahler's interest in Dvořák's music, which brings us to the general problems
that some critics had with Dvořák's symphonic poems.

The concept of the 'wilful' was formulated in the reception of Beethoven's
works, in which music was divided into two camps whose different argumentative models are applied, often unconsciously, to the music of the nineteenth century even today. Beethoven was, according to the musical attitude
of a given listener, interpreted as classical or romantic, that is, either as a con-
summate model for formal construction, whose music generated its own principles of representation in the free play of periods and symmetries, or on the
other hand as a creative genius, implying the brooding procreation of music
in an act subjected to wilful, critical reflection.

The classical line of reception adheres to the idea, found from Kant through
Hegel to Schopenhauer, that pure instrumental music is the one art in a position to represent directly the Absolute, the Ideal, the art that operates from
itself, beyond all thought-structures, that symbolizes what is natural as
opposed to the contortions of conceptual thought. This attitude extended past
the end of the nineteenth century, even for example to Schoenberg, and was
coupled with the understanding of inspiration as a gift that the Will cannot
assess.

On the other hand the view of Beethoven as a contemplative artist, working on and with the material, seeking and rejecting, achieving expression
beyond the individual instance, the concrete substance, led to the 'reflective'
practitioners of programme music. These seek to make the unspeakable speak
not by way of principle and proportion, therefore not in pure instrumental
music, but rather by way of the concrete (*Konkretion*) and therefore the conceptual.

Dvořák's main advocates in Vienna were above all the conductor Hans Richter, who performed his works again and again, and also to a decisive degree Johannes Brahms and Eduard Hanslick, starting with their function as members of the commission that awarded the stipend of the Austrian Ministry of Culture for the rising generation of Czech artists, which Dvořák received several times, the first in 1875. All of these men were at home in the paths of absolute music. Thus Dvořák was performed, was stimulated to the composition of works, and from the beginning of his public career was received as a composer of absolute music, and the conservative critics, orientated toward absolute music, took him unto themselves as a member of their party.[2] The *Musikalisches Wochenblatt*, in its review of *The Noon Witch* at Vienna, calls Dvořák the 'composer claimed by the conservative critics for themselves as the most absolute of all living absolute musicians'.[3]

Thus arose the image of Dvořák—partly supported by the composer himself—as the 'Bohemian *Musikant*', as one creating from blind inspiration without consciousness of his own genius. In reality Dvořák was already an ardent Wagnerian in the 1860s and studied closely the scores of the so-called New German School, with general results in his treatment of the orchestra as well as specific results in the form of quotations. Moreover, he hardly ever gave over a major work for final publication without revision, reworking, and critical inspection. And finally, a major portion of his work was in fact text-related. Despite all of this, the category in which Dvořák was already judged in the 1890s was that of the naïve instrumental composer. The terminology used here has its roots in the much deeper level of musical thought mentioned above, which linked the mystification of the unconscious to the idea of the absolute, and was opposed to conscious, concrete, conceptual reflection.

In an obituary notice published on 21 May 1904 in *Die Zeit*, Dvořák is characterized as a 'great artist in the field of absolute music', in which lay 'his most distinctive individual importance' (*eigenste Bedeutung*), and, carrying this idea further, it is said that 'the epithet "naïve" ' could be applied to him 'in its highest and purest sense', for music came to him 'naturally, spontaneously and self-evidently' (*selbstverständlich*), and was completely 'given over to instinct'. This view of Dvořák climaxes in the telling pronouncement: 'Music is with him only music, nothing more and nothing less.' It has 'elemental power', and that means that it springs forth from him as though without any action on his part. 'The personality seems here only an executant and vehicle for the work,

---

[2] Mahler may be counted among Dvořák's supporters at a later date, and he of course represented a more progressive orientation, but this was after Dvořák's image had already been formed.

[3] 'von der conservativen Kritik als der absoluteste aller absoluten lebenden Musiker für sich in Anspruch genommene Componist'.

who bows before the loftiness of his mission with a childlike and calm devotion, indeed perhaps isn't even aware of its true greatness.'[4]

As late as 1911, in Schoenberg's *Harmonielehre*, we find the creed that corresponds well to this common perception of Dvořák:

The artist's creative process is instinctive. Consciousness has little influence on it. He feels as though what he does were dictated to him—as though he does it in accord with the will of some power in him whose laws he does not know. He is only the executant of a will hidden from him, of instinct, of the unconscious in him.[5]

The label 'Bohemian *Musikant*' is used as a contrast to the 'philosopher' composers, the 'reflective' (*reflektierend*)—meant in a derogatory way—practitioners of programme music. To the extent that romantic thought had stylized music as a counter-world, the distortions of the real world should not be reflected in it; it should be purely separated from the thought-ghost of conceptuality. In the struggle between naturalness and the artificial striving for effect, in which tone-painting and the pursuit of concrete expression were generally decried, Dvořák was celebrated by the devotees of harmony as a firmly planted, folkish *Musikant*. Even the oft-cited national colour came to the aid of the conservatives, who praised as the 'secret' of Dvořák's art precisely the achievement and development of this 'wonderful affiliation of the Slavic temperament with the old classical tradition of absolute music'.[6]

Naturally it could not have fitted well with this stylization toward classical simplicity—not to say *naïveté*—achieved via the concept of inspiration, when Dvořák (suddenly, it seemed) took up the 'affected' programme music manner. Regarding the performance of *The Wild Dove* in Vienna, the critic of the *Musikalisches Wochenblatt* wrote: 'It is remarkable that the full-blooded musician Dvořák, who in his earlier works represented so well the prototype of the cheerfully creating 'Bohemian *Musikant*', gives himself over now more and more to the camp of the reflective programmatic composers.'[7] This ostensibly new inclination of Dvořák's is explained as resulting from a nationalistic wish to tell tales well known in the Bohemian vernacular. The

---

[4] 'Die Persönlichkeit scheint hier bloß ein Vollzieher und Träger des Werkes zu sein, der mit einer kindlichen und ruhigen Ergebenheit vor der Höhe seiner Mission sich beugt, ja ihre wahre Größe vielleicht nicht einmal kennt.' F. V. Krejčí, Prag, 'Der Fall Dvořák', *Die Zeit*, 503, 93–4.

[5] 'Das Schaffen des Künstlers ist triebhaft. Das Bewußtsein hat wenig Einfluß darauf. Er hat das Gefühl, als wäre ihm diktiert, was er tut. Als täte er es nur nach dem Willen irgendeiner Macht in ihm, deren Gesetze er nicht kennt. Er ist nur der Ausführende eines ihm verborgenen Willens, des Instinkts, des Unbewußten in ihm.' *Harmonielehre* (Leipzig and Vienna, 1911), 464.

[6] 'wundervolle Angliederung des slavischen Temperaments an die alte klassische Tradition der absoluten Musik'. 'Der Fall Dvořák'.

[7] 'Es ist merkwürdig, daß der Vollblutmusiker Dvořák, welcher in seinen früheren Werken so recht das Prototyp des schaffenslustigen "böhmischen Musikanten" vorstellte, sich neuerdings immer häufiger ins Lager der reflectirenden Programm-Componisten begibt.'

national colour in the music was received in part even joyfully and was adeptly linked with the stereotypical image of Dvořák, but the folk-tale programme on the other hand was often enough given as reason for a negative critique.

Here the circle is closed again in another way, bringing us back again to Vienna as a focal point. The Vienna performances, as compared with those in Berlin or even Frankfurt, were indeed judged with greater reservation or even negatively. And now we can add another explanation for this: Vienna was not only the city of national conflicts, but also the high temple of those who pledged themselves to so-called autonomous music. Thus even the general problems in the criticism of Dvořák's symphonic poems are in large part associated with Vienna. A telling contrast to the typical Viennese reactions is the verdict of the *Musikalisches Wochenblatt* regarding the performance of *The Wild Dove* in Berlin:

. . . programme music in the best sense of the word. In an exceedingly skilful way, the Bohemian master has utilized to good account the fairy-tale material on which the piece is based; in the formal structure, in the treatment of the orchestra, everywhere we detect the hand of a master. On the basis of striking themes, the whole is constructed very effectively in only one movement, whose tonal speech is throughout uncommonly lively and fitting in expression, interesting and characteristic in tone-colour.[8]

Likewise the critique in the *Signale* of the same performance calls *The Wild Dove* a 'piece rich in fantasy, splendidly colourful' (*phantasiereiches, farbenprächtiges Stück*).

In the positive reviews of the symphonic poems, the textual basis is neither praised nor criticized, but in those that are reserved or negative it proves to be an annoyance. The strategy by which the reviewers hope to dismiss the uncomfortable new Dvořák, without damaging the familiar one, is as simple as it is transparent: the displeasure voiced with the work is founded and justified in the selection of the text. The content of the text engenders incomprehension, even loathing, and accordingly it is denounced as the starting-point of all censure. The *Signale* describes the *Noon Witch* in Vienna as a symphonic poem with 'a gruesome, completely unmusical programme, which to preserve the honour of the composer should have remained unperformed'. Regarding *The Wild Dove* in Vienna, the critic calls the fairy-tale simply 'a ghostly horror'. The *Musikalisches Wochenblatt* speaks, regarding *The*

---

[8] '. . . Programmmusik im besten Sinne des Wortes. In überaus geschickter Weise hat der böhmische Meister den zu Grunde liegenden Sagenstoff musikalisch verwerthet, in der formalen Gestaltung, in der Behandlung des Orchesters, überall verspüren wir die Meisterhand. Auf markanten Themen baut sich das Ganze in nur Einem Satz sehr wirkungsvoll auf, und ungemein lebendig und treffend im Ausdruck, interessant und charakteristisch im Klangcolorit ist durchgehends die Tonsprache desselben.'

Water-Goblin and *The Noon Witch* in Vienna, of 'musical child-killing', which causes the works to sound 'not overpoweringly demonic, but rather just simply painful'. It further calls these symphonic poems 'only musically interesting, aesthetically offensive curiosities', and comes to the conclusion that Dvořák 'will never receive laurels in German concert-halls for this genre [programme music], unless he chooses less repulsive material'.

That this argument is only an excuse is shown not least by the parallels the critics themselves cite between the allegedly offensive programmaticism and certain 'classical' pieces, even when this argument is used to diminish the compositional worth of Dvořák's works. In its review of *The Golden Spinning-Wheel* in Vienna, the *Musikalisches Wochenblatt* makes reference to a parallel between the explanation of the action by the spinning-wheel and the 'singing bone' (playing the role of the nemesis) in Mahler's *Das klagende Lied*. In the same journal's review of *The Water-Goblin* and *The Noon Witch*, the relationship of the latter's content to 'Der Erlkönig' is emphasized, as well as the relationship of Dvořák's choral ballad *Svatební košile* (The Spectre's Bride, written in 1884 on a text of Erben), to the Leonora story. The ghostly passage in *The Wild Dove* could, in the opinion of the same journal, come from Weber's 'Wolf's Glen Scene' in *Der Freischütz*.

The contradiction between the assessment of the Erben ballads and of other subjects closely related in content is obvious. Fairy-tales are relatively gruesome not only in Slavic lands—we know the evil stepmother only too well, and the other protagonists in the Grimm fairy-tales likewise show few scruples in the choice of means to their ends. Thus for example in the story of Hänsel and Gretel not only does the witch want to fatten the boy in order to roast him at the appropriate time; in the end she herself is burned in the oven, which occasions general rejoicing. The decisive success of the opera *Hänsel und Gretel* by Humperdinck shows that in this time subjects like this were no deviation; rather, in the case of Dvořák, the choice of text only served the anti-programmatic critics as a peg on which to hang their verdict against these pieces, and against programmatic music in general, without impugning the composer.

Despite their origins in folklore the subjects are seen as inhibiting the natural freshness of the music, as is emphasized by the review in *Die Zeit* of the Vienna performance of *The Golden Spinning-Wheel*. To be specific, the reviewer on the one hand thinks that Dvořák 'loses the best part of his individuality as soon as he rejects national colour'. But on the other hand he believes that 'the programme prevents a free flow of his fantasy', so that 'finally the less successful part' so predominates 'that it makes its mark on the whole symphonic poem. . . . It really strikes one as odd, to see a composer so exceedingly happy in his style work against the nature of his being through the whole expanse of a large work.'[9] But in the end this is paradoxical: whoever would compose in a national style must write pure intrumental music.

The postulate that such programmes are not suitable for musical representation was often used as either a conscious or an inner argumentative model, but did not really hide the fact that Dvořák was being castigated for his apparent emulation of the New Germans, in particular Richard Strauss. One need only consider the revealing warning that Hanslick felt he had to give in his discussion of *The Water-Goblin*, that Dvořák should not sink into Strauss's domain.[10]

The critiques of the Berlin performances, here including the *Hero's Song*, as well as those from Frankfurt, at least praise the capable, effective, and masterful process of development in the music as well as the instrumentation and deployment of tone-colour, but several of the Viennese critics are reserved even in these respects. Since orchestrational skill is often associated with Wagner and with Richard Strauss—see for example the review in the *Musikalisches Wochenblatt* of *The Water-Goblin* and *The Noon Witch*—the praise of orchestral technique actually changes in part to a reproach. The masterful sound-technique (*Klangtechnik*) reveals itself as a pretext for criticism, used to further underpin the overall rejection. Thus the review just mentioned finds the 'tone-painting' (*Tonmalerei*) to be 'suspicious' (*bedenklich*); *Die Zeit* holds the musical depiction of the programme in *The Wild Dove*, largely dependent on instrumentation, to be too detailed and too detrimental to the sense of musical unity. Brilliant instrumentation in symphonies and concertos—by all means, yes; music as expression in the form of programme-bound compositions, which represent only the consequences of exhaustion of technical means: O God, no!

So we find contradictions even within the individual critiques. One can see clearly whose spiritual child a given reviewer is when the same review that holds the programme to be represented in such detail that the public and even the composer himself get lost in it speaks, on the other hand, of the total construction of the work as a 'successful treatment and intertwining of two contrasting subjects: a funeral march and a merry wedding dance'.

Thus the reception of the first performances of Dvořák's symphonic poems

---

[9] 'Dvořák . . . verliert den besten Theil seiner Eigenart, sobald er das nationale Colorit verschmäht. . . . Da nun das Programm ein freies Ausströmen seiner Phantasie nicht zuläßt, so überwiegt schließlich der minder gelungene Theil derart, daß er der ganzen symphonischen Dichtung seinen Stempel aufdrückt. Es berührt in der That eigenthümlich, einen in seiner Art so überaus glücklichen Componisten in einem großen Werke die ganze Zeit hindurch gegen die Natur seines Wesens arbeiten zu sehen.'

[10] 'E-moll-Symphonie und *Der Wassermann* von A. Dvořák', in Hanslick, *Am Ende des Jahrhunderts (1895–1899): Musikalische Kritiken und Schilderungen* (Der modernen Oper, viii; Berlin, 1899), 217.

in the German-speaking lands reflects the party strife between the adherents of absolute music on the one hand and those of the 'progressive party' on the other. These works could be praised only if one was in a position to acknowledge mastery of the symphonic poem by one marked as a composer of absolute music, without having to engage in verbal gymnastics and evasive action because of their programmatic alignment.

19

Music and Words in Dvořák's Symphonic Works: A Nietzschean Perspective on the 'New World' Symphony and *The Wild Dove*

DAVID M. SCHILLER

ANTONÍN DVOŘÁK'S reputation as a conservative composer no longer obscures his versatility and originality. John Clapham presents Dvořák as a versatile and progressive composer, who 'came round full circle to Wagnerian methods late in his career, by which time he was well-equipped to use them successfully'.[1] By this time, however, Wagner himself was dead, and Friedrich Nietzsche (1844–1900) had begun to publish his objections to Wagner's aesthetics, a development that Dvořák followed with intense interest as the controversy unfolded. Though Wagner's music remained influential, his aesthetics were no longer necessarily avant-garde.

In this chapter I consider the relationship between musical form and extra-musical content in Dvořák's 'New World' Symphony of 1893 and his symphonic poem *Holoubek* (The Wild Dove) of 1896. In these late works Dvořák left behind the polemics of the 'Music-of-the-Future' controversy. No longer constrained by the theoretical opposition between absolute and programme music, he arrived at a flexible compositional technique equally adaptable to the symphony and the symphonic poem. An understanding of Nietzsche's aesthetics will help to clarify Dvořák's compositional approach in these late works and provide a point of departure for the discussion.

The title of my chapter alludes to Friedrich Nietzsche's essay 'Über Musik und Wort', (1871). However, I would also like to acknowledge Miroslav Černý's more recent claim to the title in 'Zum Wort-Ton-Problem im Vokalwerk Antonín Dvořáks', in *Music and Word: Brno IV 1969* (Colloquia on the History and Theory of Music at the International Musical Festival in Brno, iv), ed. Rudolph Pečman (Brno, 1969), 139–57. I would like to thank Alan Houtchens for reading this chapter in an earlier version and David Beveridge for his editorial suggestions.

[1] 'Antonín Dvořák', *The New Grove Late Romantic Masters*, ed. Stanley Sadie (New York, 1985), 237. See also Ch. 15 above.

Primary evidence of Dvořák's interest in Nietzsche comes from the reminiscences of Josef Michl, who studied composition with Dvořák around the year 1901:

I saw that the Master was very interested in Nietzsche: He put one question after another which exhausted practically all I knew about the philosopher and a good third of his questions remained unanswered. Finally the conversation was concentrated on the essay 'Nietzsche versus Wagner' and here Dvořák said: 'I think nobody in the world has written anything like it *against* Wagner. Nietzsche must have had a great brain and in many respects he is right. But in some things he does him injustice and great injustice. You know you can talk a great deal about Wagner and you can criticize a great deal, too—but he is undefeatable. What Wagner did nobody did before him and nobody can take it from him. Music will go its way, will pass Wagner by, but Wagner will remain.'[2]

As Dvořák was clearly aware, there was a marked shift in Nietzsche's attitude toward Wagner's music between the 1870s, when 'Die Geburt der Tragödie' (The Birth of Tragedy) (1872) and 'Richard Wagner in Bayreuth' (1876) were published, and the 1880s, when 'Der Fall Wagner' (The Case of Wagner) (1888) and 'Nietzsche contra Wagner' (1889) appeared. The apparent contradiction between Nietzsche's earlier enthusiasm for Wagner and his later criticism of the composer made it difficult to abstract a consistent and positive aesthetic from his scattered comments on music. Dvořák's own frustration in the face of this difficulty can be inferred from his exhaustive interrogation of Michl and from Michl's inability to answer his questions.

Michl stops short of telling us in what respects Dvořák thought Nietzsche was right, and I will not try to show that Nietzsche's thought was a direct influence on Dvořák's compositional practice. However, as recent scholarship on Nietzsche has begun to reveal the coherence of Nietzsche's aesthetics, it does seem fair to review the musical issues that are raised in Nietzsche's writings and to reconsider Dvořák's music in the light of these issues. Chief among them are the relationship between absolute and programme music, the relationship between art music and folk-music, the aesthetic necessity of periodic phrasing and lucid form, and the aesthetic requirement that music remain pleasurable.

An article by Frederick R. Love published in 1977 argues strongly for the recognition of a positive aesthetic principle underlying Nietzsche's rhetoric, a principle denoted by the terms 'Musik des Südens', 'südliche Musik', and 'mein Süden in der Musik', which occur repeatedly in Nietzsche's writings

---

[2] 'Z Dvořákova vyprávění' (From what Dvořák Told), *Hudební revue*, 7 (1914), 440–6, as trans. in *Antonín Dvořák: Letters and Reminiscences*, ed. Otakar Šourek, trans. Roberta Finlayson Samsour (Prague, 1934), 170.

PLATES

PLATE 1. V. E. Nádherný, *Dvořák Conducts the Orchestra at the World's Fair in Chicago*, 1893. Drawing 38 × 23 cm. Courtesy the Antonín Dvořák Museum, Prague.

PLATE 2. Ludwig Michalek, portrait of Dvořák, 1891. Pastel. 72.5 × 52 cm. Courtesy the Prague Conservatory of Music, No. 261/1.

PLATE 3. Max Švabinský, *Antonín Dvořák, 1898*. Pen drawing, 33.3 × 26.5 cm. Courtesy the National Gallery, Prague, No. K-29.284.

PLATE 4. Max Švabinský, *Antonín Dvořák, 1901*. Lithograph, 60 × 48 cm. Courtesy the Antonín Dvořák Museum, Prague.

PLATE 5. Max Švabinský, Dvořák, standing figure. Pen drawing, 74.5 ×
43 cm. Courtesy the National Gallery, Prague, No. K‑6605.

PLATE 6. Max Švabinský, sketch for *Czech Spring* (writers), 1910. Oil on canvas, 105 × 100 cm. Municipal Museum, Prague, No. M-538. Reproduction courtesy the National Gallery, Prague, negative 75231.

PLATE 7. Max Švabinský, sketch for *Czech Spring* (artists and composers), 1910. Charcoal drawing, 105 × 97 cm. Municipal Museum, Prague, No. M-539. Reproduction courtesy the National Gallery, Prague, negative 75232.

throughout the 1880s. In English, the phrase 'Southern Music' serves to identify the principle. Love explains:

[Southern music] is that for which Nietzsche came to feel deep sympathy as his refuge
from Wagnerian music. . . . It hardly needs to be said that Southern Music for
Nietzsche was not necessarily music of the geographical South. Although the term
itself was generated out of the traditional polarization of 'northern' indistinctness,
romanticism and metaphysics versus the clarity, classicism and earthbound realism of
the South (a favorite cliché of German writers, at least since Goethe) . . . it is opposed
not so much to the North as such in his usage, but to all that is *German*.[3]

On the level of the phrase or period, 'Southern Music' is characterized by
rhythmic clarity, as Nietzsche explains in 'Nietzsche contra Wagner', the one
work by Nietzsche that Michl identifies by name as a subject of Dvořák's
interest: 'My foot feels the need for rhythm, dance, march. . . . It demands of
music first of all those delights which are found in *good* walking, striding,
dancing. . . . Richard Wagner wanted a different kind of movement; he over-
threw the physiological presupposition of previous music. Swimming,
floating—no longer walking and dancing.'[4] On the level of the complete
work, clarity of form is the corresponding virtue, as Nietzsche explains in
'The Case of Wagner': '[The music of *Carmen*] builds, organizes, finishes; thus
it constitutes the opposite of the polyp in music, the "infinite melody".'[5]

An earlier text, but one central to the reassessment of Nietzsche's musical
thought, is the essay 'On Music and Words'. Possibly intended as a section of
'The Birth of Tragedy', it was left incomplete and unpublished in 1871. For
Carl Dahlhaus, 'On Music and Words' formulates no less than 'a comprehensive concept of "absolute" music which reveals the latent unity of musical aesthetics in the nineteenth century'.[6] From his reading of Nietzsche and
Wagner, Dahlhaus derives the insight that the distinction between absolute
and programme music rests not on the presence or absence of a sung text or
programme but on an aesthetic judgement as to 'whether music was the
"founding" and "motivating" element or whether it was "founded" in and
"motivated" by other elements'.[7]

In 'The Birth of Tragedy', Nietzsche arrived at the premise that folksong is
'the original melody', that '*melody is therefore primary and universal*' (emphasis

---

[3] 'Nietzsche's Quest for a New Aesthetic of Music: "Die allergrößte Symphonie", "Großer Stil",
"Musik des Südens"', *Nietzsche-Studien*, 6 (1977), 180–1.

[4] See *The Portable Nietzsche*, trans. and ed. Walter Kaufmann (New York, 1968), 664 and 666.

[5] '*The Birth of Tragedy*' *and* '*The Case of Wagner*', trans. with commentary by Walter Kaufmann (New
York, 1967), 157.

[6] 'The Twofold Truth in Wagner's Aesthetics: Nietzsche's Fragment "On Music and Words"', in his
Between Romanticism and Modernism: Four Studies in the Music of the later Nineteenth Century, trans. Mary
Whittall (Berkeley and Los Angeles, 1980), 39.

[7] Ibid. 34.

in the original), and that 'melody generates the poem out of itself'.[8] 'On Music and Words' expands on this point, mentioning various concrete manifestations of the principle of absolute music, including the lyric poetry of ancient Greece, the folksongs of the people, 'a Palestrina mass, a Bach cantata, a Handel oratorio', and the choral finale of Beethoven's Ninth Symphony.[9] It is on the significance of Beethoven's Ninth that Nietzsche's aesthetics diverge most sharply from Wagner's. In opposition to Wagner's thesis in 'The Art Work of the Future' that the Ninth Symphony signalled the end of absolute music, Nietzsche insists that the words of Schiller's 'Ode to Joy' are irrelevant to the music's effect and that Beethoven's interest lies exclusively in the *sound* of the human voice:

What does Beethoven say himself when he introduces this choral ode with a *recitativo*? 'O friends, not these sounds, but let us strike more agreeable and joyous ones!' More agreeable and joyous ones! For that he needed the persuasive tone of the human voice; for that he needed the innocent air of the popular song. Longing for the most soulful total sound of his orchestra, the sublime master reached not for words but for a 'more agreeable' sound, not for concepts but the sound that was most sincerely joyous. And how could he be misunderstood?[10]

In both 'The Birth of Tragedy' and 'On Music and Words', absolute music and lyric poetry hold a privileged place. Folksong is regarded as the prototype and source of absolute music and, in a symphonic context, the 'innocent air of popular song' is likewise assimilated to the realm of absolute music. Dvořák's remarks on Schubert's use of the 'song-like' in a symphonic context provide a subtle counterpoint to Nietzsche's remarks on Beethoven. Concerning Schubert's 'Unfinished' and 'Great' C major Symphonies, Dvořák wrote: 'What is perhaps most characteristic about them is the song-like melody pervading them. [Schubert] introduced the song into the symphony, and made the transfer so skillfully that Schumann was led to speak of the resemblance to the human voice (*Ähnlichkeit mit dem Stimmorgan*) in these orchestral parts.'[11] According to Nietzsche, Beethoven had incorporated into his Ninth Symphony 'the innocent air of popular song' by using the human voice as an orchestral instrument. For Dvořák, on the other hand, Schubert had 'introduced' the song in the symphony—in *his* Eighth and Ninth—by writing instrumental parts that resembled the human voice. And speaking for himself in the same article, which coincidentally was published shortly after

---

[8] Nietzsche, *'The Birth of Tragedy' and 'The Case of Wagner'*, 53.

[9] 'On Music and Words', trans. Walter Kaufmann, repr. in Dahlhaus, *Between Romanticism*, 113–15.

[10] Ibid. 113.

[11] 'Franz Schubert', *The Century Magazine* (July 1894), repr. in John Clapham, *Antonín Dvořák: Musician and Craftsman* (New York, 1966), 300–1.

the première of *his* Ninth Symphony, 'From the New World', Dvořák wrote, 'I cordially acknowledge my great obligations to [Schubert].'[12]

In Nietzsche's later writings, his privileging of the lyric and of absolute music would be reinforced by an explicit polemic against the dramatic and the theatrical, summed up in his famous 'three demands' from the conclusion of 'The Case of Wagner':

That the theater should not lord it over the arts.
That the actor should not seduce those who are authentic.
That music should not become the art of lying.[13]

Dvořák did not share Nietzsche's hatred of the theatre; still, in his essay on Schubert, the lyrical and dramatic also appear in opposition when he characterizes Schubert's genius as 'lyrical, and not dramatic, or, at any rate, not theatrical'.[14] In his ninth and last symphony, 'From the New World', Dvořák himself had written in the lyric tradition of Schubert, taking not the romantic lied but the folksong-like melody as his raw material and model. On the whole, Dvořák's genius too might at this point in his career be characterized as lyrical and not dramatic.[15]

But Dvořák's career did not end with the 'New World'. Among other works, the symphonic poems based on ballads by Karel Jaromír Erben and the operatic masterpiece *Rusalka* were yet to come. When Dvořák made his last conducting appearance with the Czech Philharmonic in April of 1900, he chose to represent himself with the last of the Erben works, *The Wild Dove*.[16] With it he programmed Brahms's 'Tragic Overture', Schubert's 'Unfinished', and Beethoven's Eighth. The programme suggests that Dvořák was conscious of having blurred the distinction between absolute and programme music, and that he now saw the lyrical and dramatic modes of expression as complementary, not opposed. In order to demonstrate this complementary relationship, I will next discuss in general terms the relationship of the 'New World' Symphony and *The Wild Dove* to extramusical, folkloristic sources, and then compare specific sections of the two works that illustrate the principles at work in both.

Assessing the 'New World' Symphony from a formal point of view, David Beveridge concluded that it represented the end-point of a gradual process of clarification and simplification in Dvořák's handling of sonata form. According to Beveridge, 'The pursuit of "local color" . . . *required* Dvořák to

---

[12] Ibid. 300.   [13] *'The Birth of Tragedy' and 'The Case of Wagner'*, 180.

[14] 'Franz Schubert', 298.

[15] Clapham extends this generalization to Dvořák's operas: 'Lyrical rather than dramatic elements are . . . generally more prominent in his operas.' See 'Antonín Dvořák', in *The New Grove Late Romantic Masters*, 241.

[16] See Clapham's account in *Dvořák*, 156.

write simply at least part of the time. But perhaps even more importantly it *allowed* him to write simply. The "American" traits provided a kind of musical exoticism which could substitute for the complex structures of mainstream Romanticism as a source of musical interest.'[17] Beveridge's overall thesis that Dvořák manifested an ongoing concern with clarification and distillation in his sonata-form compositions remains persuasive. However, his characterization of the 'American' traits in the 'New World' as exotic and, therefore, outside mainstream Romanticism should be qualified. Classicalizing and miniaturizing tendencies had always been present within Romanticism, and emulation of folk models was central to Czech Romanticism from its very beginnings. Milada Součková's study of the Czech romantic writers has shown that they eagerly embraced the folksong as a poetic model from their earliest attempts to create a modern Czech literature. Taking their inspiration from the German philosopher-poet Johann Gottfried Herder (1744–1803), whose work became widely known to Czech intellectuals in the first two decades of the nineteenth century, they produced collections of contemporary rural folksongs, and composed new poetry in ballad style; one talented poet even forged two pseudo-medieval manuscripts that were widely accepted and admired as genuine.[18] Given Nietzsche's conception of the folksong as a prototype of absolute music, both the pervasive presence of the folksong in Czech Romanticism and Dvořák's interest in American folksong appear in a new light.

In a letter to a friend in Prague dated 27 November 1892, Dvořák wrote that the Americans were looking to him for guidance in the task of creating an American national music: 'The Americans expect great things of me and the main thing is, so they say, to show them to the promised land and kingdom of a new and independent art, in short, to create a national music. If the small Czech nation can have such musicians, why could not they, too, when their country and people is so immense.'[19] A few weeks later, in an interview with the *New York Herald* regarding the 'New World' Symphony, he explained how he had gone about the task of creating a model of national music for American composers: 'I have simply written original themes embodying the peculiarities of the Indian music, and using these themes as

---

[17] 'Romantic Ideas', 378.

[18] Milada Součková, *The Czech Romantics* (The Hague, 1958), 28. The name of the forger-poet is Václav Hanka; the two forgeries are known as the 'Králové dvůr' and 'Zelená hora' MSS. Dvořák set six poems from the former to music (No. 30 in Burghauser's catalogue, pub. variously as Opp. 7, 12, and 17).

[19] Letter to Josef Hlávka. 'Amerikáni očekávají veliké věci ode mne a hlavní je, abych prý jim ukázal cestu do zaslíbené země a říše nového samostatného umění, zkrátka vytvořit muziku národní!! Když prý malý národ český má takové muzikanty, proč by oni to mít nemohli, když jejich zem a lid je tak obrovský!' See *Antonín Dvořák: Korespondence a dokumenty—Kritické vydání* (Antonín Dvořák: Correspondence and Documents—Critical Edition), ed. Milan Kuna et al., iii (Prague, 1979), 162; trans. per *Antonín Dvořák: Letters and Reminiscences*, ed. Otakar Šourek, trans. Roberta Finlayson Samsour (Prague, 1954), 152.

subjects, have developed them with all the resources of modern rhythms, harmony, counterpoint and orchestral color.'[20] Dvořák's discussion of themes, subjects, and especially the process of thematic development situates the 'New World' squarely in the classical symphonic tradition.[21]

Given Dvořák's explicit concern for making 'From the New World' symphonic in its developmental procedures, it is noteworthy that the two inner movements were associated in his mind with ideas for a vocal work. In the same interview for the *New York Herald*, he said:

The second movement is an Adagio [*sic*: it is marked 'Largo']. But it is different from the Classic works in this form. It is, in reality, a study or sketch for a longer work, either a cantata or opera, which I purpose writing and which will be based upon Longfellow's 'Hiawatha'. I have long had the idea of someday utilizing that poem. . . . The scherzo of the symphony was suggested by the scene at the feast in 'Hiawatha', where the Indians dance, and is also an essay which I made in the direction of imparting the local color of Indian character to music.[22]

Various secondary sources claiming direct information from the composer have associated the second movement specifically with the description of Hiawatha's wooing of Minnehaha, or, alternatively, with Minnehaha's funeral.[23] In a detailed discussion of the sketches for the symphony and their association with folk material, Antonín Sychra focuses primarily on the funeral interpretation for the Largo, and quotes the following passages from *Hiawatha* in reference to the second and third movements respectively:

---

[20] 'Dvořák on his New Work', *New York Herald* (15 Dec. 1893), as repr. in John Clapham, *Dvořák* (New York, 1979), 202; also repr. in *Dvořák in America: 1892–1895*, ed. John C. Tibbetts (Portland, Oreg., 1993), 363.

[21] For an explicit statement of the link between thematic development and absolute or 'classical' music, see the remark by Franz Liszt (or Princess Carolyne Sayn-Wittgenstein) in Franz Liszt, 'Berlioz und seine Haroldsymphonie', *Neue Zeitschrift für Müsik*, 43/8 (17 Aug. 1855), 81. It reads: 'In der sogenannten classischen Musik ist die Wiederkehr und thematische Entwicklung der Themen durch Regeln bestimmt' (In so-called classical music the return and thematic development of the themes is determined by rules). The passage is excerpted and trans. in 'The "Music of the Future" Controversy', in *Music in the Western World: A History in Documents*, ed. Piero Weiss and Richard Taruskin (New York, 1984), 383.

[22] See Clapham, *Dvořák*, 202. After completing the symphony, Dvořák did indeed make some sketches for specific scenes for an opera to be based on *The Song of Hiawatha*, including settings of words, but these sketches are not clearly related to the music of the symphony. See John Clapham, *Antonín Dvořák: Musician and Craftsman* (New York, 1966), 281–2.

[23] For a careful consideration of the merits of the two interpretations, see Michael Beckerman, 'Dvořák's *New World* Largo and *The Song of Hiawatha*', *19th-Century Music*, 16/1 (summer 1992), 35–48. Regarding *Hiawatha* and the symphony's scherzo movement, see also Beckerman, 'The Dance of Pau-Puk-Keewis, the Song of Chibiabos, and the Story of Iagoo: Reflections on the Scherzo of Dvořák's Symphony *From the New World*', in *Dvořák in America*, 210–27.

Minnehaha's funeral (from book xx)

Then they buried Minnehaha;
In the snow a grave they made her,
In the forest deep and darksome,
Underneath the moaning hemlocks;
Clothed her in her richest garments,
Wrapped her in her robes of ermine,
Covered her with snow, like ermine;
Thus they buried Minnehaha.

Pau-Puk-Keewis's dance (from book xi)

First he danced a solemn measure
Very slow in step and gesture,
In and out among the pine-trees,
Through the shadows and the sunshine,
Treading softly like a panther.
Then more swiftly and still swifter,
Whirling, spinning round in circles,
Leaping o'er the guests assembled,
Eddying round and round the wigwam,
Till the leaves went whirling with him,
Till the dust and wind together
Swept in eddies round about him.[24]

Sychra must be credited with establishing the central importance of Dvořák's interest in folk materials as a common bond between his symphonies and symphonic poems. However, he sees Dvořák's interest in folklore as evidence of the composer's social realism and democratic nationalism, while I am considering it in the narrower context of Nietzschean aesthetics. As a result my interpretation tends in an opposite direction from Sychra's. Where Sychra sees the folksong as lending specificity of reference and emotional content to Dvořák's absolute music, I, taking my cue from Nietzsche, see Dvořák reshaping the folksong into symphonic form, while at the same time remaining faithful to its true nature as absolute music. But from either perspective, the special fascination of the 'New World' Symphony is that the vaguely programmatic references to funeral and dance in its second and third movements closely parallel the more explicitly representational settings of the funeral rites and wedding festivities in *The Wild Dove*, giving us a legitimate basis for comparison.

---

[24] Antonín Sychra, *Antonín Dvořák: Zur Ästhetik seines sinfonischen Schaffens*, trans. Gert Jäger and Jürgen Morgenstern (Leipzig, 1973), 300–3.

In his discussion of folksong in 'The Birth of Tragedy', Nietzsche supports his view that 'melody generates the poem out of itself' by referring specifically to *Des Knaben Wunderhorn*: 'Anyone who in accordance with this theory examines a collection of folksongs, such as *Des Knaben Wunderhorn*, will find innumerable instances of the way the continuously generating melody scatters image sparks all around, which in their variegation, their abrupt change, their mad precipitation, manifest a power quite unknown to the epic and its steady flow.'[25] In other words, an originative melodic and lyric flame may be inferred from the spark-like verbal images of folk poetry. Longfellow's *Hiawatha* may well have impressed Dvořák as an American folk-ballad in the mould of *Des Knaben Wunderhorn*, or for that matter, of Czech folk poetry.

Karel Jaromír Erben (1811–70), whose poem 'Holoubek' is the literary source of *The Wild Dove*, was a major figure in Czech Romanticism. He collected more than 2,200 folksongs, preserving the tunes as well as the words of many of them, and established the Czech fairy-tale as a literary genre. His own collection of ballads, *Kytice z pověstí národních* (A Bouquet of National Tales), originally published in 1853, provided Dvořák with the text of his choral work *Svatební košile* (The Spectre's Bride), as well as the programmes for the symphonic poems *Vodník* (The Water-Goblin), *Polednice* (The Noon Witch), *Zlatý kolovrat* (The Golden Spinning-Wheel), and *Holoubek* (The Wild Dove).[26]

In a synopsis printed in the published version of the score, Dvořák summarized the programme of *The Wild Dove* as follows:

1. ANDANTE, MARCIA FUNEBRE [m. 1]: Weeping and sobbing, a young widow follows the coffin.
2. ALLEGRO–ANDANTE [m. 70]: A young lad meets her and persuades her to cease her mourning and marry him.
3. MOLTO VIVACE, LATER ALLEGRETTO SCHERZANDO [m. 143]: The young widow soon stops her grieving and celebrates a merry and mirthful wedding with the young lad.
4. ANDANTE [m. 464]: The grave of her first husband, whom she had poisoned, is covered with grass, above his head an oak tree grows up, and from its branches the mournful cooing of a wild dove resounds through the country. This grieving sound penetrates to the heart of the treacherous woman, who, driven by the pangs of conscience to madness, finds death in the waves.
5. ANDANTE, TEMPO I. (EPILOG) [m. 499].[27]

---

[25] 'The Birth of Tragedy' and 'The Case of Wagner', 53.

[26] As a matter of coincidental interest, Longfellow's dates are 1807–82, and *Hiawatha* was pub. in 1855, just two years after the first edn. of Erben's *Bouquet*; Dvořák, not unreasonably, might have regarded Longfellow as the American Erben.

[27] See the critical edn. of *Holoubek*, ed. and with an introd. by Otakar Šourek, trans. Dr L. Dorůžka (Prague, 1955), p. xv. I have added measure nos. showing where the tempo indications occur in the score.

In addition, Dvořák copied out eighteen of the poem's twenty-six stanzas directly into his manuscript score, apparently reiterating the representational aspect of the music. By comparing Dvořák's treatment of the Andante funeral-march section of *The Wild Dove* with his treatment of the Largo in 'From the New World', and his treatment of the Molto vivace–Allegretto scherzando with the Scherzo of the 'New World', we can obtain a clearer sense of the representational dimension of the symphony and of the aesthetic values of both works.

Not only did Dvořák specify a *marcia funèbre* character for the opening of *The Wild Dove*, he also wrote the words 'Funeral procession' over mm. 5–7, and beneath this heading he copied out the first two stanzas of Erben's poem:

1. Around a narrow
   churchyard path,
   she came this way weeping
   the young, pretty widow.

2. She wept, she pined
   for her husband;
   for the last time
   she accompanied him this way.[28]

The firmly pulsed tempo emphasized by the dotted rhythms, the minor mode, and the muted horns and muffled timpani leave little room for doubt as to what is going on. Yet for all its programmatic aura, the movement's most literal reference is to a milestone of absolute music, Beethoven's Third Symphony. This is not to deny a further reference to the literally functional music of the French funeral-march tradition; however, it is the transformation of the convention into musically autonomous form that defines the second movement of the 'Eroica'. The rising minor tetrachord in *The Wild Dove*'s first theme (Ex. 19.1*a*) refers to the subject of the fugato section of the second movement of Beethoven's Third (*b*). *The Wild Dove*'s C minor tonality, too, reinforces its connection to this most famous of all symphonic funeral marches. To make matters more interesting, however, the opening period of *The Wild Dove* is immediately repeated in a transposition to C sharp minor (mm. 24 ff.). In this key the same upward tetrachord, with an added appoggiatura, occurs as a principal theme in the slow movement of the 'New World'. (Ex. 19.2). Here the starting rhythm is the same as with Beethoven. Thus the Beethovenian gesture works in two directions. On the one hand it adds a programmatic nuance to our interpretation of the 'New World' Largo; on the other hand it suggests that the opening section of *The Wild Dove* is itself a symphonic slow movement.

A similar connection can be made between the Scherzo of the 'New World' and the third section, Molto vivace, of *The Wild Dove*, both of which

[28] 1. 'Okolo hřbitova | cesta úvozová; | šla tudy, plakala | mladá, hezká vdova. 2. Plakala, želela | pro svého manžela: | neb tudy naposled | jej doprovázela.' The complete Czech text of Erben's 'Holoubek' is supplied as an insert to the score in the critical edn. (ibid.). The Eng. version offered here for the passage in question should be regarded only as an indication of the poem's contents.

Ex. 19.1 *a*. Dvořák, *The Wild Dove*, first theme; *b*. Beethoven, 'Eroica' Symphony, second movement

Ex. 19.2 Dvořák, Symphony No. 9, second movement

are also linked to Beethoven. Here the point of departure is the Scherzo of Beethoven's Ninth Symphony, with its explosive introduction of falling fourths and fifths similar, as many commentators have observed, to those that open the Scherzo in 'New World'. We may add that in both cases the loud introduction leads to a hushed main theme that strikes the dominant three times before resolving to the tonic (Ex. 19.3).

Ex. 19.3 *a*. Beethoven, Symphony No. 9, second movement; *b*. Dvořák, Symphony No. 9, third movement

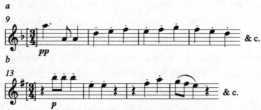

The third section of *The Wild Dove* also makes a token gesture toward the Scherzo of Beethoven's Ninth with its initial rhythmic motif of a dotted crotchet followed by a quaver and a crochet. Though these allusions to the Ninth are admittedly less persuasive on purely musical grounds than the references to the 'Eroica' funeral march cited above, I believe a similar complex of associations is at work. Indeed, the point is not to establish that the Beethoven Scherzo is a direct model for either of the Dvořák works, but rather to suggest that Beethoven's 'raising' of dance to the level of absolute music may operate at a distance to influence our perception of the scherzi in both the 'New World' and *The Wild Dove*.

The third section of *The Wild Dove* is identifiable as a symphonic scherzo by its tempi and dance-like character, and it fits the conventional scherzo–trio–scherzo form of a symphonic scherzo, with the trio coming at 'Un poco meno mosso' (m. 294) and the scherzo returning at Tempo I (m. 376). The opening tempo of this section is identical to that of the Scherzo of the 'New World' (Molto vivace), and if one accepts Clapham's observation that a *meno mosso* tempo is required for the Trio in the 'New World', then the tempi are identical for the two trio sections as well.[29] Clearly the third section of *The Wild Dove* is much weightier than it needs to be to fulfil its dramatic function in the symphonic poem. Though it is over 300 measures long, comparable to the Scherzo in the 'New World', it represents only two stanzas of the poem:

8. Around the merry
   churchyard way,
   they go this way,
   bridegroom and bride.

9. There was a wedding
   it was noisy and festive,
   the bride in the embrace
   of a new bridegroom.[30]

Formal, indeed symphonic, considerations seem to be uppermost in Dvořák's mind, as Šourek observed in his introduction to the work in the critical edition. In fact, in the two paragraphs that Šourek devotes to the form of *The Wild Dove*, he offers three different formulations of the relationship between its programme and its musical form. First, he refers to 'the five paragraphs into which Dvořák divided the main ideas of the work' as '*a sufficient basis* [my emphasis] for the organically accomplished form of the work'. Next he proposes that the subject '*makes it possible* [my emphasis] to give the work a marked and plastic shape organized in accordance with the cyclic form of a symphony'. Finally, he concludes: 'The whole composition, the fruit of a genial musical-architectonical inspiration, vaults like a boldly extending arch, which, after the introductory mourning music culminates in the broad melodic lines of dance frolic, to return in the conclusion to the mood of the beginning, even if in a different conception and colouring.'[31] Ultimately, the programme of *The Wild Dove* exerts no more control over the form of the

---

[29] *Antonín Dvořák*, 91.

[30] 8. 'Okolo hřbitova | veselejší cesta: | jedou tudy, jedou | ženich a nevěsta. 9. Byla svatba, byla | hlučná a veselá: nevěsta v objetí | nového manžela.'

[31] Introd. to Dvořák, *Holoubek* (see n. 27), pp. xi–xii. Janáček employed a similar organic metaphor in his analysis of *The Wild Dove*. See Leoš Janáček, 'A Discussion of Two Tone Poems Based on Texts by Karel Jaromír Erben: *The Wood Dove* and *The Golden Spinning Wheel*', trans. Tatiana Firkušný, in *Dvořák and his World*, ed. Michael Beckerman (Princeton, NJ, 1993), 264.

work than allusions to *Hiawatha* exert over the form of the 'New World' Symphony. It is the five-paragraph programme that reflects the musical architecture of the tone-poem, rather than the other way round. Music is the founding and motivating element.

All this Nietzsche would certainly approve, for formal lucidity and rhythmic clarity are precisely the aesthetic criteria that he had insisted on in 'The Case of Wagner' and 'Nietzsche contra Wagner'. In summary and in conclusion, we can recognize that Dvořák continued in *The Wild Dove* the process of distillation and clarification that David Beveridge saw as culminating (in so far as it was manifested in sonata form) in 'From the New World'. What is most progressive about *The Wild Dove* is not anything Wagnerian, but the formal lucidity, marching and dancing rhythms, and song-like melodies that are typically Dvořák's own. By moving beyond the oppositions of the Brahms–Wagner controversy, as Nietzsche had done in his aesthetic thought, Dvořák asserted his own aesthetic principles.

20

Dvořák and Elgar

GRAHAM MELVILLE-MASON

BRITISH scholars of Dvořák have made passing reference to Elgar playing under Dvořák at the Worcester and Birmingham festivals of 1884 and 1886 respectively, and Jitka Slavíková also has mentioned this in her new study *Dvořák a Anglie* (Dvořák and England).[1] English writers on Sir Edward Elgar (1857–1934), from the composer's friend William Henry Reed to the present-day scholar Jerrold Northrop Moore, have made slightly more reference to their composer's deep interest in the music of Dvořák. Further examination of surviving written evidence, as well as the music itself, shows Elgar to have sustained a special place in his heart for Dvořák and his music. This is to be found in Elgar's own writings, recollections of his contemporaries, and the works of Dvořák that Elgar chose to conduct in his later life, as well as those in which he performed and upon which he subsequently commented very favourably. To this we can add the evidence of the influence of Dvořák in a number of Elgar's works from the late 1880s onwards. Of course, unlike the Brahms–Dvořák relationship, the traffic between Dvořák and Elgar was all one-way. As far as I am aware, Elgar's name does not feature in any writings of Dvořák.

As early as 1884, when Elgar was 27 years old, we find him writing most enthusiastically about his discovery of the Bohemian composer's music. In a letter of 28 September from Worcester, he wrote to Dr Charles William Buck (1852–1932), a medical doctor from Yorkshire, keen amateur violist and cellist, and early champion of Elgar's music, 'I wish you could hear Dvořák's music. It is simply ravishing, so tuneful and clever and the orchestration is wonderful: no matter how few instruments he uses it never sounds thin. I cannot describe it, it must be heard.'[2]

This letter followed only days after Dvořák had conducted his Stabat Mater and Sixth Symphony at the Three Choirs Festival in Worcester during the second of his nine visits to England between 1884 and 1896. Elgar had played

[1] (Prague, 1994).   [2] Percy M. Young, *Elgar O.M.: A Study of a Musician* (London, 1955), 56.

in the Festival Orchestra since 1878 and was promoted from the second to the first violin section in 1881. By 1884 he shared the third desk with Charles Hayward and so would have been in quite close proximity to the conductor.[3] The impact of Dvořák, both the man and the musician, was great and, as is seen from Elgar's letter to Buck, immediate, although, as far as is known, the two men never met face to face nor corresponded.

Elgar had started to include Dvořák's first set of Slavonic Dances in his own local orchestra's concert programmes straight after he had first heard them at the Three Choirs Festival in Worcester in 1881, that is only three years after Dvořák had orchestrated them.[4] From that time, as the early Elgar scholar Percy Young says, 'the warmth of this new Bohemian music infused his whole nature and his creative genius saw more clearly in what direction his objective lay.'[5] From then on Elgar always expressed a great affection for Dvořák's music, as is evident from the chronicle of his musical activities throughout the rest of his life, as well as from those clearly discernable influences to be found in his own music.

Just how early in his life Elgar became aware of Dvořák's music is not recorded. It may have been earlier than the festival of 1881. Northrop Moore has drawn attention to Elgar's five early Intermezzi for wind quintet, written in the spring of 1879, and comments on the style of the last of these as being a mixture of Schubert and the 'homely strains' of Dvořák.[6] Whether Elgar could have known any of Dvořák's music so early is uncertain; the Moravian Duets and the first set of Slavonic Dances had been published by Simrock in 1878, and on 15 February 1879 August Manns conducted the Slavonic Dances Nos. 1–3 at the Crystal Palace in what was probably the first public performance of Dvořák's music in England. At that time Elgar was living in Worcester, but he did travel to London from time to time if concerts interested him.

It seems that the 27-year-old Elgar may have been too reserved to address the 43-year-old composer and conductor at Worcester in 1884, since Elgar was virtually unknown as a composer at that time, although he had written a few instrumental and vocal pieces. (His first composition to bring him any wide public recognition was his 'Salut d'amour' of 1888.) A chance for Elgar to meet Dvořák might have occurred on the Wednesday before the concert in 1884, when Charles Pipe—Elgar's brother-in-law—gave a dinner party to which Three Choirs musical worthies were invited. However, Moore tells us

---

[3] J. Northrop Moore, *Edward Elgar: A Creative Life* (Oxford, 1984), 109.

[4] The Three Choirs Festival is the oldest and longest-surviving music festival in European history, having been founded in 1715. It takes place alternately in one of the English West-Country cathedral cities of Gloucester, Hereford, and Worcester.

[5] *Elgar O.M.*, 56.

[6] *Edward Elgar*, 84.

that 'The great composer was elsewhere in Worcester that evening.'[7] But Elgar's awareness of Dvořák's presence was strong, on and off the podium. He records the contrast of seeing 'among those placidly English faces' Dvořák's 'fierce peasant's jowl . . . striding down Foregate Street' and it seeming 'as much out of place in Worcester as did his fervent Slavonic music when heard amidst the sedate hymn-tunes of the cantatas then being written for the festivals by English composers.'[8]

Edward Wulstan Atkins, son of Elgar's great friend Sir Ivor Atkins, has been generous in making his father's notes available to me. He says that he remembers his father and Elgar often talking about the festival of 1884 and how Dvořák made such a great impression on them both—not only as a composer and in his handling of orchestration, but also as a conductor. He says that it was clear to him as a young man that Elgar was highly stimulated by this first direct encounter with Dvořák and that it was not only the undoubted highlight of the whole festival for him but had a lasting effect on him as a composer.[9]

Another long-standing close friend of Elgar was William Henry Reed, a noted solo violinist and leader of the London Symphony Orchestra. He too made an interesting observation concerning the immediate effect of the visit in 1884: 'One of the results of this visit of Dvořák and the impression made upon Elgar by the Stabat Mater was that he began to devote himself more seriously to the composition of music for his [own parish] church of St. George.'[10]

Dvořák made the fifth of his nine English visits in October of 1886, principally to conduct the première of the oratorio *Svatá Ludmila* (St Ludmila) at the Leeds Festival[11] but going on to Birmingham later in the month to conduct his Sixth Symphony in D. Again Elgar was in the first violin section of the orchestra, but even though two years older than at the Worcester encounter, he seems not to have introduced himself to Dvořák. That he was excited at the prospect of playing under Dvořák again is clear from more letters to his friend Charles Buck. In a letter from Worcester, dated 14 October, seven days before the Birmingham concert, he wrote, 'Dvořák is coming to conduct his Symphony in D at Birmingham on Thursday, so we are on our mettle somewhat.'[12] After the event he wrote again, on 15 November, 'Stockley's first orch. concert was grand; Dvořák (I intersperse a few accents

[7] Ibid. 110. It seems that his invitation to the official reception was also overlooked.

[8] R. Burley and F. Carruthers, *Edward Elgar: The Record of a Friendship* (London, 1972), 78.

[9] Letter from E. W. Atkins to the present author, 7 July 1984.

[10] *Elgar*, rev. edn. (London, 1949), 20.

[11] Founded in 1858, triennial from 1880 and biennial from 1970.

[12] *Letters of Edward Elgar and Other Writings*, ed. Percy M. Young (London, 1956), 26.

but forget the real ones) came & conducted his symphony and Fanny Davies played Schumann's p.f. concerto.'[13]

The *Birmingham Daily Post* of 22 October gave a very good review of the Stockley concert of the previous day, commenting:

When the renowned Bohemian master entered the orchestra he was received with a hearty outburst of applause. It was evident before many bars of the symphony had been executed that a perfect understanding existed between the composer-conductor & his orchestra, and that the latter were on their mettle, determined, apparently, that Birmingham players should come out of the ordeal with triumph . . .

and concluding that the orchestra 'never had been heard to greater advantage than in Dvořák's [*sic*—without *háček* on 'r'] symphony last night.'

By the end of 1886, Brahms had become an international giant for Elgar. He wrote an article for the *Malvern Advertiser* of 21 December that year, prior to a concert of Brahms's music to be given there in the following January. In Brahms, the enthusiastic Elgar saw none of the 'expression of natural dialect (the charming characteristic of lesser men: Gade, Dvořák, Grieg)' as he put it.[14] But, for all that, the evidence in his correspondence and in his music that he conducted shows that there was never any lessening of the esteem in which Elgar held Dvořák's music.

Elgar, as he commented himself, was much captivated by Dvořák's great sense of orchestration, the clever juxtaposition of instrumental colours, the placing of the instrumental parts, and the variety in selection of individual instrumental groups—so avoiding the orchestral thickness of some other nineteenth-century composers. For example, Dvořák never automatically used four horns if three would do, as we see in works like the Serenade in D minor, the Mass in D major, and the Violoncello Concerto in B minor. Such clarity Elgar applied in many of his own orchestral works, demonstrating an understanding of Dvořák's methods as early as the overture *Froissart* (Op. 19) of 1890. Elgar referred to Dvořák's horn writing in a letter to Walford Davies in 1909.[15]

As is seen from Reed's remark quoted above, the effect of Dvořák upon Elgar's choral writing was immediate after he heard the Stabat Mater in 1884, but it became more profound after he experienced *Saint Ludmila* two years later. This is audible in Elgar's works involving chorus and orchestra from the 1890s—*The Black Knight* (1890–2), *King Olaf* (1894–6), and *From the Bavarian Highlands* (1895).

---

[13] *Letters of Edward Elgar and Other Writings*, ed. Percy M. Young (London, 1956). William Cole Stockley was the promoter of this concert series and conductor of this Birmingham orchestra.

[14] Moore, *Edward Elgar*, 117.

[15] *Edward Elgar: Letters of a Lifetime*, ed. J. Northrop Moore (Oxford, 1990), 209.

Of course, Elgar's best-known choral work is *The Dream of Gerontius* (Op. 38, 1899–1900), and something must be said about the connection it has with Dvořák for reasons other than stylistic influence. The original proposal that Dvořák should set Cardinal Newman's text as a commission from the Birmingham Triennial Festival (founded in 1768) seems to have come about during a Birmingham visit, according to an account by the Revd Robert Eaton which was in the possession of W. H. Reed (now unfortunately lost):

Antonín Dvořák happened to be in Birmingham to conduct a performance of one of his works and visited Cardinal Newman at the Oratory after attending High Mass. When he left, the Cardinal presented him with a copy of *Gerontius* and Dvořák left in high glee, saying that it would inspire him. It was indeed suggested to the Festival Committee that he should be invited to write a setting for the 1888 Birmingham Festival. This they refused to do, however, partly on financial grounds, but moreso on religious ones, for they found that the poem was 'too Catholic'. It was felt at the time by many people that a great opportunity had been missed by the rejection of this idea and there the matter rested for a time, although the wish was being constantly expressed that *Gerontius* should be set to music by some great musician, and, indeed, it began to be rumoured that Elgar was thinking of the subject.[16]

This was probably unlikely at that time, since it is thought that Elgar knew the text only after he had been given a copy on his wedding-day in 1889, by Father Thomas Knight, the priest at Worcester who had instructed the future Mrs Elgar in the Catholic faith, and that it was this man who put the idea of setting it into Elgar's head, even helping him to adapt the text. Indeed, the first evidence of Elgar setting any music for this work does not appear to date from before January 1900.

The Dream of Gerontius does not seem to have been proposed to Elgar as a commission for the Birmingham Festival until 1899. Rosa Burley and Frank Carruthers, in *Edward Elgar: The Record of a Friendship*, comment that Elgar was rather scared that the subject had excessively Roman Catholic overtones and therefore was not likely to be welcomed by the Protestant community. He told them 'in fact that Dvořák, who had planned a setting of the work for the 1888 Festival, had been discouraged from making it for this very reason.'[17] And so Dvořák had turned down the request. However, all these festivals regularly performed and commissioned Catholic Masses and Requiems—including Dvořák's own Requiem for Birmingham in 1891. Of course, in the three years since 1888, Church of England attitudes (if not more extreme Protestant

---

[16] Reed, *Elgar*, 59. According to information from Jarmil Burghauser, Dvořák's copy of the poem is currently kept at the composer's country home in Vysoká; it bears the dedication 'Antonín Dvořák | with the kindest wishes and respects | of Cardinal Newman', dated 24 Oct. 1886. Dr Burghauser is currently working on a hypothesis that Newman's poem was the inspiration for Dvořák's Requiem.

[17] p. 134.

opinion) had begun to change sufficiently to make *Gerontius*, if not innocu-
ous, at least far less offensive and incense-laden to Protestant ears than it would
have been when Dvořák had first considered it. What is interesting in the
context of this work is a newspaper cutting at Elgar's birthplace which reports:
'The matter, indeed, was about fifteen years ago discussed between [Cardinal
Newman] and Dr. Dvořák, who afterwards found the subject too placid and
lyrical for his special style.'[18]

Of course, it is possible to make detailed comparisons between the scores
at various points in specific works by Dvořák and Elgar. This would require
more space than is available here. However, as a guide to further study, there
are a number of parallels which do repay closer examination in matters of
form and orchestration in particular, as well as some occasional thematic similarities. These are offered as a starting-point.

The concertos for violin and for cello are a case in point. Perhaps the two
finest concertos for the cello are those of Dvořák and Elgar, and there can be
little doubt that Elgar had Dvořák's B minor Cello Concerto in mind (as well
as Schumann's Cello Concerto—as Tovey has pointed out) when writing his
own. Among Elgar's writings is an account of him hearing the Dvořák concerto performed under Rodewald at Brighton on 28 May 1899,[19] although he
did not write his own concerto for the instrument until 1919. Indeed, it must
have been a strong catalyst for Elgar, still retaining his youthful enthusiasm for
the Bohemian master. He chose also a minor key (E minor). In both works
the solo instrument is heard throughout and the orchestral parts are laid out
so that the lower parts never submerge or obscure it. The parallels of approach
in the final movements of each also serve to emphasize the connection: both
nostalgically recall earlier themes from the slow movements toward the ends
of their respective finales.

Elgar chose the key of B minor for his other concerto, the Violin Concerto
of 1909–10. His 'nobilmente' theme in the slow movement has more than an
echo of a theme from the slow movement of Dvořák's Violin Concerto in A
minor of 1880, as may be seen in Ex. 20.1.

The early overture *Froissart* does sound like a 'mixture of Dvořák with short
but vivid bursts of the real Elgar', as Michael Kennedy calls it.[20] However, the
bombastic 'Empire Elgar' (often thought of in connection with his name,
although this was not his true nature) is little heard in Dvořák, even though
Alec Robertson could hear a parallel in the ending of Dvořák's symphonic
poem *Píseň bohatýrská* (A Hero's Song) of 1897 with some of the patriotic
writing of Elgar.[21]

[18] Moore, *Edward Elgar*, 291.   [19] Reed, *Elgar*, 58.
[20] *Portrait of Elgar*, 3rd edn. (Oxford, 1987), 49.   [21] *Dvořák*, rev. edn. (London, 1964), 156.

Ex. 20.1 *a*. Elgar, Violin Concerto, slow movement; *b*. Dvořák, Violin Concerto, slow movement

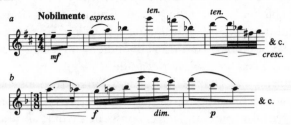

On 31 March 1892 Elgar began work on his Serenade in E minor for string orchestra, and here we find more parallels with Dvořák, whose own Serenade in E major dates from May 1875. The 'string serenade' concept was one shared also with Tchaikovsky and many other European composers of the second half of the nineteenth century, as well as later with Dvořák's fellow countrymen Janáček and Suk and Scandinavians like Dag Wiren.[22] To cite just two comparisons between the examples of Dvořák and Elgar, consider the two Larghetto slow movements and the way the opening themes of each work return toward the end of their respective finales.

Soon after Elgar's marriage in May 1889, he and his bride moved to London and were quickly caught up in the musical life of the capital. They attended concerts conducted by Hans Richter in the St James's Hall, at the second of which Dvořák's Symphonic Variations of 1877 was played. Elgar had written in variation form in a number of works by that time but never in a symphonic way. In 1897 Hubert Parry had written his Symphonic Variations in E minor, also possibly influenced by Dvořák's set. It is doubtful whether Elgar heard the première of this work, given at the Philharmonic Society's concert on 3 June 1897, as it seems that he was living in Malvern throughout May and June of that year. (He conducted at Worcester on 4 May, and spent the weekend of 5 June in Hereford.) Although the Enigma Variations did not appear until 1898–9, it is questionable whether he had a further opportunity of hearing Parry's new composition, but acquaintance with Dvořák's work undoubtedly sowed the seeds in Elgar's mind and, as Northrop Moore says, showed the possibilities of a long series of variations 'capped with an extended finale'.[23]

Internal parallels between the two works can be observed: for example, Dvořák's Variation 19 holds a surprise when he brings in a graceful waltz in B flat major which has little connection with the work so far but which he then chooses to develop considerably over the next five variations. Compare this

---

[22] See Graham Melville-Mason, *The Bohemian, Moravian and Slovak Contribution to the European String Orchestra Repertoire* (Edinburgh, 1977).

[23] *Edward Elgar*, 133.

with Elgar's introduction of his Variation 10 ('Dorabella') and its contrast with the melodic basis of much of what has gone before. The evidence of Elgar's letters to his publisher Jaeger of the Novello firm (Dvořák's British publisher!) shows that initially Elgar was thinking of calling his work Symphonic Variations, and not until 28 April 1899 does the word 'enigma' enter into the correspondence. Even then it is not as a title.[24]

Both Schumann and Dvořák had greater long-term influences on Elgar than did Wagner or Brahms. Elgar's instrumentation, his aesthetic approach, his romantic lyrical expression and contrasts in rhythm all feature in both Schumann and Dvořák. Some examples of this can be found in comparing Elgar's approaches with, say, the initial climax in the opening movement of Dvořák's Seventh Symphony in D minor or, again, with the passage toward the end of the finale of the Eighth Symphony in G—both of which might just as well have been scored by Elgar. Michael Kennedy has pointed out also the remarkable similarity to Elgar in the slow movement of Dvořák's Fourth Symphony in D minor of 1874, which, he says, 'might almost be by Elgar and contains an extraordinary anticipation of the "New Faith" theme in *The Kingdom* (1901–6)'.[25]

Both Dvořák and Elgar were symphonists, and both wrote concertos for violin and cello, concert overtures, and symphonic poems, as well as large-scale choral works. Some other points of comparison may be made between Dvořák's Slavonic Dances and Elgar's Bavarian Dances, or Dvořák's cantata *Svatební košile* (The Spectre's Bride) and Elgar's *King Olaf* or *Caractacus*. In chamber music Elgar was less prolific in his mature years than Dvořák, and he did not turn to opera as Dvořák had done, except at the very end of his life with the unfinished *Spanish Lady*. However, as a young man he had partaken in much domestic and local chamber music-making, which gave him an experienced hand when writing for small forces. His Piano Quintet in A minor of 1918–19 owes much to his intimate knowledge of the quintets of Dvořák, Schumann, and Brahms. The finales, for example, of the famous Dvořák Quintet in A major and Elgar's show similarities, not only in their introductions.

Elgar's interest in Dvořák's music was enhanced by his participation in performances of Dvořák's orchestral works in the years up to 1897, as well as his playing in the Piano Quintet at home. From 1897 his conducting career developed greatly, and his London years saw him in front of the Queen's Hall Orchestra and London Symphony Orchestra, with whom he made a number of gramophone recordings. Among the works of Dvořák that we know he

---

[24] *Letters to Nimrod from Edward Elgar, 1897–1908*, ed. Percy M. Young (London, 1965), 27 ff. Jaeger was to be Nimrod in Elgar's set of variations.

[25] *Portrait of Elgar*, 35.

conducted are: the overtures *Carnival*, *V přírodě* (Amid Nature), and *Husitská*, the Sixth, Seventh, Eighth, and Ninth Symphonies, the Symphonic Variations, the B minor Cello Concerto, the Nocturne in B major, and the choral works Stabat Mater, *The Spectre's Bride*, and Te Deum, as well as the Slavonic Dances, which featured often in his concert programmes. Concerning the Nocturne, there is an amusing note of Elgar's on his copy of the programme from a Crystal Palace concert on 28 October 1889, to which he had gone specially to hear the work. Alas, the work was 'omitted' he wrote, 'owing to the howling of the dogs arrived for Show tomorrow!'[26]

Dvořák made an impression on other English composers of the time, notably Charles Villiers Stanford (1852–1924), who was born in Dublin and was Dvořák's host at Cambridge, Samuel Coleridge-Taylor (1875–1912), Charles Hubert Hastings Parry (1848–1918), and the young Ralph Vaughan Williams (1872–1958). England had been without a great national composer since the time of Henry Purcell (if we omit any claim to Handel!) until Elgar appeared on the scene and gave rise to a new flowering of creative talent that has continued unbroken in a line through Holst and Vaughan Williams, Walton, Britten, Tippett, and Simpson. Dvořák played some small part in this regeneration through the undoubted influence that he had upon Edward Elgar over a period of fifty years.

[26] Reed, *Elgar*, 24. This was the Great Dog Show of the Kennel Club, a forerunner of the now famous Crufts Dog Show, which started in 1891.

VI

THE IMPACT OF AMERICA
ON DVOŘÁK

21

Dvořák among the Yankees: George Chadwick and the Impact of the Boston School

MARK GERMER

CLEARING the path for an American musical idiom was not Dvořák's initial objective in coming to New York, but once arrived, he does not appear to have declined any invitations to pontificate on the subject. His now famous pronouncements, carried in newspapers and in *Harper's New Monthly Magazine*,[1] may have been variously motivated, and a good argument can be made that some of them, at least, were not well considered. An insouciant enthusiasm lends sparkle, perhaps, to what otherwise could be taken as press exposure for the National Conservatory and the agenda of its founder. Certainly he wished to do well by Jeannette Thurber, whose seriousness of purpose he genuinely admired; and there is nothing invidious in positing the existence of commercial advertisement in the public remarks Dvořák made in his official capacity as director. Indeed we might now take the position that, more important than the words themselves, the intellectual attitude conveyed by those remarks constitutes Dvořák's true gift to the Americans, for the path that Dvořák actually helped to clear was the one midway between the highbrow and the lowbrow—a path that scarcely two decades later would be widely perceived as lying midway between Boston and New York.[2]

---

[1] The *Harper's* art. (vol. 90/537 [Feb. 1895], 428–34) is 'Music in America'—see Charles Hamm's discussion of it in Ch. 25. Several of the newspaper pieces are repr. in John Clapham, *Dvořák* (New York, 1979), 197–203; several more, incl. the *Harper's* art., appear in *Dvořák in America: 1892–1895*, ed. John C. Tibbetts (Portland, Oreg., 1993), 355–84. Henry Krehbiel's art. 'Dr. Dvořák's American Symphony', *New York Daily Tribune* (15 Dec. 1893), may be found in an annotated edn. by Michael Beckerman in *Notes*, 49/2 (Dec. 1992), 447–73.

[2] MacDonald Smith Moore documents the increasingly pervasive association of New York City with lowbrow culture in the public and private discourse of many American writers and musicians in his *Yankee Blues: Musical Culture and American Identity* (Bloomington, Ind., 1985); see his ch. 5 for explicit denouncements by, among others, Oscar Thompson and Thomas Hart Benton. Always implicit in such discourse is the contrast to genteel New England with Boston at its hub, and the sense of a national cultural mission that New Englanders of Anglo-Saxon heritage often assume to be their monopoly. I use the term 'Yankee',

Still, there is something cavalier, even offhanded, in certain exaggerated comments—the most curious of these being the paragraph from December 1893 in which Dvořák proclaimed the music of 'Indians' and 'Negroes' to be 'practically identical'—that are known to have rankled leading American composers of the time.[3] Several of these had at least flirted with 'Indian' or 'Negro' materials in their music before Dvořák's advice on the matter. Indeed, what first sent me back to Dvořák's stay in America was puzzlement over, on the one hand, the lack of evidence for personal interchange between Dvořák and the American composers in the North-East with whom he most likely would have come in contact and, on the other, the lack of any incisive discussion of the Native-American and African-American elements that such interchange could have inspired. Of course there were journalistic responses, whose motivations, like Dvořák's, varied according to personal agendas.[4] But I have not discovered serious contemporaneous reflections on Dvořák of, for example, Henry Gilbert, Charles Sanford Skilton, or Arthur Farwell, composers whose works based on 'ethnic' fragments make them potentially instructive commentators. (Later on, in the early 1900s, some of them would take credit for answering Dvořák's call, while inveighing against the forms and models of the Germanocentric concert tradition—which, it is important to say, Dvořák also represented.)[5]

We do have a strong sense of Edward MacDowell's response; his much-quoted rejection virtually presaged the sort of reception accorded such concerts as that of December 1896, which presented a programme of orchestral

incidentally, in this cultural and not primarily geographical sense of Anglo-Saxon backgrounds and aspirations. Dvořák's role as director and his relationship with Thurber are described briefly in Emanuel Rubin, 'Jeannette Meyers Thurber and the National Conservatory of Music', *American Music*, 8 (1990), 294–325, esp. 307–8, 311.

[3] Miroslav Ivanov suggests in *Novosvětská* (The 'New World' [Symphony]) (Prague, 1984) that the reporter may have misunderstood Dvořák, and that in reality Dvořák may only have said that African-American and Native-American musics were linked by their use of the pentatonic scale. The passage in question is preceded by a discussion of pentatonic patterns in Scottish folk-music and the music of Mendelssohn.

[4] Adrienne Fried Block quotes some of these and summarizes others in 'Dvořák, Beach, and American Music', in *A Celebration of American Music: Words and Music in Honor of H. Wiley Hitchcock*, ed. Richard Crawford et al. (Ann Arbor, Mich., 1990), 258–60. See also now her essay 'Dvořák's Long American Reach', in *Dvořák in America*, 157–81, which I had not seen when formulating my remarks here.

[5] Arthur Farwell, 'The Struggle Toward a National Music', *North American Review*, 625 (Dec. 1907), 570; Henry Gilbert, 'Nationalism in Music', *The International*, 7 (Dec. 1913), 369. See also the relevant passages on Farwell and Gilbert in Barbara A. Zuck, *A History of Musical Americanism* (Ann Arbor, Mich., 1980), 61–5 and 75–8. Excerpts from some privately held letters of Farwell, recently made available, amplify the point somewhat; see Farwell's claim to be 'the first composer in America to take up Dvořák's challenge' in a letter to Quaintance Eaton (12 June 1935), quoted in Evelyn Davis Culbertson, *He Heard America Singing: Arthur Farwell, Composer and Crusading Music Educator* (Metuchen, NJ, 1992), 109. However, such remarks as this belong primarily to the climate of the 1930s, not to that of the 1890s, related as those decades may be; see Thomas Stoner, ' "The New Gospel of Music": Arthur Farwell's Vision of Democratic Music in America', *American Music*, 9 (1991), 183–208.

works on 'Negro' themes: 'If judgement were to be passed on what was heard at this concert as results of Dr. Dvořák's "negro melody" theories it would hardly be favorable.'[6] MacDowell's own adoption of 'Indian' material in the early 1890s, incidentally, must be regarded as tenuous at best.[7]

For Dvořák's part, he would almost surely have known the music of MacDowell.[8] MacDowell's mother worked with Jeannette Thurber at the National Conservatory, and he knew Harry Burleigh, perhaps Dvořák's best-known American associate[9] (unless that epithet more rightly belongs to Dvořák's student and colleague at the Conservatory Rubin Goldmark, another composer whose music Dvořák knew).[10] And I will argue presently that he had more than a passing acquaintance with the music of George Chadwick.

Indeed we know that Dvořák studied some American scores, for he adjudicated two competitions for American composers at the National Conservatory, and even requested more time for study during the course of the first of these.[11] However, the names of all but the winning entrants have so far eluded me,[12] the disposition of the Conservatory's papers being something of an enigma; in any case they did not elicit any critique by Dvořák of which there remains a known record.

Only one prize appears to have been awarded the second year, and the reason why the outcome holds some potential interest is that the selection of that

[6] Anonymous review, *The Pianist*, as quoted by Sumner Salter, 'Early Encouragements to American Composers', *Musical Quarterly*, 18 (1932), 97–8. For MacDowell's negative response to Dvořák's recommendations, see most recently Francis Brancaleone, 'Edward MacDowell and the Indian Motives', *American Music*, 7 (1989), esp. 360 and 379, nn. 7–8.

[7] Robert Stevenson, 'The First Published Native American (American Indian) Composer', *Inter-American Music Review*, 4 (1981–2), 79–84.

[8] Incidentally, it does not appear to be reported in the Dvořák literature that MacDowell was offered the position of Director of the National Conservatory several years before it was offered to Dvořák (MacDowell papers, Music Division, Library of Congress, Washington, DC; information kindly supplied by Margery Lowens); it is an interesting point, in that the nationalist agenda of the Conservatory would presumably not have been implemented, since MacDowell did not support it.

[9] Burleigh worked for a time as Frances MacDowell's secretary, according to Anne Key Simpson, *Hard Trials: The Life and Music of Harry T. Burleigh* (Metuchen, NJ, 1990), 12. Burleigh appears not to have studied in any formal sense with Dvořák, but did work as his MS copyist (ibid. 15).

[10] See David Beveridge, 'Rubin Goldmark: Dvořák's American Pupil', in *Dvořák-Studien*, ed. Klaus Döge and Peter Jost (Mainz, 1994), 234–47.

[11] Letter from New York, 1 Nov. 1892, in *Antonín Dvořák: Korespondence a documenty—Kritické vydání* (Antonín Dvořák: Correspondence and Documents—Critical Edition), ed. Milan Kuna et al., iii (Prague, 1989), 158. The impression left by this letter contradicts that of another, from 1892, to Josef and Zdeňka Hlávka (available in Eng. trans. in *Antonín Dvořák: Letters and Reminiscences*, ed. Otakar Šourek, trans. Roberta Finlayson Samsour [Prague, 1954], 151–3, here at p. 152); there is commentary on this letter in Merton Robert Aborn, 'The Influence on American Music of Dvořák's Sojourn in America', Ph.D. diss. (Indiana Univ., Bloomington, 1965), 116–20.

[12] Given the amount of recoverable documentation that has not yet seen the light of day, there is reason to believe that we shall learn more of this episode. The winning entrants are listed in Rubin, 'Jeannette Meyers Thurber', 307.

work, Chadwick's Third Symphony, over all the others may bring us the clos-
est we ever come to knowing Dvořák's opinion, formed after two years on
the American scene, of an established American composer. It was an opinion
quickly broadcast, incidentally, through the publication of Dvořák's congrat-
ulatory notification in the *American Art Journal*.[13]

It seems highly improbable that this was Dvořák's first encounter with
Chadwick and his music, though no proof of a meeting has come to light.
The obvious point of contact between them would have been Franz Kneisel,
a close friend of Chadwick in Boston. Members of the Kneisel Quartet, of
which Kneisel was the founder and first violinist, earned fame in the 1890s as
the foremost interpreters of chamber music in the country through their
annual concert series in Boston and New York; they also gave the world première performances of works by both Chadwick and Dvořák,[14] and we know
that Dvořák attended their New York performances.[15] Kneisel was also the
leader for the programme that Dvořák conducted on his visit to Worcester,
Massachusetts, in September 1893,[16] and there can be no doubt that the violinist was well acquainted with both composers.

But there is also a strong likelihood that Dvořák would have come across
Chadwick's music directly. The second of Chadwick's symphonies had
recently acquired the distinction of being the first orchestral work by an
American to be published without subscription in the United States; and the
same publisher, Arthur Schmidt of Boston, followed this début in 1890 with
the publication of Chadwick's Quintet for Piano and Strings, a work the
Kneisel Quartet had taken on tour at home and abroad. Alerted by the Kneisel
Quartet's performances or perhaps by the personal association with the
group's leader—if not by notoriety in the musical press—the Czech composer
could hardly have failed to recognize the name of the young American composer just hitting his stride in the early 1890s.

Now we would have to imagine Dvořák possessed of virtually no intellectual curiosity were we to believe that he did not interest himself in these and
other newly published scores during his American tenure. Yet, having said
this, I must back away from the idea somewhat. For it will not hurt us to limit
speculation about the intellectual curiosity of an eminently practical man.
Dvořák went to America for a perfectly good American reason, namely to
earn an attractive salary. He said as much when he wrote that he hoped to put

---

[13] 21 Apr. 1894.

[14] Chadwick's Piano Quintet (1887) and String Quartet No. 4 (1896); Dvořák's String Quartet in F
major and String Quintet in E flat major (1893), and apparently also the string quartets in A flat major (1895)
and E major (first performed 1889, composed 1876!).

[15] Clapham, *Dvořák*, 118.

[16] John Clapham, 'Dvořák's Visit to Worcester, Massachusetts', in *Slavonic and Western Music: Essays for
Gerald Abraham*, ed. Malcolm Hamrick Brown and Roland John Wiley (Ann Arbor, Mich., 1985), 207–14.

away a sizeable portion of his New York earnings for the future. In the main, the evidence suggests that his thoughts and deeds were directed by two principal interests: composing and supporting his family.

Though as attentive a tourist as anyone—witness his delight in observing Indians in Iowa—Dvořák offers us little evidence that he arrived eager to imbibe of Americana, musical or otherwise, and in fact he confessed utter surprise when confronted with the expectation, voiced in certain philanthropic quarters, that he should discover the way to create an identifiably national American idiom.[17] He was engaged to lead, moreover, by example and *not* through the promotion of American works already in circulation, as that would necessarily have altered the angle of Jeannette Thurber's Conservatory enterprise, throwing its nationalist justification into question. It is in this light that the composer's remarks on musical nationalism and its raw materials may realistically be cast.

Dvořák had deliberated at length while negotiating the terms of his American employment and now set about fulfilling his contract, not forgetting the inclusivist social agenda of the Conservatory's founder and guiding spirit. The sincerity of Dvořák's recommendations need not be called into question; but neither should they be overvalued as spontaneously original utterances.[18]

This may seem a circuitous route, but I believe that placing Dvořák's comments on 'Negro' and 'Indian' musics in this perspective frees us to consider other means by which the composer might have taken the musical pulse of his American surroundings. Though, as I have cautioned, it does not seem to be the case that Dvořák actively schooled himself in American music, we need not fall to the opposite extreme of imagining him somehow possessed of immunity to outside influence. I believe, furthermore, that to find the American pentatonicism that he described in the *New York Herald* of December 1893 he would have needed to look no further than the music of Chadwick, to which he plainly had easy access. (See Ex. 21.1, showing two excerpts from the Scherzo of Chadwick's Second Symphony.) To make this point is to take nothing away from Dvořák, whose pentatonicism in the American chamber works penetrates the texture in a way that is never attempted by Chadwick.[19] But the use of themes constructed of gapped

---

[17] Letter of 12 Oct. 1892 to Emil Kozánek. See *Antonín Dvořák: Korespondence*, iii. 152–3, and *Antonín Dvořák: Letters*, 150.

[18] The *Harper's* art. ('Music in America') bears the note: 'The author acknowledges the cooperation of Mr. Edward Emerson, Jr., in the preparation of this article.' Thomas Riis has suggested that Emerson may be a pseudonym for Henry Edward Krehbiel.

[19] On the subject of Chadwick's (mainly melodic) pentatonicism, see Victor Yellin, *George Chadwick: Yankee Composer* (Washington, DC, 1990), 92 ff., 104 ff., and *passim*. On Dvořák's application of 'pentatonic structures to the whole texture', see David Beveridge, 'Sophisticated Primitivism: The Significance of Pentatonicism in Dvořák's American Quartet', *Current Musicology*, 24 (1977), 25–36, esp. 28–9.

Ex. 21.1 Chadwick, Symphony No. 2, second movement, tunes with gapped tetra-chords

tetrachords by, arguably, the most prominent of Yankee composers in the 1890s bids for our attention as much as do the African-American and Native-American melodies that Dvořák allegedly heard as 'practically identical'.

More important, perhaps, are the aspects of musical personality and world view that highlight this small parallel. The Czech guest's principal recommendation to American composers—that they seek inspiration in the music of the peoples congregated around them, regardless of the music's ultimate origins—seems strangely prefigured not in Farwell or Gilbert but in the *œuvre* of Chadwick (and one cannot help but wonder whether Dvořák might have ventured to speak so boldly among his hosts largely because he expected his words would fall on receptive ears). We should not let Chadwick's prize-winning Third Symphony, with its tone of academic high seriousness, deflect us from the good humour and buoyant tunefulness (of, for example, the Second Symphony) that is, at the same time, a most representative strain of this composer. It was the Chadwick of the early 1890s, moreover, who—already practised in the introduction of popular dance elements here and the quotation of a drinking-song there—did not shy away from the sentimental and the manic (he would later write for Broadway!) in such musical comedies as *A Quiet Lodging* (1892) and *Tabasco* (1894).

The latter work, incidentally, contains among its several ethnic numbers a parody of the plantation songs of the sort Dvořák heard in New York and alluded to in his *Harper's* interview, a point that brings us back to the attempt to place Dvořák's pronouncements on a likely American musical idiom in the context of what he had learned about American music thus far. In admiring such songs as a point of departure for the future, Dvořák never postulated that openness to vernacular inspiration necessitated a sacrifice of method or a lowering of tone. Taking a line remarkably similar to Chadwick, he anticipated a naturally occurring American idiom primarily as the logical outcome of technical mastery over the forms of European concert music. This is not the comparatively radical line that would be developed a decade later by more self-conscious nationalists.[20] Neither Dvořák nor Chadwick assumed an explicitly populist outlook. Indeed, as Zoltan Roman has reminded us,[21] Dvořák did not approve of a certain 'light and trashy' music (the same mass-commercial music once deprecated by Chadwick?);[22] but both shared a practical interest in the opportunities presented by materials immediately reflective of their time and place. It would be hard to imagine two more compatible musical temperaments.[23]

[20] See n. 5 above.

[21] 'Music in Turn-of-the-Century America: A View from the Old World', *American Music*, 7 (1989), 315–23, at 318–19.

[22] Yellin, *George Chadwick*, 23–5, 224 n. 40.

[23] I would like to thank Thomas Riis, Charles Hamm, and Adrienne Fried Block for their criticisms of the working draft of this paper, and David Beveridge and Victor Yellin for comments on its next incarnations.

22

Dvořák's Pentatonic Landscape: The Suite in A major

MICHAEL BECKERMAN

ON 20 April 1894 Dvořák wrote the following in a letter to his publisher Simrock: 'I have the Sonatina for violin and piano (easy to play), a Suite in A major for piano (of medium difficulty), then ten new Songs (two volumes) taken from the Bible, and I think that the Suite for Piano and the Songs are the best things I have written in these genres.'[1] Although most critics have validated Dvořák's estimation of the *Biblical Songs*, his evaluation of the Suite, Op. 98, has not been confirmed. Indeed, no mature work of Dvořák's has come in for more frequent trashing than this one. Paul Stefan finds that it has neither the immediacy of appeal nor the significance of the other American works,[2] while Gervase Hughes says that 'it is a work of little character which apart from a few "Negro" touches in the finale might have been produced by any competent composer.'[3] Alec Robertson is utterly snide, speaking of it as a 'poor work',[4] and John Clapham places it among the composer's 'slighter compositions' in his first monograph[5] and ignores it in his second.

Part of the problem seems to be that, according to the critics, the piece exhibits no serious compositional touches; thus František Bartoš (using data from Otakar Šourek) in the critical edition: 'Apart from the finale of the last movement which repeats some of the musical material contained in the first movement, there are no signs of a closer thematic relationship which would link the movements into a complete whole.'[6] Though the premise is a bit

---

[1] 'Ich habe die *Sonatina* für Viol[ine] und Piano (*leicht aufführbar*), *eine Suite* in A dur für Pianoforte (*mittelmäßig schwer*), dann habe ich zehn neue *Lieder* (zwei Hefte), *aus der heiligen Schrift entnommen*, und glaube, daß ich in dieser *Suite für Piano* und in den *Liedern* das Beste geschrieben, was ich bis jetzt auf diesem Gebiete geleistet habe.' *Antonín Dvořák: Korespondence a dokumenty—Kritické vydání* (Antonín Dvořák: Correspondence and Documents—Critical Edition), ed. Milan Kuna et al., iii (Prague, 1989), 260–1.

[2] *Anton Dvořák*, transl. from the Ger. by Y. W. Vance (New York, 1941), 220.

[3] *Dvořák* (London, 1967), 172.   [4] *Dvořák* (London, 1945), 109.

[5] *Antonín Dvořák: Musician and Craftsman* (New York, 1966), 150.

[6] Pref. to Dvořák, *Suite, Op. 98: Piano*, trans. G. Thomsen (Prague, 1957), p. viii.

peculiar—we do not necessarily expect close thematic relationships in Mozart in order to have a complete whole—it is totally incorrect. In this study I shall argue that the work, though its tone may seem relaxed and informal, is at least as carefully composed as any other work by Dvořák, and moreover I will suggest that it was precisely the work he wished to compose. I shall further propose that, far from being a slight occasional piece, it may well be the most characteristic and revealing work of the American period.

First I would like to articulate some of the elements that unify the piece; then I will proceed to a discussion of its overall character. The opening movement has two main ideas, which I will designate 'A' and 'D' in honour of the composer. 'A' is a four-note figure beginning on F♯ with a pentatonic inflection, while 'D' is a static minor arpeggio with a scale passage leading to a triple articulation of E. I have compiled a table of thematic material throughout the work which shows these two primary ideas and, under each of them, several different transformations (Ex. 22.1). There are also numerous penta-

Ex. 22.1 Thematic relationships in the Suite in A major

'A'   'D'

First movement, main theme   First movement, theme of middle section

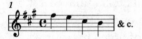   

Second movement, theme of middle   Second movement, main theme
section

Third movement, main theme   Fourth movement, main theme

Third movement, first contrasting   Fourth movement, countermelody to
theme   main theme

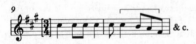   

Fifth movement, variant of main theme

Ex. 22.2 Pentatonic flourishes at ends of movements: *a*. second movement; *b*. third movement; *c*. fifth movement

tonic flourishes that conclude movements throughout the work (Ex. 22.2), and great care is taken to link various movements together by key and motif. Finally, almost all the subsidiary (non-tonic) key-areas exploited in the work derive from the first three notes of motif 'A', as shown here in the order in which those notes occur in the melody:

F sharp minor	Third movement, first contrasting key-area (mm. 9–24)
F sharp major	Fifth movement, last contrasting key-area (mm. 53–58)
E minor	Fifth movement, first contrasting key-area (mm. 17–25)
C sharp minor	Second movement, main key of movement
	Third movement, second contrasting key-area (mm. 33–56)
C sharp (D flat) major	Second movement, middle section (mm. 61–125)

Thus despite its relaxed atmosphere, this does not appear to be a loosely constructed work, a claim that I believe will be strengthened by further detailed exploration.

The other problem critics such as Clapham, Šourek, Antonín Sychra, and others have articulated is that the work seems to lack any sense of drama or scope, the often-voiced implication being that the master rested after his great labour with the 'New World' Symphony.[7] Thus, it must be considered an occasional work, perhaps at best a kind of salon titbit, long on sentiment and

---

[7] Perhaps Šourek summarizes this viewpoint best when he says: 'This small little work certainly cannot be compared, in its significance and value, to Dvořák's previous American compositions. It does not seem to possess their strength of ideas or their spontaneous expansiveness in terms of structure and design.' (Toto drobné dílko skutečně nemůže býti ve svém významu i hodnotách srovnáváno s předcházejícími americkými skladbami Dvořákovými. Nemá jejich myšlenkové síly ani jejich spontánního rozmachu v práci i stavbě.) *Život a dílo Antonína Dvořáka* (The Life and Work of Antonín Dvořák), 2nd edn., iii (Prague, 1956), 196–7.

short on craft. Before responding to such viewpoints, though, we might look at what exactly the work does do, and for this I would like to explore what is arguably the most static and least dramatic part of the suite, the fourth movement.

The fourth movement is an Andante which some have referred to as an Indian lullaby, though Lord knows it doesn't sound like any Indian music you or I might ever have heard, Kikapoo, Ojibway, Apache, New Delhi, or otherwise. It opens with a retrograde of the second to fifth notes of 'D' (see Ex. 22.1 above, comparing the first and third entries under column 'D'). The character of the movement is determined by the alternation of chords a minor third apart—first A minor and C major (Ex. 22.3*a*), then, beginning at m. 11,

Ex. 22.3 Fourth movement: *a*. opening; *b*. continuation

C minor and E flat major (*b*). C thus acts not so much as a relative major, a goal to be attained, but rather as a brief stopping-point on the way to yet another third-relation. When C is finally tonicized in m. 30, one can hardly speak of a traditional tonic, since the approach touches only fleetingly on the dominant harmony (G), and the C major section is entirely over a tonic pedal (featuring a new theme accompanied by a major-key variant of the opening material). See Ex. 22.4. The dominant, as an emphasized harmony or a key-area, never shows up for work. In the principal key of A, as well, the only dominant chords are the E major chords occurring just prior to the return of the primary material in mm. 19 and 41, not sounding on the downbeat in either case. Finally, we may note that in keeping with the careful compositional procedure described above, the opening theme is treated slightly differently each time it occurs.

What then is the effect of the tonal ambiguity of the opening and closing

Ex. 22.4 Fourth movement

and the pedal that dominates the middle section? In a sense, the piece is in C major, yet it begins and ends on A. Rather than moving forward tonally, despite its chromatic elements, it has the appearance of standing still. We interpret the chromaticism in mm. 3 and 4 as secondary—it merely serves to reinforce the effect of the primary material when it recurs. The realm of functional tonality, with its implications of forward movement toward a goal, is completely destabilized. It may seem overly dramatic to call this little movement subversive and revolutionary, but in its own way it disrupts the tonal universe almost as forcefully as atonality a decade later.

Indeed, this process is present throughout the suite as a whole. The harmonic motion, if it can even be called that, is either between parallel major and minor (first, second, and last movements) or to key-areas up or down a third (third and, briefly, last movements). This further increases the sense of stasis, for it is third-relations that most effectively foil the sense of forward drive in tonal music, invariably created by root-movement of a fifth or a second. Even the opening movement of the work, quite clearly in A major, begins with an ambiguous F sharp minor chord which threatens the tonal stability whenever it occurs. The second theme involves no harmonic change, and even when there is some kind of tonal movement the work seems to stress harmonic colour over motion. Thus it seems that Dvořák is trying to make a piece that, relatively speaking, stands still.

Dvořák is certainly not the only composer to work with static musical materials. It should be obvious that composers, from Monteverdi to Stravinsky, are not only in the business of creating high drama. There is an equally significant drive to work against the illusion of forward movement in time by creating what might be called 'stases', or illusions of motionlessness. Whether they occur in 'Morning' from Grieg's *Peer Gynt*, the Shrovetide Fair scene from *Petrushka*, Beethoven's 'Pastoral' Symphony, or Borodin's *In the Steppes of Central Asia*, such moments suggest tableaux rather than action, and picture rather than drama. It is my contention that the Andante, and indeed the suite as a whole, must be seen in this tradition to be fully understood. And so, we must ask, what kind of pictures is Dvořák offering us?

This brings us, finally, to America. No one has yet been able to articulate what, precisely, is American about Dvořák's works, and I shall fail as well, although I hope in a new way. The discussion usually begins with allusions to pentatonicism, which, it is grudgingly acknowledged, could well have evolved in Bohemia, and continues with mysterious and inscrutable Indians, Scotch snaps, and references to Black singers who may or may not sound like cors anglais. Yet when we try to escape the question of Dvořák's 'Americanness' the composer's comments about his music inevitably drag us back. He writes about Black music and Indians, especially the Hiawatha legend. He says, about the 'New World' Symphony, 'Bude snad trochu americká', ('It will perhaps be a bit American'), and speaks elliptically about a new style growing out of the American soil.[8] And when we wish to dismiss this as too vague and even misleading, we have the very real changes in the composer's style to contend with.

Unfortunately, in historical studies, as distinct from scientific experimentation, we have no control group. If we could only have had two Dvořáks, one who stayed at home and another who went abroad, we could more easily chart the impact of his voyage, and the exercise would leave the realm of speculation. Yet, we may ask, is there any possible factor that has been left out of the discussion?

In his analysis of the F major Quartet in *Studien zu Dvořáks Streichquartetten*, Hartmut Schick speaks about the work's bucolic and pastoral character: 'Like no other of the American works, the quartet seems to belong to a bucolic-pastoral sphere'.[9] Though he is correct about the pastoral character of that work, he is wrong to neglect the rest of the American works, for from the Largo of the 'New World' Symphony to the Adagio of the Cello Concerto, from the 'waterfalls' in the Sonatina to the Andante pastorale in the sketchbooks, and from the Quintet in E flat major to the A major Suite, this period

---

[8] Letter of 14 Apr. 1893 to Antonín Rus in Písek (*Antonín Dvořák: Korespondence*, iii. 188–9). In an earlier letter (12 Apr.) to Emil Kozánek he had written 'Inu, *vliv* Ameriky, každý, kdo má "čuch", musí vycítit.' (The *influence* of America will be felt by anyone who has a 'nose'.) Ibid. 186. And as early as 24 Jan. of the same year he writes, in a letter to Jindřich Geisler, 'Zdá se mi, že americká půda na mou mysl blahodárně bude působit a skoro bych řekl, že již v té nové sinfonii něco takového uslyšíte.' (I seem to feel that the American soil will reflect on my mind favourably, and I should almost say that in this new symphony you will hear something of it.) Ibid. 177.

[9] 'Wie kein anderes der amerikanischen Werke Dvořáks scheint das Quartett einer bukolisch-pastoralen Sphäre anzugehören'. (Neue Heidelberger Studien zur Musikwissenschaft, ed. Ludwig Finscher and Reinhold Hammerstein, xvii; Laaber, Germany, 1990), 268.

is dominated by pastoral tone. And this is perhaps a hint for us. I do not mean to minimize the significance of a whole range of influences, Indian, Negro, and otherwise, nor do I find the issue of pentatonicism uninteresting, especially as discussed by Schick and by David Beveridge (although I am bothered by the 'ism'),[10] yet there must be something that animated this language, that caused a series of tendencies, already present in Dvořák's work in Bohemia, to become magnified. I would like to focus on one factor that is still with us and that is something Dvořák noticed: the landscape.

On 15 December 1893, the day of the première of the 'New World' Symphony, an interview with Dvořák appeared in the *New York Herald*. The composer made it clear that the second and third movements of the symphony were based on *The Song of Hiawatha* by Longfellow. Equally surprising, Dvořák said that he had encountered that work thirty years before, and that he had always been enchanted by it.[11] The most casual perusal of *The Song of Hiawatha* makes it clear that Dvořák must have had vivid imaginings of the American landscape decades before he saw the prairies.

Even more revealing is the fact that the Largo of the 'New World' Symphony was based, at least in part, on 'Hiawatha's Wooing', book x of Longfellow's poem. This book, like many others in the poem, is rich in descriptions of nature. Although Dvořák never specified the exact place he used in the chapter (it is over 280 lines) he quite possibly based the outer sections of the movement on the pleasant homeward journey of Hiawatha and Minnehaha:[12]

> Pleasant was the journey homeward,
> Through interminable forests,
> Over meadow, over mountain.
> Over river, hill, and hollow.
> Short it seemed to Hiawatha,
> Though they journeyed very slowly,
> Though his pace he checked and slackened
> To the steps of Laughing Water.

---

[10] Schick, *Studien*, 264 ff.; Beveridge, 'Sophisticated Primitivism: The Significance of Pentatonicism in Dvořák's American Quartet', *Current Musicology*, 24 (1977), 25–36.

[11] Both Šourek and Sychra assume that Dvořák first encountered the poem some time after 1870, since it was trans. into Czech by his friend Josef Sládek.

[12] For a detailed discussion of all the evidence see my art. 'Dvořák's *New World* Largo and *The Song of Hiawatha*', *19th-Century Music*, 16/1 (summer 1992), 35–48. In short, there is convincing evidence that Dvořák, only days before the première, told the music critic Henry Krehbiel that the Largo was based on 'Hiawatha's Wooing'. An exploration of that chapter yields several possibilities, of which the depiction of the homeward journey seems the most plausible. It also seems that the C sharp major section corresponds to the words 'All the birds sang loud and sweetly,' coming after the passage quoted here. Regarding *Hiawatha* and the Scherzo of the symphony, see also my essay 'The Dance of Pau-Puk-Keewis and the Song of Chibiabos: Reflections on the Scherzo of Dvořák's Symphony *From the New World*', in *Dvořák in America: 1892–1895*, ed. John C. Tibbetts (Portland, Oreg., 1993), 210–27.

Dvořák didn't say a great deal about his conception of the American landscape before he travelled outside New York, to Spillville, Minnehaha Falls,
and other places west, but he certainly made some revealing statements after
he had seen the open spaces. This comment, from a letter to Kozánek, is perhaps Dvořák's most telling and detailed description of the American landscape:

It is very strange here. Few people and a great deal of empty space. A farmer's near-
est neighbor is often four miles off. Especially in the prairies (I call them the Sahara)
there are only endless acres of field and meadow and that is all you see. You don't
meet a soul (here they only ride on horseback) and you are glad to see in the woods
and meadows the huge herds of cattle which, summer and winter, are out at pasture
in the broad fields. . . . And so it is very 'wild' here and sometimes very sad—sad to
despair. But habit is everything. I should have to go on and on telling you things and
you would hear many curious things about this America.[13]

He closes the letter with a discussion of his new works—the Symphony, the
F major Quartet, and the Quintet—saying: 'I know I never would have written
these compositions in this way if I had not seen America!' He continued to discuss these open spaces when he returned to New York. According to his pupil
William Arms Fischer, 'He told me after his return that he had been reading
Longfellow's *Hiawatha*, and that the wide-stretching prairies had greatly
impressed him.'[14]

If indeed, as I suggest, Dvořák's American works are coloured by pastoral
style, we might well ask how this pastoral differs from earlier pastorals by
Dvořák and others and what it might have to do with the American landscape. The pastoral style evolved for many reasons, too numerous to discuss
here, and yet at its core was the attempt to give shape to images of idyllic
motionlessness, an urban view of country life. But what was country life? It
was nature, to be sure, but always populated, always with an inn nearby, peas-
ants dancing. And so pastorals, whether in Grieg, Mozart, Beethoven,
Smetana, or earlier Dvořák, are invariably marked by melodies of a narrow
range, mainly stepwise, with parallel thirds or sixths—the outdoors—but
domesticated by centuries of noisy and bustling settlement.

Dvořák clearly encountered an American landscape that was open, and

[13] 'Je to zde divné. Málo lidu a mnoho prázdných míst. Jeden sedlák od druhého třebas 4 míle vzdálen,
zvláště v *prériích* (já tomu říkám Sahara), nic než veliké lány polí, luk—a to je vše, co uvidíte. Člověka
nepotkáte (zde jen jezdí) a jste rád, když uvidíte v lukách a v lesích ty nesčíslné řady dobytka, který neustále
v zimě v létě je v širých polích a pase se. . . . A tak je to zde vše velmi *divoké*, někdy až velice smutně,
člověk by si zoufal. Ale zvyk vše přemůže. Musel bych Vám povídat dlouho a dlouho a divné věci by jste
o té Americe slyšeli.' Letter to Emil Kozánek, 15 Sept. 1893, *Antonín Dvořák: Korespondence*, iii. 207. Trans.
here according to Roberta Finlayson Samsour in *Antonín Dvořák: Letters and Reminiscences*, ed. Otakar
Šourek (Prague, 1954), 166; this letter repr. therefrom in *Dvořák in America*, 399.
[14] From the Pref. to Fischer's arrangement of the main theme of the Largo for voice (Boston, 1922).

often silent, symbolized, as in *The Song of Hiawatha* or the pastoral novels of Fenimore Cooper, by the prairie. Although Dvořák had encountered the prairie in Longfellow before he left Bohemia, he came face to face with it only after his arrival in the New World, and it was then that he felt a need to assimilate it. His letters are replete with allusions to distance, we see sketch-book notations referring to the 'wildflower of the prairie', he visits Minnehaha Falls, and struggles to portray this new sense of space.

And so, on the basis of these encounters, Dvořák creates an American pastoral—the motifs become more drawn-out, relaxed, resulting in increased use of the types of patterns we term 'pentatonic', and the range becomes wider. For example, it seems certain that the language of the Largo from the symphony, with its drones, pentatonic flavour, widely spaced intervals (tenths instead of thirds), and delicate orchestration, is an attempt to create an image of the primeval American spaces, an image that Copland later popularized in *Appalachian Spring* and *Billy the Kid*. And yet Dvořák also discovered a sadness in the stillness of the prairie, and he invented a kind of exotic minor pastoral as well, such as we see in the Andante of the suite, and elsewhere, as in Ex. 22.5 from the third movement. It is almost unrecognizable as a conventional pastoral, but it embodies the same general principle: working against the illusion of forward motion in order to create the illusion of standing still.

Ex. 22.5 Third movement

This new and expanded approach to tonality may suggest to us why Dvořák composed the work as a suite. It is clearly a genre that does imply a cyclic whole, a series of interrelated pictures, but one that is free from the fairly rigid tonal and formal expectations of symphonies, sonatas, and quartets, which carry with them considerable historical implications. That Dvořák wrote the work for solo piano further suggests that he wished to separate this utterance from the public grandeur of symphonic work and the private technical world of chamber music, with its contrapuntal traditions. Though chamber music is always considered especially intimate, there is nothing more personal than a solo piano piece.

I do not think Dvořák's sensitivity to extramusical elements is being overemphasized in this case. We would do well to remember that after his return to Bohemia Dvořák almost ceased to write 'absolute music'. His major works from 1895 until his death consist almost entirely of operas and tone-poems, all richly concerned with images of landscape, especially *Rusalka* and such tone-poems as *The Wild Dove* and *The Water-Goblin*.

The fact that the composer bragged about the suite to Simrock, and later lovingly orchestrated it, suggests that he had no doubts about its value, that he had said what he had to say. And I believe this work most vividly reflects the true American contribution to Dvořák's style: this pared-down, clear, and unpretentious vision, devoid of romantic flourish and cliché, rejecting Teutonic bluster, and offering a simple yet subtle and variegated series of powerful and resonant landscapes. In his letter to Kozánek he alluded to the 'many curious things' he could say about America; I believe he said at least some of them in his suite.

VII

THE IMPACT OF DVOŘÁK
ON AMERICA

23

Dvořák and the Historiography of
American Music

RICHARD CRAWFORD

SHORTLY after the death of James Russell Lowell in August 1891, Henry James wrote an appreciation of his mentor and friend. James observed that after a man dies, those who knew him 'find his image strangely simplified and summarized':

The hand of death has smoothed the folds, made it more typical and general. The figure retained by the memory is compressed and intensified; accidents have dropped away from it and shades have ceased to count; it stands, sharply, for a few estimated and cherished things, rather than nebulously, for a swarm of possibilities. We cut the silhouette, in a word, out of the confusion of life, we save and fix the outline, and it is with his eye on this profiled distinction that the [writer] speaks.[1]

James was writing here about biography, but his words also apply to history. For historians explore all possible ways to reveal the truth behind their facts: summarizing, intensifying, and casting certain events into relief by omitting others—by 'cut[ting] the silhouette . . . out of the confusion of life'. Every bit as much as gathering and compiling, the writing of history involves simplifying, compressing, and surgery.

The notion that the historian is a maker of silhouettes reminds us that the final image depends upon his or her predilections. Historical 'silhouettes', formed from the facts seen and heard, are summoned by the historian's own habits of seeing and hearing. Who historians are, the motives behind their studies, the stake they hold in the outcome—all these things shape the history they write.

Historians of American music have tended to line up in one of two camps. The first has seen the United States as simply one among many western nations. Thus, the writing of its music history has been chiefly a matter of tracing continuities that link American musical life with that of the Old

[1] *Literary Criticism: Essays on Literature: American Writers; English Writers* (New York, 1984), 516.

World, as the writer understands it. The progress of music education and concert life, the founding of choral societies, conservatoires, orchestras, and opera
companies, and the acceptance of European forms and aesthetic principles as
the starting-point for American composers—these events are taken as signals
of growing artistic vitality. Let's call historians in this camp 'cosmopolitan'.

The second camp has seen things differently. Taking American music as an
emanation from a unique, democratic society, these historians have centred
their attention chiefly on discontinuity with Europe. They have found special
value in the work of American musicians who have resisted, or reinterpreted,
or failed to receive messages from creative and intellectual centres abroad.
Originality, experimentation, and eclecticism have been their touchstones of
worth, as well as a conviction that American music is to be valued especially
for its uniqueness—its difference from Old World practice. Let's call the outlook of this school of historians 'provincial'.[2]

Now let's call in Dvořák and observe the role for which historians of
American music have fitted him. Or, to put it another way, let's trace
Dvořák's historiographical 'silhouette' through general histories of American
music. Historians have based their Dvořák silhouette chiefly on three ele-
ments: (1) his American compositions; (2) his teaching at the National
Conservatory in New York City (1892–5); and (3) his public statements about
American 'folk-music', reported in newspapers and popular periodicals.

The first general history of American music written after Dvořák's visit was
that of Louis C. Elson, published in 1904. Elson finds Dvořák's visit important chiefly for its impact on Dvořák himself. For Elson, the 'New World'
Symphony would 'always remain Dvořák's chief achievement in this country'. Here was no 'Bohemian masquerading as a plantation darky . . . but an
idealization of the typical music of the South'.[3] Elson makes only brief mention of Dvořák's teaching, nor does he quote his public statements.

In the book *Music in America* (1915), edited by Arthur Farwell and W.
Dermot Darby, all three elements of Dvořák's historiographical silhouette
come into play. Dvořák's American compositions are found to be untrue to
the spirit of the 'Negro music' they borrow. 'Dvořák himself placed our negro
themes into a setting unmistakably Slavic.'[4] More significant for Farwell than
America's impact on Dvořák was Dvořák's on America. Noting the composer's 'brilliant regime' at the Conservatory, Farwell mentions the composition prizes and the school orchestra's improvement under Dvořák, praising

---

[2] The foregoing comments are adapted from Richard Crawford, *The American Musical Landscape*
(Berkeley, 1993), 7–9. Ch. 1 of that book, 'Cosmopolitan and Provincial: American Musical
Historiography', presents an overview of the subject.

[3] *The History of American Music* (New York, 1904), 348.

[4] *Music in America* (New York, 1915), 332.

especially 'the superior training it afforded poor young men of talent'.[5] But for Farwell, Dvořák's stance on folk-music and American composition was the key to his importance. According to him, it had been Dvořák's 'proclamation' that first stirred public discussion of 'whether the basis of a characteristic national American musical art was to be found in the music of the negroes or Indians'.[6] Then, noting 'attempts to weld from the several folk-song elements of this continent a truly national music', Farwell credits Dvořák with having 'first counselled the American composer to thus employ the methods from which alone could be formed a distinctive school'.[7] Farwell also prints an extract from the article in *Harper's Magazine* of 1895 in which Dvořák praises American plantation and slave songs and suggests their role in the creation of 'truly national music'.[8]

Like Elson, John Tasker Howard in his book of 1931 (and its later editions) finds honour in America's impact on Dvořák. For Howard, the 'New World' Symphony is both masterpiece and exemplar. 'Because it is a great work, and a highly popular one,' Howard writes, 'it focused attention on the use of American folk songs.' Howard also acknowledges Dvořák's teaching but finds his attempts 'to develop a nationalistic school of music among his American pupils' something of a dead end:

Arthur Farwell, Henry F. B. Gilbert, Harry Burleigh, Harvey Worthington Loomis, Charles Wakefield Cadman, Charles S. Skilton, Carl Busch, all were among the pioneers who turned to folk music of the North American continent around the turn of the century. Some of them lost their enthusiasm in later years, or at least decided that they did not care to limit themselves to folk material. They came to realize the subtlety of Americanism in art, and that while the essence of folk music is native, it alone cannot produce a nationalist idiom.[9]

With *America's Music* of 1955, by Gilbert Chase, we cross the historiographical divide into a thoroughly 'provincial' view of American music history. Where 'cosmopolitan' histories make much of 'growth', 'development', and signs of 'maturity', Chase's story hangs chiefly on American musicians' efforts to shake off what he sees as the German yoke. Dvořák's American compositions count for little in Chase's book. But as a teacher and a public presence, Dvořák is a major player whose role is described in five crucially positioned pages.

Chase's book is cast in three large sections: 'Preparation', 'Expansion', and 'Fulfillment'. 'Fulfillment' begins with a chapter called 'Nationalism and

---

[5] Ibid. 256. [6] Ibid. p. xvi. [7] Ibid. 332.

[8] 'Music in America' (with the 'co-operation' of Edwin Emerson, Jun.), *Harper's New Monthly Magazine*, 90/537 (Feb. 1895), 428–34. Repr. (with slight discrepancies) in *Dvořák in America: 1892–1895*, ed. John C. Tibbetts (Portland, Oreg., 1993), 370–80.

[9] *Our American Music*, 4th edn. (New York, 1965), 700.

Folklore', and on its second page Chase begins his brief for Dvořák. Painting with broad strokes, he argues that it was Dvořák who connected American music to the strain of European Romanticism most likely to promote distinctiveness. That strain was 'nationalism', and 'Dvořák was one of its leading representatives'. Romanticism, Chase explains, 'exalted liberty' and 'recognized the artistic value of folklore'. In America, however, 'German influence' had inoculated composers *against* Romanticism. Hence, America had failed to find stylistic freedom, as had Poland, Bohemia, Norway, and Russia through their composers' encounters with indigenous folk-music. It was Dvořák, Chase claims, who first offered a cure for the Teutonic virus. Thanks to his example, American composers were finally shown a new path, 'a definite impetus to the formation of a "national" school of composers in the United States'.[10] Chase continues, 'Dvořák was not offering a pattern. He was pointing to a potential source of inspiration. And more important than any particular source he mentioned—Negro spirituals or Indian melodies—was the attitude of mind, the spiritual message, that he conveyed to American musicians.'[11] Dvořák is the pivot on which Chase's book turns. From here on, *America's Music* is a chronicle of fresh New World voices.

H. Wiley Hitchcock, in the preface to his *Music in the United States* (1969), names Chase as one of two scholars whose ideas have 'influenced [him] most'. But not on our subject, for Hitchcock reduces Dvořák to the role of a minor character. The 'New World' Symphony is mentioned only in passing, and Dvořák's teaching isn't mentioned at all. In Hitchcock, Dvořák is invoked, though not discussed, both as an exponent of 'Negro melodies' and, as in Chase, as the man who according to Farwell challenged American composers 'to go after our folk music'.[12] But Romanticism, nationalism, and folklore, which for Chase converge on Dvořák, are dispersed elsewhere in Hitchcock's text.

Like Hitchcock, Charles Hamm in his *Music in the New World* cites Chase as a major influence. A quotation from Dvořák provides an epigraph for Hamm's chapter 15, 'The Search for a National Identity'.[13] Then Hamm uses Dvořák's career to introduce a long chapter on American music written to 'reflect the musical and cultural life of America in the first half of the twentieth century': first Dvořák himself; then Edward MacDowell (with his ambivalence about nationalism); then Dvořák's own pupils' embrace of it; then composers like Farwell, inspired by Dvořák to use folklore; then composers who drew upon other American vernaculars, including Gilbert, Gershwin, Ives, Thomson, Copland, and Harris; and finally, genres—operas

---

[10] *America's Music* (New York, 1955), 386–7.   [11] Ibid. 390.
[12] *Music in the United States*, 2nd edn. (Englewood Cliffs, NJ, 1974), 144.
[13] *Music in the New World* (New York, 1983), 410.

and art songs—in which national identity was explored. Thus, Hamm inter-prets Dvořák's impact in much broader terms than his predecessors. He explains how American Indian and Negro singing are linked to Dvořák's American works. As for teaching, Hamm seems most interested in the way Dvořák described his duty: 'not so much to interpret Beethoven, Wagner, or other masters of the past, but to give what encouragement I can to the young musicians of America'. With that as a starting-point, Dvořák's comments on 'nationalism' merit a long quotation from the *Harper's* article. In Hamm's opinion, 'Dvořák did not urge American composers to base their composition on Indian and Negro melodies. Instead, he urged them to be receptive to whatever music was taken most to heart by their fellow citizens.'[14]

It's instructive to compare Chase's and Hamm's final 'silhouettes' of Dvořák. The two men agree that Dvořák's message has invited misinterpre-tation—that the issue was not really one of Indian vs. Negro melodies, or even that American composers 'must turn to . . . folk songs of America', as Hitchcock had written (though he would delete this statement from his *Music in the United States*, third edition, of 1988). Rather, the key lay in attitude, in receptiveness to what folk-music could offer American composers. For Chase, however, it's a matter of composers finding American source material; for Hamm it's a matter of their finding American music that will connect with an American audience. Chase's reading of Dvořák's public pronouncements leads to the following precept: 'American composers should turn their atten-tion to the indigenous products of American culture[;] . . . they should value and cultivate—by assimilation rather than by imitation—the idiosyncratic ele-ments of musical culture in America.'[15] Hamm, in contrast, has Dvořák urging composers to 'be receptive to whatever music was taken most to heart by [your] fellow citizens'. When we compare the rest of Chase's chapter 19 with Hamm's chapter 15, we see that Chase limits himself to folk-music as a source (Farwell and his Wa-Wan Press, Gilbert and his interest in Indian and Negro melodies, other 'Indianist' composers like Cadman and Skilton, and John Powell's Anglo-inspired works), while Hamm's account, as noted, ranges much farther afield.

Hamm's case for Dvořák depends heavily on two sentences in the *Harper's* article and his view of the composer as a Czech nationalist. In the article, Dvořák asks: 'What songs . . . belong to the American and appeal more strongly to him than any others? What melody could stop him on the street if he were in a strange land and make the home feeling well up within him, no matter how hardened he might be or how wretchedly the tune were played?'[16] As for musical nationalism, according to Hamm, Dvořák

---

[14] Ibid. 412.   [15] *America's Music*, 390.   [16] 'Music in America', 432.

knew the popular and folk songs and dances of Czechoslovakia from his youth and kept in touch with this music throughout his life. Melodic and rhythmic elements of his pieces grow out of this music; many of his own compositions capture the essence of Czech life and culture. As a result, his compositions were taken to heart by the Czech public and struck audiences in other countries as being significantly different from the products of German, Russian, Scandinavian, British, and Italian composers.[17]

The key phrase, 'taken to heart by' the public, the people, or citizens, is not Dvořák's phrase but Hamm's—a distillation based on his reading of Dvořák, Chase, maybe Farwell, certainly John Clapham's earlier book on the composer (1966),[18] and his listening to many kinds of music, American and non-American. A composer seeking to capture the spirit of a society 'reads' his or her 'fellow citizens', determines what music they love, and makes that his starting-point. Hamm takes this conclusion and runs with it: from Dvořák not just to Farwell but to Ives, to Gershwin and Copland, and, by the end of the chapter, to Virgil Thomson's *Four Saints in Three Acts* and Ethelbert Nevin's 'The Rosary'. Of course, Hamm doesn't claim Dvořák's direct influence on all these composers and works. But by attributing to Dvořák an insight so all-encompassing, and by setting it, and him, at the head of a chapter that ranges so broadly, Hamm makes Dvořák the proverbial 'eye of the needle' through which passes a vast and motley parade of nationalist aspirations. His view of Dvořák's place in American music history seems an excellent example of what an imaginative historian can construct from a selection of facts, a firm historiographical stance, and an apt 'silhouette'.

And now the final twist. Between 1955 and 1987, when his revised third edition of *America's Music* appeared, Chase changed his view of Dvořák's place in American music history dramatically.[19] In Chase's third edition, Dvořák is summarily dropped: he's cited in three passing references but stripped entirely of the key role he played in the first and second editions. The book's structure is completely revamped: no 'Preparation', 'Expansion', and 'Fulfillment'; no 'Romanticism'; no chapter on 'Nationalism and Folklore'. The 'German hegemony' against which American composers earlier had had to 'revolt' has evaporated, taking Dvořák with it.

Chase doesn't explain in his third edition why he's changed his tune on Dvořák, but one can guess from articles he published in the late 1970s and early 1980s. I think the change was sparked by his reading in the social sciences, which made him think hard about how time is represented in history-writing. And when he took to heart the notion of time's flexibility— the interaction, in history, of 'diachronic' or linear time and 'synchronic' time,

---

[17] *Music in the New World*, 412. [18] *Antonín Dvořák: Musician and Craftsman* (New York).
[19] (Urbana, Ill., 1987.)

which grapples with simultaneous strands of activity—his earlier view of American music history as a teleological chronicle came apart. Dvořák's fate suggests that, for Chase—the first historian to make him a featured player in American music history—the Bohemian composer's role hung almost entirely on the author's historiographical stance. Looking for an agent to act in a particular historical moment, he found Dvořák. But after he lost faith in that moment's casual connection to events that followed, Dvořák lost his key position in Chase's chronicle.

I'm not sure how much our review of American music historiography tells us about Dvořák. But we can certainly take this saga of his changing role as proof, a century after his visit, that although the so-called 'provincial' view of American music history is firmly in the saddle, consensus remains elusive. According to our leading historians, Dvořák was either a famous but historically insignificant visitor or he was a seminal force on the American musical scene. Take your choice. The subject, as the saying goes, awaits further study.

24

Dvořák and his Black Students

THOMAS L. RIIS

WHEN Dvořák was brought to New York in 1892, cajoled by the idealistic and open-handed Jeannette M. Thurber, to become the director of the National Conservatory of Music (the only federally chartered school of music ever in the United States), he could not have foreseen the impact that his presence would make, although it certainly was not unanticipated by his patron. Mrs Thurber's move to create a national school of music where admission was based solely on talent without regard to race, colour, or the ability to pay was in itself a radical social gesture in 1885, when the school was founded. It testified to her fearless artistic commitment and organizational spirit. The idea of employing a European to enhance the Americanness of her school reveals yet more astuteness. Dvořák's arrival in America proved to be a catalytic event.

Dvořák's generally positive statements to the press about 'national songs' plunged him immediately into the centre of a controversy about the relative merits of African-American slave songs and their relationships to 'cultivated' products. What seemed eminently sensible to Dvořák—that national airs and folk-melodies could and should become the basis of a national American symphonic style—sparked hostility for Americans whose racism could not encompass the idea that Black or Indian music might be found worthy of integration into formal concert music.

How were Dvořák's Black students involved in this controversy? Indeed, who were his Black students, and what does the nature of their work tell us about Dvořák's impact on them and theirs on him?

One reminiscence of Dvořák in the African-American press in January 1904 noted that opera producer Theodore Drury and singers Desseria Plato and Margaret Scott attended the National Conservatory in Dvořák's time;[1] but these three, if they knew Dvořák at all directly, probably sang or played

A slightly different version of this chapter appeared in Czech trans. as 'Dvořák a afroamerická hudba' (Dvořák and African-American Music) in *Hudební rozhledy*, 14/5 (1991), 226–9.

[1] 'Stage', *Freeman* (Indianapolis, 4 Jan. 1904), 4.

under his baton in the school orchestra. They were not in his composition class. Thurber's protegé James Gibbons Huneker mentions the names of two students in a piano class at the Conservatory comprising only African-Americans, Paul Bolin and Henry Guy.[2] But for neither of these men do we have any further information in connection with Dvořák.

The two most eminent African-Americans to have worked with Dvořák were Will Marion Cook (1869–1944) and Harry T. Burleigh (1866–1949). Cook became famous as a writer of musical comedies, and we shall return to him presently, but it is Burleigh who has always attracted the most attention. Already an experienced singer at the age of 26, Burleigh reportedly inspired Dvořák's curiosity and admiration by his singing of Black spirituals in the composer's home in New York. He appears not to have been Dvořák's student but rather his amanuensis or music-copyist, a position for which he was paid[3] and which he secured partly through the assistance of Edward MacDowell's mother (Frances Knapp MacDowell), who served as the Conservatory Registrar. Burleigh had made her acquaintance years earlier in his home town of Erie, Pennsylvania.[4]

The influence of Black spirituals on the music of Dvořák has been variously conceded and denied by numberless critics from 1893 to the present, and Dvořák himself made several well-known comments on this matter. So let us hear from Harry Burleigh on this issue first of all. In a letter that appeared in 1918, he speaks clearly. The 'New World' Symphony, which is mentioned, was of course by this time an acknowledged masterpiece, and Dvořák long dead.

There is a tendency in these days to ignore the Negro element in the 'New World' symphony, shown by the fact that many of those who were able in 1893 to find traces of Negro musical color all through the symphony, though the workmanship and treatment of the themes was and is Bohemian, now cannot find anything in the whole four movements that suggests any local or Negro influence, though there is no doubt at all that Dvořák was deeply impressed by the old Negro 'spirituals' and also by Foster's songs. It was my privilege to sing repeatedly some of the old plantation songs for him at his house, and one in particular, 'Swing Low, Sweet Chariot', greatly pleased him, and part of this old spiritual will be found in the second theme of the first movement of the symphony, in G major, first given out by the flute. The similarity is so evident that it doesn't need to be heard; the eye can see it. Dvořák saturated himself with the spirit of these old tunes and then invented his own themes. There is a subsidiary theme in G minor in the first movement with a flat seventh, and I feel sure the composer caught this peculiarity of most of the slave songs from

[2] Arnold T. Schwab, *James Gibbons Huneker: Critic of the Seven Arts* (Stanford, Calif., 1963), 52.

[3] Eileen Southern, *Biographical Dictionary of Afro-American and African Musicians* (Westport, Conn., 1982), 56.

[4] Ibid. 56.

some that I sang him; for he used to stop me and ask if that was the way the slaves sang.[5]

Burleigh's comment is not unlike Dvořák's own analysis, provided to the *New York Herald* in December 1893:

Since I have been in this country I have been deeply interested in the national music of the Negroes and Indians. . . . In both there is a peculiar scale caused by the absence of the fourth and seventh or leading tone. In both the minor scale has the seventh invariably a minor seventh, the fourth is included and the sixth omitted.[6]

Dvořák seems to be describing familiar pentatonic and Dorian scales; both are found of course in a variety of folk styles. Neither Dvořák nor Burleigh claimed that these scales are used exclusively in the spirituals. Both strongly suggested (in other passages) that while the language of the spirituals and Dvořák's American works may share certain technical points, it was the mood or aura that linked the symphonic and folk styles.

But let us come back to Dvořák's implied question to Burleigh, 'Is that the way the slaves sang?', and consider the sound itself. How *did* the slaves sing, and how did Burleigh sing for Dvořák? Perhaps there is something more here than a series of intervals, omitted sixths or flatted sevenths.

In the year following Burleigh's birth the first collection of spirituals with music notation appeared in print, *Slave Songs of the United States*, by Allen, Ware, and Garrison (1867). The fascinating preface by the collector William Allen eloquently describes the difficulty of notating precisely the strange sounds of the slave songs. He says, in part:

The difficulty experienced in attaining absolute correctness is greater than might be supposed by those who have never tried the experiment and we are far from claiming that we have made no mistakes. . . . The best we can do, however, with paper and types, or even with voices, will convey but a faint shadow of the original. The voices of the colored people have a peculiar quality that nothing can imitate; and the intonations and delicate variations of even one singer cannot be reproduced on paper.[7]

How much did Burleigh, a descendant of free people of colour, in Pennsylvania, know of the slave songs? His grandfather was a former slave, which gave Burleigh, so to speak, a direct line to the old style. But he was also the son of educated parents and had high aspirations and helpful, well-placed White friends. He was certainly aware of the conflicting views among free

[5] Maud Cuney-Hare, *Negro Musicians and their Music* (Washington, DC, 1936), 59.

[6] John Clapham, *Dvořák* (New York, 1979), 201–2.

[7] (New York, 1867), pp. iv–v. Repr. in *Readings in Black American Music*, ed. Eileen Southern, 2nd edn. (New York, 1983), 151.

Blacks and former slaves about the appropriate use or exposure of the slave songs after the American Civil War. Burleigh advocated their dissemination but saw an alternative to their being presented in a 'raw' state, straight off the plantation. His eulogist, Ellsworth Janifer, quotes his words:

In the old forms the spirituals were just simple tunes. Only the Negroes could sing them because they understood, instinctively, the rhythms. They could harmonize them with their voices and produce some of the strangest, most subtle effects. They had no accompaniments. There was nothing in the tune to guide the singers. . . . They were really hidden from the world. You know that they have been in print for years, but it is only since they were arranged that they have become widely known.[8]

A sampling of Burleigh's own vocalism can be heard on the so-called Broome Special Phonograph Records. (This rare recording of spirituals was probably made in the 1940s; though not commercially available, one excerpt was supplied to me by Paul Charosh.) A study of, for example, 'Go Down Moses', a minor-key tune with the sixth omitted, *à la* Dvořák, tells us many things. Even without knowing Burleigh's identity or background, we could conclude that the singer is a strong one. He is classically trained. All of his final consonants are audible; his vowels are clear, his tone sustained and full. There is but little discernible folk or blues timbre in his voice, although it is free of extreme vibrato. His rhythms are precisely executed. Syncopations are crisp rather than swinging or crooning. The piano accompaniment is appropriately present and, from the singer's point of view, appropriately subdued.

Although certainly made after his student days, the recording may be reasonably representative of Burleigh's singing for Dvořák. It was only a year after his meeting with Dvořák that Burleigh landed the plum job of his career: he was selected over several dozen other applicants for the soloist's position at the prestigious and mostly White St George's Episcopal Church in New York. The St George's music committee was not looking for a slave singer. This recording, as beautiful as it may be, surely does not show how the slaves sang.

The manner in which Burleigh sang for Dvořák we will never know. Perhaps it was with a more folk-like sound. But it was Burleigh also who first arranged the spirituals to be performed as concert vocal solos with piano accompaniment, rather than as choral works or quartets as had been done in the 1870s by the Fisk Jubilee Singers. At any rate it seems beyond serious doubt that Burleigh brought a high level of polish to his renditions for Dvořák.

Burleigh and Dvořák were agreed that the principle of borrowing motifs and sharing scales could be maintained, but also that the adaptation of an emotional sound and a spiritual attitude, not merely a line of notes, should be

---

[8] 'Harry T. Burleigh Ten Years Later', *Phylon*, 21 (1960), 149.

prized. It was Dvořák's whole experience in America, as he himself said, that led to his Symphony 'From the New World', not any one song, sound, or event.

Dvořák was not alone among European composers in being impressed by African-American songs, but if he and others were so powerfully moved by sounds from America, their openness was matched by the resistance of Americans themselves to recognizing the worth of folksong sources. The racism of the 1890s was so intense that even allowing Blacks to stand dignified on a public platform, as either performers or speakers, was difficult to achieve except in select company.

The World's Columbian Exposition in Chicago, which Dvořák attended in 1893, purportedly demonstrated the progressive, forward-looking attitudes of Americans, but African-Americans were all but excluded entirely from the exhibitions.[9] The alleged savageries and primitiveness of exotic West African dancers were allowed as an entertainment in an ersatz Dahomean village on the Midway Plaisance, the outdoor promenade, but the central exhibition of 'civilized' activities and achievements was all too aptly named 'The White City'.

The civil-rights crusader Ida Wells wrote a tract to excoriate the fair, calling her pamphlet *The Reason Why the Colored American is not in the World's Columbian Exposition*.[10] The 25th of August 1893 had been declared Colored People's Day, but Wells railed against it as a meagre and insulting sop. And if Black crowds did not stay away, they could not have been encouraged by the fun the press took at the day's expense; it had been advertised that watermelon vendors would be on hand to help draw a large turnout.[11] The single event of Colored People's Day that merited and received attention was a rousing oration by the leonine, practically legendary Frederick Douglass, followed by poetry read by Paul Laurence Dunbar and music by Douglass's grandson Joseph and by Will Marion Cook, soon to become a pupil of Dvořák. In fact, it is probable that Dvořák and Cook first met at the fair. Dvořák journeyed from Spillville with his family to conduct music for Bohemia Day on 12 August, just two weeks before Colored People's Day, and Cook was already in town. Maurice Peress has recently located a letter of introduction for Cook from Harry Burleigh to Dvořák which suggests the strong likelihood of their having met at Dvořák's lodgings near the fair.[12] At any rate, Cook later came to New York and enrolled in the National Conservatory.

Cook's musical training up to this point had been extensive. After studying

[9] William S. McFeely, *Frederick Douglass* (New York, 1991), 366–72.
[10] Ibid. 366.   [11] Ibid. 370.
[12] Unpub. letter found among the Dvořák correspondence and documents in the Muzeum české hudby (Museum of Czech Music), Prague, and shown to Mr Peress by courtesy of Dr Milan Kuna.

the violin for years and attending Oberlin Conservatory, he was accepted for study with Joseph Joachim, and he travelled to Berlin for that purpose in the mid-1880s. While from all appearances Cook enjoyed and benefited from his European studies, cherishing his memories of Joachim, his comments about Dvořák do not create the impression that he was on especially friendly terms with him by 1898. In a memoir published towards the end of his life he recalled:

I was barred [for a time] from the classes at the National Conservatory of Music because I wouldn't play my fiddle in the orchestra under Dvořák. I couldn't play; my fingers had grown too stiff. Dvořák didn't like me anyway; Harry Burleigh was his pet. Only John White, the harmony and counterpoint teacher, thought I had talent, and insisted that I attend his classes.[13]

Aside from occasionally trading on his famous teacher's name, Cook did not discuss in print the specifics of his relationship with Dvořák elsewhere. After studying with Dvořák he went on not to classical performance work but into popular music. He created two of the most important Black-cast musical comedies on Broadway, *Clorindy* (1898) and *In Dahomey* (1902). Despite his jealous cut at Burleigh they remained friends; Cook was later reported to have worked on his musicals in Burleigh's New York flat.[14]

Although Dvořák seems to have liked Burleigh, Cook may have been confusing Dvořák's fondness for him with that for another Black student, Maurice Arnold Strothotte (1865–1937). Strothotte was a student in Dvořák's composition class in whom there seemed to be much potential. Dvořák told the *Chicago Tribune* (13 August 1893), during his World's Fair visit:

At present I have studying with me in New York seven pupils; next year I shall have a much larger number. I take only those far advanced in composition; that is, understanding thorough bass, form and instrumentation. The most promising and gifted of these pupils is a young Westerner, Strothotte by name, a native of St. Louis. A suite of 'Creole Dances' written by him, and which contain material that he has treated in a style that accords with my ideas, will be given in New York during the winter.[15]

Dvořák was as good as his word, and the concert alluded to took place on 23 January 1894 at Madison Square concert-hall. An ensemble of Conservatory students and singers from St Philip's Church, the most élite of New York's Black Protestant congregations, formed a virtually all-Black cast. The group performed Dvořák's arrangement of Foster's 'Old Folks at Home', and Maurice Arnold Strothotte (his name now simply shortened to Maurice

---

[13] 'Clorindy, the Origin of the Cakewalk', *Theatre Arts* (Sept. 1947), 61, Repr. in *Readings in Black American Music*, 228.

[14] James Weldon Johnson, *Along this Way* (New York, 1933), 175.

[15] 'For National Music', as quoted in Clapham, *Dvořák*, 201.

Arnold) conducted his own *American Plantation Dances*, the 'Creole Dances' referred to by Dvořák.[16]

Will Marion Cook and Maurice Arnold followed strikingly similar paths in their musical development. Both enjoyed conservatoire-level training in the American Midwest, Cook at Oberlin and Arnold in Cincinnati. Both made an extended stay in Germany, Cook in Berlin with Joachim and Arnold in Berlin, Cologne, and Breslau, where he studied with many teachers including Max Bruch. Arnold was just old enough to have missed crossing Cook's European path. Neither ever mentioned the other in letters so far as I have been able to tell. Arnold appears to have been at the Chicago fair in the same summer as Cook and Dvořák (he was noted as Burleigh's accompanist in newspaper advertisements for Colored People's Day). He also composed an orchestral work, *Danse de la Midway Plaisance*, that at least confirms his awareness of the Exposition fever that had taken hold in many regions of the country that summer.[17] Unlike Cook, Arnold was appointed as an instructor at the National Conservatory. W. L. Hubbard credits him with '[using] the Negro plantation idea, not by introducing Negro melodies but by embodying the African spirit in his own work'. An unpublished violin sonata is also said to be 'in the African style'.[18] Arnold wrote two operas, a dramatic overture, a cantata, works for piano eight hands, and songs.[19]

In at least one important respect Arnold was not like Cook or Burleigh: he apparently did not seek fame as a Black nationalist artist. Although he was not in fact White, it is not unreasonable to guess that he could have passed for White. His name, with a brief description of his life and works, appears in a few American sources from early in the twentieth century, but none makes direct reference to his skin colour or ethnicity, an omission that would be almost unheard-of if he were Black in a highly race-conscious era. He is not recorded by Maud Cuney-Hare in her landmark chronicle *Negro Musicians and their Music* of 1936. He died in 1937, and, though his name was preserved in Czech biographies of Dvořák as one of the master's pupils, he disappeared from history in the English-speaking world until 1979, when John Clapham noted him as a Black student of Dvořák's.[20] His midwestern roots and early turn to non-racial genres may account for his relative invisibility to

---

[16] Ibid. 133.

[17] 'Arnold, Maurice', in *Musical Biographies*, comp. Janet M. Green (The American History and Encyclopedia of Music, ed. W. L. Hubbard, i; New York, 1910), 21.

[18] Ibid. 21.

[19] 'Arnold, Maurice', in *Baker's Biographical Dictionary*, 8th edn., ed. Nicolas Slonimsky (New York, 1992), 791.

[20] See Šourek, *Život a dílo Antonína Dvořáka* (The Life and Work of Antonín Dvořák), 2nd edn., iii (Prague, 1956), 103–4 n., 146 n., 193, and Clapham, *Dvořák*, 133.

biographers centred around New York and Washington. His fate is ironic, given Dvořák's high hopes and personal tribute to him.

Burleigh and Cook remained the Black composers for whom great expectations were held. The *Negro Music Journal* in 1903 declared, 'The Negroes, and the Negroes alone, have the songs of the American soul and soil, and Dvořák was not long in discovering the fact. . . . Burleigh and Cook are the men who lent Dvořák the opportune suggestions. . . . They form a shrine around which our future music must encircle.'[21] This deification of course proved to be premature. The writer could not have guessed at the impending and far greater impact of the blues and jazz, with which Cook and Burleigh had comparatively little commerce. Nor could he have realized the power of prejudice and habit to keep Blacks from rising too quickly in the fields of musical comedy and symphonic performance. Integration was still a rarity on the New York stage in 1903 and would remain so through the first decades of the twentieth century.

Burleigh turned to writing art songs that, while attractive, have no special 'folk' flavour. Most are now out of print. He wrote no important symphonic music and is today known chiefly as an arranger of spirituals. Cook garnered accolades for his musical comedies in 1903, and helped to foster other young talents in the 1920s, but he died almost forgotten in 1944 after a long decline. While Dvořák's words and goodwill were remembered, albeit selectively and with varying emphasis, the realization of his dreams of an American symphonic music created by his students was not directly achieved.

But the story does not end with Arnold, Burleigh, and Cook. In a recent essay entitled 'Dvořák's Long American Reach', Adrienne Fried Block has documented far more completely than I the influence of Dvořák among American musicians.[22] Block and Rae Linda Brown have pointed out to me the remarkable similarities between Dvořák's 'New World' Symphony and the Symphony in E minor of Florence Price, America's first Black woman writer of symphonies.[23]

The last chapter of my tale has a pleasantly mythical or legendary ring, so I'll tell it this way. Once upon a time Dvořák had a rebellious student named Will Marion Cook, who grew to manhood and who himself became a teacher after a fashion. And one of *his* students did eventually become a great American composer. Duke Ellington, although he never attended a conser-

[21] As quoted in William Austin, '*Susannah*', '*Jeannie*', *and* '*The Old Folks at Home*': *Stephen Foster's Songs from his Time to Ours* (New York, 1975), 298.

[22] In *Dvořák in America: 1892–1895*, ed. John C. Tibbetts (Portland, Oreg., 1993), 157–81.

[23] Rae Linda Brown, 'William Grant Still, Florence Price, and William Dawson: Echoes of the Harlem Renaissance', in *Black Music in the Harlem Renaissance*, ed. Samuel A. Floyd, Jun. (New York, 1990), 80. Incidentally, Price's symphony was performed by the Chicago Symphony Orchestra under Frederick Stock at the next World's Fair in Chicago after the Columbian Exposition, in 1933.

vatoire as Cook urged him to do, nevertheless was one of Cook's greatest admirers. Ellington characterized his days 'browsing around Broadway', asking for Cook's musical advice about developing themes, as 'one of the best semesters I ever had in music'. Ellington recalled Cook's words, 'First you find the logical way, and when you find it, avoid it, and let your inner self break through and guide you. Don't try to be anybody but yourself.'[24] Ellington took the advice to heart, and the results of his labours were rich indeed: thousands of works spanning all genres, settings, and moods, vocal and instrumental, symphonic as well as solo music. Dvořák's own early declaration that he 'came to discover what young Americans had in them and to help them to express it'[25] would seem to have found a parallel in Cook's treatment of Ellington. And so we might finally agree that Dvořák's hope for American students was fulfilled at last, but in the second generation rather than the first after his own.

[24] Edward Kennedy 'Duke' Ellington, *Music is my Mistress* (Garden City, NY, 1973), 96–7.
[25] 'The Real Value of Negro Melodies', *New York Herald* (21 May 1893), 28, as repr. in Clapham, *Dvořák*, 198.

25

Dvořák, Nationalism, Myth, and Racism in the United States

CHARLES HAMM

NATIONALISM in music is defined by *The New Harvard Dictionary of Music* as:

the use in art music of materials that are identifiably national . . . in character. These may include actual folk music, melodies or rhythms that merely recall folk music, and nonmusical programmatic elements drawn from national folklore, myth, or literature. This concept of musical nationalism has most often been employed [for] music of the later nineteenth and early twentieth centuries.[1]

This notion of national style emerged just as many large new nation-states were taking shape in Europe. King Wilhelm I of Prussia was proclaimed Emperor of Germany on 18 January 1871, ruling a new German Reich made up of twenty-five states (including the former kingdoms of Prussia, Bavaria, Saxony, and Württemberg), for instance, and a similar unification occurred in Italy at almost the same time.

In the process, previously autonomous villages, districts, regions, city-states, and even entire kingdoms and nations were swallowed up by new modern nation-states, and for political reasons it became expedient to develop a new mythology of 'national race', according to which the entire population of a given nation-state was imagined to have a common language, religion, history, and cultural heritage. I am using Roland Barthes's concept of mythology as a process whereby ideologically based arguments and explanations are put forward to 'overturn culture into nature', that is, to make a given situation seem natural, self-evident, commonsensical.[2] In various European countries it was argued that entire national populations were unified, across class lines, by a national character and culture, which found expression in each country's history, myths, sagas, and folklore—particularly folksong.

A slightly different version of this chapter appeared in Czech transl. as 'Dvořák, nacionalismus, mýtus a rasová otázka v USA', in *Hudební rozhledy*, 14/4 (1991), 183–6, and also in Charles Hamm, *Putting Popular Music in its Place* (Cambridge, 1995).

[1] ed. Don Michael Randel (Cambridge, Mass., 1986), 527.   [2] *Mythologies* (London, 1973).

Folk song is essentially a communal as well as a racial product. There is no music so characteristic of the German people as German folk song, so characteristic of the Russian people as Russian folk music. . . . English folk song is distinctively national and English, and, therefore, inherently different from that of every other nation in the world.[3]

'Deutsch' is the title given to those Germanic races which, upon their natal soil, retained their speech and customs. . . . In rugged woods, throughout the lengthy winter, by the warm hearth fire of his turret chamber soaring high into the clouds, for generations [the German] kept alive the deeds of his forefathers; the myths of native gods he weaves into an endless web of sagas.[4]

The greatest artist belongs inevitably to his country as much as the humblest singer in a remote village—they and all those who come between them are links in the same chain, manifestations on their different levels of the same desire for artistic expression, and, moreover, the same nature of artistic expression.[5]

The dark side of this developing ideology of nationalism lay in its necessary exclusion of individuals or groups within a nation-state who did not belong to the dominant 'race' or culture. Thus Richard Wagner could write:

The Jew speaks the language of the country in which he has lived from generation to generation, but he always speaks it like a foreigner. [This] makes it impossible for him ever to speak colloquially, authoritatively, or from the depths of his being. A language, its expression and its evolution are not separate elements but part of an historical community, and only he who has unconsciously matured in this community can take any part in what it creates. . . . Our entire German civilization and art have remained foreign to the Jew; for he has taken no part in the evolution of either. . . . The cultured Jew stands alien and alienated in the midst of a society he does not understand, with whose tastes and aspirations he is not in sympathy, and to whose history and evolution he is indifferent.[6]

Though the population of the United States of America was anything but homogeneous in the late nineteenth and early twentieth centuries, arguments for a national character and national culture, based on the myth of 'national race', were put forward as vigorously here as in Europe.

The only possible root upon which we can engraft our [national] culture is the Anglo-Saxon root . . . because those ideals upon which our republic was based are characteristically and distinctively Anglo-Saxon. The Anglo-Saxon spirit of good

[3] Cecil Sharp, *English Folk Song: Some Conclusions*, 4th (rev.) edn. (Belmont, Calif., 1965), 164–5. 1st edn. 1907.

[4] Richard Wagner, 'Was ist deutsch', in *Bayreuther Blätter*, 1 (1878), 29–42. Originally written in 1865.

[5] Ralph Vaughan Williams, *National Music and Other Essays* (Oxford, 1987), 7. From lectures given at Bryn Mawr in 1932; 1st edn. London, 1963.

[6] 'Das Judentum in der Musik', *Neue Zeitschrift für Musik*, 32 (1850), 101–7, 109–12.

sportsmanship and sense of fair play and justice have been, up to this time, the basis of everything that is fine, that is liberal, that is progressive in our past and in our present.[7]

The reserve, the dislike of ostentation, the repressed but strong emotion masked by dry humor, that belong to our New England type—this Anglo-Saxon element in our heterogeneous national character is of crucial significance in determining what we call the American temper.[8]

The most articulate proponents of an American national identity and culture based on Anglo-Saxon roots were a group of composers from New England and the South, described as 'humanist Victorians' by MacDonald Smith Moore, who says of them:

[They] rationalized their musical calling on the basis of redemptive culture: the doctrine that musical culture could redeem the American spirit. . . . [They] portrayed redemptive culture primarily as a potential American civil religion. As Yankees, they considered themselves leaders of a progressive movement peculiarly American and, therefore, universal. By directly experiencing the ordering principles of redemptive culture, audiences could understand the meaning of their identity as Americans.[9]

Here as in Europe, the relationship between 'alien' groups and America's 'national culture' was questioned and challenged:

Can the Negro and the Jew stand in the relation of a folk to our nation? And if not, can the music they create be the national music? There is this possibility: that as the American winds himself around layer after layer of civilization, he diminishes the vigour of his specific characteristics.[10]

We Americans are no more black Africans than we are red Indians; and it is absurd to imagine that the negro idiom could ever give adequate expression to the soul of our race.[11]

The insidiousness of the Jewish menace to our artistic integrity is due to the speciousness, the superficial charm and persuasiveness of Hebrew art, its violently juxtaposed extremes of passion, its poignant eroticism and pessimism. . . . For how shall a public accustomed by prevailing fashion to the exaggeration, the constant running to extremes, of eastern expression, divine the poignant beauty of Anglo-Saxon sobriety and restraint? . . . How shall it value as it deserves the balance, the sense of proportion, which is the finest of Anglo-Saxon qualities, and to which, like the sense of humor to which it is akin, nothing is more alien than the Oriental abandonment to excess? Our public taste is in danger of being permanently debauched, made lastingly

---

[7] John Powell, 'Lectures on Music', *The Rice Institute Pamphlet*, 10/3 (July 1923), 127.
[8] Daniel Gregory Mason, *Tune in, America* (New York, 1930), 159.
[9] *Yankee Blues: Musical Culture and American Identity* (Bloomington, Ind., 1985), 44.
[10] Gilbert Seldes, 'The Negro's Songs', *Dial* (Mar. 1926), 249.
[11] Powell, 'Lectures on Music', 162.

insensitive to qualities most subtly and quintessentially our own, by the intoxication of what is, after all, an alien art.[12]

When Dvořák arrived in America in 1892, this debate over American character and national style was in its first stages. He is commonly supposed to have suggested that a national American music might emerge out of elements of Indian (Native American) and Negro (Black) music, and *The New York Herald* of 21 May 1893 reported him as saying 'I am now satisfied that the future music of this country must be founded upon what are called the Negro melodies.' But all evidence suggests that the 'Negro melodies' he heard in New York were of two types, European-style arrangements of spirituals and the commercial 'plantation' songs of Stephen Foster and other white songwriters, and that he had no contact with and no knowledge of more 'authentic' Black music. This point is made quite explicit in his extended and often-quoted essay 'Music in America', published in *Harper's Magazine*. After an initial disclaimer of his right to speak to the subject:

It would ill become me . . . to express my views on so general and all-embracing a subject as music in America, were I not pressed to do so, for I have neither travelled extensively, nor have I been here long enough to gain an intimate knowledge of American affairs. I can only judge of it from what I have observed during my limited experience as a musician and teacher in America, and from what those whom I know here tell me about their own country.[13]

Dvořák nevertheless proceeded to predict that:

the music of America will soon become more national in its character. This, my conviction, I know is not shared by many who can justly claim to know this country better than I do. Because the population of the United States is composed of many different races, in which the Teutonic element predominates, and because, owing to the improved methods of transmission of the present day, the music of all the world is quickly absorbed by this country, they argue that nothing specially original or national can come forth.

. . . All races have their distinctively national songs, which they at once recognize as their own. . . .

It is a proper question to ask, what songs, then, belong to the American and appeal more strongly to him than any others? . . . The most potent as well as the most beautiful among them, according to my estimation, are certain of the so-called plantation melodies and slave songs. . . . The point has been urged that many of these touching songs, like those of Foster, have not been composed by the Negroes themselves, but

---

[12] Daniel Gregory Mason, 'Is American Music Growing Up? Our Emancipation from Alien Influences', *Arts and Decoration* (Nov. 1920).

[13] (With the 'co-operation' of Edwin Emerson, Jun.), *Harper's New Monthly Magazine*, 90/537 (Feb. 1895), 429. Repr., with slight discrepancies, in *Dvořák in America: 1892–1895*, ed. John C. Tibbetts (Portland, Oreg., 1993), 370.

are the work of white men, while others did not originate on the plantation, but were imported from Africa. It seems to me that this matters but little. . . . Whether the original songs which must have inspired the composers came from Africa or originated on the plantations matters as little as whether Shakespeare invented his own plots or borrowed them from others. The thing to rejoice over is that such lovely songs exist and are sung at the present day. . . . Just so it matters little whether the inspiration for the coming folk-songs of America is derived from the Negro melodies, the songs of the Creoles, the red man's chant, or the plaintive ditties of the homesick German or Norwegian. Undoubtedly the germs for the best of music lie hidden among all the races that are commingled in this great country.[14]

Though Dvořák's message could not be clearer, let me summarize what he actually said, as opposed to what he is often alleged to have said:

1. There is no such thing as an American 'race', since the country's population is made up of the 'commingling' of many different nationalities. Furthermore, modern communications make music from elsewhere in the world readily available in the United States.
2. As a consequence, the music of no single national or ethnic group can be considered 'American'.
3. Nevertheless, a national style can come about in the United States, from a 'commingling' of the musics of the various groups cohabiting in the country.
4. Such a style had in fact already emerged, in the 'plantation songs' of Stephen Foster and others, which Dvořák clearly understood were not the 'folksongs' of Southern Blacks but rather the contemporary products of White, professional songwriters.
5. The future would bring similarly 'American' songs derived from other national or ethnic groups.

The truly radical aspect of his comments lies in his suggestion that American 'national song' could be the product of commercial songwriters, reflecting and at the same time shaping the complex, multicultural contemporary life of the United States, rather than folksongs dredged up from the midst of the past, mystically echoing some unitary American character or spirit.

Dvořák, then, did not urge a 'national' school of American composition drawing self-consciously on one strain or another of folksong. In fact, his comments are not concerned with 'folksong' at all, and he nowhere uses that term. Arthur Farwell's *Navajo War Dance*, Henry Gilbert's *Negro Rhapsody*, and John Powell's *Natchez-on-the-Hill* were not what he had in mind for the future of America's music. He predicted instead a continuing school of national song, drawing on different elements of the country's diverse

---

[14] 'Music in America', 432–3; *Dvořák in America*, 376–7.

population, and possibly a classical music growing out of—not based on—this American song. What he proposed would in fact become the Anglophiles' worst nightmare, when it did come about: music by immigrant urban Jewish composers, with names like Irving Berlin and George Gershwin and Aaron Copland, drawing on Black, Jewish, Irish, and Italian styles, accepted both at home and abroad as the most distinctive American music of its time.

Dvořák's most important contribution to American music, then, was his vision, his foresight and audacity in suggesting that contemporary, commercially produced popular music might be the 'national song' of the United States. This came at a time when his American peers were blinded by ethnocentricity, and a quarter-century before anyone else was to develop such an argument.

APPENDIX: DVOŘÁK'S INTERVIEWS WITH BRITISH NEWSPAPERS

WITH CRITICAL COMMENTARY BY
DAVID R. BEVERIDGE

Jarmil Burghauser, in his important study 'Concerning One of the Myths about Dvořák: Dvořák the Apprentice Butcher', cites several valuable but neglected early sources of information on Dvořák's life;[1] among them are two interviews given by the composer to newspapers during his visits to England in 1885 and 1886. These interviews have recently been issued for the first time in modern reprints—but only in German translation! (They are found in Klaus Döge's *Dvořák: Leben, Werke, Dokumente*.)[2] Here, for the first time, the interviews are reprinted in their original English texts, with annotations.

We can spot some errors of fact in the interviews, but for spontaneous recollections (as they appear to be) by a 45-year-old composer reaching back to his childhood, they are remarkably well in accord with data otherwise confirmable. On some points they correct misinformation that has been widely circulated in the secondary literature, and in general they help to 'flesh out' our picture of what Dvořák the man was like. Moreover, quite apart from their historical significance, they make thoroughly enjoyable reading.

Enthusiasts Interviewed
Sunday Times (London), 10 May 1885, p. 6.

This interview was given by Dvořák to Paul Pry during the composer's third visit to England, which lasted from 19 April until 14 May 1885. His previous visits had been in March and September of the preceding year, lasting about three and two weeks respectively. The highlight of this third sojourn was the world première of the Seventh Symphony, commissioned by the Philharmonic Society of London and performed by it under the composer's direction on 22 April 1885. But there were many other concerts featuring Dvořák's music as well. Based on references in the interview to performances that occurred 'this week' and would occur 'next week' (and whose

---

[1] Trans. by and rev. in collaboration with David Beveridge, Karel Janovický, and Graham Melville-Mason, in *Czech Music: The Journal of the Dvořák Society*, 18/1 (spring 1993), 17–44.

[2] (Mainz, 1991), 331–8. I wish to thank Klaus Döge for supplying me with photocopies of the original interviews.

actual dates we know), the interview appears to have taken place very close to the date of publication, that is, 10 May.

The interview undoubtedly took place in the German language, as is clear from Pry's mention of having translated the composer's words, and the many German words and German spellings that remain. Dvořák knew some English by this time, but was still much better at German and generally used this language to communicate with his British hosts. The narrative is very colourful, and the description of events may be assumed to have been embellished a little by Dvořák and/or by Pry in his translation.

More than one brief sketch of Antonín Dvořák's[3] life has been written since his first visit to this country a year ago, but in no case have we had a complete history of the events that make up his singular and interesting career.[4] It has been my good fortune to obtain from the famous Bohemian composer, during his present stay, a verbal account of those events, which I here translate as nearly as possible from his own words.

'I was born,' said 'Pann'[5] (Mr.) Dvořák, 'in 1841, at Mühlhausen, or, as we call it in Bohemia, Nelahozeves, a village four miles from the town of Pralup.[6] My parents were poor. My father (who is still living) was a butcher, and as is often the case in our country, combined the occupation of innkeeper with his regular business.[7] I helped him in both, for I learned as a boy to buy, kill, and cut up the sheep and oxen.[8] At the same time I attended the village school, and there learned the violin and singing and the rudiments of music. Every child in Bohemia must study music. The law enacting this is old; it was once repealed, but is now in force again. Herein, I consider, lies one great secret of the natural talent for music in my country. Our national tunes and chorales come, as it were, from the very heart of the people, and beautiful things they

---

[3] Apparently the *Sunday Times* could not print the háček over the 'r' in Dvořák's name. The same applies to the *Pall Mall Gazette* interview which follows.

[4] By the 'brief sketches' of Dvořák's life written since his first visit to England (Mar. 1884), Pry probably means sketches in British newspapers or journals, identity unknown. The most significant biographical essays on Dvořák up to this time had been published in German and Czech. They were Hermann Krigar's 'Anton Dvořák: Eine biographisches Skizze', *Musikalisches Wochenblatt* (Leipzig), 11/1–8 (Dec. 1879–Feb. 1880)—see Ch. 1 n. 13—and the opening pages (7–11) of Václav Juda Novotný's booklet *Dvořákovo 'Stabat Mater': Rozbor proslulého díla s krátkým životopisem skladatelovým* (Dvořák's 'Stabat Mater': An Analysis of the Famous Work with a Short Biography of the Composer) (Prague, 1884). The *Sunday Times* interview contributes a number of interesting details not found in either of them.

[5] Pan. The double 'n' is probably a German spelling.

[6] Should be Kralupy, lying actually about two miles south-south-east of Nelahozeves.

[7] 'Tavern-keeper' would probably be a better phrase than 'innkeeper'. The principal function of Dvořák's father's 'inn' (in Czech 'hospoda') at Nelahozeves seems to have been to dispense beer. Overnight accommodation was not provided.

[8] However, Dvořák did not, as has often been reported, engage in any formal training in the butcher's trade. The extent of his activities as a butcher has tended to be exaggerated in the literature, and the extent of his early musical activities understated. See Burghauser, 'Concerning One of the Myths' (n. 1 above).

are. I intend some day writing an oratorio into which I shall introduce some of these chorales.[9] The Slavs all love music. They may work all day in the fields, but they are always singing, and the true musical spirit burns bright within them. How they love the dance, too! On Sunday, when church is over, they begin their music and dancing,[10] and often keep it up without cessation till early in the following morning. Each village has its band of eight or ten musicians—I belonged to ours as soon as I could fiddle a little. It is supported by the dancers, who pay nothing to go in, but in the middle of their polka or waltz a couple is stopped by one of the musicians and not allowed to continue until they have paid as many kreutzers as they can afford. When all is over, the band divide their earnings, and mine, of course, used to be handed forthwith to my father.

'At the age of thirteen I went to live with my uncle at the village of Zlonic, near Schau.[11] There I studied with the school-teacher and organist, Anton[12] Liehmann, a good and clever musician. I should tell you that in Bohemia every school-teacher is bound to know sufficient music to give instruction in it. Well, I sang in the choir and began to learn the organ a little. I used to help to copy out the parts from the little scores that Liehmann wrote for the performances of the village band, and I remember how puzzled I got over the various keys in which the parts for wind-instruments were written. These things were not explained to me. I had to find out their meaning for myself. Once, I recollect, I determined to try my hand at a score myself. I wrote a polka for strings, 2 clarinets, 1 cornet, 2 horns, and 1 trombone. With great pride I carried it home to Mühlhausen and had it tried by our band there. How anxiously I waited for the opening chord! It was all right, bar the cornet part, which I had got quite in the wrong key. The mistake was soon remedied by transposition, but I leave you to guess its effect.'[13]

[9] Indeed, Dvořák had already in the previous year accepted an invitation from the Leeds Musical Festival to compose a choral work, and had determined that it should be an oratorio based on the story of the Czech heroine St Ludmila. This work, which he composed from Sept. 1885 to May 1886 and whose première he conducted at Leeds in Oct. that year, features a magnificent chorus based on the oldest known Czech liturgical melody, 'Hospodine, pomiluj ny' (Lord, have mercy on us).

[10] As in the opening scene of Dvořák's later opera, *Jakobín*.

[11] Zlonice, near Slaný. The move quite definitely occurred not at the age of 13, but rather around Dvořák's 12th birthday on 8 Sept. 1853. Though 1854 is commonly reported in recent literature as the year of the move, Pry's is the only source pub. during Dvořák's lifetime that gives this information. The others all state or imply that the move occurred in 1853, as Burghauser points out in 'Concerning One of the Myths'. We might add that Dvořák himself in a letter of 1895 to his family, recently pub. for the first time, referred to having been in Zlonice in 1853–6. See *Antonín Dvořák: Korespondence a dokumenty—Kritické vydání* (Antonín Dvořák: Correspondence and Documents—Critical Edition), ed. Milan Kuna et al., iii (Prague, 1989), 392.

[12] Antonín. Anton is the Ger. form.

[13] Dvořák apparently loved to tell this story, in progressively more colourful variants, and others loved to retell it. Cf. Krigar's earlier biographical study based on information from the composer (see n. 4 above), 214–15, and the *Pall Mall Gazette* interview from 1886 (below). In the much later words of H. L. Mencken,

'When did you first begin serious study?'

'Not yet. However, while at my uncle's I went on acquiring musical knowledge after a fashion. When I was fifteen[14] I began to learn the piano and counterpoint. As I have already told you, Liehmann was an excellent musician, but he left his pupils to find out a great deal for themselves. For instance, I had to teach myself entirely how to read a "figured bass." I can scarcely tell how I managed it, but after a little time, when I played the organ for services, I used to read whole Masses from old copies written with a "figured bass." Of course, they were not all such Masses as we gave on the yearly Church Festival, when works like Cherubini's D minor, Haydn's D minor, or Mozart's C major were performed.[15] Ah! those yearly performances. They might excite a smile now, but how lovely I thought them then! Indeed, it was being ever in the midst of this musical element that developed the feeling within me and made me long to become a real musician.

'At last my father's friends persuaded him not to bring me up to business, but to send me to Prague to study there in right good earnest. In 1857 I went, and was lodged with some relatives, receiving from home for my "keep" the scanty allowance of 8 florins [about 15s.] per month.[16] I was placed at the Organists' College, then under Joseph Pitsch,[17] an institution where organists and conductors are instructed. Here my great difficulty at first was that I could scarcely speak a word of German, for, although a Bohemian institution, the

who briefly sketched Dvořák's biography in an essay about the 'New World' Symphony: 'The polka itself seems to have been very creditable, but in scoring it the boy forgot to transpose the trumpet part, and so the first performance ended with yells for the police.' [!] See the repr. of this essay in *Dvořák and his World*, ed. Michael Beckerman (Princeton, NJ, 1993), 187.

[14] Earlier, actually. In the *Pall Mall Gazette* interview and elsewhere it is confirmed that he studied the piano and counterpoint in Zlonice, but around his 15th birthday he left Zlonice for Böhmisch Kamnitz (now Česká Kamenice).

[15] The Dvořák Memorial in Zlonice preserves a major portion of the musical archives from the church there dating from the time of Dvořák's childhood, but none of the mentioned works by Cherubini, Haydn, or Mozart are included. The archive does contain a D minor Mass probably by the Czech composer Vincenc Mašek (1755–1831) but attributed on the copy at Zlonice to Cherubini. It also contains fragments of a work in C major labelled as a Mass by Mozart, which is actually a Litany and evidently not by Mozart. (I have not been able to determine who the composer might be.) Dvořák thus may only have *thought* that he performed in the works mentioned; but then, too, the scores and parts at Zlonice may have been lost since his time, or he may have been remembering performances at Böhmisch Kamnitz (Česká Kamenice), where he lived next, and where we know there was a copy of Mozart's 'Coronation' Mass in C Major. (The Museum of Czech Music in Prague holds a MS list evidently made by Jan M. Květ of contents of the old church music archive at Böhmisch Kamnitz, though the archive itself is for the most part not traceable.)

[16] The British monetary equivalent is given in square brackets in the original art., as are the equivalents in round brackets in the next long paragraph; all probably represent insertions by Pry. A florin was the same as a gulden or, in Czech, *Zlatý*. Dvořák's allowance of 8 florins per month would have been at the bottom end of the scale for a factory worker's wages, according to information from Christolph Stölz, *Die Ära Bach in Böhmen: Socialgeschichtliche Studien zur Neoabsolutismus* (Munich, 1971), 343–4, as cited in Döge, *Dvořák*, 62–3 n.

[17] Actually Karl Franz Pitsch.

professors were then compelled to speak German—a rule which was simply scandalous.[18] However, if I could not speak, I managed to show that I could do something, and in time I got on very well, especially after Pitsch died, and a remarkably clever musician named Krejci[19] became head of the college. He was organist of a large church, and I was chosen with some of the best pupils to sing in the choir. Now it was that I first heard of Mozart, Beethoven, and Mendelssohn as instrumental composers; previously, indeed, I had hardly known that the two last-named had existed. Still I learned no instrumentation at the college. The first real orchestral performance I ever heard—I shall never forget it—was a rehearsal at the Conservatoire, when I contrived somehow to slip in. The work performed was Beethoven's 'Choral' Symphony, and the conductor was Spohr.'[20]

'How long did you remain at the College?'

'Nearly three years. I left in 1860,[21] when I was nineteen, and then came the important question, How to earn a living? First I tried what I could do as a fiddler, and got a place as viola-player in a band of eighteen or twenty, which played at various cafés and public places, doing the usual dances, potpourris, and overtures—among the last "Maritana," always a favourite. Well, by this I earned the huge sum of 22 florins (about two guineas) a month, then a little fortune to me; but I added to it by playing with our bandmaster in sextet performances at a lunatic asylum, where in time I became organist also. I had not much to spare for luxuries, and I longed, above all, to hear an opera. I remember one Sunday afternoon standing outside the theatre, when "Der Freischütz" was announced. Only ten kreutzers (a few pence) to go in, and I hadn't the money. A companion came up and I asked him to lend me as much. He was as badly off as myself, but said he would run and fetch what I wanted. I waited and waited, but, alas! he did not come back, and ultimately

---

[18] Apparently spurred by his nationalist, anti-German agenda, Dvořák here perpetrates what must surely be a gross exaggeration of his difficulties with the German language at the Organ School in Prague. His schooling at Zlonice had been in the German language, and afterwards he had spent a year in the border-town of Böhmisch Kamnitz (Česká Kamenice), where almost all the inhabitants were German-speaking, and where again he attended classes in German, achieving a perfect academic record and classification into the 'Vorzugsklasse' (superior category). When possible Dvořák liked to hide the fact that he spoke German even as an adult, as may be seen from a letter of 21 Aug. 1885, when just three months after the present interview he wrote to his friend Josef Zubatý during yet another visit to England, and asked him not to mention (in the Czech press) that he had conducted rehearsals for *Svatební košile* (The Spectre's Bride) at Birmingham in Ger., with Alfred Littleton translating into Eng. 'I'd rather have you write that I spoke, say, Turkish! You know how it is with these things in our country.' ('Napište třebas, že jsem mluvil turecky! Víte, jak to u nás chodí.') See *Antonín Dvořák: Korespondence*, ii. (Prague, 1988), 86. It is worth noting that his nationalistic effusions, while undoubtedly sincere in essence, apparently involved an element of posturing; he was, at any rate, highly conscious of how his statements would 'play' with the Czech public at home. See also n. 53 below.

[19] Josef Krejčí, later director of the Prague Conservatoire.

[20] Louis Spohr (1784–1859). The concert was on 9 July 1858.

[21] Should be 1859, after two years' study.

I had to leave the spot, my eyes full of tears, without having seen "Der Freischütz."[22] However I managed from time to time to hear a good concert. This I did by slipping into the orchestra and hiding myself behind the drums. I enjoyed myself, too, by spending most of my leisure hours in composing. In 1861 I wrote a quintet and quartet, both for strings, and to my intense delight succeeded in getting some friends to play them.[23] They were pleased with the works, and so was Krejci, my old master, to whom I showed them.[24] This encouraged me immensely.

'A year later an event of great importance to us happened in Prague—the opening of the new Bohemian Theatre, under the direction of Mayer.[25] The band in which I played was engaged as the nucleus of an orchestra of 36, and I must leave you to imagine how we dance-music players got on during our opening season with such operas as Bellini's "Montecchi e Capuletti" and "Norma," Rossini's "Otello," and Cherubini's "Deux Journées." But we were very proud of our national theatre, I can tell you, and now we are more so still. Whilst yet in the band I made the acquaintance of my friend Karl Bendl, who was well off and the possessor of a large quantity of scores, to which I had been unable up to that time to obtain access. He lent me some, among the first Beethoven's septet and the quartets of Onslow. I studied them with avidity, constantly composing all the while, and gradually I began to get ideas on scoring and instrumentation. None but the friends who shared my apartments knew how much I wrote, tore up, and burnt. These good fellows laughed at me, of course, but still I persevered, until in 1871 I made up my mind to leave the theatre and try to get private lessons, in order to get more time for composition. In this object I succeeded. Two years afterwards came my first reward. It was then that I wrote the "Patriotic Hymn," which is to be performed in London next week.[26] Given by the "Hlahol Gesang-Verein of Prague," and conducted by my friend Karl Bendl, it gained a great success, and gave me vast encouragement.'[27]

'You have written some operas, I believe?'

[22] But cf. the version of this story in the *Pall Mall Gazette* interview, according to which he heard *Freischütz* from the gallery.

[23] The quartet (in A major) was written in 1862, not 1861.

[24] An MS copy of the quartet, though not the original autograph, bears a dedication in Dvořák's hand to Krejčí.

[25] Jan Nepomuk Maýr (1818–88). Pry has again used a German spelling.

[26] The work was performed by Geaussent's Choir under Dvořák's direction on 13 May 1885.

[27] The full title is *Hymnus z Hálkovy básně 'Dědicové Bílé hory'* (Hymn from Hálek's Poem 'The Heirs of the White Mountain'); the work glorifies the Czech rebellion in 1620 against the repressive (and German) Habsburg regime. The première took place in March 1873. 'Gesang-Verein' was not part of the performing organization's title, but rather represents here (ironically) another Germanization. Dvořák had composed the work a year previously (May–June 1872), thus one year after his departure from the theatre orchestra, not two as the interview states.

'Yes; one of my chief ambitions when I began to compose was to write an opera. My first attempt was one called "König und Köhler."[28] The influence of Wagner was strongly shown in the harmony and orchestration. I had just heard "Die Meistersinger," and not long before Richard Wagner had himself been in Prague.[29] I was perfectly crazy about him, and recollect following him as he walked along the streets to get a chance now and again of seeing the great little man's face. Well, my opera. The parts were copied out, and it was to be done at the theatre. The piano and choral rehearsals began. But with one assent all complained that the music was too difficult. It was infinitely worse than Wagner. It was original, clever, they said, but unsingable. Persuasion was useless; my opera was abandoned. In 1875 I took the score up again, destroyed it, and re-wrote the whole opera afresh.[30] It was brought out and, being not only easy but national instead of Wagnerian, it had a genuine success.

'Meanwhile my position had been slightly improving; I had married, and had been appointed organist of the Adalbert Church,[31] in Prague, a welcome if not very lucrative post. Later on, I was much assisted by the "artists" stipend, a grant for one year at a time from the Government to artists whose works reveal talent and to whom assistance is of value. As examples I sent to Vienna my first symphony, in F, Op. 25 and my opera.[32] The grant amounted to 400 florins. A year later I tried again and sent in my "Stabat Mater" and a new grand opera "Wanda;" but nothing resulted.[33] At the third attempt I

[28] This is a Ger. trans. of the work's Czech title *Král a uhlíř* (The King and the Charcoal Burner). It was actually his second opera, after *Alfred*. Dvořák never mentioned *Alfred* in his lists of works, though he allowed word of it to slip out in Novotný's biographical sketch mentioned above (n. 4). Jan Smaczny, in 'Alfred: Dvořák's First Operatic Endeavour Surveyed', *Journal of the Royal Musical Association*, 115 (1990), 81–2, speculates that Dvořák may have wanted to suppress *Alfred* as an immature work, or have been sensitive about the fact that its libretto was in Ger., in a period of strong Czech nationalist sentiment.

[29] Actually Dvořák is probably referring to an event eight years before, in 1863, when he played the viola in a concert of Wagner's works conducted by the composer.

[30] He did completely reset the libretto, but in 1874, not 1875. And though he rejected the first setting, he did not destroy it: the autograph score survives for the first and third acts, and the second exists in performing parts. Jiří Berkovec has recently prepared a vocal score for publication.

[31] i.e. the church of Svatý Vojtěch.

[32] Dvořák is probably referring to his second setting of *The King and the Charcoal Burner*, which however had not been completed when he first applied for the stipend. He may have submitted it with one of his later applications. The committee's report on his first application does mention that he had submitted symphonies, which were probably his Third in E flat major and Fourth in D minor. By his 'first symphony, in F, Op. 25' Dvořák must mean what we now know as his Fifth Symphony in F major, which on its autograph MS bears the op. no. 24 though it was pub. (not until three years after this interview) as Op. 88. (To complicate matters further, it was pub. as Symphony No. 3!) This work, composed in 1875, was in fact submitted with Dvořák's *third* application for the stipend, as may be seen from his covering letter dated 30 July 1876. See Milan Kuna, 'Umělecká stipendia Antonína Dvořáka', *Hudební věda*, 29/4 (1992), 298, 303–4. See also Döge, *Dvořák*, 161–2.

[33] The supposed failure of the second application, though reported as fact in John Clapham's *Dvořák* (New York, 1979), seems to represent some kind of confusion. Both Hanslick and Krigar, in their biographical sketches published before the *Sunday Times* interview, had reported five successive awards in as many years, and Hanslick was a reliable authority, since he was himself a member of the jury throughout

succeeded in getting 500 florins. Subsequently I tried once more, and sent in some vocal duets, a string quartet, some variations for piano, and the pianoforte concerto that was played this week by the Philharmonic Society.[34] I waited some months, and at last one day a letter came from the famous critic, Dr. Eduard Hanslick, informing me that the committee, consisting of Johannes Brahms, Herbeck, and himself had recommended a grant of 600 florins. My delight at receiving a letter from such a man as Hanslick was doubled on the receipt of one from Brahms, expressing deep interest in me and telling me that he had recommended Simrock, the well-known Berlin publisher, to print some of my compositions.[35] Thus, by kind assistance on all hands, was I put on the road to the success for which I am so grateful. And let me not end without telling you how deeply I appreciate the welcome which the English people have given to myself and my works.'

From Butcher to Baton: An Interview with Herr Dvořák
Pall Mall Gazette (London), 13 Oct. 1886, p. 415.

This unsigned interview was conducted during Dvořák's fifth visit to England, ?4 October to 7 November 1886, during which he conducted the world première of the oratorio *Svatá Ludmila* (St Ludmila) at the Leeds Musical Festival on 15 October. Since the *Sunday Times* interview of May in the previous year he had paid one other visit to England, for two weeks in August 1885, to conduct the British première of the cantata *Svatební košile* (The Spectre's Bride) in Birmingham.

It is possible that Dvořák gave this interview with the *Pall Mall Gazette* directly in the English language: in the previous year he had switched from German to English in his ongoing correspondence with Francesco Berger, secretary of the Philharmonic Society, beginning with the letter of 13 October 1885. Moreover he had developed

---

the period in question. Milan Kuna, ('Umělecká stipendia', 302) confirms after examining the committee's records that not only was Dvořák's second application successful, but he ranked first among all the applicants. The *Sunday Times* interview is again mistaken about the works submitted in the second year: neither the Stabat Mater nor *Vanda* had been composed or even begun. Dvořák's application letter for the third year lists the Stabat Mater as a submission, though it could only have been in piano–vocal score as he had not yet orchestrated the work. The same letter discusses *Vanda* (spelled by Pry again in Ger. style) and refers the committee to published reviews of the work, without listing it among the enclosures.

[34] 6 May 1885, with F. Rummel at the piano, under Dvořák's direction. Dvořák's application letter dated 26 July 1877 lists as enclosures a volume of chamber music, the duets (Moravian Duets), the Serenade for strings, and the variations for piano; the Piano Concerto is not mentioned. See Kuna, 'Umělecká stipendia', 308. Dvořák in fact applied a fifth time, again successfully, in the following year, and it may have been then that he submitted the Piano Concerto; unfortunately his application letter for that year seems to have been lost (ibid. 310–13).

[35] Hanslick had reported Brahms's interest to Dvořák, and suggested that he write to Brahms, which he did. Thus it was Dvořák who initiated the direct correspondence between the two composers. His first letter from Brahms, from Dec. 1877, was a reply. See David Beveridge, 'Dvořák and Brahms: A Chronicle, an Interpretation', in *Dvořák and his World*, 60–2.

an extensive correspondence in English with Alfred Littleton of Novello & Co., and had even thumbed his nose at his German publisher Simrock, with whom he had got into a dispute about the use of Czech vs. German titles on his publications, by writing to *him* more than once in English![36] (Their usual language of correspondence was of course German.) However, Dvořák's wording could not have been as polished as that found in the interview, so we may assume that the reporter took some liberties.

To-day sees for the English musical world the beginning of the great event of the present season, the Leeds Festival, which hundreds of performers and thousands of music-lovers have been anticipating. Among the great musicians who will take part in the festival is Herr Dvořák,[37] the well-known Bohemian composer, who has come to this country to conduct the first performance of his new oratorio, 'St. Ludmila,' published by Messrs. Novello and Co. The name of Dvořák as a composer has been familiar to the British public ever since his 'Stabat Mater' was for the first time performed at Birmingham,[38] and since his minor compositions, characteristic as they are of the man in their ever-varying originality and vivacity, their wild enthusiasm and spontaneity, have charmed and pleased; but of the man, apart from the composer, little enough is known. Through the kindness of Messrs. Novello and Co. an interview between a representative of this paper and Herr Dvořák was arranged, and it was at Mr. Littleton's charming villa at Sydenham, which is becoming famous as a resort of distinguished musicians, that Herr Dvořák gave the following interesting account of his past life and career. Pan Antonín Dvořák is a man of middle age, whose Slavonic extraction is apparent in every feature of his face. He is of somewhat above middle height, very dark, and cheerful and lively in his conversation, which he accompanies with intensifying gesticulations:—

'You want me to tell you something about myself,' said Herr Dvořák to our representative, 'and of my work and career? First of all, then, let me tell you that I am the son of a butcher and innkeeper, which two occupations generally go together with us in Bohemia. I was born in 1841 in a small village called Nelahozeves, near Prague, where I spent my childhood. When about ten years old I began to play the violin, without any instructions or without

---

[36] *Antonín Dvořák: Korespondence*, iii, includes a total of nine letters written by Dvořák in Eng. between Oct. 1885 and Oct. 1886. See pp. 106, 109, 126, 133, 144–5, 161, 170, 171–2, 173.

[37] Dvořák may have resented this use of the Ger. form of address, which would have reminded him of the forced Germanization imposed on his countrymen. (Cf. his attitude toward the use of German in the Prague Organ School in the *Sunday Times* interview above) Either the Czech 'Pan' or the English 'Mr' would have been more appropriate in this context.

[38] The Stabat Mater received its Birmingham première on 27 Mar. 1884. Its first performance in England, which caused a tremendous sensation, was on 10 Mar. 1883, at the Royal Albert Hall in London under Joseph Barnby. Many other works by Dvořák had been performed in England before this.

even the most elementary knowledge of music.[39] It is the custom in my country that children, when they are about eleven or twelve years old, are sent to a German-speaking town or village, where they learn to speak German; while German parents send their children into the Czech villages to learn our language, for it is impossible to get on in Bohemia without either of the two. The village to which I was sent is called Zlonic,[40] and it was there where I received my first instruction in pianoforte playing. It was not much, but it enabled me on returning home to play my fiddle among the bands of musicians who play in the streets and public-houses. This I did for a long time, till the time came for me to choose whether I would be a butcher or a musician;[41] and, though my parents were very poor, I decided to leave butchering alone and devote myself to music. Prospects I had none whatever; I knew my notes and that was all; but I kept to my colleagues, playing valses and polkas for a few kreutzers all the evening, sometimes, when there was a village fair or other festivity, till the next morning. One day it struck me that I might compose a new dance, and accordingly I sat down and wrote and wrote till it was finished, when, with great satisfaction, I went to my colleagues, and the performance of my first composition took place. The results were disastrous, for, innocent of any idea that the music ought to be written differently for different instruments, I gave the same sheet to one and all, and, oh, heavens! the shrieking discord! For some time I did not offer any more of my productions to the public, but I puzzled and puzzled over the reason for this failure of my work.[42] Meanwhile the time came when I ought to have become a soldier, which, however, never came to pass, because I was not strong enough.[43] My father, seeing that I really had some talent, now sent me to Prague, and it

[39] Dvořák in fact probably learned the violin from his teacher Josef Spitz at the school in Nelahozeves, and probably somewhat earlier than the age of 10. Cf. the *Sunday Times* interview on this point, and also the biographical essay by Krigar (in *Dvořák and his World*, 214). See also Burghauser, 'Concerning One of the Myths', 21 n.

[40] Actually Zlonice. Zlonice is a Czech town, not German, but Dvořák attended a German-language school there. He was indeed sent to a German town a little later, 1856–7: Böhmisch Kamnitz (now Česká Kamenice).

[41] Dvořák did not return home to Nelahozeves for any extended period; his family moved from there to Zlonice about two years after he did. In saying 'This I did for a long time, till . . .' he may be referring to the time he spent in Zlonice between leaving school there (an unknown date) and his departure for Böhmisch Kamnitz in the autumn of 1856, by which time he may have already resolved to enter the Prague Organ School a year later.

[42] Dvořák is clearly 'milking' his story here. Cf. the more matter-of-fact account in the *Sunday Times* interview.

[43] He actually was not eligible to be drafted into the army until several years later, at which time he was indeed released from service. The reason for his release is unknown, but evidently it was not that he was too weak. On the other hand there is evidence from several sources that through his mid-teens, i.e. through the period described in the *Pall Mall Gazette* passage, he was physically slow to develop. These issues are discussed in detail in Jarmil Burghauser's MS work in progress, *Chlapecká léta Antonína Dvořáka* (The Boyhood Years of Antonín Dvořák).

was then that I heard the names of any great composer for the first time. At Prague I also went to the opera for the first time in my life, and listened to Weber's "Freischütz" from the gallery.[44] My daily work was still to play in a band sometimes in a soldier's uniform when the occasion was particularly grand. I made now enough money to hire a piano by the month, and I gave a few lessons in piano playing, using all my spare time to write enormous volumes of original composition, all of which I have now long ago destroyed.[45] I was still puzzling over the secret of the unsuccess of my first composition,[46] but light was dawning, and I began to see. So the years went by. In '73 I married, and still I was nothing but a poor, obscure musician. Then, in '74, I went in for a competition[47] for a musical scholarship at Vienna, and my manuscript gained £40.[48] Next year I tried again, and got £50; the year after £60; but the "Stabat Mater" which I sent was not even noticed, and beyond sending the prize to me, nobody took any further notice. At home in my own circles I was by this time pretty well known as the composer of a Bohemian Patriotic Hymn, but not till '78 had my name been heard in the musical world as a composer. At that time my Moravian duets were published at Berlin by the well-known firm of Simrock, and there appeared in the feuilleton of the *National Zeitung* an account of them, written by Professor Ehlert, the ablest critic in Germany at the time, which not only brought me a good deal of money, but after a day or two a multitude of letters from publishers in all parts of Germany and Austria, asking me to write for them.[49] Since then I have been working on; my dances, songs, and symphonies have found a public, and among my larger works the "Stabat Mater" and the "König und Köhler"[50] are perhaps the most popular.'

'Now, Herr Dvořák, to come back to your own work. If it is not an indiscreet question, I should like to ask you how you compose?' With a good-natured smile and a humorous twinkle in his eyes, Herr Dvořák said: 'That is rather a difficult question to answer. When I was young I composed very quickly indeed; I had a real fury for writing, and I cared not what they were like as long as I could only get my ideas on paper. In time, however, I have

---

[44] But cf. the version of the story in the *Sunday Times* interview, according to which he was not able to hear *Freischütz*.

[45] He destroyed many works from this time, but not all!

[46] Obviously an over-dramatization—his two symphonies from 1865 have some problems, but transposition of instrumental parts is not one of them!

[47] i.e. applied by post.

[48] MSS of fifteen compositions, actually. The award was 400 florins, given here in British equivalent.

[49] This review, pub. by Louis Ehlert in Berlin, 15 Nov. 1878, included the first set of Slavonic Dances as well as the Moravian Duets.

[50] *The King and the Charcoal Burner*. It is surprising that Dvořák ranked the popularity of this work, unpublished until after his death, above that of his three operas already published at that time: *Tvrdé palice* (The Stubborn Lovers), *Dimitrij*, and *Šelma sedlák* (The Cunning Peasant). The last-mentioned was his only opera at the time to have been performed outside Bohemia—in Dresden, Hamburg, and Vienna.

learned to be more careful, and at present, after I get a new idea, I try to get it clear in my own mind before I write anything at all. I play it over twenty, thirty, nay, a hundred times, till I have got exactly what I want. After that the writing does not take long, and what has been in my mind for some months is on paper in about a week, or even less.'

'And your new oratorio, is it the first time that it will be performed at Leeds, and what is the subject of it?'

'Yes, it has never been performed before. The subject is a poem by a young Bohemian poet, Yaroslav Vrchlicky,[51] who, though not yet thirty years old, is already an eminent man, whom at home they have called a second Byron. The subject is the conversion of the Bohemians to Christianity by one Ivan, who caused Ludmila to become a Christian, while she, in her turn, persuaded her countrymen to adopt the new faith.'

'And what is your opinion of the English as a musical nation? Are they so utterly devoid of a sense for music as is generally assumed?'

'Of this I am only an imperfect judge, but as far as my experience of English audiences goes I can only say that people who had not a good deal of love for music in them would hardly sit for four hours closely following an oratorio from beginning to end, and evidently enjoy doing it. As to their being good musicians, I judge them by the orchestras who have played my compositions under my own direction, and it has struck me every time. With regard to music it is with the English as it is with the Slavs in politics—they are young, very young, but there is great hope for the future. Twenty years ago we Slavs were nothing; now we feel our national life once more awakening, and who knows but that the glorious times may come back which five centuries ago were ours, when all Europe looked up to the powerful Czechs, the Slavs, the Bohemians, to whom I, too, belong, and to whom I am proud to belong.'

The words of the magnificent chorus at the end of 'St. Ludmila'—

> Thou that rulest all creation,
> Guide of every faithful nation,
> Open Thou Thy willing hand:
> Guard Thy true Bohemian land—[52]

came into my mind as the torrent of eloquent patriotism burst forth, and I took leave of the man who by his music has done much to bring the 'true Bohemian land' once more into honour.[53]

---

[51] Jaroslav Vrchlický.

[52] Actually the words of the penultimate number (44) of the oratorio, introduced by Svatava and affirmed by the chorus. In Vrchlický's original Czech: 'Ty, jenž jsi vesmíru vládce, | ostříhej své věrné stádce, | roztáhni své lásky dlaň! | věecky věrné Čechy chraň!'

[53] There is some evidence that the outburst of nationalist sentiment at the close of this interview was intended for the Czech audience at home as much as for the British. Dvořák sent the interview to his friend

Joseph Zubatý with a letter of 18 Oct. 1886, asking him to translate it into Czech and 'give it especially to [the newspaper] *Národní listy*; I think it will have a good effect among our countrymen. Leave out the biographical data, but transmit especially *the whole* of the further conversation toward the end of the article. *The nation will rejoice.*' He betrays his press-consciousness in another way in his next sentence: 'The article is under the title "*From Butcher to Baton*", thus very catchy.' ('Dejte to zejména do *Národ[ních] listů*, myslím, že to v národě dobře bude působit. Životopisná data vynechte, ale zejména další rozmluvu ku konci článku *dejte celou. Národ bude jásat.* Článek je pod názvem "*Od řezníka k taktovce*", tedy *velmi působivý.*') His previous letter of 15 Oct. 1886 to the journalist Václav Juda Novotný is in a similar vein: 'I think the last sentence of this article will meet with hearty approval all over our nation.' ('myslím, že poslední věta z toho článku najde po celém našem národě vřelého souhlasu.') *Antonín Dvořák: Korespondence*, ii. 184, 188–9. See also n. 18 above. I do not mean to suggest, however, that Dvořák's effusions were insincere.

CONTRIBUTORS' PROFILES

MICHAEL BECKERMAN teaches music history at the University of California at Santa Barbara, while residing in San Francisco. He is the editor of *Dvořák and his World* (Princeton University Press, 1993) and *Janáček and Czech Music* (Pendragon Press, 1995), and author of *Janáček as Theorist* (Pendragon Press, 1994). His articles concerning Czech music and other topics have appeared in various scholarly journals, and he also contributes to *The New York Times*. He is currently working on an edition of the 'New World' Symphony with analysis and commentary for the Norton Critical Score series.

DAVID R. BEVERIDGE is working in Prague on a projected four-volume study of Dvořák's life and work. His doctoral dissertation on Dvořák's sonata forms (University of California at Berkeley) is to be published by Pendragon Press, and his articles on various musical topics have appeared in a variety of American and European publications. In 1991 he was director of the Dvořák Sesquicentennial Festival and Conference in America, held in New Orleans.

JARMIL BURGHAUSER is a freelance composer and scholar in Prague, where for many years he has been president of the Antonín Dvořák Society. He is author of the Dvořák thematic catalogue (recently prepared for publication in a new expanded edition), and is one of the chief editors for the ongoing complete edition of Dvořák's works. His published essays and monographs on Dvořák, Smetana, Janáček, and other topics are innumerable. Of his symphonic, chamber, vocal, film, television, and stage works, the ballet *Sluha dvou pánů* (The servant of two masters) has achieved the greatest popularity, with numerous stagings in Czechoslovakia and abroad.

MIROSLAV K. ČERNÝ teaches musicology at Palacký University in Olomouc (Moravia), though residing principally in Prague, and has also taught at the Charles University pedagogical college and at the Academy of Performing Arts in Prague. He was for many years a member of the Institute for Musicology of the Czechoslovak Academy of Sciences. His research interests include the music of the nineteenth and twentieth centuries, especially Dvořák, and also the music of antiquity, on which subject he is shortly to publish a book with Palacký University Press. He has also published many articles in a wide range of Czech scholarly journals.

RICHARD CRAWFORD is Glenn McGeoch Collegiate Professor of Music at the University of Michigan in Ann Arbor. His research has focused on music in America, with books and articles on subjects ranging from New England psalmody to nineteenth-century parlour song, to George Gershwin, Duke Ellington, and jazz. He is a past president of the American Musicological Society and editor-in-chief of the society's Music of the United States of America (MUSA), a national series of scholarly editions (1993-). His most recent book is *The American Musical Landscape* (1993), and he is now at work on *A History of Music in the USA*.

JAROSLAVA DOBRINČIĆ is a freelance scholar in the fields of art and sociology, residing in Rijeka, Croatia. After studying sociology and pedagogy at Charles University in Prague, she taught art appreciation at Prague's National Gallery from 1968 to 1985, serving as head of the education department during her last four years there.

KLAUS DÖGE has been working since 1992 as an editor for the Richard Wagner Gesamtausgabe in Munich. Over the years he has also produced editions of works by Haydn, Rossini, Mahler, and Dvořák, and published studies of Arnold Schoenberg, Anton Webern, and especially Dvořák, including his 1991 monograph *Dvořák: Leben, Werke, Dokumente*. He studied musicology and history at the Albert-Ludwig University in Freiburg, and has taught music history at both the Pädagogische Hochschule in Freiburg and the Musikhochschule in Würzburg.

JARMILA GABRIELOVÁ has taught in the Musicological Institute of Charles University in Prague since 1976, after studying piano and musicology both there and at the Prague Conservatory. Her areas of interest have been nineteenth- and early twentieth-century music and music aesthetics, especially in Bohemia, and recently the music of Scandinavia. She has published many musical articles as well as a book on the compositional issues presented by Dvořák's early instrumental works. In spring 1994 she taught as a visiting lecturer at the University of Copenhagen.

MARK GERMER is a freelance musicologist residing in Havertown, Pennsylvania. His doctoral dissertation (New York University) investigates the relationship between church and folk music in eighteenth-century Bohemia. He has taught in the music departments of Rutgers University (New Brunswick, New Jersey) and of Temple University, Philadelphia, and recently completed a term as contributing editor to the Music Library Association's journal, *Notes*.

MARKÉTA HALLOVÁ has served since 1990 as Director of the Antonín Dvořák Museum in Prague, also supervising its branches at Dvořák's birthplace in Nelahozeves and at the composer Josef Suk's home in Křečovice. She is the author of many articles in leading Czech musical journals and in the *New Grove Dictionary of Music and Musicians*, and of a study (1983) of young Czech contemporary composers, and editor of a number of collections of essays and bulletins on Dvořák published by the Czech Music Society from 1982 to 1990; she has also served on the editorial team for the complete critical edition of Dvořák's correspondence and documents.

CHARLES HAMM is Arthur R. Virgin Professor of Music Emeritus at Dartmouth College, New Hampshire. A past president of the American Musicological Society, he has held Woodrow Wilson, Guggenheim, and Fulbright fellowships. His books include *Yesterday: Popular Song in America*; *Music in the New World*; *Putting Popular Music in its Place* (a collection of his essays); *Opera, Afro-American Music, South Africa, and Apartheid*; and a complete critical edition of the early songs of Irving Berlin. He resides principally in Norwich, Vermont and is currently writing a book on Irving Berlin for Oxford University Press.

ALAN HOUTCHENS has taught music history at Texas A&M University since 1989. His research activities have focused primarily on Czech culture, especially Dvořák, and have yielded articles in a variety of scholarly journals and books. His doctoral dissertation on Dvořák's *Vanda*, for the University of California at Santa Barbara, laid the groundwork for the preparation currently under way, in collaboration with Jarmil Burghauser, of the critical edition of this unjustly overlooked opera. He is presently preparing a book entitled *The Dvořák Companion* for Greenwood Press.

MILAN KUNA has been a member of the Institute for Musicology of the Czechoslovak (now Czech) Academy of Sciences in Prague since 1963, and is currently chief editor of the institute's journal *Hudební věda* (Musicology). He is also the head of the editorial team for the ongoing ten-volume critical edition of Dvořák's correspondence and documents. As well as a long list of articles, he has published books dealing with film music, Czech musical life during the Nazi occupation, experimental research in musical performance, Tchaikovsky's stays in Prague, and the Czech musicians Václav Talich and Karel Boleslav Jirák.

GRAHAM MELVILLE-MASON resides principally in London, but teaches music history as a visiting professor at Charles University in Prague, the Janácek Academy in Brno, and the Bratislava Academy. His is president of the International Advisory Board of the Prague Spring Festival, chairman of the Dvořák Society for Czech and Slovak Music of Great Britain, and vice president of the British Czech and Slovak Association. In the past he has taught at Edinburgh University, where he also worked with the Edinburgh International Festival. Through the 1980s he served as a member of the senior music staff of the BBC in London.

JOHN K. NOVAK recently completed a sabbatical replacement appointment in music theory at the Oberlin College Conservatory, Ohio. He has published articles on Janáček and Dvořák, and recently completed a doctoral dissertation for the University of Texas at Austin on Janáček's programmatic orchestral works. He has often been a guest of the Foreign Institute of Czechoslovakia for language and cultural programs in Prague. He performs on the piano and the accordion.

MIROSLAV NOVÝ is a freelance musicologist in Prague, and member of the editorial teams for the complete critical editions of both Dvořák's correspondence and his musical works; in the latter capacity he edited the Nocturno for String Orchestra and a number of piano works. He has also edited Dvořák's *Čtyři sbory* (Four choruses) for mixed voices for Carus-Verlag in Stuttgart. He studied musicology and aesthetics at Charles University in Prague, following which he held positions with Czechoslovak radio, the Czech Music Fund, and, from 1969 to 1988, the library of the Bedřich Smetana Museum in Prague where he worked as a musicological expert.

MARTA OTTLOVÁ has taught since 1990 in the Musicological Institute of Charles University in Prague, following many years of service in the Institute for Musicology of the Czechoslovak Academy of Sciences. She has published many articles on Czech music of the nineteenth century and on the history of opera. In 1981 she co-founded an annual interdisciplinary symposium on the nineteenth century in the Czech lands, held in Plzeň. She was co-organizer with Milan Pospíšil of the International Dvořák Congress in Dobříš, Czechoslovakia, in 1991, and co-editor of the conference proceedings.

LEON PLANTINGA is Henry L. and Lucy G. Moses Professor of Music and Director of the Division of the Humanities at Yale University. Besides many articles on music of the late eighteenth and the nineteenth centuries, he has published *Schumann as Critic* (Yale University Press, 1967), *Clementi: His Life and Music* (Oxford University Press, 1977), and *Romantic Music: A History of Musical Style in Nineteenth-Century Europe* (W. W. Norton, 1985). His latest book, *Beethoven's Concertos: Style, Genre, and Meaning* (W. W. Norton) is shortly to be published.

MILAN POSPÍŠIL is a member of the Institute for Musicology of the Czech Academy of Sciences in Prague, conducting research focused on opera of the nineteenth century with special attention to Dvořák and Meyerbeer. At present he is preparing the critical edition of Meyerbeer's *Les Huguenots* for the Meyerbeer-Werke (published by the Meyerbeer Institute in Thurnau with Ricordi & Co. in Munich). He studied musicology in Prague and (with Heinz Becker) in Bochum. He was co-organizer with Marta Ottlová of the International Dvořák Congress at Dobříš, Czechoslovakia, in September 1991, and co-editor of the conference proceedings.

THOMAS L. RIIS is Director of the American Research Center at the University of Colorado at Boulder, where he has taught music history since 1992. He writes and lectures widely on a variety of topics, concentrating his research on musical theatre and African-American popular music. His book *Just before Jazz: Black Musical Theater in New York, 1890-1915* (1989), has just been reissued in paperback, and he has recently completed an edition of the music of the first major African-American musical comedy, *In Dahomey* (1902) by Dvořák's pupil Will Marion Cook.

HARTMUT SCHICK has been teaching and conducting research at the Musicological Institute of Tübingen University since 1989. He studied musicology, history, and philosophy at the universities of Tübingen and then Heidelberg, where he completed his doctoral studies under Ludwig Finscher with the dissertation 'Studien zu Dvořáks Streichquartetten' (published by Laaber Verlag in 1990). He is currently working on his *Habilitationsschrift* concerning musical form in the Italian madrigal.

DAVID M. SCHILLER teaches music history at the University of Georgia, where he is completing a doctoral dissertation entitled 'Assimilating Jewish Music: *Sacred Service, A Survivor from Warsaw, Kaddish*'.

JAN SMACZNY has taught music history at the University of Birmingham since 1983. He was educated at the University of Oxford and Charles University, Prague, writing his dissertation on the early operas of Dvořák. He has published on many aspects of Czech music although his main area of interest is the life and work of Dvořák.

KARIN STÖCKL-STEINEBRUNNER is a freelance music scholar residing at Herrischried in the Black Forest, following teaching appointments at the universities in Freiburg and Karlsruhe. She has undertaken research on a wide range of musical topics, especially music of the late nineteenth century and vocal music with emphasis on the word–tone relationship, but also literature, philosophy, and aesthetics. She is (with Klaus Döge) co-editor of the Goldmann-Schott critical score of Dvořák's 'New World' Symphony with analysis and commentary (1982).

INDEX